Grace through Fire

Jessica Berg

Grace through Fire
Red Adept Publishing, LLC
104 Bugenfield Court
Garner, NC 27529
https://RedAdeptPublishing.com/

---

1.   http://StreetlightGraphics.com

To my parents, David and Barbara, who taught me the value
of hard work and the importance of family

Chapter 1

The sun kissed the dewy grasses tickling the belly of a mother bison as her calf nursed.

Nikki Lancaster held her breath, savoring the moment, hoping that the hitch in her breathing didn't disturb mother and calf in the quiet of the Custer State Park morning. She hid behind her camera lens, three hundred yards from the nine-hundred-pound prairie behemoth, and clicked a few more pictures, adjusting the lens, zooming in on the calf as it nudged its mother, demanding more milk.

Her camera captured the moment the mother bison's tongue licked her calf's tiny, furry ear. A blood-orange sky kissed the wildflower-embroidered prairie grasses. If this didn't get her a spot in *National Geographic*, nothing would. She was only a few spectacular shots like this away from getting closer to her dream job: world-famous wildlife photographer.

With a snort and a tail flick, the mother ushered her baby away, their hooves thundering over the ground. The moment and her photo shoot ruined, Nikki stood and craned her neck to see what had disturbed her award-winning, million-dollar, adventure-guaranteeing career shot.

A tourist.

She glared at his form as he walked out of a copse of trees. *Idiot.* She zoomed in her camera, but the man's red baseball hat, covering his facial features, shadowed most of his face. Decked out in jeans, T-shirt, and red-and-green-checkered flannel—despite the warm morning—he trudged through the long grasses. He carried

1

nothing with him, but something hung from the back of his jeans pocket. She zoomed in farther. Leather work gloves.

Odd.

Tourists weren't out and about this early in the morning, and there were no hiking trails in this area. Most sane people knew to stay away from buffalo, but he had to have seen the pair before emerging from the trees. Despite the humid breath of a June morning, she shivered at his furtive looks. Just a few more clicks. Evidence of his stupidity to show her best friend, Sara Kelly. As a resident of the Black Hills area, Sara detested moronic tourists mucking up the status quo.

The man glanced in her direction and stilled. She knew he couldn't see her well. Three football fields of prairie grasses separated them, but her body froze, her camera rooted between her whitened knuckles. Without the aid of her camera lens, she could only make out a human form with a baseball hat, but his misplaced presence leached through the distance. The recent reports about missing women in the area reeled through her mind. Shoving those horrible stories to the back of her mind, she concentrated on the idiot in the distance.

Nikki stashed her camera back in its case. She would have to come back again, and that was a gamble. The wild animals of Custer State Park did as they pleased. They didn't care if she lived on steak or canned tuna.

He lunged into action. His long legs ate up the distance, which now didn't feel far enough.

Her heart skipped a beat and thundered blood through her body, fueling her into a sprint. Halfway to her car and full out of breath, Nikki second-guessed herself. *Maybe he needs help?* He must be parked near her, but she hadn't seen a vehicle when she'd parked her car. *Maybe he's stranded?*

The second her feet slowed, her brain, like a television banner, scrolled the names of the missing women in the state park. *Run, you idiot!*

With lungs and thighs on fire and a stitch in her side, she jumped into her VW bug, turned the key, and stomped on the accelerator. Gravel spit out from her squealing tires. In her rearview mirror, the man's form decreased until he disappeared from sight.

Catching her breath, she ripped off the ugly flame-orange fishing hat her father had given her and threw it in the back seat. His irrational fear of her being shot by hunters, on or off season, was a symptom of the traumatic brain injury he'd received years ago in a vehicle accident. Even though he would never know if she wore it or not, she had promised. Although, this time, the hat had highlighted her presence with all its neon glory to someone who either wanted to flag her down for help or—the missing women's names popped up again. *Lucy, Michelle, Hallie, Alexis.* An oily sensation swirled through her gut.

Nikki shifted her VW into a higher gear, determined to forget the disturbing man who trespassed on her photo shoot and her sense of security. She had another perfect spot planned for the late-afternoon sun as soon as she finished her shift at the Dakota Chuckwagon. The tourist brunch crowd was a good way to keep a roof over her head and food in her belly, and occasionally, it prompted a future photo session. The green numbers on the dashboard clock advised her to shift into overdrive. If she were a bird, she would be entering Custer in no time, but the twisting winding roads through the state park added a good thirty minutes, and if the buffalo created a traffic jam, it could be an hour.

Zooming around a curve, she checked her rearview mirror. A dark-green SUV was following too closely, the dark-tinted windows blocking her view of the driver. Just wait until the Park Rangers stopped him. Or the HPs. They didn't have a sense of humor. Not that she had any personal experience. She eyed her glove box, where she had stashed her speeding ticket receipts.

The road lengthened out again, and Nikki stepped on the accelerator, hoping to lose the bumper kisser. The SUV sped up as well. Goose bumps exploded over her arms. She pressed the pedal more. The SUV bumped into her.

What the...?

Another set of curves, more vicious than the last, was coming up. It was suicide to take the curves any faster than the marked thirty-five mph. The SUV tapped on her bumper again. As the bug's tires hit the curve going way too fast, the left side of her car left the ground, and she prayed that there was no oncoming traffic. Fighting down panic, she eased off the gas, and once her tires hit pavement, the car twisted into the shoulder of the road, smashing the passenger side into a large boulder.

Her head slammed into the driver's-side window, and she saw stars. The airbag exploded, punching her in the face. Her eyes welled with tears, and for a second, she thought she'd gone blind. But her vision blurred to normal, and her gaze followed the swiveling hips of the hula-dancing woman on her dashboard that Nikki's Marine brother, Nathan, had sent her as a practical joke from his Oahu Marine Corps Base in Hawaii.

She dabbed at her left temple and her nose.

Blood.

The SUV roared past her, but with blood trickling in her eye, she couldn't make out any more details than she had before. The driver had either meant to kill her or had been drunk. Either was enough to still her heart and then send it hammering blood through her body. She thanked God it still beat. A tad too fast, but that was better than not at all.

She jumped at the tap at her driver's-side window. It was a miracle the glass wasn't shattered. Her headache was proof of that.

Nikki squinted into the face of a white-haired old lady, a Stetson-hat-clad man at her elbow. Nikki tried opening the window but no luck. She tugged at the door handle, and the door creaked open.

"Are you all right?" the woman drawled in a Southern voice.

"I don't know." Nikki prodded her wounds again. "I think so."

"I don't think so, honey." The woman's cool hands rested on Nikki's forehead. "You're pretty banged up. Can you move?"

Nikki tested her major appendages, and all felt normal. "I think so."

"Dwayne, help this young lady out of her car. I'll call 911."

"No." Nikki flushed. "I mean, I feel fine. If you give me a minute, I'll be okay to drive."

The woman tutted. "But your car won't."

When Nikki took stock of her beloved car, she saw red. Well, she saw her happy yellow bug looking as if a giant had taken a club to the passenger side. If she ever saw the green SUV again, she'd—"Did you get a look at the SUV following me?"

"We noticed it driving all funny, but we were too far away to get any pertinent information." The woman eyed her. "Did he drive you off the road?"

Nikki bit her lip and nodded.

"Well, I wonder who peed in his Cheerios." Dwayne spoke for the first time, his Southern drawl deeper and slower.

"Dwayne, language. Anyway, he sped off after we got closer, then we saw you. Poor dear." The woman fit her hand over Nikki's forehead again. "Name's Delilah."

The edges of Nikki's world were fuzzy and gray. "Do you mind if I sit in your car for a while?"

"Of course, dear. Come. Lean on Dwayne. He's good for something. Occasionally."

Wordlessly, the tall, older man assisted Nikki to their car.

"Oklahoma, huh? Long ways from home."

"We love it here. We tour the Black Hills area whenever we get a chance. A hidden gem." Delilah messed with Nikki's hair, which had come undone from her chignon. "Here. Have some water." She passed Nikki an unopened bottle of water and pulled out her phone and called 911 before Nikki could stop her.

Darn it. This was not good. Hopefully, his police radio was off or he was on vacation in Bora Bora or he was busy buying drugs for his next drug bust. Anything but listening to his radio.

Delilah snapped her Jitterbug phone closed. "There. The posse is on its way."

"Great. Just great." Nikki took another swig of water and waited. Waited for help that didn't come in the form of Xavier Palinski.

Author Note: Custer State Park in South Dakota is one of my favorite places in the world. When people think of South Dakota—if they ever do—they automatically think of Mt. Rushmore. While this monument is a true national treasure, the western part of the state offers beautiful mountain vistas and green rolling grasslands to make any nature lover's heart hum, just like Nikki Lancaster's. Don't worry, though, about sharing the same fate as Nikki. Normally, Custer State Park's only dangers are buffalo (please don't try to pet them) and rattlesnakes (also, please don't try to pet them)! If you're catching this story without reading its older sibling, Amber Waves of Grace, it might not be a bad idea to head on over to that novel and get acquainted with seventeen-year-old Nikki and her older sister, Corrie, who also found herself in a spot of trouble. Hmm... trouble-finding must run in the Lancaster family.

Chapter 2

Xavier Palinski loved the Hills on his days off when he could drive with the doors off his Jeep, not a care in the world except where he'd stop to eat or fill gas. He'd come from a winning streak in Deadwood and had money to burn and time to burn it. Question was where.

Hit and run. State Highway 87. Mile marker seven. Needs medical attention.

He should have turned his police radio off. Really, he should have. He could ignore it, but as he was three miles from the scene, he'd never be able to look at his badge with honor again. Well, the least he could do was wait at the scene, be sure everyone was okay, and jet out when the cavalry showed up.

He pulled up behind a white Lincoln Continental with Oklahoma plates, called in the information, and readjusted his concealed weapon before hopping out of his Jeep. His heart slid to his toes at the sight of the yellow Bug with no less than five Save the Elephants bumper stickers on the back. That car could only belong to one person.

His saunter quickened into a jog, and he skidded to a halt as a tall, aging cowboy untangled himself from the driver's seat and gave a brisk nod of greeting. "Afternoon."

Xavier, at 6'5, didn't know what it was like to look up at somebody. But he assessed the man's stance and gaze and within seconds stretched out his hand. "Agent Palinski, Department of Criminal Investigations. Got the alert over the radio. Stopping by to check if everything's okay."

The tall cowboy jerked his head in the direction of the backseat to the tune of a woman's curse.

Yup, only one driver of the yellow Bug. And she hated him.

Swallowing his own stew of emotions, he crouched down at the opened back passenger door and met the eyes of Nikki Lancaster. He would love to lose himself in their blue depths as he once had, but there was no welcome in them and besides, the blood running in them had his gut twisting.

He reached for her hand, and she pulled back as if he'd burned her. Maybe he had. His skin tingled. "What happened?"

The woman sitting next to her chirped up, her gray eyes flashing with anger under the stormy cloud of white hair billowing around her head. She looked like an avenging angel. If avenging angels wore lemon-slice shirts and candy-apple red lipstick.

It took him a few seconds to compute her thick accent and slang, but he got the gist. Some loser had run his Nikki—no, she wasn't his anymore—off the road and had driven off. The only information: it was an SUV. And it was green. No license plate number. Not even the state. During the tourist season, this wealth of information did nothing to weed out potential suspects.

His experience in law enforcement had trained him to assess the situation, evaluate the issue, ignore emotion, and make the right call. It had served him well until now. Now all he could take in was Nikki's blond hair, usually tamed into place and styled in what he used to refer to as the *Anne of Green Gables* style, pouring over her shoulders, streaked in her own blood. Her face was white with fear and pain, streaks of blood marring her tanned complexion.

"Nikki, are you alright?"

She skewered him with a look, one that was not all that unfamiliar, although the love used to outweigh the exasperation. Now, the exasperation heightened her disdain for him. They hadn't spoken in three years, had ignored each other's existence until they'd bumped into each other at Mount Rushmore a couple of months ago. She'd been there with her family; he'd been there on official business. To say the meeting had been awkward would be an understatement.

The Lancasters had tried to lighten the blow, pretending to be interested in his new life. Corrie had been especially kind, her eyes twinkling with kindness and warmth. That might have had something to do with the four-year-old boy playing peek-a-boo with him. Corrie's husband, Aaron, had slapped him on the back, asked if he'd killed anyone lately, and moved on to keep his son from smearing ice cream on an unsuspecting tourist.

Nikki's scoff brought him back to reality. "You never did listen to me. Some things never change."

That was fair. He hadn't been listening now, and probably not before either. One notch amongst many of why he'd lost her.

"I'm sorry." *For everything.*

"Yes, well, I was saying that I think the vehicle was a Chevy, but I can't be certain. Dark green. And very tinted windows. Illegally so, I'd wager."

There she was. The girl who never missed a thing. The girl who saw a version of the world no one else ever thought to explore. That's what made her an excellent photographer. That's what made her an excellent lover. Would have made her an excellent wife.

"That's good. Something to go off of. Have you ever seen the vehicle before?"

She screwed up her face, a movement that crinkled her long, straight nose and planted furrows in her forehead. He had the sudden urge to kiss her. Pull her into his arms, feel her against him, and drink her in. She'd probably slap him, would have every right to.

"No. At least, I don't think so."

"Anything odd happen today?"

"Is this your case?"

"Excuse me?"

Her ice-blue eyes met his. "I didn't think DCI agents dealt with petty little things like hit-and-runs."

A wail of sirens cut off his reply. Again, that was fair. She was right. He didn't deal with hit-and-runs. Usually. But this wasn't just any hit-and-run. Someone had tried to kill her, and from the looks of her car, if she hadn't acted cool-headedly, she'd be dead.

But she didn't belong to him. Not anymore. This would not be his case. Not that that would stop him. He would do what he could to protect her. Even if she hated him more for it.

The combined wailing of a police cruiser and an ambulance in the background spiked through Nikki's head. What she wouldn't give for ibuprofen and a chaser of whiskey. Oddly enough, Delilah and Dwayne had both, but refused to share on account of "not knowing if it would kill her or not."

With Xavier, her ex-fiancé, outside the couple's car, she didn't care if it would. She held her water bottle to her unmarred cheek, the cool plastic refreshing against her hot skin. Scratch that. She didn't want to die. She wanted to find whoever had run her off the road and almost killed her and her Bug. And she most certainly did not want Xavier looking at her like he used to. Like he wanted to kiss her. She'd slap him. Maybe.

"Well, honey, your heroes have shown up. Up and at 'em." Delilah shoved her out of the backseat and into Xavier. His arms came out to steady her, and for a split second, she wanted to curl into his chest, inhale his scent, his strength. She pushed away from him and wrapped her arms around her middle.

His gentle gaze shuttered, and the Xavier that stood before her was all cop, all business. He motioned with his arm and ushered her to the parked ambulance. The paramedics helped her into the back and assessed her injuries. A lanky deputy sauntered over, exchanged a few words with Xavier, and turned his attention to her.

"Deputy Morrison, ma'am." He pulled out a notebook and pen and, after asking her a gazillion questions, snapped his notebook shut and left her to the ministrations of the paramedics.

Feeling like a deflated balloon with enough oomph to let out a weak raspberry, she signed her life away in the back of the ambulance and now stood in the shadow of a tow truck, signing her Bug's life away and entrusting it with a stranger. Delilah and Dwayne had stayed with her even though she'd insisted she was fine. They obviously could see through her lie. She was not fine. But she held herself together with grit and the tight squeeze of her arms. She could not, would not, fall apart in front of Xavier.

"You need a ride home, honey?" Delilah crooned from behind her.

Unwelcome tears burned hot behind Nikki's eyes. She squeezed them shut and shuddered out a breath. "Yeah."

"Good. I think that handsome blond wants to take you home."

A harsh laugh scraped at Nikki's throat. "That's not such a great idea." Her eyes betrayed her and scanned Xavier as he stood, probably talking about her to the deputy. His tall frame encased in board shorts and tank top did nothing to hide his muscular, tanned physique. Blond hair, the color of ripened wheat, stuck out from his backward ball cap and flowed over his shoulders. He belonged on the beach somewhere, his toes sinking into salty sand. It's where they should have spent their honeymoon. Had planned to spend their honeymoon.

His gaze caught hers, and he raised his eyebrow in question. She averted her gaze and pretended to care about a prairie dog chirping from atop its domed home.

Delilah touched Nikki's shoulders. "We're finished giving our statements. Me and the hubby need to get going. You okay?"

Nikki nodded.

"Here." Delilah stuck a piece of paper into Nikki's clammy palm. "My number. We'll be around for a couple of days. Call if you need anything."

"Thank you." Nikki clutched at the paper as if it were a lifeline as the older couple climbed in their car and drove off, leaving Nikki alone with the deputy and Xavier.

"Miss Lancaster, make sure you come down to the station later this afternoon. I would like to ask more follow-up questions." He pulled away from the scene, leaving Nikki, Xavier, and bits and pieces of her car.

"Let's get you home." Xavier offered his arm to help her hobble back to his Jeep when she stumbled. She hadn't realized how sore her leg was until she'd stood for a while on it and had tried to move.

"What makes you assume you will be taking me home?"

Xavier looked around them. Nothing but pine trees and prairie dogs. "Unless you plan on hitchhiking, I am your only option. I promised Deputy Morrison I'd take you home."

"He mustn't know that you suck at keeping promises."

His silence confirmed her judgment, ceded her the win. His piercing blue eyes made hers look like an overcast wintery day. Her chest constricted. Most women would punch her in the throat for breaking Xavier's heart two days before vowing to love him forever. Years after that fated decision, standing before him, his hand a breath away from hers, she wished with all her might she hadn't.

He had always played the gentleman, the devoted lover, the quintessential best friend, but overall, he had played the protector. *To a fault.* In the end, he had chosen her father's fear over her joy.

Xavier remembered the exact moment his heart had shattered. Until that moment, he had scoffed at that saying, chalked it up to hormones and hyperbole. But he had never figured Nikki for a heart-crusher. He had smelled it on her that morning before her words could even escape her, a pheromone he hoped to never experience again. If he avoided women and never trusted his heart to one again, he wouldn't.

She had been wearing a strapless sunflower dress, her curly hair spiraling over her shoulders, her eyes betraying a smile so tight it should have cracked her face. And then it was over. She had spouted things like "I don't need you to protect me all my life," "I feel boxed in," and other revelations that left him reeling, physically and emotionally, as she sped out of his parents' farmyard, Save the Elephant bumper stickers the last he would see of her for years.

Now she stood before him, skinny jeans and tank-top splattered with her own blood, her blond hair stained rusty with blood, squatting like dreads over her shoulder. Her eyes, too, betrayed her. Her ferocious scowl did not match her gaze. *Regret?* He squashed the thought before hope could blossom in his chest. She had questioned his honesty. *Defend yourself!* He couldn't. But lying to protect her, lying to keep her safe had been the noble thing to do, had been what her family had expected him to do. If only he could go back in time, not have broken a promise sealed with a kiss and the sacred pinky swear.

"You have two choices. You can either stay here and commune with the prairie dogs or you can hitch a ride with me." Not giving her time to respond, he ambled to his jeep, careful to keep his pace even and steady even though his emotions were anything but. He slid into the driver's seat, clicked on his seatbelt, and turned the key, his Jeep's engine purring to life. *One. Two. Three. Come on, Nikki! Four. Five.* He would drive away at ten. He would. *Six. Seven.*

"Didn't get to ten fast enough, did you?"

Xavier gritted his teeth. He shouldn't have added "Mississippi" to each number. But fair was fair, and Nikki did more than march to the beat of her own drum, she danced to the carefree melody of a Jamaican kettledrum.

"I gave you some time for that hitch in your get-a-long."

"Such a gentleman, aren't you?"

"That's what I've been told." After she buckled up, he pulled away from the shoulder of the road and zipped along the curves through granite hills carpeted with scrappy ponderosa pines, some clinging to the hillsides with nothing but grit and determination and a root.

"Thank you."

He spared her a glance. Fifteen minutes of silence broken by her whispered acknowledgment. He had barely heard her over the rush of wind and the roar of the engine. "You're welcome."

Again, nothing but a whirlwind of wind and the zoom of passing cars. He itched to say something. Anything. But his throat closed on social niceties and pointless chitter-chatter. What he wanted to ask her would start an unquenchable inferno. *Why? Why did you leave?* But it didn't matter now. He knew why she left. And he couldn't blame her. He would drop her off, say goodbye, and work in the background to find her attacker.

"Turn here."

Xavier took a left on Highway 385, a road that led to the Crazy Horse monument north of Custer. Before the monument came into view, Xavier followed Nikki's directions and took a gravel road running west and turned into a driveway hidden by towering pines and granite boulders. It wound up a slight hill and ended in a red-pebbled parking area. A rusted-out Ford Ranger squatted in front of a rustic cabin crowned with a green tin roof.

"Sara's home." Nikki made no move to exit the Jeep. Instead, she fiddled with her seatbelt button, not quite clicking it for release.

Up here, away from civilization, nature ruled with a silent majesty that was anything but quiet. Pine trees whispered, cottonwoods chattered, insects chirped, and somewhere in the distance a creek, which had yet to dry up with the summer heat, burbled. A romantic spot if ever there was one. Except, the woman sitting next to him resembled a ticked-off mannequin more than a touchable, kissable woman.

"Do you want me to come in with you?" Not sure who Sara was, Xavier moved to undo his seatbelt.

"No!"

His fingers stilled, and he clenched his teeth shut.

Nikki closed her eyes and took a deep breath. She finally opened them, and without looking at him, said, "Sorry."

He waved away her apology. "You've had a rough morning. No problem."

Without another word, she hopped from the Jeep and limped to the cabin, shutting the bright red door behind her.

Xavier tore his gaze from the cabin and drove away. He wove through tourist and local traffic and parked in front of the sheriff's office. His vacation had ended early.

*A*uthor Note: *Ah, yes, thwarted love. For those of us who have not experienced heartache, we can live vicariously through Nikki and Xavier. They won't mind; they're pretty cool like that. I'm sure you're wondering what could have possibly broken up high school sweethearts prepared to vow to love each other until death do them part, especially if you've read Amber Waves of Grace and experienced the powerful connection between them. Well, for that, you'll have to wait, but I promise, it's worth it!*

Chapter 3

Nikki leaned against the door, her breath hitching in her throat. *Do not fall apart.* She gulped in a breath and let it out slowly, her nerves ending their spasms as Xavier's jeep grumbled out of her space.

"Nikki?" Sara's voice sailed down from the loft area, a space littered with a thousand fairy lights and rainbow-colored bead curtains hiding the wide opening from the ground floor.

"Yeah?" She was breathless and hated that Xavier still made her blood simmer like cooking caramel.

"You better hurry or you'll be late for your—" Sara clambered down the steep steps and latched on to Nikki's shoulders. "What happened?" She petted the air beside Nikki's wounds, covered with gauze and bandages, and stared at the bloody polka dots spattered on her tank top. Sara straightened to her full five-foot, one-inch height and planted her hands on what she called her "luscious hips" and repeated the question. Being short and fluffy—Sara's words—never stopped her from being a force of nature. It could have been her Type A personality or her flaming red hair, but if one wanted to remain in Sara's good graces, one never referenced either of those attributes.

Nikki willed herself to scream, to stomp her feet, anything but do what her body demanded. She hated crying. She always felt like death warmed over after a crying spell, and her face would be blotchy for hours. Besides, the headache tightening screws in her skull left no room for the after-crying migraine she would inevitably suffer.

Pushing away from the door, Nikki stumbled to the tiny kitchen, ripped open the door, and grabbed the bottle of Moscato that she and Sara had failed to finish the night before. After unplugging the cork with her teeth, she spit it on the floor and drank directly from the bottle.

"Finally succumbed to day-drinking, huh?"

Nikki took another swallow. "Nectar of the gods."

"It has grapes in it. Let's call it juice if anyone asks." Sara yanked the bottle away from Nikki. "Talk."

As if she were telling someone else's story, Nikki relayed the morning's events.

In response, Sara took a swig from the now-communal bottle. "Girl, you got problems."

Nikki glared at her friend as best friends can do and not get punched in the eye. She made a grab for the bottle.

"Nah-ha. Not going to be your enabler. Next thing I'll know, the whole Lancaster family will descend upon us." She planted a hand on her jutted-out hip. "Now, your brothers-in-law are hot enough for me to endure it all, but your mother scares me."

"No different than your mom."

Sakura Kelly, Sara's adoptive mom, was notorious for her green tea and "her feeling." On their first meeting, Sakura, a trim Japanese woman, had demanded Nikki call her Mama Kelly, and used her feeling to predict Nikki's love of the outdoors and rocky road ice cream. With M.D. behind her name, her feeling carried medical weight. After that, it didn't take long for Dr. Sakura Kelly to narrate how she'd met Aidan Kelly, a captain in the Irish Army, through Doctors Without Borders, married him, and adopted a red-headed infant. Either Sara or Nikki got daily texts about Sakura's feeling. What power lay behind the woman's ability to always be right, they could never figure out.

Sara's phone buzzed. She glanced at it and smiled. "Did you have to conjure her up? Here I thought I could go at least one day without a feelings text."

"What does she say?"

"She says, and I quote, 'tell Nikki to stay out of trouble.'"

Nikki's shoulder blades touched. "I love your mom, but she's spooky."

"Try being her daughter. That feeling has haunted me my whole life. I don't think I even had the option of trying to get into trouble." Sara whipped her red dreads into a sapphire scrunchie.

"And now I don't either, apparently." Nikki limped to a couch with upholstery crawling with mama black bears and cute baby bears and collapsed, hugging a bear pillow to her chest. When she and Sara had first moved to the Black Hills area, they had sworn they would never succumb to cabin-y decorating. Within a few weeks, they had thrown that stupid idea out the window and the entire cabin screamed I'm A Cabin In the Woods. They even had a moose toilet paper thingy.

Nikki's ears buzzed with Sara's voice, and she knew faintly that her friend was on the phone. After a few minutes, Sara sank down beside her and gave her a half-hug. "I called into work for you."

"What?" Nikki jumped up and sat back down with an "umpf."

"Just as I thought. Don't cry. You know how you feel about crying, remember?"

Nikki nodded wordlessly, her vision blurring with moisture. Not tears. Moisture. Maybe that thought would make a difference.

"Come on. Let's get you cleaned up. I'll try to wash your hair, at least, in the sink. You can't get those bandages wet yet."

Nikki followed Sara and relinquished her hair to the gentle ministrations of her friend, her thoughts abuzz with the green SUV, the near brush with death, and the all-too-real presence of Xavier Palinski.

"Hey, what's wrong?" Sara's fingers stopped their massaging.

"Nothing."

"Liar."

Nikki stared at the tattoo on her arm that she got her first year in college, her first year away from the often-paralyzing fear of her father and coordinating nagging of her mother, reminding Nikki to "be careful because you know how your father gets." *Yeah, just when it deals with me.* After tracing her finger over the scrawled script, she spiraled her fingernail back over her favorite Biblical quote: There is no fear in love.

Much like a tombstone, the ink reminded her of a time when fear had no sway over her life. That was until her sixteenth year when a semi-truck slammed into her father's pickup, leaving a stranger in his wake. Gone were the moments of praise when she defied danger, lived life on the edge. In its place lived a shell of a man violently ruled by irrational fear.

Warm water from the rinsing process dripped down her neck. Her lungs constricted and froze.

"Dad!" Nikki sprinted into the house and stood, dripping mud and blood on the entryway's tiled floor. "You'll never guess what happened."

Jake's gaze never left the contestants vying for one million dollars on Who Wants to be a Millionaire.

"Dad?" She hoped her mother didn't catch her in the house looking as if she'd rolled through a mud puddle. Well, she hadn't just rolled through it, she had plunged off her bike in the midst of an awesome trick and splatted in. And ripped a huge gash in her shin. "You know Mom's not good with this kind of thing. Hurry before she sees and has a connip-tion."

He tore his gaze off the television and stared at her. His dull gaze, which haunted his eyes ever since the accident, sharpened, his face flushed, and within seconds he crossed the living room floor, his body trembling. Without another look at her or a word, he ran out the door to the crooked-framed bike. With a roar she had never heard before, he latched on to the bike and threw it to the ground.

"Dad, no! What are you doing?" She gripped his forearm. "Stop!"

He pushed her away, lifted the bike again, and threw it harder. Bike parts scattered at his feet.

Nikki screamed but dared not touch the man before her. This was not her father. Couldn't be her father.

Her mother sprinted from around the back of the house and froze at the sight before her. Nikki ran to her.

Jake dragged the bike to the dumpster, and with a guttural cry, slammed the bike into the metal container, and stalked back into the house without a glance at his daughter and wife.

Nikki reached for her mother. "Mom—"

"What did you do?"

The harshness in her mother's voice stopped Nikki from seeking comfort in her arms.

"Get in the house, get washed up, and for the love of God, quit upsetting your father with your stupid antics."

With eyes blinded by tears, Nikki ran into the house and sat in the shower until the hot water scalding her skin ran cold, numbing her from the outside in.

Nikki jumped as a water droplet dripped a cold trail down her spine.

"Sorry, almost done." Sara cupped around Nikki's ear and rinsed the edge of Nikki's hairline. "There. All done."

After helping Nikki rinse her hair and tucked it up in a turban, Sara dragged her out to the bear couch. "Spill it."

"I'm scared." The words stung her throat.

"Of course, you are. If someone would have tried to run me off the road, I'd have crapped my pants. Say, can we hunt this loser down and... you know?"

Nikki concentrated on Sara's played-up squinted eyes and creased lips, a warrior face if she ever saw one. "Those are the words of a true friend."

"Don't you forget it." Sara fussed with the slipping turban. "Back to you being scared."

But words would not squeak by her tight chest and even tighter throat. She couldn't give voice to her fear. Voicing it might make it come to life. Voicing it might make it real. She'd lived so long under the shadow of fear, both her father's unrealistic reality and her fear of doing more damage to her father's already unstable healing brain. The moment she had left the farm, she had taken off the stifling mantle and vowed she would never let fear rule her life again. She would live.

Up until that morning, she had never anticipated her plan going awry.

After a much-needed change of clothes, a two-hour nap, and a hearty meal of tomato soup and a cheese sandwich, Nikki stepped out the cabin door and waited for Sara to latch and lock it before heading to her friend's pickup.

"I think Sampson misses your Bug." Sara patted the battered hood.

The pickup did look sulky. "I hope for his sake, and mine, that I get her back soon. Or if at all."

"Shhh." Sara placed her finger on her lips. "Don't say it too loudly." She ignored Nikki's eye roll. "You want to go to the sheriff's station right away?"

"I better. Get this over with sooner." Nikki's leg bounced as if the appendage had read the word *prestissimo* from her body's inner sheet music. She pressed down on her thigh, hoping to quiet the movement to a reasonable *tardo*. No such luck.

Her leg bounced her all the way to the sheriff's office and jiggled and fiddled throughout the interview. No matter what question the deputy asked her, she had no new insights, nothing to add to the case.

She walked out from the air-conditioned building into the dry heat of Custer and into Sara's awaiting pickup.

"It's sure a cooker out there." Nikki adjusted the vents to blow on her face.

"At least it's not humid. It's the humidity that gets you."

Nikki chuckled at Sara's exaggerated "Fargo" accent, making fun of the Midwestern way of demonizing the moisture in the air. She rested her palm over the bandage on her temple and sucked in a breath. "Apparently, laughing is out for the near future."

"Good thing your doctor's appointment is next."

"Since when?"

"Since I called when you were napping, Sleeping Beauty."

"Are you my mother?"

"No," Sara slid her a glance, "but I could call her. I'm sure she'd be here in a heartbeat. Or at least six hours."

"You drive a hard bargain. I give up. Do what you want."

"Always do."

Nikki let that comment dissolve into silence and watched the businesses, from little tourist traps to diners to mom-and-pop stores held afloat by the tourist economy, whiz by. From the eastern side of the state, she'd always heard how different West River was and didn't quite believe it until she set down semi-permanent roots in Custer. *Not bad different.* Slower paced, an economy held together by the influx of strangers and nature-seekers, and in August, bikers from all over the world. Nestled in the middle of granite and ponderosa forests, Custer's beauty never failed to awe her. From peaks to valleys, Nikki trekked and hiked, capturing moments when nature stood still and smiled.

She fiddled with the window knob. The passenger window hadn't opened since Sara took pity on the old truck and bought it from an old man who wove some fairy story about how the pickup had once saved his life, blah, blah, blah. Nikki had stopped listening to the rambling, but within an hour, her friend was the proud owner of a truck old enough to be her father with a burned orange paint job. Thankfully, nature had done her part, and rain and snow had eaten away most of the ugly paint, leaving better-looking rust in its place.

Sampson, as Sara lovingly called the pickup, jerked into a parking spot at the clinic.

"You don't need to come with me."

Sara struggled out of the seatbelt. "Oh yes, I do. I don't trust you as far as I can throw you."

"What do you think I'd do? Go to the bathroom, wait for twenty minutes, and come back out?"

"That's exactly what you would do."

Not responding to that truth, Nikki stalked to the clinic door.

An hour later, with a diagnosis of a concussion and a see-I-told-you-so look from Sara, Nikki pouted in the front seat of Sampson.

"Are you going to pout all day?"

"Yes. And probably tomorrow too." Nikki glared out the window, ignoring the BOGO Fudge sign enticing passersby into a local chocolatier shop.

"Does that mean I should start advertising for a new roomie?"

"As I'll be unfit to live with for the foreseeable future, you might as well."

Silence held them hostage until Sara brought Sampson to a creaking halt in front of the cabin. The canopy of trees brought an earlier evening than the wide-open prairie, and Nikki shivered. She wasn't cold. The person who tried to kill her was still out there. And she did not know who or why. She couldn't protect herself from a danger she didn't know existed.

"Come on. I'll buy you an ice water." Sara all but pulled her from the passenger seat.

Nikki stumbled out. "I'd rather have wine."

"You heard the doctor. No alcohol with a concussion."

Mumbling about the ineptness of the medical profession, Nikki followed Sara into the cabin and collapsed on the couch. She must have dozed off because she awoke to the soft pressure of her friend's hand on her shoulder.

"Here. Drink."

The cool water healed the cracks on her parched tongue and throat and refreshed her spirits. She owed her friend the rest of the story.

"I didn't tell you everything."

Sara's gaze pinned her like a butterfly to a display board. At Nikki's lengthy pause, she motioned with her hands. "Well?"

"Remember me telling you I never planned on getting married?"

"Yeah, but I thought you were being your overly dramatic self."

Nikki slid her a glance and finished the rest of her water. "I'm never 'overly dramatic.'" She waved off Sara's retort. "Do you want to hear the story or not?"

Sara dropped next to her on the couch, tucked her feet under her, and stuffed her magenta-colored maxi skirt over her toes. "Spill."

Nikki started repeating the facts of the accident when Sara interrupted her. "I've heard this. Cut scene. Move on."

After scowling at Sara, Nikki dove into the past. "I was getting there. The person who first came upon the scene after the Oklahoma couple was a DCI agent." And dang, he had looked mighty fine. Nikki curled her fingers into her palms until she branded the soft flesh. His hair had been just as she remembered, his eyes just as warm and open, until he had shuttered them to her.

"Earth to Nikki." Sara waved her hand in front of Nikki's face.

Nikki blinked. "Sorry. Anyway, the DCI agent is—" she took a deep breath and spoke quickly, "my ex-fiancé."

Sara peered owlishly at her and placed the back of her hand on Nikki's forehead. "How is it that I, your best friend, do not know this? Are you keeping other nefarious secrets? Do you hate puppies? Torture children?"

"And I'm the overly dramatic one, huh?"

"But, but, when, how, why... why?"

"Three years ago. I called it off." Picking at an invisible speck on the couch, Nikki mumbled, "He lied to me."

"Do I need to make sure this cheating so-and-so can never make babies?"

"If you had asked three years ago, I probably would have said yes."

"But now?"

"I don't know." Nikki scrubbed her face.

Sara pointed to Nikki's phone. "Have a picture of him?"

For the past three years, Nikki would occasionally work up the courage to delete the photos of Xavier. Every time her finger would hover over the "Are you sure you want to delete this picture?" warning, she'd chicken out. Part of her hadn't wanted to make his removal from her life permanent.

Knowing Sara would never let this go, she scrolled through her pics and paused on one of her favorite pictures of them. Xavier's arm slung possessively around her shoulder. Her skin tingled at the memory of his naked chest against her bikini-clad one. That day had been blistering, but the water, ice-cold beverages, and tubing had cooled her off, only for Xavier to bring her back to a boiling point with one of his smiles or his kisses or his touch. His smile, wide and unassuming, crinkled the skin around his blue eyes. His cheeks sharpened in that smile, bringing out his chiseled facial features. This was Xavier in his element. Free. Open. Wild. All the things she had wanted to be, but his loyalty to her father's irrationality overcame his promise to help her escape it. In the end, his ultimate betrayal split them apart.

"If you don't show me that picture, I'll snatch it from you and look at whatever I want." Sara's hand reached for Nikki's phone.

"Here." Nikki shoved her phone at Sara. "Happy now?"

"Kiss my ever-loving grits. You said no to this?" She pointed to Xavier's glistening abs with a black-painted fingernail and frowned. "Sorry. He's obviously a lying jerk. What'd he do?"

The urge to spill everything overwhelmed her. She was tired. Tired of plastering a smile on her face, pretending everything was hunky-dory, tired of pretending her father's accident hadn't turned her life upside down and inside out, tired of convincing herself that she had stopped loving Xavier when in truth she never had. This time, she couldn't stop the burning tears and suffocating sobs. Through the tears and snot and hiccups, she dumped her emotional garbage on Sara's shoulder. From her adventurous father championing her escapades morphing overnight into a timid stranger who raged any time he thought her in danger to Xavier's daring promises to protect her from her father's fear.

Promises he failed to keep.

Nikki pressed a tissue against her nose and sniffled. "I found out what he'd done when the travel agent, who was helping me plan all the details for the honeymoon, called me. I assumed there were some changes to the plan... not—" She hiccupped. "Not something that would change the trajectory of my life, you know?"

In silent solidarity, Sara rubbed circles over Nikki's back.

"She told me that... uh... due to 'unforeseen circumstances,' all the activities I'd planned earlier were no longer available."

"What?"

"That was pretty much my reaction too. One after the other, canceled. Paragliding—nope; scuba diving—nope; surfing lessons—nope. By the time I was done striking a Sharpie through my list, I felt like someone had struck a large slash through me. Sounds stupid, I know, but I don't think I ever felt so numb, so…"

"Are you saying that he went behind your back and canceled everything you planned?"

"Everything. Everything he'd promised we could do." Her heart stung in memory of the first skewering pain of his betrayal. "After I found out what he'd done, I… ah… I knew… no matter how much I tried to convince myself that he'd done it out of love… that if I said yes…"

"You would never be free from your father's fear."

She closed her eyes and soaked in the healing balm of someone finally understanding her decision. Guilt slipped in through the balm's cracks. "You know the crazy thing? I never even gave him a chance to defend himself. Just walked in, threw some words at him, and walked out. I don't even remember what I said. And the other crazy thing? I never stopped loving him."

Sara brought Nikki into her side. "Would you say you're a different person today than you were three years ago?"

A laugh scraped from her throat. "I would certainly hope so, but I'm probably the same old trouble-making, stubborn old cow."

"You don't give yourself enough credit. It takes guts to do what you did, to reveal long-hoarded secrets." Sara squeezed Nikki's shoulder. "And if you changed, don't you think Xavier did as well? Maybe the stupid boy finally became a noble man? Don't you think it's worth finding out, at least?"

An after-crying-session-headache clawed at Nikki's brain. "Add that to the list of things I'm terrified of right now. Odd man in the park plus could-have-been-deadly car accident squared by not knowing what in the heck to do with Xavier's return. Want to know what that equals?"

"Massive headache?"

Nikki massaged her temples and worked her fingers backward over her scalp. "Mind if I cancel our *Death in Paradise* date?"

"Promise we get to watch two episodes tomorrow night. And extra popcorn. One bag for each one?"

Nikki stifled a yawn. "Promise."

Sara clapped her hands. "Alexa?" She clapped her hands again, louder. "Alexa, you pay attention now."

If Alexa could give the middle finger to a human, it would pick Sara. Nikki liked to imagine the blue ring along Alexa's rim was that.

"Maybe you should be nice to her."

Sara scowled at Nikki, then at the tiny computer. With a silky, sweet voice, Sara crooned, "Alexa, my darling, please add Mike and Ikes, mini marshmallows, and Skittles to my shopping list?"

Alexa repeated back the list, and Sara grinned.

"What are we going to do with all that?" Nikki shuffled to the bathroom.

"Those, my friend, are key ingredients to Sara's Spectacular Popcorn Salad."

Nikki's teeth hurt thinking about it, but if she survived the morning's events, she should survive her friend's concoction.

Author Note: Where would we be without friends? I'm not talking about the acquaintances who get the occasional head nod or obligatory "how are you?" I'm talking about the friends who stick with you, no matter the stupid or misguided decisions made. I've had several of those friends in my life, and I have no clue where I would be without them today. Perhaps you are fortunate enough to have a friend like Sara, who will create extremely unhealthy but yummy concoctions and threaten to avenge your adversaries. If you are curious about Sara's Spectacular Popcorn Salad, it's simple to make. Make sure you start with a marshmallow-based microwaveable popcorn (major popcorn

brands have variations of this). Then, add your favorite candies. My favorites, like Sara's, include Mike and Ikes and Skittles. I've added Swedish Fish before and haven't regretted it! This is a movie-night tradition with my four kiddos and one of the only times we agree on the tastiness of what's on the menu.

Chapter 4

Xavier exited the sheriff's office, a chip on his shoulder and a boulder sitting in his gut. Something felt off about the whole thing. If he weren't so invested in the victim, he could think clearer, but every time he brought back to mind the crime scene, his stomach twisted, and his chest constricted.

According to Deputy Morrison, Nikki had offered no new insights into the case. With nothing to chew on besides old facts and anxiety, he drove through the dusky evening to his favorite watering hole. An out-of-the-way spot, virtually unknown to tourists unless they stumbled upon it, the Other Place boasted cold beer, edible dill pickle chips, and an old jukebox that played nothing by Creedence Clearwater Revival.

Estella, a server past her prime and preserved by the makeup and Aqua Net of the eighties, brought him his usual: a chokecherry brown ale and a side of dill pickle chips. He went out on a limb and risked ordering a cheeseburger, hoping the cook, who preferred his cow to still moo on the bun, had called in sick.

No such luck. Xavier forced a smile when Estella asked him mid-chew how the burger was. She called him "hun," refilled his water, and left him to contemplate a future bout of food poisoning.

A thick, dark hand the color of leather slapped him on the shoulder, and his best friend and partner in crime plunked down on the empty seat across from him. "Must be hungry enough."

Xavier ignored Thaddeus's pointed look at his plate. "We must all take risks. Want half?"

"Not on your life." Thaddeus leaned back in his chair to nearly to its tipping point. At a little over six foot with the build of an offensive lineman, it was a wonder he hadn't toppled over yet, but in the four years Xavier had known DCI Agent Thaddeus Cornwall, the man had never once even wavered.

"Estella won't like you if you break her chairs."

"These things? If they survived the last three decades, they are indestructible." Xavier's skin had found the rips and tears in the lime-green plastic that passed for fabric. Indestructible was a kind assessment.

After Estella brought Thaddeus his Coors Light, Xavier hid the last three quarters of his burger under a napkin. "Thought you were out of town until next week."

"Plans changed. You know how it goes."

Xavier nodded in silent commiseration. The world of DCI agents often shifted with the slightest criminal breeze. This breeze, however, had a bite to it. He rubbed his thigh, knowing that under his shorts lurked a nasty scar, a reminder of his first run-in with a man wielding a knife.

Thaddeus stole a dill pickle chip and chewed. "Heard from Morrison you're poking your nose in county business."

"More like county business poked its nose in me."

"I told you to keep your radio turned off during your off days." Thaddeus scratched at his goatee.

"Advice I will take from here on out."

Thaddeus motioned for refills, and Estella obliged them and added two winks.

"She must want an extra tip. She's never winked at me before."

"Maybe she finally got her eyes checked and found out how ugly you really are. That is her type." Despite the insult, Xavier knew that women found Thaddeus attractive. He had overheard, more times than he cared to remember, whispered women's voices gushing about

Thaddeus's "sexy hazel eyes," "coppery full lips," and "the cutest afro they'd ever seen." Between that and the James Earl Jones voice, Thaddeus often had a horde of ladies fighting for his attention. Not that Xavier minded the competition. There was one woman he wanted fighting for him, and he knew she had stopped doing that years ago.

"She winked at you too."

Xavier swallowed his beer and his bitterness. "She likes my hair. Says it reminds her of her first Barbie."

Thaddeus's chest rumbled with laughter. "That should be enough to persuade you to cut it off."

"Women like it." One woman in particular, but she no longer cared. *Or did she?*

He couldn't forget that look of regret. It had quickly morphed into disdain, but it had been there. Well, if she was sorry for breaking off their engagement and breaking his heart, she could remain so for the rest of her life. Which had almost been cut too short this morning. Blood roared in his ears at the memory of her blood staining her hair and splattering her clothes. His hands fisted. He needed to gain control of his feelings.

"Want to talk about it?"

Xavier followed Thaddeus's gaze and unclenched his fists. "Nope."

And like a good friend, Thaddeus sat with Xavier, drinking, talking, and listening to John Fogerty sing "Who'll Stop the Rain." Everything except talk about what mattered: Nikki was back in his life, and someone wanted her dead.

Author Note: These are a few of my favorite things: fried dill pickle chips (dipped in ranch, of course) courtesy of a trip to Nashville, Tennessee; a good cheeseburger grilled to perfection medium rare, thanks to my mom, who taught me how to grill; and any song by Cree-

dence Clearwater Revival due to my father, who essentially raised me on rock-n-roll. As for the chokecherry ale, I can't attest to the taste of this beer, but I remember eating chokecherries as a kid until my tongue tingled and went numb with the sour/bitter combination of this tart berry. If you've never eaten a chokecherry, you probably aren't missing out on much, and you can probably figure out the sensation of eating one of these by their name alone.

Chapter 5

" *Nikki, do you want to send your father back to square one? Do you know how hard I have to work to keep him—"* Cynthia pinched the bridge of her nose. Her inhale shook her body. *"I know this is hard on you. It's hard on all of us. It's just that every time you go off half-cocked and—"*

"Do something stupid? I know." Nikki swirled her spoon in a bowl of soggy Honey Nut Cheerios. She knew better than to glare at her mother, so she made do with staring down a drowning Cheerio. *"What do you want me to do? Change everything about me? Quit being myself? Be more like Corrie?"*

"That's not what I said."

"But it's what you meant."

A roaring pickup zooming up the drive saved Nikki from a tongue-lashing.

"Xavier's here." Without giving her mother a hug or even a cursory goodbye, Nikki snatched her backpack, sprinted from the house, and hopped in Xavier's Ford Ranger. *"Promise to take me far away from here?"*

His lips greeted her with a smoldering kiss. "Name the place."

"Tahiti?"

"Is that before or after school?"

"Let's skip school and go right now."

"How about we compromise? I'll take you after we graduate."

She held out her pinky finger. "Deal."

The instant Xavier wrapped his pinky around hers, a red ball cap faded into view, hiding his topknot. His yellow Sandy Mustang shirt morphed into a red-and-green-checkered flannel, and his smiling mouth transformed into a gaping black hole rimmed with jagged teeth. The sound of crunching metal and glass reverberated out of the abyss.

Nikki bolted up in bed. Sheets stuck to her clammy skin. Lightning illuminated her bedroom for a millisecond.

When her room descended into darkness, the remaining dregs of her nightmare vanished. She switched on her bedside lamp and rubbed her eyes, hoping to erase the image of Xavier transforming into the man who stalked her thoughts. There was no way to plug her ears to the conversation between her and her mother in Dreamland. Sadly, that had been part of the daily routine for one and a half years—up until she had left the farm. But even then, her father's fear lurked in the periphery of her life.

She glanced at the opening in the bedside table. Somewhere amidst her lotions, a bushel of hair ties, a few bobby pins, and a nail file, a Bible suffocated under a blanket of dust. She grunted. Her soul probably resembled the dusty cover. But perhaps it wasn't suffocating. Perhaps it was as she thought: broken. Only a soulless teen would have continued making the same mistakes, bringing chaos into her family's life, living out her father's imaginary nightmares.

She slid the book out from under the flotsam and jetsam and cradled it in her hands. The cracked binding harkened back to days when she'd packed it along for her adventures—bike, four-wheeler, camping under the stars, it didn't matter. Without revealing its rice-papery innards, she knew what she would find: a dot of dried chocolate over Saul's name, a tragic victim of a s'more gone wrong; an epic grass stain obscuring Jonah's complaints about having to do his job, courtesy of Nikki not being able to read and walk at the same time; the words "He wept" blurred by her own tears at Jesus's heartbrokenness over the death of his best friend.

With shaking hands, she opened the cover and traced her fingers over the scrawling inscription from her father: *For my Nikki on her twelfth birthday. May God keep you safe—! Love, Dad*

Her throat tightened at the black Sharpie slash through the original text. She could almost hear her teenage self sniveling as her father nearly tore through the paper as he slashed out the words *on all your adventures.* That black ink stamped the moment her Bible quit joining her on adventures. Never again would the wind play with the pages or the sun warm the ink until the faint smell wafted up to Nikki's nose. And just as her Bible moldered away on a shelf in her bedroom, her soul did as well.

She gripped the book until her fingers numbed and her knuckles whitened. No matter how she had emulated Corrie in church, no matter how much or how loud she had sung the hymns, God never felt as close as when His sun shone down on her or when His grass cushioned her feet. Something was clearly wrong with her. She set the Bible down and plucked at a loose thread on her gingham quilt. Her gaze fell on her tattoo. It wasn't the end of the story. Flipping to 1 John 4:18, she focused on the rest of the verse: "but perfect love casts out fear."

She had tried to love her father to the point of sacrificing her own happiness for his, trying to be more like Corrie, Nathan, and the rest who seemed content with church walls and hymns and timed sermons. She had ultimately failed, failed so hard even God had abandoned her. It had been years since she'd felt His presence. *I'm still broken, aren't I?* She cradled her face in her hands and yelped when her fingers pressed against her bruised nose and bandaged forehead.

Sweat beaded on her skin. Air thickened in her lungs. Nikki shoved the blankets off and slipped her bare feet into her bear slippers—a gag gift turned treasured possession from her nephew, TT—and marched out of her room to the front door. A resounding boom shook the house. *Fear does not own you!* She ripped the door open and, under the protection of the front porch awning, stood in her bear slippers and underwear and black cami, watching the rain cascade off the roof. Heaven forbid someone see her like this, but then again—

Someone could be out there, the same someone who had tried to kill her less than twenty-four hours ago. She gripped the hewn porch railing harder, not caring that her fingernails bent inward against the wooden surface.

Tracing the inked scripture with her index finger, she dug her toes into her bear paws and leaned against the porch railing.

Light shattered the darkness. A crash of thunder broke over the cabin.

Nikki added her own resounding answer to the lightning, to her attempted murderer, to the fear swirling in her gut and yelled, "I am not afraid!"

Another thunderous boom swallowed up her response. And instead of running back to her room, she stood there amid the storm. She would conquer her fear.

Author Note: As a Christian, I have, like Nikki, wrestled with God's presence in my life. I believe most Christians have, but there is often a stigma around being honest with our individual faith journeys. This stigma causes people to be silent because they fear what those "perfect" Christians will say about their doubts, their fears. Well, I'm far from a "perfect" person and often have to wipe the dust off my Bible. It's taken me forty years to realize two truths that Nikki must slowly learn (because I'm the mean author): there is no one right way to act out a faith journey, and no matter how inconsistent we are, God never is. He is always constant. Nikki is not the only Lancaster to learn a valuable

lesson about God; her older sister, Corrie, had to learn a lesson or two, as well, in Amber Waves of Grace.

Chapter 6

How dare the happy little annoying birds not care about his headache. Xavier groaned into his pillow and smashed the ends of it over his ears. He hadn't slept at all except in fits and starts. Dreaming, he thought of Nikki. Awake, he thought of Nikki. He needed coffee, black and strong.

His phone pinged a news alert. He read it and groaned. Another woman had been reported missing in the Custer area. None of them were his cases, but he knew the anxiety churning in the investigating officers' guts. Everyone was on edge. Things like this didn't happen in South Dakota.

Shuffling to his tiny kitchenette, which held a dorm-size fridge, hot plate, and his grandmother's microwave from the seventies, he scratched at his chest hair. Coffee. The most modern appliance in the space burbled and hissed out liquid from a K-cup, and within minutes, Xavier brought his Three Stooges mug with the words "To Serve and Protect" to his lips and took a bracing sip of the black brew. It would take a while for the caffeine to leach into his system. Until then, a hot shower would have to do.

Scalded and towel dried, he dressed and talked himself out of pouring a shot or five of Baileys into his coffee. He snatched a banana and a protein bar on his way out the door and bumped into Mrs. O'Malley, his neighbor with a penchant for peeping from and into peepholes. To be fair, she was as nearsighted as a—whatever type of animals were nearsighted—and not light enough to keep the hall floorboards from squeaking an alert.

When the apartment manager had informed Xavier of his new neighbor, Xavier had expected a waddling old lady with an Irish burr. The one thing he had guessed right was the lady part. The rest of Mrs. O'Malley defied the odds. And gravity. From her too-perky chest to her spiky blond pixie cut sharpened into pink spikes and her too-long eyelashes, which looked as if butterflies fluttered whenever she blinked. Now and then, he would find a bottle of Baileys with a bow on it outside his apartment door. That kept the fortysomething widow in his good graces and put his tongue in check when she flirted with him, like now.

"Well, good morning, Officer."

"Good morning, Mrs. O'Malley. And it's Agent. I'm a DCI agent, remember?"

She adjusted the strap on her workout tank top. "Members of law enforcement are all the same to me." Tucking her phone into the waistband of her hot-pink yoga pants, she looked up at him through her butterfly lashes. "I sleep so much better knowing there's an officer of the law right next to me." She glanced to her right and her left and leaned in to whisper, "Especially with a maniac on the loose."

Xavier swallowed a snort. "You know to call 911 first, right? Before you hop across the hall and knock on my door."

She swatted at him. "Silly. Of course I know that." She plugged an earbud into her ear. "Well, gotta run. Going to complete my 5K this morning. Don't worry though. I've got a secret weapon with me today." She dangled a tiny canister of what looked like pepper spray attached to her wrist by a plastic armband.

She saved Xavier from answering when she plopped the other earbud in and darted down the hallway. He would put all his winnings from Deadwood that her 5K ended within two blocks and at Custer's Coffee and Cakes. Smart woman. Running was for morons, and the only reason he sweated through it was so he could still have the occasional slice of pizza and beer and meet his fitness requirements.

He double-checked that his door was locked and trotted to his Jeep. He was already late for his meeting with Deputy Morrison. His phone buzzed. *Change of plans. Grab wit and bring to office. Wouldn't say no to coffee.*

Deputy Morrison could get his own coffee. Xavier grumbled and swung through Custer's Coffee and Cakes and left with a Mrs. O'Malley sighting and three cups of steaming nectar of the gods. By the time he got to Nikki's cabin, his mood had soured to rotten and his coffee—now, Morrison's coffee—had spilled on him. Twice.

He knocked on the door, counted to five, and knocked again.

"Hold your horses. I'm coming."

Another thirty seconds, and the door opened to a whoosh of Des'ree's "You Gotta Be" and a lovely scent of vanilla bean.

"You must be Sara." Xavier held out his hand in greeting.

Nikki's roommate tucked a lotion bottle under her arm and shook his hand. "You'll smell like cookies all day."

"I've smelled worse."

Sara cocked her head, sending her red hair, dreaded with black and white beads, swinging about her shoulders. "I doubt that." She moved aside. "Come in. You must be Nikki's ex-fiancé."

Not sure if that statement needed a response, he stepped over the threshold. The small cabin living space acted as one universe containing two entirely different planets—one with bright colors and beads and lava lamps, the other with soft flowers and vintage lace and cherished old things, all tied together with bears and moose. He had seen nothing like it and doubted he would ever again.

"I'm here to pick up Nikki." Xavier glanced at a decorative teacup and a mini lava lamp sharing shelf space.

"For a morning date? How cute."

"It's not that. I need to—"

"Doesn't matter. She's not here."

"What do you mean?"

"She's. Not. Here."

She'd be perfect for Thaddeus. He blinked at that sudden thought and brought his attention back to her. "Do you know where she went?"

"Back to where she took her photos yesterday. She showed me the pictures she took of that weirdo prancing around with the buffalo. Moron. I hope he got skewered."

Xavier left Sara with her hopes and dashed out of the cabin and into his Jeep. Dratted woman. His heart thumped in odd rhythms as he drove faster than the speed limit and common sense allowed. *Why does she put herself in harm's way? Why can't she ever play it safe?*

His fists tightened on the steering wheel. Being stuck behind a lumbering tourist on a good day was frustrating enough. Being stuck behind one when a nagging fear was poking his conscience was swear-word inducing. "Don't tell me, Montanans, that you've never seen a buffalo before." He decorated the rest of his diatribe with colorful and creative adjectives.

At a scenic outlook, he zipped past the minivan and, within minutes, parked behind a rusted piece of motorized metal. No sign of Nikki.

He adjusted his concealed handgun and picked his way through the prairie grasses. Dew soaked through his tennis shoes after ten steps. If he had known about this impromptu nature walk, he would have dressed for the occasion. Anger mingled with fear, and it was in this emotional state that he found Nikki, her face as white as lead.

"What in the he—"

She stared through him. Her dilated pupils made her eyes black instead of blue. She shivered in the sunshine, and goose bumps gathered in the thousands on her skin.

"Nikki?" He reached out to touch her, but she started and backed away. "What's wrong?"

She didn't answer. Her lips moved, but no sound emerged. With a shaky finger, she pointed to a spot a couple of feet from where they stood.

Hand on his weapon, he crept up to the spot and froze. The animals that had dug it up and devoured it had left little behind except for half a face, random body parts, and the tattered clothing of what used to be a woman.

Author Note: Custer, South Dakota, is a beautiful spot tucked away in the Southern Black Hills. From here, visitors have easy access to Crazy Horse, Mount Rushmore, hiking, and scenic highways that wind up into the heart of the Black Hills. To echo the sentiments of Delilah and Dwayne from Chapter One, the Black Hills is truly a hidden gem. These ponderosa-pine-laced granite hills and the communities nestled among them offer touristy things for those who crave that entertainment and the beauty and splendor of nature to those who want to escape the realities and trials of life. Unfortunately for Nikki and Xavier, the beauty of where prairie and mountain collide cannot and will not shield them from the ultimate tragedy of life: dealing with death.

Chapter 7

Even nestled in one of Xavier's sweatshirts unearthed from the bowels of his Jeep, Nikki could not stop shivering. Whenever she closed her eyes, she saw the ruined remains of a person, someone who used to be alive. Tears slipped down her cheek. She bit her lip. If she cried now, she would never stop.

Warmth seeped through her skin, and she noticed a pair of arms encircling her waist and a muscular chest against her back. Minutes after her gruesome discovery, she had lost track of time. It could have been hours, but she knew minutes had passed between that and Xavier's arrival. Then the peaceful prairie had come alive in whirls of blue and red. Crime scene investigators snapped pictures and took measurements, and law enforcement officials strung a perimeter of yellow crime scene tape. It all felt rehearsed. But this was all too real.

She struggled from his embrace and immediately wanted back in. Jutting out her chin, she heaved a breath. "Why would someone do this?" His silent, sad gaze told her what she already knew. "There will be no justice for her, for the others, will there?"

"I wouldn't say that." He pointed to the CSI team combing over every inch of the scene. "They know what they're doing. I've worked with most of them, off and on. Good people. They'll do everything in their power to find justice—for all of them."

"But what if they don't?" Her voice ended with a high squeak, and she bit the inside of her cheek.

"A wise man once said that justice comes for and to all in the end."

Nikki smiled softly at the mention of Pastor Luke Tuttle. He had married Violet seven years ago, and as Violet was her sister in spirit, Luke was her brother-in-law in spirit. Between him and Corrie, they had polished Xavier until he had sparkled with squeaky-clean goodness. If Nikki could do it over again, she would burn that stupid book of poetry that Corrie had forced upon teenage Xavier. Poetry and flowers had been nice, but she had witnessed the wilting of Xavier's inner rebel, the thing that had made him irresistible and slightly dangerous. The squeeze of his hand on hers brought her back to the present.

"What if that's not good enough? What if..." *What if I can do something?* Her skin prickled at the thought. Adrenaline pumped through her body, heating her skin.

"You will not involve yourself in this. Do you understand me?"

Nikki ground her teeth. "Last time I checked, you are not my father or my hus—"

"Yeah, I know. You don't have to remind me." He stuck his hands in his pockets and watched the crime scene technicians work their magic. "But you do you. I can't stop you any more than I can stop the rain." By the stoop in his shoulders to the flatline of his voice, it was clear he'd given up on her.

Panic skittered up her spine. "Really? That's it? You're not going to stop me from doing something stupid or reckless?"

"And have you accuse me of meddling with your dreams and crushing your independent spirit? You've already done that once, and I don't plan on making that same mistake twice."

"But—"

He walked away.

Nikki clenched her fists at her sides and squeezed them until her fingernails bit into her palms. Deputy Morrison interrupted her internal monologue on the idiocy of men, especially men with the name Xavier Palinski.

"Miss Lancaster, is there anything else you can tell me about your discovery of the remains?"

Nikki shivered at the term "remains." "I already told you all I know."

"One more time, please. I want to be sure I didn't miss anything." He pulled out his notebook and pen. "From the beginning, if you don't mind."

Nikki collected her emotions and thoughts and went back over the morning's events. Something about the mysterious man had niggled at the back of her mind after she had gone to bed. To shake the funny feeling, she had come back to the scene of the photobomb. No, there was no one else around. Yes, she remembered the exact spot because she was that good. And, no, she suspected nothing "peculiar" at the time because who would, on a bright morning full of possibilities?

A CSI technician zipped what was left of the woman into one large evidence bag. Nikki felt her head empty of blood and pool at her feet.

Deputy Morrison gripped her upper arm. "You okay?"

Nikki closed her eyes and dragged in a deep breath, held it, and released it slowly back into the morning air. Her clammy skin felt translucent, and she had the sensation that if she could look at her own body, she would see right through it. But as Deputy Morrison was looking at her with a little concern and not total alarm, she figured she had simply gone pale.

"I'm fine."

"Lying to an officer is a crime."

She held out her wrists. "Then cuff me."

"No wonder he likes you."

Before Nikki could ask for clarification, Deputy Morrison gestured for her to stay and marched over to Xavier. After a minute or two, they both walked back to her, Deputy Morrison with a big grin exposing a gap between his front teeth, and Xavier with an equally big scowl.

"I have ordered Agent Palinski to take you home, Miss Lancaster."

"But I don't need a ride. I have a—"

"I will have your"—Deputy Morrison shot the hunk of rusty junk a wary glance—"vehicle taken back to your cabin." His hand shot up to quell her retort. "You are as white as a ghost and unfit to drive. End. Of. Story." His clipped tone had Nikki tucking her tongue firmly behind clenched teeth. "Agent Palinski would like nothing more than to take you home. Isn't that right, Agent?"

Xavier looked anything but. "Pleased as punch."

He certainly looked like he would like to punch something, or someone.

Deputy Morrison's face softened. "Get some rest, Miss Lancaster. Get something in your stomach and come down to the office. I want to make sure we have every detail. Okay?"

All she could do was nod. Maybe it was a good thing that an officer of the law had taken away her keys. Literally, as they now, sans house key, jangled from Deputy Morrison's utility belt.

She somewhat felt Xavier's warm hand guiding her back through the tall grass and wildflowers, dimly heard his warnings about a gopher hole, and barely registered the swift relocation of her body as he saved her from a twisted ankle.

After being tucked in the passenger seat of Xavier's Jeep and clicked into safety, Nikki stared out the window, twitching to the slam of the driver's-side door. If she could remain in her mental fog, she wouldn't mind it. But she knew that before she was ready, the fog would lift and reveal the truth: something or someone had destroyed a woman thoroughly enough to fit into nothing more than a two-gallon Ziploc baggie. As mental Novocain didn't exist, maybe caffeine would work as a substitute. There were three cups of what she assumed was coffee in the Jeep, and she chose one.

"I wouldn't drink—"

Nikki forced herself to swallow the cold liquid. "Why didn't you warn me?"

Xavier slid her a look but didn't respond. For the rest of the long trip, thanks to one large buffalo who refused to give up in the game of chicken, silence filled the Jeep's interior. Xavier said nothing, and Nikki couldn't. Nothing would pass the large lump of emotions jumbled at the back of her throat.

"Is Sara home?" Xavier's voice was as gravelly as the sound of the Jeep's wheels crunching the pebbles in her cabin's driveway.

"Yes. I took her means of transport. Remember?"

"I'll still come in with you, though, to make sure you get all settled."

"There's no need."

"Direct orders."

Nikki squelched a scream. Instead of retorting with some childish version like "orders shmorders," she hopped out of the Jeep and stormed to her cabin. The door was locked. This time she didn't bother holding in a squeal of frustration. Nikki's hand shook as she tried to jiggle the key into the tricky lock. Xavier's shoes crunched on the gravel and tapped on the wooden planking of the porch behind her.

His warm hand wrapped around her cold and clammy one, and he slipped the key from her fingers. "Breathe."

"Don't tell me what to do."

"Fine, don't take my advice. I'll just have to load your sorry, passed-out hind end back in the Jeep. And you know how I'll do it? Swing you over my shoulder like a sack of potatoes."

Nikki breathed—two big breaths for good measure. "Anyone ever tell you you're a donkey's patoot?"

Author Note: Even though I use Custer State Park to frame the death of an innocent woman, the state park is home to abundant life. Here are some fun facts about Custer State Park:

First, 1,300 bison roam the park. As majestic as these animals look, please do not ever approach one.

Second, Custer State Park offers 71,000 acres of nature to roam around. Whether you are into fishing, hiking, or driving through picturesque landscapes, Custer has you covered.

Third, for hikers or those who love to be on the top of the world, hike Black Elk Peak, the highest point east of the Rockies.

Fourth, make friends with the park's "begging burros". These animals are notorious for sticking their heads in tourists' cars in search of a petting hand or, more commonly, a free snack handout.

And lastly, of course, visit Mount Rushmore. While this monument is not in Custer State Park, it is a hop, skip, and jump away ... and they have awesome ice cream too!

For more information visit, like I did, the Black Hills and Badlands webpage.

Chapter 8

Xavier jammed the key into the lock and twisted it. The lock clicked open, and so did his anger.

"Only you, darlin.'" He swung the cabin door open and gestured for her to enter. "Ladies first."

If looks could kill, he would be dead, but it took a lot more than a death glare from an enraged woman to kill him. *Maybe.* The ignoramus part of him wanted to press her against the doorframe and kiss the glare right out of her. The other two percent of him that wasn't corrupted with thoughts of her wanted to expand that kiss on the couch, on the counter, on the—

He had to deny himself the taste and feel of her for several reasons. First, she would slap him. Second, she would kiss him back. Third, he wouldn't be able to let her run away again. She would well and truly break him into a million pieces. He would have to deal with his anger in a more productive way.

He slammed the door behind him and pointed to the bear-bedazzled couch. "Sit."

She sat without a comment, without a sigh, without even an eye roll.

His heart hummed with pity. Ignoring his conscience, he filled a glass with ice water and offered it to her. "Drink."

She did. All of it.

His Nikki was broken. His anger turned on him and gnawed away at his gruffness. He sank down beside her on the couch. The cushions squished together and tacoed Nikki against him.

"This couch sucks." Xavier pushed himself away but to no avail. The cushions did not care that he hadn't been this close to Nikki for years. And they certainly didn't care that he had wanted nothing more than to touch her for that eternity of time.

"We keep it because of the cute bears."

The absurdity of the situation and the debacle of the couch transformed Xavier's scowl into a grin. "You're kidding, right?"

"I don't kid about bear couches. Besides, Sara would kill me if I got rid of it. She says it brings people closer."

"Your roommate is a loon."

"Yup."

"Where is she? You said she was home."

"Must be out for a hike or something." By the way Nikki traced a cute bear cub with her pinky finger, Xavier could guess at her thoughts.

"She'll be back."

"She always locks the door when she goes out. Claims there're weirdos around every corner and that you can't be too careful. I hope she..."

Thigh to thigh, shoulder to shoulder, they sat, staring at a blank and dusty television screen. Xavier's mind was nothing like the screen, though. Several images zoomed through his head: the destroyed human body Nikki had found, the photos of the missing women running through his mind like a police lineup. All of them were pretty, all of them blond—like Nikki. If anything ever happened to the woman he loved—

Love? His thoughts slowed. *When will I—can I... ever stop loving her?* He knew the answer, and his shoulders hunched. His stomach flipped at the touch of her hand on his.

"You okay?" she whispered.

"I should be the one asking you that."

"I'm okay. Now." Her hand squeezed his and let it go. "Thank you."

That one admission broke him, and his anger quit chewing away at him and salivated to devour the unknown evil that had tainted Nikki with fear and bled her of her zest for life and her sass.

"Want me to whip up some lunch? I can make a mean grilled cheese sandwich."

"I don't think I could eat even if I wanted to."

He understood that. "Well, when you feel up to eating, make sure you do. Until then, rest."

The old Nikki would have argued. This Nikki nodded without comment.

Xavier struggled from the couch's gravitational pull and tucked a magenta afghan around Nikki. The bright color accentuated her pale skin and the purple rings under her tired eyes. On impulse, he leaned down and pressed his lips to her hair. Her silken blond hair hadn't changed, and the scent of her shampoo that used to intoxicate him hadn't lost its power.

A tiny sigh escaped her lips, and Xavier froze. Slowly, so as not to frighten either of them into a stupid decision, he backed away, his fingers trailing a wayward lock of her hair. His hand itched to encircle it around his finger, as he would have done when an abyss of brokenness and heartache hadn't separated them.

"I, uh, will swing back by around four."

A blush stained Nikki's cheeks. "You don't have to."

"I want to." *Please slam the door to my heart. Shut me out.*

"Okay."

He forced himself to smile. He, like an idiot, had offered, and Nikki, very un-Nikki-like, had taken him up on his offer.

Before he could say or do anything else that would have him questioning his sanity, he walked out and closed the door softly behind him. He had a lot to do before coming back. First on the list: back to the scene of the crime to get some answers.

Author Note: Love, or at least a whiff of it, is in the air! And what could be more romantic than a cabin in the woods? From personal experience, nothing, as my husband and I spent our honeymoon in a cabin near Glacier National Park. Wait, I'm feeling a national park vibe going on. Apparently, I really love nature and state and national parks. If you could recommend one state or national park, which one would you pick and why? Tell me where I should go next at Jessicabergbooks.com/contact.

Chapter 9

Nikki emerged from a nap five years later. Or at least, that's how she felt. She fought her way out of the blanket, left it slumped and defeated on the floor, and shuffled to the kitchen. She needed food, caffeine, and a shower, not necessarily in that order.

While she waited for the ancient coffee maker to struggle to life, Nikki nabbed a cookie on her way to shower.

Fifteen minutes later, hair turbaned in one of Sara's psychedelic hair wraps, with two grilled cheese sandwiches and a cup of coffee clutched in her hands, Nikki relaxed in an Adirondack chair on the porch. An inquisitive squirrel tightroped across the roof eave and, gripping with its little toes, leaned forward, shook its bushy tail, and chattered at her.

"Nikki, come here. Quick!" Jake hollered from the tree belt.

Nikki sprinted as quickly as her six-year-old legs could take her out the back door of the barn. She skidded to a halt and bent over, her dirty hands clutching her thighs as she caught her breath.

"Look." He pointed to a pile of fallen tree limbs, victims of the past winter's ice storm.

Nikki squatted and squinted at what looked like a bird's nest. Something shivered in the center of it.

She gasped. "A baby squirrel."

Her father gently grasped her hand when she went to touch the tiny ball of shivering fawn-colored fur. "No. If we touch it, the mother might not want it anymore."

"But... but it's scared, and it's getting dark. Can we take care of it?"

"How about we wait to see if the mother comes back?"

"But... the cats. They'll eat him."

He scratched at a couple days' worth of stubble. "How about we compromise? You and me. We'll sit a watch." He held out his pinky finger.

Her pinky wrapped around his. They made their plan. He took charge of shelter; she handled snacks. That night they sat huddled together in sleeping bags, ate bags upon bags of fruit snacks, and quenched their thirst with juice boxes. Nikki had claimed the nine-to-midnight watch, but she awoke at dawn, curled up in a sleeping bag, a tiny squirrel smaller than her hand tucked up next to her.

Little Ash had been her and her father's first adventure.

The squirrel chattered, and its thumping tail echoed off the tin roof. Nikki shook off the memories of Ash and brushed the crumbs of two grilled cheese sandwiches off her shirt. The midafternoon sun warmed her skin. Coffee wisps rising from her cup steamed her face. Despite the caffeine facial, her nerves twinged, and her synapses fired, recreating the grisly image she had witnessed that morning.

Jane Doe needed Nikki to be strong, not a ninny like this morning. And whatever had happened between her and Xavier should never happen again. Her scalp tingled at the memory of his lips on her hair, the way his finger had seduced it to curl to his bidding. She checked the time, threw the bread crusts on the ground, and hustled into the cabin.

After pulling up her hair into a messy bun, she filled up her travel coffee mug, grabbed her camera, and locked the cabin door as Xavier drove up the driveway. He hopped out and opened the door for her.

Nikki raised an eyebrow.

"Trying to make up for being a 'donkey's patoot' earlier." He shut the door and trotted to the driver's side.

"I never thought you'd take that to heart."

There was a moment's pause. "I take everything you say to heart."

"Well—" Nikki fiddled with her seat belt to buy herself some time. *Nothing.* "Just take me to the sheriff's office, please."

"As you wish." He drove out of the driveway and merged into traffic on Highway 385.

It didn't escape her attention that he used the line from her favorite movie, *The Princess Bride.* She ignored him and settled her sunglasses on her face.

"Were you able to rest?"

"Yeah."

Xavier must have sensed her lie, but he didn't accompany his furrowed forehead with advice or scolds. "You must have had grilled cheese, too, huh?"

She brushed at the front of her shirt.

"You don't have crumbs. I saw a squirrel run off with a piece of cheesy crust. Still not eating those?"

"It's not worth the calories." She hated that he remembered the little things about her.

"That's my favorite part."

"Well, you weren't around to toss it to, so some lucky squirrel got your prize."

Xavier's right cheek twitched.

"What?" Nikki demanded.

"Nothing."

"You have something on your mind. Spill it."

His cheek twitched again. "I think it's better if I keep what I was going to say to myself."

She played his words through her head. "Oh, you... you... jerk!"

"I didn't say anything."

"You didn't have to. You were thinking that it is my fault you weren't around to scavenge my bread crusts."

Xavier braked for a slow-moving tour bus. The moment slowed as well. Nikki studied Xavier with her peripheral vision. His strong jaw tensed to breaking point. His cheek twitched to some inner metronome.

"I'm sorry. That was unfair of me. You don't have to answer me. Actually, feel free to ignore me the rest of the way."

To her surprise and dismay, he took her up on her offer, making the five minutes to the Custer County Sheriff's Office feel like hours. Regret and guilt morphed into anger and stubborn righteousness.

As soon as Xavier parked his Jeep, Nikki jumped out and slammed the door a little harder than necessary. Getting to the glass door of the sheriff's office before him, she yanked it open and didn't bother holding it for him.

She forced a smile for the desk clerk then waited in an orange plastic chair and thumbed through a year-old copy of a gossip magazine. Xavier sat two chairs away, and she felt the yawning abyss between them. Her and her stupid mouth.

Deputy Morrison rescued her from her depressing thoughts, and she and Xavier followed him to an interview room. Spartan in decor, the room housed one table etched with angst and despair and a few metal folding chairs stenciled with "Property of Custer Sheriff's Office." If she was a person of interest, Nikki would have added her own fear to the markings graffitied on the fake wood surface of the table.

"Have a seat and make yourselves comfortable." Deputy Morrison rubbed at his bald head and eyed the room as if seeing it for the first time. "As much as possible. I'll be right back."

Nikki plopped into a folding chair and drummed her fingers on the table.

"I wouldn't touch that if I were you." Xavier crossed his arms and leaned into a corner of the room. Above his head, a CCTV camera blinked.

Her fingers danced a tune on her thigh. She couldn't ignore the goose bumps that broke out on her arms at the sound of his voice. She gave credit to the overall gloom of the room.

"Here we are. Three coffees." Deputy Morrison kicked the door shut. "I'd like to fulfill the stereotype of bad-tasting cop coffee, but I can't. It's some of the best coffee you'll ever have."

Nikki took a tentative sip and sighed. "You didn't lie. That is pretty good."

"Palinski, take a seat. You're making me nervous."

Xavier sat and scooted his chair a few inches away from Nikki.

Deputy Morrison opened his laptop, typed a few things, and asked Nikki to recount the events of that morning. Jane Doe needed her to be strong, so Nikki swallowed and retold how she came across her gory find.

"And why did you go back?" Deputy Morrison stopped typing her words and glanced at her.

"I thought there was something off yesterday with the tourist popping out of nowhere. I didn't give him much thought after that, but last night, I kept replaying the oddity of his location. Tourists rarely walk that far off the road. So, I wanted to see if something had drawn him to that spot. And I can't shake a feeling I have about this guy." *Great, now I sound like Mama Kelly.* "Never mind. Just me over-thinking things again." She placed her camera on the table and slid it over to the deputy. "I took pictures of him yesterday—more to show my roommate another example of annoying tourists. I'm thinking now he is more than that. Maybe he's the guy responsible for the missing women. Maybe more of them are out there." Nikki shivered at the thought and hugged her arms around her middle.

Deputy Morrison finished his hurried typing and took a sip of his coffee. "This man you photographed. He was in the exact spot that we found the woman's remains?"

"Yes." She swallowed the bile rising in her throat. A warm hand enveloped hers. She looked down at her and Xavier's intertwined hands.

"Mind if I keep your camera?"

"That's why I brought it." She'd downloaded the images on her computer.

Deputy Morrison tapped his keyboard. His eyes narrowed in thought. "This is a good breakthrough. Whether or not you got his face, we have something to go off of." He stood and shook her hand. "Thank you, Miss Lancaster. I'll be in touch."

"You go ahead, Nikki. I want a word with Deputy Morrison." Xavier held the door open and closed it after she'd left.

She stood outside the uninviting door, her arms crossed and foot tapping. Seconds ticked by, then minutes. Eventually, the door opened, and Xavier's feet stuttered to a stop at the sight of her.

"Sorry to keep you waiting. You could have waited out front."

"And read gossip about people I don't know from a year ago? No thank you. I'd rather wait patiently right here."

He eyed her tapping foot and crossed arms. "Patiently, huh?"

"Take me home. Please."

"As you wish."

Nikki squelched the urge to kick him down a steep grassy hill, but as there were none in sight, and Deputy Morrison would arrest her for assault, she compromised by jutting out her chin and enclosing herself in his Jeep without his help.

They became part of the stream of traffic making a pilgrimage to the Crazy Horse Memorial but turned off the road before Crazy Horse's stone face came into view in the distance. She had hiked that monument before and had stood under the stern gaze of the Indigenous leader. Sweaty and breathing harder than she should have, Nikki had completed the Volksmarch with a record-breaking fifteen thousand other people on a mission to connect to nature and a past in the process of being set in stone.

Xavier parked the Jeep in front of her cabin. "You did well today."

She opened her mouth to thank him only to be thankful she hadn't wasted those words when he continued with the unsolicited advice of keeping her nose out of police business and letting the professionals do what they did best.

Without waiting to hear more of Xavier's "wisdom" or safety recommendations, Nikki scooted out of the Jeep and entered the safety of her cabin. Stupid man and his brilliant words of advice. Because he was right. She should keep out of it, but it couldn't hurt to study the pictures she had taken. No harm ever came from looking at pictures.

Xavier's goal of finishing his mini vacation with a cold beer and hot pizza ended with a swig of lukewarm coffee and a stale donut. He kicked back in a beige cloth-covered chair that hadn't had its innards replaced since the seventies. At least that was the age he'd estimated the lumps and bumps poking him in the backside to be.

"So, Morrison, you owe me a beer and pizza."

Xavier wasn't sure what Morrison's first name was. He wasn't sure anybody knew it. All he knew was that the letter E preceded the deputy's last name. Bets were still out, and Xavier had ten bucks on Eugene. It fit the bald, gap-toothed, lanky individual sitting upright at the desk across from him.

Deputy Morrison grinned, showing off the gap between his two front teeth. "After this conversation is over, you might want to up the ante and opt for something stronger." He pulled eight-by-ten photographs from a manila envelope and spread them over his scarred desk. "We developed these from Miss Lancaster's camera."

Xavier sat forward in his chair and plied the corners of one with his index finger. "Not a lot of detail on the face, huh?"

"From the looks of it, a male wearing a red ball cap."

"Better than nothing."

"Nothing's about it. Flannel, T-shirt, and jeans, nothing special about those. Even the hat. Just a red hat, no insignia, nothing." Morrison jabbed his finger at one of the pictures. "Who walks around with such nondescript clothing?"

"Someone who doesn't want to be noticed."

"Bingo."

Xavier grabbed a zoomed-in photograph of the unknown man. Nikki apparently had wanted to get a close-up, but the angle of the hat and subsequent shadow hid any distinguishable features of the man's face. "Can we get an estimated height and weight? The flannel looks bulky. It'll be hard to get decent body measurements."

"We'll see. I sent these in for processing." He clicked a pen shut and used the end to point out a detail on another picture. "Tell me, though, who goes for a nature hike in the middle of the summer in flannel with leather gloves hanging from one's back pocket?"

Xavier whistled between his teeth. "That's my clever girl." He ignored Morrison's questioning glance and studied the picture closer. "They look like standard leather work gloves. And you're right. No tourist would walk around with these unless they had a specific purpose for them."

"You think he's a hiker?"

"No. Besides, hikers wouldn't use these types of gloves, anyway."

"Palinski." Morrison squared his shoulders. "I don't think Nikki Lancaster took pictures of an annoying tourist. I think she was right when she said she took pictures of a killer."

Author Note: I will be the first to admit that my photography skills are less than exemplary. Still, that does not keep me from taking my cell phone out into the wide-open prairie. One would think that the middle-of-nowhere South Dakota would offer nothing for an amateur photographer's lens. I disagree and have photos to prove it. From pur-

ple-and-pink alfalfa to yellow clover to the black-spotted, red ladybugs crawling along the green stalks of the wildflowers, the prairie shows its beauty to those willing enough to capture it. One of the most unique places in South Dakota to photograph, and one that is on my bucket list is the Badlands. Despite the at-times hostile environment, this rugged, awe-inspired place conjures up images of the past, of adventure, and of endless possibility and endurance. If you're ever on I-90, going through South Dakota, consider getting off the beaten trail and taking the scenic route through the Badlands. Don't worry, it takes you back to the real world and back on track, but I can't say you won't be sorry when you see the rust-and-cream striated rocks in your rearview mirror.

Chapter 10

Normally, Nikki felt safe in her homemade photo lab, a liberal term for the dark dirt hole of the cabin's basement, made darker with its sole window sealed off by a heavy-duty tarp and duct tape. Usually, freshly developed photos clipped with clothespins filled the space whenever she felt the urge to use her film camera.

Currently, her skin crawled. As it wasn't the dank darkness around her, it was probably the unknown man sporting a red ball cap in the photo she was manipulating on her laptop. The more she studied it, the more she knew that man didn't belong there. He had trespassed on nature. She couldn't fight the feeling that he had also encroached on someone's life.

She needed sunlight and air. After snapping her laptop shut and tucking it under her arm, she climbed the ladder and pushed at the storm shelter doors. They parted, and Nikki darted out into the small area of patchy grass and pine cones behind the cabin. The space between the back of the cabin and the first layer of forest allowed two lawn chairs and a grill. She needed more than sunlight and air. Her soul craved wide-open spaces, empty highways without a curve, a road so straight that on a good day, she could see fifty miles.

The urge to go home overwhelmed her. Maybe if she heard her sister's voice—no, she would end up blabbering all about her grisly find, and within six hours, the entire Lancaster-Tuttle relations would descend in force. And her father—her breathing hitched, and she pressed a fist to her sternum. If he ever found out what happened to her... Bile snaked up her throat. He could never know. It would kill him. For the first time, she was grateful she wasn't on her parents' car insurance plan.

"Nikki?" Sara called from the front of the cabin.

"In the back. Coming." Nikki traipsed to the front porch, entered the kitchen, and stopped short.

Sara sipped the last of her lemonade from her glass and grabbed her rainbow-splattered unicorn lunchbox for her night shift at Custer Clinic. "What?" She brushed at her scrubs. "It's a full moon tonight. Lucky scrubs are a must."

Nikki cringed. Sara's lucky scrubs were rather unlucky, as they still bore a few holes from when a patient had set her on fire, but Sara had taken it as a fortuitous sign and wore them on Friday the thirteenths, full moons, and Halloweens.

"Stay out of trouble," Sara reminded Nikki as she closed the door behind her.

"Why do people keep telling me to stay out of trouble?" she mumbled to the empty cabin and opened the fridge devoid of anything unhealthy and chocolaty. Time for a trip to town.

She grabbed her purse, waltzed out the door, and froze. The driveway was empty. Gritting her teeth, Nikki marched back into the cabin, slammed the door, and contemplated making a meal out of carrot sticks and ranch. And even though she could drink ranch with a straw, her tummy rumbled for something more, something Chinese.

Is it worth the Lyft fare?

For the Chinese food the Woon family created at their restaurant, she would pay the hefty fee. After arranging a ride, she called the mechanic shop and barely maintained her composure with the news that Bug wouldn't be able to come home for another week. The man she spoke to must have sensed her negativity and offered a loaner vehicle. After getting into her Lyft, she finalized the details of her new ride and had her driver drop her off at the mechanic's shop.

The proud driver of a baby-blue Lincoln Continental the size of a boat, she parked a few blocks away from Woon's Family Chinese Restaurant and ordered her usual. It felt good to sit in her typical booth facing the large picture window looking out onto Custer's Main Street. She doused her beef and broccoli with noodles in soy sauce and, with chopsticks, dove into her meal.

Next stop, the grocery store to stock up on essentials. After making gibberish small talk with the owner's two-year-old daughter, who toddled around and visited with all the customers, Nikki exited the restaurant and entered the flow of tourist traffic on the sidewalk. It never ceased to amaze her how every corner of the planet met in the least populated state in America. Maybe the Indigenous tribes of the Black Hills area were right; this place was powerful and mystic. In a span of two city blocks, she overheard five different languages and brushed shoulders with people of different ethnicities and races.

She slid onto the Continental's driver seat and started up the engine, which resembled that of a lion with laryngitis. She didn't have a choice until Bug was healthy again, so she dampened her pride and pulled out into traffic. A car horn blared coming from the opposite direction. Nikki glanced out her passenger window at an SUV that hadn't been there seconds ago when she had looked. It must have come barreling down the street. The windows were too tinted to see the driver. Probably a stupid teenage boy.

Nikki glanced in her rearview mirror at the vehicle. An SUV. A dark-green SUV. With tinted windows. Her mind flashed to the SUV that had purposely driven her off the road, almost killing her. Her palms dampened with sweat, and she clutched the steering wheel a little tighter. Even though her stomach roiled, Nikki could not be the victim anymore. She turned into a parking lot, whipped a U-turn, and followed the green SUV, keeping a buffer of at least three cars between them. The nagging words of warning from Xavier and Sara replayed like a broken record in her head. She shook them off. Besides, she hadn't found trouble. Trouble had found her.

Author Note: There are two things I can identify with Nikki from this chapter. Well, three, if you consider my love of ranch ... yes, I totally hit the Midwest stereotype on that one. But, back to the two similarities. I love open spaces. The wide-open prairie, the long stretches of road. seemingly never-ending, far outweigh the tight, confined spaces of woods and mountains. While I love visiting these places and find them beautiful, I could never live in them. However, I know people from mountainous or wooded areas who say the same about the prairie, that the expansive openness makes them feel vulnerable. Which landscape are you more comfortable in? Or are you a beach-type person who needs the ocean? The second deals with finding trouble and my children. If you have kids, maybe you can relate to this one. I have four children, each with differing personalities. When it comes to trouble, my oldest boy is often a victim of unforeseen circumstances. Not that I let him off the hook for it! My youngest son, however, is a different story. Trouble doesn't find him; he finds trouble and then wallows in it until he's covered from head to toe.

Chapter 11

Xavier gripped his cell phone until he feared the screen would crack. He slammed his Jeep door closed and stalked over to a blue Lincoln Continental parked in the parking lot of Lynn's Dakotamart, the grocery store in Custer.

He rested his forearms on the open driver's-side window. "What in the blue blazes do you think you are doing?"

Nikki jumped and clutched at her chest. The look she gave him should have turned him to stone. "Xavier! You gave me a heart attack."

"What are you doing here?"

"Grocery shopping."

"Really? From your"—he gave the blue behemoth a once over—"car?"

"First of all, it's a loaner until Bug is fixed, and second, I was making the list in my head. You know what they say about shopping without a list. You end up buying things you don't—"

"Nikki, someone called in a blue Lincoln Continental for suspicious activity."

Her skin flushed, and she traced the car's insignia engraved on the steering wheel. "Probably a lot of those driving around."

Xavier hauled himself to an upright position and walked around the front of the car and slid into the passenger seat. "The driver of a green SUV—yeah, the one you're parked behind—called you in from the grocery store. Apparently, you've been following her around town for half an hour."

"Fancy DCI agent doing the grunt work now, huh? Kind of—wait. Did you say 'her'?"

"Yes. For some reason, the woman in question does not appreciate being followed." Despite Nikki's asinine behavior, he wanted nothing more than to kiss the frown off her face. "When she called in, Morrison connected the dots and called me. He figured you wouldn't want the flashing lights and handcuffs."

"Handcuffs? Really?"

Xavier gave her what he hoped was the perfect authoritative stare. "Yes."

Her bottom lip poked out, not in a full-on pout but enough to pull at his heartstrings. *Darn it! Why on God's green earth did this woman bumble back into my life?*

"I didn't mean any harm. I wanted to see who had..."

Xavier's heart tripped. "Whoa. Hold on. You thought the person driving the SUV was the guy who tried to kill you? The same guy who probably killed the woman in the park? And probably more?" Xavier pushed his fingers through his hair and pulled. Hard. "What in the hell were you thinking? You were going to what? Go up to him and ask him his name and if he killed anybody recently? Are you insane—"

Her sobs broke his stride. His Nikki never cried.

"I'm sorry, Nikki." He reached across the seat for her hand.

She yanked her hand away and smashed it on the steering wheel. Hissing in pain, she cuddled it to her chest and rocked back and forth in the driver's seat, tears streaming down her blotchy red face.

"Nikki, please, I—"

"Go away! I don't need your scolding. I already feel foolish enough without your help."

"I didn't mean to make you feel foolish. But what you did is. Don't look at me like that, Nikki. Seriously, think about what you were about to do." His stomach lurched at the thought of her idiotic plan. "You could have become the next—I can't tell you how much—" He clamped down on his emotions and swallowed the rising panic. "Just don't do anything stupid, again."

"You don't understand," she whispered.

"What don't I understand?"

She scoffed. "You never have. I don't want to sit back and do nothing."

"But you haven't. Your pictures shed some light on a case that has been going nowhere. You took such detailed pictures we should be able to get something from them." If there was anything specific to get.

"But what if I can help more? This guy doesn't know who I am. I wore that stupid, ugly hat, remember? Besides, I'm not driving the same car, and if I found him, I could—"

"No. No. No." Xavier ground his teeth, a habit his mother and his dentist warned him against. He usually did well unless under duress or stress or dealing with pigheaded, stubborn women. "I will arrest you myself and stick you in a jail cell until this blows over."

"You can't. You wouldn't."

He reached into his back jeans pocket and pulled out a set of zip-tie handcuffs and dangled them between his thumb and forefinger. "Try me."

Her face bleached of the red blotches. "I'll scream."

"Parking lot's empty."

"I'll punch you. In the face."

"I've had worse."

Nikki growled.

Xavier growled back.

"Fine." She held out her hand in a truce.

Xavier eyed it as if it would bite him. "Really?"

"Scout's honor."

"You were never a Girl Scout. Doesn't count."

She huffed and stuck out her pinky finger. "I pinky swear to not make any more stupid decisions."

He knew there was a loophole somewhere in there, but he entwined his pinky with hers. "I take my pinky swears seriously." He held up the handcuffs again. "Very seriously."

Nikki held his gaze, but her right eye twitched. "Maybe I like the idea of handcuffs."

Fire coursed through his veins. *This is what it must be like to spontaneously combust.* He prayed the heat on his face remained internal and would not betray him in a blush. "I make them tight."

"Good. I like them tight."

Xavier clamped down on a swear word. This infernal woman was going to make him lose his mind. And as she already had his heart, he needed to put distance between them. A whole state's worth. His cell chirped at him. He dug it out of his pocket and read it. "Morrison wants to know if I have the situation under control."

"Am I the situation?"

"Yup. And do I? Have it under control?"

She snorted. "Probably not. But a pinky swear is a pinky swear. You can trust me."

He squinted at her twitching lip. "I'm going to leave now, and so are you."

"But I have groceries to get."

"No, you don't. At least not until the offended woman leaves the premises and is assured that no creepy car is stalking her."

"Did you get her name?" She scoffed at his negative answer. "But I never had time to look at the SUV for scratch marks or anything from—"

This time Xavier didn't hold back a swear word. "You have until I get out and get in my Jeep to get this car started and out of the parking lot. I will follow you back to the cabin, and that is where you are to stay the entire day. Do you understand?" He held up a finger to stem the retort he could see forming on her lips. He scrambled out of the passenger seat and jogged to his Jeep. He didn't miss Nikki's neck craning as she attempted to get a good look at the green SUV on her way out of the parking lot.

He followed her home, made sure she got out of her vehicle, and escorted her to her door.

"Gonna lock me in too?" Her eyes flashed at him. Well, they were about to do a lot worse after he completed the next step in the keep-Nikki-out-of-trouble scheme.

"Don't tempt me." Afraid of his own reactions to her and his inability to control his tongue, he pointed to her door. "Get in."

She rolled her eyes and almost stomped her foot but, in the end, did as demanded. And slammed the door as an exclamation point.

He jumped in his Jeep, and before leaving the driveway, he dialed a house phone number he hadn't dialed in years. It was strange how the brain held on to information the heart no longer cared to know.

Four rings.

"Hello?"

"Corrie? It's Xavier. We need to talk."

Author Note: This scene was a blast to write. I found myself, as I was typing, taking on Nikki's and Xavier's voices. Oddly enough, Xavier sounded Irish. Not sure why as if his last name means anything, you'd think he'd sound Polish. Despite my ineptness at doing any accent apart from a hyperbolized Midwest accent, it was fun to "hear" my characters. To add to the fun, I went back through their scenes in Amber Waves of Grace to "hear" their teenage voices. It just wasn't the same. Does it make me crazy to be slightly saddened that my characters have grown up?

Chapter 12

After sitting in the cabin for hours, sans snack food and Sara's sunny personality, Nikki felt like the proverbial little black rain cloud. Between bouts of self-pity and humiliation at being caught following an innocent person, she forced herself to think of the repercussions Xavier tried pointing out to her. *What would have happened if the person was the killer?* She scrubbed her face, winced at the stinging pain of her wounds, and reached for her wineglass. Empty. She glared at the dot of wine at the bottom of the glass.

By now the wronged woman would be safely home. Xavier could not arrest Nikki for going back into town for provisions. She glanced at the time on her cell phone. She had thirty minutes before the store's closing time of nine. Briefly, she thought about calling him and apologizing. But that lasted a nanosecond before she flicked it away, grabbed her purse, opened the door, and stared into the face of her sister, Corrie.

Nikki slammed her hand over her heart and took two steps back. "Corrie! What are you doing here? Where's Aaron? TT?" She paused and cocked her head at Corrie's scowl. "Did I forget something? Did we make plans? I'm going into town to get wine and—"

"We need to talk." Corrie swept past her with a wave of indignation and authority only an older sister could possess. "Now."

Nikki took a couple of seconds to shut the door and gain her composure. Gluing a smile on her face, she plopped next to her sister, who had plunked down on one end of the couch. "So, to what do I owe the pleasure of your visit?"

"A six-hour drive after the phone call I got is not something I would call a pleasure." Corrie readjusted her ponytail keeping her waves of brown hair confined. Her mocha-colored eyes pierced Nikki, and Nikki relived the feeling she'd experienced after Corrie had caught her and Xavier in the semitruck cab years ago.

"What phone call? Who called—" Nikki clenched her fists so tight her fingernails bit into her palms. "Xavier. I'll kill him. Slowly. Painfully."

"You can't kill him if you're across the state. And that's where we're going. Home."

Nikki sprang from the couch. "No."

"I'm not sure you have a choice."

"Quit treating me like I'm a child. I'm not a scared seventeen-year-old anymore. I am more than capable of taking care of myself and—"

"Nearly getting yourself killed." Corrie's voice hitched at the last word. Her eyes shone with tears. "Can you imagine..." She grabbed a tissue from her purse and blew her nose.

Nikki sat back down and clutched her sister's hand. "I'm sorry. I really am." She jerked on Corrie's hand until her sister looked at her. "Do you believe me? I never meant to put myself in harm's way. I wanted to make a difference for that poor woman. I want to help give her justice."

Corrie sniffled. "I understand, but that's not your job."

"No, you don't understand. I'm the one who found her, the one who watched some crime scene tech zip what was left of her in a Ziploc bag... the one who saw the killer."

"Which means he saw you too—and tried to run you off the road, for heaven's sake. Do you hear yourself?"

"He probably only saw that ugly hat I promised Dad I'd wear. There's no way he saw me. Besides, Bug is in the shop. He wouldn't recognize the car I'm driving now, anyway. And I already pinky swore Xavier that I would behave. I have a better chance of being eaten by a rabid shark than coming face-to-face with a murderer."

Corrie pinched the bridge of her nose and muttered under her breath.

Nikki did not ask for clarification. "I'd offer you some wine, but my shopping was derailed." She waited a beat and asked, "Does Mom know?"

"No. But if you don't come home with me tomorrow, I swear I will call her." Corrie wagged her cell phone in front of Nikki's face.

Nikki made a grab for it and missed. "Dad! We can't. What about Dad? He can't... this will... break him." Her voice cracked.

"He's stronger than you give him credit for. Years of therapy have helped him, and besides, Mom's the Dad Whisperer now. Aaron calls it voodoo. If he does start to freak out, she'll talk him down."

A spark of hope warmed Nikki's heart. Not trusting it for a second, though, she rested her hand on Corrie's forearm. "Please, I'm so close to making my dreams come true. I can't up and leave. Why, the other day, I got a solid lead that could break me into National Geographic. I thought you'd be prou—"

"Your boss has already been spoken to."

"What the—" Nikki gaped at Corrie. "I am not your farm. You have no right to barge into my life and order me or my life around."

"Done pitching a fit?" Corrie held up her hand to quell Nikki's retort. "I didn't call your boss. Xavier did." Corrie covered Nikki's hand and didn't blink when Nikki jerked away. "This is for the best. If you can't keep yourself out of trouble, I will do it for you. You can come back when this maniac is caught."

Heat seared Nikki's skin. He'd done it again—gone behind her back, made choices for her. Her palms stung. She released her tight fists. "That could be months. Years... I can't leave Sara here all by herself." Even though she knew Sara would never leave this cabin or her patients because of some madman running around, killing people, Nikki wouldn't—couldn't—leave without trying to convince her.

"Ask her to come with." Corrie jerked her head in the direction of Nikki's bedroom. "You better pack enough clothes for an extended stay at the farm." Corrie's phone rang. "It's Mom." She held up a finger and walked out the cabin door.

Knowing Corrie and Xavier held the winning hand, Nikki trudged to her room and hauled out her largest suitcase. *I'm only packing for two weeks.* After that, she would be back.

Author Note: As you can probably tell by now, family plays a huge role in my story—all my stories, really. I am the oldest of five siblings with my youngest brother being twenty-one years younger than me. Yup, you heard me right. Twenty-one years! I have no clue what I would do without my crazy, awesome sisters and brothers. With so many different personalities making up the fabric of my family, sometimes I worry about my parents' sanity. Not that they had that in the first place. Due to being part of such a large nuclear family and extended family (I have about 50 first cousins), family dynamics have always intrigued me. Add imperfect humans into the mix and family drama is sure to arise.

Chapter 13

Xavier sipped his beer and held the cold bottle to his temple.

"Rough day?" Thaddeus shuffled a deck of cards and dealt two to himself, Xavier, Morrison, and Cody Boyd, a new game warden invited to Poker Night Friday at Xavier's apartment. The new officer had handled the grisly crime scene two days before without losing his breakfast or his cool and, thusly, had earned Morrison's respect. By proxy, he had earned Xavier's and Thaddeus's.

Xavier glanced at the cards in his hand. Two hearts, one of them the queen. *That must mean I am the joker.* "You can say that again." At the big blind, he had already put in his chips, so he checked. As the rest of the guys contemplated their hands, Xavier snuck his phone out of his pocket and read the text from Nikki. It was short, sweet, and to the point. And it tore at his soul. *Thanks for narcing me out. You have proven why I could never marry you.*

Thaddeus flipped over the first card on the table. The flop revealed another heart.

"Want to talk about it?" Cody upped the ante.

Thaddeus choked on his sip of beer, and Morrison looked downright ashamed of the young man.

Xavier smiled. "You are new, aren't you?"

Cody's face turned crimson, giving his red hair a run for its money. He swallowed so hard that his Adam's apple bobbed at least two inches. "Sorry. I, uh, was trying to... help. Sometimes talking about things helps me, so..."

Xavier waved a dismissive hand. "No worries. Nothing I can't handle." *Liar, liar!*

Cody looked as if he wanted to argue, but a side glance from Morrison had the young game warden snapping his mouth shut and fiddling with his remaining chips.

Morrison played a poker chip between his thumb and pointer finger. "Cody here will eventually learn the ropes. It's not his fault Bryce put in for an extended leave of absence, forcing Cody up in the ranks. Surprised all of us, didn't he?"

If Morrison expected a response from the clearly chagrined game warden, he would be disappointed.

"Bryce? I don't recognize the name." Not that Xavier knew every law enforcement officer by name in the area, but he did pride himself on knowing most of them.

As a DCI agent, he worked with and headed up investigations that included a variety of municipal, county, and state law enforcement offices. Having an excellent rapport with his comrades often made his "intrusion" on local cases smoother. The less head-butting, the better.

"He was a good guy." Morrison scratched at his bald head. "Can't figure out why he left."

Cody gained the ability to speak. "He mentioned something about an uncle or something like that."

Morrison took the information in stride and shrugged. The poker game continued. The turn and the river lay on the table, displaying two other hearts. All but he and Cody had folded. Cody added to the pile of chips. Xavier met Cody's amount and raised the stakes. A pile of chips awaited either of them. If Xavier played his cards right, he would end this round a winner. He mentally grunted. With his luck, he would screw even this up.

Cody met his wager, and they flipped their cards.

Cody hissed through his teeth and pushed the pile of chips to Xavier. "Nice hand. I thought I had a good one with three of a kind."

"Thanks." Xavier stacked his chips according to color and awaited the next deal.

Morrison's phone rang. He answered it. His face paled. "Be there in fifteen... yeah, I'll tell them." Morrison slammed his phone back in his pocket. "Palinski, Boyd, saddle up."

Glad he hadn't even finished his first drink, Xavier grabbed a light jacket embroidered with the DCI's logo and tucked his gun in its holster.

"Anything I can do?" Thaddeus asked.

"Yeah, tally the chips." Xavier stuttered to a stop. Nikki, Corrie, and Sara were alone in a cabin in the middle of the dark woods. "Could you do me a huge favor?" He gave Thaddeus directions to Nikki and Sara's cabin.

Within ten minutes, the whirling lights of Morrison's cruiser and the headlights of Xavier's Jeep and Cody's vehicle joined the light show already illuminating the night sky. Generators powered spotlights, and if Xavier didn't know any better, it could have been the scene for some impromptu party. But it wasn't.

All three men joined the assembled law enforcement on the edge of the park. Grass that hardly ever felt the touch of a human shoe was trampled under heavy boots except for a ring of grass still standing knee-high fifty yards away. Only a select few would be allowed in. The fewer people, the less crime scene contamination. Flashes of light emerged from the tall grass. Xavier shivered. It was one thing to see the destruction of human life, but to photograph it was personal.

"Palinski!"

Xavier held his hand out to his boss, DCI Special Agent Supervisor, Cal Magee. "What's going on?"

"Another body. We've been called in to assist."

Xavier slipped on gloves offered by Cal and walked into the grass. Despite the bright lights keeping the darkness at bay, nothing could dispel the evil before him. He had seen some awful things in his life, had learned to turn the emotion off, but the body of the young woman lying in a fetal position and nestled almost tenderly on a pile of grass, her palms pressed together and resting under her cheek, ignited a rage deep inside his gut. Checking his reaction, storing it for later, he methodically searched for evidence. Long blond hair, bloodstained a dull rust color, hung in tendrils over the bruised and battered face.

Xavier could not erase the image of Nikki's blond hair from his mind. His stomach clenched at the thought of finding her like this—and that she'd actively sought out the killer.

"You're grinding your teeth." Morrison tucked a rope that had theoretically bound the woman's hands as evidenced by the snakelike bruising on her wrists into an evidence bag. After a deputy, who had photographed the scene, informed them he was done, Morrison asked, "What gives?"

Xavier ignored him and flashed his light over the tattered remains of the dead woman's butter-yellow shirt. Nikki often wore a shirt with the same off-the-shoulder style. He closed his eyes against the thought. *Get ahold of yourself.*

Morrison wrote on the evidence bag encasing the rope he'd found wound neatly and placed it a foot away from the body, closed it, and reached for a smaller one. "Maybe Cody's right. You need to get something off your chest." Morrison glanced around. "No one around 'cept you and me"—he looked down at the body, his gaze a mixture of anger and sympathy—"and this poor girl."

Xavier trailed the beam of light down the angle of her bruised cheekbone and along her left hand tucked under her cheek. A white line around her ring finger glared at him from the surrounding tan skin. Either she had taken the ring off herself recently, or the killer stole it. *A memento of the kill?* He sat back on his haunches and rubbed his upper arm across his forehead. "It's Nikki." At Morrison's prompting, Xavier elaborated. "She hates me."

"How is that different from before?" Morrison plucked a piece of ribbon entangled in some long grass and tucked it in a bag, wrote on it, and placed it with the others.

"You're real helpful." Xavier bent down and picked up a piece of red flannel cloth that did not match any of the victim's clothes. After storing it away and writing all the information required, he continued his hunt for evidence and brought Morrison up to speed on the Nikki situation.

"Dude, you called her sister? I'd hate you too."

Xavier didn't have time to reply. The coroner arrived, asked a few questions, collected the body, and wheeled it away, encased in a black body bag, on a gurney. After that, Cal Magee posted officers around the scene to secure it and announced the time to reconvene in the morning.

Daylight always brought a new perspective to a crime scene, and Xavier wanted more than anything to find all the perspective he could to catch this demented maniac, put him behind bars, and make it safe for Nikki to come back. Even though she would never be part of his life, knowing that by tomorrow afternoon she would be on the other side of the state made his heart ache. But she would be safe... *and hating me for it.*

Author Note: When most people think of South Dakota, they probably have nothing to say or a lot to say. Either way, most could probably agree that nothing bad happens here, that murder and mayhem seem to skip this little-known Midwest state. While this is probably true as South Dakota's crime rate is one of the lowest in the nation, this state claims a few encounters with some well-known historical criminals

and overall bad boys/girls who made the notorious Wild West town of Deadwood a living legend. Wild Bill Hickock, Calamity Jane, Poker Alice, and Jack McCall—to only name a few—put Deadwood on the map. Modern Deadwood, while maintaining the historical flavor of its bygone heyday, has lost its infamous smell, and boasts excellent accommodations, close access to all the "bucket list" items of visiting the Black Hills, and, of course, the chair that Wild Bill spent his last moments on this earth in.

Chapter 14

Nikki's heart thumped against her ribs like a bird struggling to escape its cage. She pressed her hand over her quivering chest. She always thought she would come back a famous photographer, one who had captured all the world had to offer. Instead, her big sister had packed her up with the threat of tattling to their mother and removed her from danger.

Only two people in the world understood her need for adventure and excitement. One of them, by proxy of a life-altering accident, had forgotten that knowledge and erased the possibility of ever sharing an adventure again. The other, a man who, no matter how hard she tried, she could not scratch off his name etched on her heart. A man who had succumbed to her parents' notion of bubble wrapping her from the world when all she wanted to do was burst all the bubbles keeping her from touching the world.

She huffed, crossed her arms over her chest, and glared out the window. Wheat fields blurred past in a sea of green. It would be several weeks until the wheat heads turned golden. *Hope I'm not around to see it.* Unlike her sister, Corrie, Nikki did not have the farming gene.

In fact, she was nothing like her sister—a fact she'd known all along but the rest of her family hadn't discovered. She had lost track of how many times she'd heard her name in reference to Corrie's. Usually, hers was the exception, the name burdened with being less than. Even after she graduated high school and left Sandy with the hopes of being free from expectations she'd wanted nothing to do

82

with, her family had still questioned her choices and cast a shadow on her dreams.

She would never forget the phone call to her parents when she'd decided what she wanted to do with the rest of her life. After jabbering on and on about traveling the world as a wildlife photographer, she had wilted, dejected, on the couch in her dorm room and stared unseeing at the oatmeal-colored cinderblock wall as her parents listed all the reasons she shouldn't. The top two: it wasn't safe, and Corrie had never felt the need to go waltzing off to unknown parts, so why did Nikki?

Nikki's hands ached. She stared at her fists kneading into her thighs. Apparently, she hadn't dealt with the pain of rejection from her family, as she had thought.

After loosening her fists and wiggling her fingers, Nikki glanced at Corrie's stony face. They had made the six-hour trip without saying more than ten words to each other.

With the farm's large grain bin in sight, Nikki broke the silence. "What are we telling Mom and Dad?"

"The truth."

"What? You said that if I came with you, you wouldn't tell Mom that I... I..."

"Tried to hunt down a supposed killer?" Corrie flicked the blinker on, which never made sense to Nikki. If County Road 55 saw two cars an hour, it was having a rocking good time.

"Yeah, that." She clutched at Corrie's upper arm and received a glare. At least, that was what she assumed Corrie slid her, as Corrie's aviators covered her mocha-colored eyes. "Please, for now, let's tell them I ran into some money problems"—*which isn't too far from the truth*—"and I wanted to come home for a while, and seeing as Bug is in the shop, you needed to come and get me."

"They'll see right through that." Corrie drove up the driveway.

Despite Nikki's embarrassing circumstances for being home, she loved her family's house with its colonial steadfastness and interior filled with love and trust. That word, trust, blinked with neon-sign intensity until it burned a hole in her consciousness. "Fine. But you're telling them."

For the first time since standing on Nikki's cabin porch, Corrie grinned. "Good. I tell a story better than you, anyway."

A child shot out from the barn with a string attached to nothing and Bacon, the family's elderly dog, in tow. A John Deere hat shaded his face, but nothing could hide his smile when he realized who pulled up in the yard. He waved, his entire body moving with the force. Much like Bacon's body when the poor dog tried to wave his nonexistent tail.

"At least someone's happy to see me." Nikki waved at her nephew and ignored her sister's snort before hopping out of the pickup and swooping up the little boy in a hug. "Hey, TT."

"Auntie!" Terrance Tuttle wrapped his arms around Nikki's neck and squeezed.

"Hold up there, little dude." Corrie rescued Nikki from TT's death grip. "Mamma wants a hug too."

TT melted into his mother's arms and wrapped his dirty legs around her waist like a monkey. "Missed you, Mamma."

"I missed you too." Corrie brushed a kiss on the boy's cheek and sputtered. "What have you gotten yourself into?"

"Daddy's soap." TT squirmed from his mother's arms, gathered his string, and ran back into the barn, yelling, "Daddy, Mamma is home!"

Corrie wiped at her mouth, and she grimaced. "This is what I get for leaving the boy in his father's care."

"What did I do now to get into trouble?" Aaron Tuttle sauntered over from the barn.

His hat matched TT's, but instead of shading chubby cheeks and a dirty face, Aaron's hat shielded a stubbled jaw, sharp cheekbones, and green eyes.

Hot on his heels was Kentucky, his ancient pet chicken. Saved from Mary Tuttle's cooking pot after outliving the egg-laying years, Kentucky had relocated from Aaron's parents' farm and spent her retirement at Aaron's feet. Aaron wrapped one arm around Corrie's waist and squeezed her to him and kissed her.

Nikki looked away. She couldn't bear the tenderness between Corrie and Aaron. And how he looked at Corrie made Nikki want to pout in jealousy. Only one man had ever looked like that at her, and she'd given him the boot. Before she could feel sorry for herself, she reminded herself of Xavier's phone call, tattling on her. She would not be standing there in front of the Lancaster barn with a kissing couple if it weren't for Xavier. Stupid, moronic buffoon of a man. *When I see him again, I'll—*

Corrie nudged her. "Earth to Nikki."

Nikki blinked. "Sorry. Did you say something?"

"No, but Aaron did."

Nikki smiled an apology and hugged Aaron. "Sorry. Got lost in my own thoughts for a moment."

"No worries." Aaron released her from the hug and clasped her upper arms. "But from the ticking of your jaw and the twitching of your eye, I'm not sure your thoughts were pleasant. Everything okay?" His gaze flicked between Nikki and Corrie.

Nikki circled her toe in the graveled driveway. "Go ahead, Corrie. You're darn near quivering."

Corrie, with plenty of wild gesticulations and eye rolls, announced Nikki's stupidity and carelessness. At the end of the five-minute recap, Nikki felt two feet tall, and Aaron stood, putting weight on his right foot, his left hand scratching at his facial stubble.

Corrie flailed her arms. "Well?"

Aaron took off his hat, scratched his scalp with the brim, and snuggled it back on. "Well… I don't know what to say." He looked at Nikki. "Is Corrie being Corrie and embellishing the story for a bit more flavor?"

"I don't—" Corrie clamped her mouth shut at the twin looks from Nikki and Aaron. Even Kentucky, busy pecking the dirt at Aaron's feet, looked up at Corrie, cocked her head, and clucked low in her throat.

Nikki now felt an inch tall. "No, she's telling the truth. I'm an idiot." She held her arms out, palms facing the ground. "Might as well put me in the stocks and throw rotten vegetables at this village idiot."

"They're in the back of the Quonset. Too hard to get out right now." Aaron tousled Nikki's hair and was rewarded with a swat and a huff.

"Nikki? Is that you? What a pleasant surprise!" Nikki's mother, Cynthia, ran from the porch to the barn and enfolded Nikki in an embrace.

Nikki inhaled her mother's scent—one part flowers, one part cleaning product, one part whatever was cooking for supper. Nikki sniffed again. Pot roast was on the menu. She clung to her mother for several seconds and bit her cheek. She would not, could not cry. Not here. Not now.

Cynthia untangled herself from Nikki's grasp and cupped her daughter's cheek. "Nikki? What's going on? Where's your car?" When Nikki failed to answer, Cynthia pinned Corrie with a questioning look. "Corrie?"

Before Corrie could explain, Jake, holding the other end of the rope clutched in TT's hand, walked out of the barn and toward them. He beamed a bright smile, and Nikki bit her cheek harder to stem her tears. Here she was again, bringing chaos to her father's life. *Put on a brave face.* Her lips twitched up into a smile, but the weight of the past couple of days weighed them down.

Jake's gaze flickered between Nikki, Corrie, and Aaron. Even TT, normally oblivious to adult-world issues, paused. His shoulders hunched and nearly touched his ears. Moving to his wife's side, Jake latched on to Cynthia's hand.

When Nikki stepped in to rescue her mother's whitening fingers, Cynthia shook her head. Cynthia faced Jake, brought one of his hands to her cheek, and allowed the other one to keep anchoring on to her. Maintaining eye contact, Cynthia murmured to Jake. Nikki couldn't make out the words, but within minutes, her father's shoulders relaxed, and his grip on her mother's fingers loosened.

Without breaking her gaze from Jake's, Cynthia motioned Nikki forward. As soon as Nikki stepped to her parents, Cynthia placed Jake's hand on Nikki's cheek. "Now, Jake, I want you to look at Nikki." He slid his gaze to Nikki's.

Her heart fell.

The fear and panic pinching his facial features and creating shadows under his eyes were as real to him as her fear of the man who had run her off the road. While her enemy was real yet unknown, his was an imaginary one that played games on a damaged but healing brain. If he knew the reason Corrie carted her home, he might never recover.

She couldn't do this to him. *I need to go back.*

Her mother's tug on her hand stopped her retreat. While Nikki gazed back into her father's eyes, her mother continued her murmurings.

Jake drew in a shaky breath, brought his other hand to Nikki's face, planted a kiss on her forehead, and whispered, "You are not in danger." After repeating this mantra several times, he moved his hands from her face to her hands.

She bowed her head and stared at her and her father's clasped hands. Minus the calluses that used to mar his farm-worked hands, they were smooth and unstained by grease or oil or worked-in dirt.

These were not the hands of the man who had welded a bike ramp together when hers of cardboard and nail-riddled two-by-fours collapsed. These were the hands of a man haunted by an irrational fear, a fear she'd nearly made reality with her ridiculous stalker stunt.

"Come on." Cynthia herded them into the house. "After having something to eat and a good lie down, we will all feel much better."

A tiny, grimy hand clasped Nikki's free one. TT smiled up at her.

Oh, TT, your aunt is an absolute idiot.

And somewhere, three hundred forty-seven miles away, Xavier probably wished her three thousand four hundred and seventy miles away.

Author Note: In the words of Dorothy from the Wizard of Oz, there is truly "no place like home." For me, no matter where I go or the houses I've lived in, my parents' farm feels like home. Even though my parents bought the farm after I graduated high school and left my parents' "nest," there is something about the white-and-red house that calls to me. Perhaps it is the wide-open spaces surrounding the farm or maybe it is the quiet of the night only broken by croaking bullfrogs. Or it could be the night sky resplendent and shimmering with stars. Either way, the farm offers me what city dwelling can't: peace, quiet, solitude—except from my four children-and a place where I am free to be me. What is your place, that even though you might not live there, feels like home? Where are you free to be you? Let me know at Jessicabergbooks.com/contact.

Chapter 15

Nikki dried the last pot and hung the damp, squirrel-embroidered flour-sack dish towel over the oven's handle. If it had been like the old days, she would have swatted Nathan with it. Of all the Lancasters, she could flick a towel louder and—if the whining complaints of Nathan were true—harder than anyone. Not a true talent, but she had to take what she could get.

Alone for the first time since arriving in a flaming ball of shame, Nikki escaped out the glass patio door, which led to the backyard and her mother's garden. Unlike Corrie, who'd had her tire swing for solace, or Nathan, who'd sought Bacon in the barn, Nikki didn't have a *place*. She had bounced around between Corrie's and Nathan's sanctuaries far too often to establish one of her own.

Her mother's garden would have to do for now. *Until I can get the heck out of here.* A twinge of guilt heated her cheeks. Her family had minimally scolded, but that wasn't the issue. They may as well have patted her on the head and given her a treat for learning a valuable lesson. All they cared about was that she was home and *safe*. Her gut twisted at that word.

Nikki picked through her mother's tomato patch with the agility of a gymnast. As a child, she had dedicated hours to the trampoline, copying moves Olympic gymnasts did on television. Her father had pretended to be her coach, even bought gaudy American flag jackets for both of them. Those moments, of course, shattered into pieces, joining the other shrapnel of what-used-to-bes. Even though his and her jackets were crammed in a tote of memories in the attic, Jake had dismantled the trampoline and hauled it off to the dump.

Her phone buzzed in her back pocket, and her heart maintained that buzz when Xavier's name popped up on her screen. She squinted at his text: *I'm sorry I had you kidnapped, but it's my job to keep you safe.*

Nikki stuffed her phone back in her pocket and suckered a tomato plant with force. The plant whiplashed back into place. She kept suckering the plants with a gentler touch and cursed the day Corrie gave Xavier a book of poetry.

"Who in the heck courts a woman, anyway?" Nikki mumbled to a frog, which hopped out from under a tomato plant. It didn't stop long enough to give an answer, but Nikki didn't need one.

She knew who courted a girl. Xavier Palinski. It hadn't taken long for the devil-may-care Adonis with golden hair to be tamed into a mere mortal. Nikki gritted her teeth. She had wanted a tiger, not a house cat. Gone were the risky nights in the back of her father's semitruck, the drives down empty country roads going way too fast, the midnight walks along the river, after sneaking out, of course, and double-dog daring each other until they were both breathless with laugher.

What wasn't gone were the electric moments when Nikki didn't think she could survive Xavier's compelling aura. He'd always had the power to overcome her senses. Even years couldn't dim that. Her still-buzzing heart from seeing his name reminded her of that.

Swallowing against something a little too close to regret, she suckered the last plant in a row of tomatoes strung up on pig paneling—a brilliant idea by her mother, who liked to keep her tomatoes in order and... *safe.* After years of being coddled and kept from forbidden, unsafe things, she had snapped. Snapped so hard, she had called off her dream wedding to a man who loved her more than anything. Loved her so much he wanted to keep her—

Bile rose in the back of her throat.

"Nikki?"

Nikki hunched her shoulders and waited for another lecture, another sermon, another ministration about the importance of safety and blah, blah, blah. "Look, Corrie, I don't feel like having another—"

Corrie enfolded Nikki in a hug and said nothing. Nikki clung to her sister. After several moments, she sniffed. Pulling back, she crinkled her nose.

"Now what's the matter with you?" Corrie cocked her head to the side and frowned.

"You smell."

Corrie raised an arm and smelled her armpit. "I do not."

Nikki snorted. "Not BO, silly. You smell like that orange degreaser stuff dad uses in his shop."

Corrie rolled her eyes. "You've been off the farm too long. I like that smell." Corrie tapped Nikki on the nose. "And so does Aaron."

Nikki batted away Corrie's hand. "Gross. Just gross."

Corrie's grin flattened into a serious line. "Can we get out of the garden, please? The smell of these tomato plants is killing me."

"I thought you loved the smell of them. Since when do you—" Nikki's mouth stopped moving, but her observation skills kicked into overdrive. Corrie had not celebrated Nikki's safe return with a glass of wine like everyone else, and Corrie had touched her belly more since dragging Nikki home than in the entire time Nikki and she had shared a house. "Wait a minute. Are you—"

"Yes."

Nikki squealed, and after pulling her sister from the evil-smelling garden, smothered her in a bear hug. "That's so awesome. Does Aaron know? Does Mom know? Am I the last to know?"

"You're the second to know." Corrie, her arm entwined with Nikki's, walked across the lawn to where a once-magnificent weeping willow tree had shaded a tattered and much-loved tire swing.

In its stead stood a baby one planted the day Terrance Tuttle entered the world. Even though no swing adorned its branches, Nikki knew that the next generations of Lancasters would enjoy its shade and comfort.

"Is it odd that I still come to this spot?" Corrie asked.

"Not one bit. I think it's sweet." Nikki tightened her hold on her sister's arm. "How have you been feeling?"

"Good. Tired but good. I was going to tell Mom a couple of days ago, but plans kind of changed."

"Don't tell me. I'm those plans."

"And I wouldn't want it any other way." Corrie sat cross-legged on the ground and pulled Nikki down with her. "I came out here to tell you the news of another impending niece, or God help us all, another nephew for you, but I also wanted to apologize."

Nikki quit plucking at a blade of grass. "You? Apologize?"

"Hey, now. Don't be dumb."

"What? Me be dumb? Never."

Corrie stilled Nikki's hand plucking another blade of grass. "Nikki, look at me." She kept her hand on Nikki's until Nikki relented and met her sister's gaze. "I am sorry. I should not have dragged you home like some naughty schoolgirl caught smoking in the girls' room. You deserve better than that. I guess I never understood, still don't understand, your need for adventure, your need for the unknown."

Through tear-blurred eyes, Corrie hunted for Nikki's hand until she found it again and clutched it. "But that doesn't make you wrong. It's taken me too long to realize that God created you not as my mini-me but as your own person. He's also given you a specific part of the world in which to be His hands and feet. And how can you do that if I—and other people who shall remain nameless—fence you in and chain you to our ideal of Nikki instead of God's ideal of Nikki? So, no matter the risk, if you wish to travel the world, commune with nature, live off the grid, I can't say that I won't worry or understand, but I will no longer stand in your way." Corrie turned Nikki's arm over and tapped her tattoo. "Fear has never been part of love, and I forgot that. I allowed my fear—my fear of our father's fear—to crush who you are and your dreams. I chose Dad over you, and I know now that I could have chosen both. But I didn't, and I am so sorry. Forgive me?"

Those words, that statement was one Nikki had yearned to hear for years. They washed over her in a tidal wave. For the first time in a long time, she inhaled a breath of air not tied to who she should be but who she was. No words could pass the lump in her throat. She leaned into her sister despite the smell of chemical oranges due to Corrie's recent snuggles with TT.

"Do you want me to take you home?"

Nikki straightened. "I am home."

"Yes, this place will always be your home. We will always be your home, but this farm is not your dream." Corrie twirled a piece of Nikki's curly blond hair around her finger. "I used to sit for hours, when you were little, and twirl your hair like this. And now here you are, all grown up with a desire for adventure and to make waves in the world. You can't do that from here."

Nikki's heart jumped a beat at the thought of returning to her cabin and capturing the wild of the Black Hills. That in itself wouldn't change the world, but she needed to beef up her portfolio before her dream of capturing the world's wildlife became a reality. There she could change the world, one picture at a time.

A picture.

Nikki's stomach flipped. She had photographed a killer, had captured an image of death himself. She didn't have to escape halfway across the globe to make a difference. She had made a difference here. If only she could do more. But she remembered the look on her family's faces.

"Earth to Nikki."

Nikki blinked. "Sorry, got lost in my own thoughts for a second."

"Well, are we loading up for a road trip?"

"I want to. I do. But there's a difference between seeking adventure and being plain old stupid and reckless." The image of her mother's hands on her husband's gray-stubbled cheeks, the echo of the incantation whispered to calm him, stabbed Nikki's heart. She couldn't—wouldn't—bring any more pain to her father, her family. "I'll hang out here for a while, molting away."

Corrie grinned. "Are you saying Xavier was right?"

"Let's not get too far ahead of ourselves."

Snorting a laugh, Corrie hauled herself to her feet. "Want me to talk to Mom and Dad for you?" She stopped herself at Nikki's arching eyebrows. "See? Old habits die hard." Placing her index fingers to her temples, she closed her eyes and repeated, "Nikki is a big girl and can take care of herself. Nikki is a big girl and can take care of herself. Nikki is—"

"The wicked part of me wants to leave you out here talking to yourself all day about how I'm right for once."

After squeezing Corrie in a bear hug, Nikki made a beeline to the old windmill on the edge of the property. Yellow clover, some stalks five feet tall, carpeted the area around the metal base. This windmill had once hidden Violet's violent ex-fiancé, an arsonist bent on destroying the Lancaster farm. But ever since Frank's conviction and subsequent jail time, the rusting metal skeleton no longer felt dangerous, at least to Nikki. According to family gossip, Corrie never stepped foot within fifty feet of the windmill. Unlike Nikki, who saw it as a voice of the past, Corrie saw it as a memorial to violence and hidden evils.

A slight breeze coaxed the blades, and the windmill sang the same song it had sung generations before, albeit a little huskier and creakier. This was the life-giver to the homestead. The original soddy had collapsed years ago, and nature had reclaimed what was once hers.

Upset she'd left her camera behind, Nikki wrestled her cell phone from the back pocket of her skinny jeans and positioned herself on her stomach. Angling the lens of the phone's camera just right, she captured the yellow clover bowing down to an ancient metal god with blades of metal slicing through the air.

Her phone pinged a text alert. She smiled at Sara's name.

I'm assuming your parents and Corrie have let you out of Lancaster prison, or do they have you locked up in a dungeon somewhere?

Nikki toyed with her bottom lip and typed: *Does a guilt trip count as a dungeon?*

Knowing your parents, yes!

Not wanting to talk about her parents or her imminent prison sentence, Nikki tapped out: *So, heard from Thaddeus? He definitely was your knight in shining armor!*

It hadn't taken long for Corrie and Nikki to exchange knowing glances the night Thaddeus had acted as bodyguard. Within minutes, Sara had the man wrapped around her pinky finger, and while Corrie and Nikki whittled away the evening with a game of Bananagrams, Sara and Thaddeus had rocked away the time on the porch swing. According to Sara, they had talked about "everything," and by the time he drove away from the cabin, Sara had dubbed him her "teddy bear."

OMG! He is the cutest. And, no, he hasn't texted, so we must hate him now.

Nikki grinned. *That's too bad!*

His loss!!

Before Nikki could swipe out a return text, she heard her mother's voice sailing through the yard. No one in the tri-county area could summon a herd of children—or whatever group name scientists had given them—like Cynthia Lancaster. Nikki shivered at the memory of her high school job of babysitting. *More like a murder of children.* Neighbors often joked that kids on surrounding farms followed Cynthia's calls to go home and were scolded by their own mothers to get back outside.

Gotta go! Prison warden is on the loose and yodeling roll call.

Not waiting for a return text, Nikki shoved her phone back in her pocket and hightailed it home before her mother called out a search party.

Author Note: As I've mentioned before, I have a large family. As the oldest of five, I probably relate more to Corrie than to Nikki. And, like Corrie, I've often made the wrong assumptions about my siblings. We all have, I'm guessing. Family relationships and dynamics can be fraught with angst and misunderstanding and downright fights. However, family is precious and an entity that should be celebrated whenever possible. This is why I incorporate family-centered plots into my stories. I have no clue where I would be without mine, and I'm certain you could say the same about yours. And as I found out through the school of hard knocks about the importance of family, Nikki is about to experience that herself! I hope you continue on with Nikki as she learns that even though families might not be perfect, and are often quite the opposite, they still matter and often come in clutch to save the day. And if you've read Amber Waves of Grace, you know the strength hidden in this rather ordinary-looking Midwest farming family.

Chapter 16

Xavier rolled his eyes at Thaddeus's early-morning text, pleading that the next time Xavier sent him into a cabin full of women, that Xavier would kindly warn him of red-headed firecrackers. He must have met Sara. *Hope she made an impression.* Thaddeus needed some excitement in his life that didn't include criminals. Sara would do nicely.

After asking when the wedding was, Xavier glanced at the report on his desk—his desk being the passenger seat of his Jeep parked in a Casey's gas station parking lot. That was what happened when he checked up on every lead from here to Timbuktu. The two victims had been identified as two of the four reported missing women. Michelle Osbourne, the woman found the other night, was a twenty-five-year-old baker from Tulsa, Oklahoma. She was last seen in Sturgis.

Xavier thanked his lucky stars it wasn't Sturgis Motorcycle Rally week. It was much easier asking questions in a small, quiet town of seven thousand residents than fishing for information among half a million die-hard motorcyclists and the tourists that converged on the small town's streets and bars.

The other victim, the one Nikki had found, was Lucy Porter, another young woman in her twenties, and like the other women, she had been lithe, beautiful, and blond.

Biting into a piece of breakfast pizza, Xavier flipped open his notepad and read his scribbled notes. The gas station attendant, a young man with a slight Southern drawl, had been a wealth of information if Xavier cared two rat butt hairs about the seven-day forecast or the odds of winning the three-hundred-sixty-five-million-dollar lottery. Xavier took another bite and chewed. The attendant, however, had recognized Michelle from a photo taken several months before her death but insisted that the woman had come in alone, bought a Diet Coke, a bag of Takis, and a fifth of Jack Daniels. After IDing her and seeing she was also from Oklahoma, the attendant had tried to strike up a conversation, but she had rebuffed any attempts at conversation.

Xavier finished the slice of pizza, sipped at his coffee, and sent off a quick text to the medical examiner. *Did vic have alcohol in her system?*

Well, Michelle, where did you go after buying that odd assortment, and more importantly, were you with anyone?

A knock sounded on the side of his Jeep. "Agent Palinski?"

Xavier eyed the gas station attendant through the open window. "Yes?"

"I forgot to tell you that the woman came in alone, but she wasn't driving."

Xavier clicked open his pen and poised his hand to write. "How do you know? What did you see?"

"Well, I was a little ticked off that she wouldn't give me the time of day. I wasn't going to do nothing, I swear, but after she left, I wanted to see what vehicle she drove." He paused, licked his lips, and patted Xavier's Jeep door. "You can tell a lot about a person by the car they drive. Trust me. I've worked this gig for years. So, I expected her to slither into a fire-red convertible and roar off in a Southern huff. But no. She hopped into the passenger side of an SUV."

Xavier's cop antennae quivered. "Did you see the driver?"

"No. Windows were tinted."

"Color?"

"Dark green."

Xavier made the last notation and handed the attendant his card. "If you think of anything else"—Xavier held the card an inch from the man's hand and made direct eye contact—"anything, I don't care how insignificant you think it is, I want to hear about it. Do you understand me?"

The attendant took it and placed it in his pants pocket. "I will. I hope you catch him."

"Him? What makes you think it's a man? You said you never saw the driver."

"Not trying to be sexist, but that wasn't an SUV driven by a woman. That was a man's vehicle."

Xavier knew several women who drove "man" vehicles. Before pulling out of the parking spot, Xavier checked his messages. The ME had gotten back to him. Just as he had thought. Michelle Osbourne was not a whiskey drinker, at least not hours before her death.

So, who is?

By the time Xavier pulled into the parking area closest to the Silverado Franklin Hotel and Casino in Deadwood, he was in the mood for a drink. *Must be five o'clock somewhere.* He glanced at his watch. For him, though, it was one p.m. and a perfect opportunity to grab a bite to eat and ask a few questions.

Lucy Porter had worked at the Legends Steakhouse, housed within the Silverado Franklin Hotel, as a hostess. Xavier walked through the hotel's front doors and approached the hostess booth. In the background, tinkling and flashing slot machines promised the gamblers seated in front of them a chance at the next big jackpot. Lucy would never get that chance.

As he approached the hostess booth, Xavier swallowed the anger and, if he wallowed in negativity, fear. Lucy and Michelle had been blond, stunning, and in their twenties. So was Nikki. He gritted his teeth. She had probably seen the killer, had evidence of him, had survived a hit-and-run, and had been on the hunt. But she was safe now. It didn't matter that she hated his guts. His stomach twisted at the lie he told himself.

Forcing a smile, he flashed his badge to the hostess, a tall African American woman. "Afternoon. Agent Xavier Palinski. Is the manager around? I need to ask a few questions concerning Lucy Porter."

"My mom's the manager. She had to step out for a while. She should be back within the hour." The hostess's gaze dropped to her hands clasped together on top of the erasable table seating chart. "Ever since I heard about Lucy's... death, I—"

"Is there a quiet corner we can talk? I'll need to speak to all the staff and your mom when she gets back. Is that okay?"

The hostess checked the table chart. "A good spot is open right now." She grabbed a menu and led the way down a set of stairs and into the farthest corner of the restaurant, tucked away from the prying eyes of patrons at nearby tables.

Xavier waited until the hostess had seated herself then scooted into the opposite bench. "First, may I have your name?"

"Kiara Armstrong." The woman smoothed back a swath of black hair that had escaped from the towering messy bun on top of her head. "Can I get you anything to eat? The cook that's in today is a master at grilling steak. Don't want to miss out."

"You leave me with no other option." Xavier ordered a baked potato as his side and an unsweetened iced tea and played with a sugar packet while Kiara went to put in his order.

"Here you go. Sorry that took so long. We have a new trainee today." Kiara set down a large glass of tea in front of him and slid into her booth, a tall glass of iced water clutched in her hand. She took a sip. "Can't quite find someone to fill Lucy's shoes. She is...

was"—Kiara swallowed—"so great. Everyone loved her. Customers, fellow waitstaff, everyone."

Xavier jotted down notes in his notepad, took a sip of his tea, and waited. He had learned over the years that silence sometimes garnered more pertinent information than point-blank questions.

Kiara poked at a folded cloth napkin in front of her. "You know, the first day she walked in for training, I wondered what in the world my mother was thinking when she had hired her. I was prepared for yet another immature college student who was only interested in flirting with the customers and making bank in tips..."

"And?"

"And then she smiled." Kiara grabbed the napkin and dabbed at the corner of her eyes. "I've never met anyone before who genuinely loved and cared for everybody. I have to admit I was jealous sometimes. She seemed to have everything. Beauty, brains, talent, and a work ethic that could put any one of us under the table."

"Did someone on staff maybe begrudge her, hate her even for her supposed perfection?"

"That's the thing. No one hated her. If she had tooted her own horn and shoved people's faces in it, I could see where someone might snap, myself included, but Lucy wasn't like that. She was as humble as they come. In fact, she'd recently taken someone under her wing and was asking if we had any extra jobs for her new friend." Kiara sucked in an unsteady breath. "We didn't."

"So, she had no enemies?"

"Not that I know of, but we didn't socialize outside of work. I'm a thirty-five-year-old mother of three. I don't quite move in the same circles as the young, single twenty-something-year-olds." Kiara's rueful smile slipped.

"What is it?"

"Two weeks before... before she went missing, she was excited and chattering away with some of us while on our break. Said she'd met someone who got her. 'A proper gentleman.' Yeah, those were her exact words."

"Did she mention his name? Where he worked? Anything?"

Kiara held out her hands, palms up, and shrugged. "If she did, she said nothing specific to me. Like I said, we were in much different phases in our life." She checked her watch. "I'm sorry, but I've got to get back to my post. I'll check on your meal, see what's taking so long."

Xavier handed her his card. "Please, if you think of anything else, call me—night or day. Send back anyone else who knew Lucy, please."

Kiara took his card and pressed it to her heart. "I swear. I want this monster found. A girl like Lucy—" Her voice broke. "She didn't deserve what happened to her."

Xavier sipped his tea and silently corrected Kiara. *No one deserves it.*

His steak came perfectly medium-rare, and as he ate, a constant stream of waitstaff filed in and out of the bench opposite him. Over and over, he got the same story. Everybody loved Lucy. No one knew the mystery man's name, but there was one nugget amongst the sluicing process. Someone had seen him, not enough to be specific on details, though. The server who had spied them in the alley behind the hotel and casino hadn't seen his face because of the dim alley lighting, but she guessed he was about six feet tall and athletically built.

Xavier left Deadwood with a full stomach and the satisfied feeling that police had in their custody a picture of the man behind the murder of at least Lucy Porter. Time to see what voodoo the tech guys could work on expanding the pictures Nikki took of what she had thought was an annoying tourist. For the first time since coming across Nikki, bloodied and bruised from the hit-and-run, he smiled. He was hot on the trail of a killer. He was in his prime. And his Nikki was safe.

Author Note: Sturgis, South Dakota, is home to the Sturgis Motorcycle Rally, the largest motorcycle rally in the world. For ten days out of the year, Sturgis's population explodes from a rather sleepy little town of about 7,000 people to a thundering, sleepless population of hundreds of thousands. In fact, for the 75th anniversary, 773,000 people descended upon this small town. If motorcycles are your thing, Sturgis won't disappoint. If concerts and people-watching are your thing, Sturgis is up for the challenge of giving you more than you bargained for. If sharing the winding roads of the Black Hills with thundering and purring motorcycles sounds like an adventure, then you better plan to visit the area the first two weeks of August.

Chapter 17

"If I have to sit around here anymore, I will go postal." Nikki slapped one of her dad's old farm hats on her head and pulled her ponytail out the small opening in the back.

"Where on earth are you going?" Corrie inserted a dishwasher pod in the dishwasher, hit start, and hung a washcloth over the edge of the double farmhouse-style kitchen sink.

The soft whirring of the machine filled the silence as Nikki tried to come up with something to do. Corrie's kitchen, decorated in shabby-chic style, fit Corrie's personality: rustic, yet girly, and flowery with a tinge of twine and tin. Nikki stemmed the jealousy blooming in her heart. She could have had a home, too, by now, all decorated and a kitchen table where she and Xavier could have sat with at least one child. But she had chosen a different path.

And now, for the past week and a half, she had divided her time between her parents' house and Corrie and Aaron's house, a football field away. Built in the same colonial style to match the original house, Corrie and Aaron's was larger plus a bedroom, making the two-story brick farmhouse perfect for the Tuttles and their expanding family.

As if on cue, TT, Kentucky and Bacon trotting behind him, ran past the window facing the front yard, pushing his bubble mower, and trying to catch the bubbles at the same time. It wasn't often that a kid had both a pet chicken and a pet dog, but TT had won the animal friend lottery.

"Mow."

"You mowed the yard yesterday. And that was twice in one week."

"Trim."

"Not only did you trim around the Quonset and barn and miscellaneous grain bins, but when the trimmer broke, you took darn scissors and used them to finish."

Nikki stretched out her right hand. She had probably done permanent damage too. "Weed the garden."

"You've single-handedly eradicated every weed known to man in the garden. I think they are too frightened of you to grow anymore."

Nikki sank into a chair at the kitchen table and rested her head on her folded arms. "Give me a job, any job." She eyed Corrie owlishly. "Isn't there a tractor to drive or a combine to operate?"

"I suppose if you want to take them out and drive them around the farmyard, but you know as well as I do that the planting is done and harvest is quite some time off."

Nikki burrowed her head in her arms and mumbled.

"What did you say? I can't understand you when you talk into the table."

Nikki brought her head up enough to be understood. "I said I'm so bored I'm tempted to go pick rocks in the driveway."

Corrie snorted. "The gravel driveway, you mean?"

"The very one. I noticed some bigger rocks. I could also sort by color and size and—"

"Stop." Corrie sat next to her and ruffled the top of her hat. Ignoring Nikki's growl, Corrie tugged on her ponytail. "If you're done with your brilliant ideas, maybe you'll shut up long enough to hear what I have to say."

"Never stopped you from talking before."

"Fine. I won't tell you." Corrie got to her feet.

Nikki latched on to Corrie's arm and yanked her back into the chair. "Please, pretty please. Give me a job!"

"I hear Mabel's hiring a waitress. Someone up and quit on her. She's desperate for help at the café. It's not an adventurous gig, but it will get you out of the house and out of my hair. Besides, I think you two will get along great."

Nikki wasn't so sure about that. *What could I have in common with a woman who could have possibly come over here in a covered wagon?*

"Why the scowl? I thought for certain you'd steal my truck and head on into town." Corrie gave one last tug on Nikki's ponytail. "Where's your sense of adventure?"

"It's bored too."

"Get on with you. Go. Shoo. Or I will lock my door, and you'll have to live at Mom and Dad's for the rest of your—"

"No need to get mean. I'm going. Geez, you got impatient in your old age." Nikki dodged a well-aimed swat and sprinted up the steps to her temporary bedroom. She changed clothes, sprayed dry shampoo on her greasy roots, teased some life into her curls, and dashed back down the steps. "Bye!"

"Come back with a job. Please."

Nikki waved away Corrie's pleading and did as her sister predicted. She commandeered Corrie's pickup and headed into Sandy. Working at a small-town café might not be the most glamorous job, but it was better than trimming grass with scissors. And hopefully, it would keep her mind off the adventures she wasn't having.

Author Note: This scene is a shout-out to my mom, who really did make her children pick rocks in the gravel driveway. In her defense, my dad had just resurfaced the driveway with new gravel, leading to large rocks scattered about what should have been a smooth driving surface. Still, me and my siblings have never let her live this infamous

mother-moment down. If you had to label your mother's—or father's—craziest moment, what would it be?

Chapter 18

Nikki felt every whisper scratch into her soul. Every. Last. One. Shutting her eyes, she gritted her teeth, wishing the old biddies behind her would hurry and finish their coffee, forget the tip, and waddle out the door.

"Nikki!"

"Coming." After working with Mabel for four days, Nikki understood that Mabel's gruff voice did not forecast grumpiness. Mabel sounded as if she'd smoked a pack a day from the time she left her mother's womb. Nikki shoved the receipt book into the pocket of her apron and entered the kitchen through a pair of swinging saloon doors. "Sorry, Mabel, I got sidetracked."

Mabel's hand paused in midair before thumping a lump of dough. "Never mind those old crows," she puffed as her thick arms pounded and kneaded the sticky white mass before her. "They're just upset over what you did to Xavier Palinski."

"That was years ago. How do they still remember that, and more importantly, why do they still care? Or ever cared?"

Mabel took up the lump of dough, slammed it to the flour-covered counter, and gave it a good whap before twisting it with her fists. "Part shock that you could send a man like him packing. Part jealousy."

"Jealous? They're like ninety."

Mabel pinned her with eyes the color of swamp water. "You saying us old folk are dried up old hags?"

"Ah... um... no?"

Mabel's face crinkled like scrunched tinfoil. She placed a floured hand on Nikki's cheek. "Because you'd be right." She cackled and resumed beating the lump before her into a tamed and malleable substance. "Although Xavier Palinski sure is a sight for sore eyes. I'll tell you that much. In fact, if I were"—she peered over her glasses at Nikki—"how old are you again, girl?"

"Twenty-five."

"Huh, anyway, what was I saying? Oh, yeah, if I were fifty years younger, I'd be giving you a run for your money."

Nikki studied her employer. Mabel either couldn't subtract, or she'd shaved ten years off her age. Penciled-on eyebrows gave her the look of being surprised, and if her permed snow-white hair didn't give her age away, her liver-spotted arms could tell a tale or two.

"I'm sure you could," Nikki muttered, escaping when the bell above the door tinkled.

They were gone.

With a damp washcloth, she cleaned the tables littered with crumbs and coffee stains before trudging over to where the old biddies had sat. She slumped her shoulders at the tip. After plucking the quarter off the black Formica tabletop, she dropped it into the slotted Cool Whip container designated for the Sandy Community Beautification Fund.

"These cheese buttons aren't going to make themselves, you know."

"Hold your granny panties," Nikki huffed under her breath. She slapped the washcloth back into the bucket and watched it drown. "Be right there."

"Aunt Nikki!" A little girl's voice chimed with the doorbells, making for a welcome distraction.

"Iris, I was wondering when you'd come visit me." Nikki enfolded Violet's eight-year-old daughter in a hug. "Mabel's got a caramel roll for you."

"Want to share it?"

"If you're willing to share one of Mabel's delicacies, I won't be the one to say no."

Iris smiled, showing off two missing front teeth and the reason for her current and sudden speech impediment. "I also brought four quarters."

"Let me guess. You want four Airheads." Nikki glanced around the empty café. "Where's your mom?"

"She's not feeling well, so she kicked me out. I'm supposed to make myself scarce and not come back until I can learn to be quiet and less energetic."

Nikki ruffled Iris's black hair. Thankfully, Iris had inherited almost all of her mother's characteristics. There wasn't anything different between mother and daughter except for the eyes. Iris's were so dark brown that people often mistook them for being black. But the similarity to her estranged father's ended with the color. Where Frank's had been shark-like in their darkness, Iris's were alive and sparkled with the intensity only possible for an eight-year-old girl who was the darling of a small town.

"So, who have you bothered since being kicked out?"

Iris scooted onto a barstool at the counter and twirled one rotation. "I first visited Daddy at his office."

Nikki smiled and scooped a large caramel roll dripping with extra caramel onto a plate. From the moment Violet and Luke had tied the knot seven years ago, he had adopted Iris as his own.

Everywhere Luke went, Iris was soon to follow, which had included the pulpit on Sunday mornings. As soon as the little girl had learned to walk, no one, not even her mother, could keep her from following Luke to the front and sitting at his feet. No one minded, though, seeing Iris's beaming face while her daddy preached. While she hadn't done that for years, Iris had claimed the front pew as hers and sat there, the perfect little princess, every Sunday morning. If only Iris could sit still on any other day as well.

Nikki set two forks next to the plate and leaned across the counter. "Then who did you terrorize?"

Iris faked a scowl and took her first bite. "Mabel is the best cook ever."

"Don't tell Nana that."

"Nana already knows. I told her."

"I'm sure she took that in stride." Nikki forked a good-sized chunk of roll into her mouth and chewed. Her eyes rolled. "You're right. Mabel is a better cook than Nana." She swallowed. "But don't tell her I said that."

"It'll cost you."

"How much?"

Iris eyed the rows of clear glass candy jars on a shelf behind the counter. "Two Airheads."

Nikki dug in her pocket and plunked two quarters on the counter. "You drive a hard bargain."

Iris added them to her quarter stash. "Pleasure doing business with you."

Nikki chuckled. "Where do you come up with half the stuff that comes from your mouth?"

"Oliver says that to me all the time."

"Who's Oliver?" It had been a while since Nikki had prowled the streets of Sandy, and more often than not, she didn't remember names as much as faces.

"Mr. Beaumont. He lives on Cherry Lane. I pull weeds for him. I want to mow, but my mom says I'm too little." Iris stabbed the roll with her fork. "He gives me a penny for every weed I pull."

Nikki glanced at Iris's hands. *Should have had her wash her hands before eating.* She shrugged the thought away. She remembered many days in her childhood when dirt and grass amplified the taste her food. "Is that where you went after your daddy kicked you out of his office?"

Iris huffed. "I chose to leave."

Nikki didn't scoff at the idea, at least externally. "It's one in the afternoon. Where else have you been?"

Iris listed off ten more names between bites of caramel roll, which Nikki left to her. It had been a long time since she had accepted dirt and grass clippings as scrumptious seasonings.

"Where are you off to now?" Nikki asked as Iris scooted off the barstool.

"Miss Henderson has kittens. Says I can have one if I weed her flower patch." Iris scooted six quarters across the counter. "One of each flavor, please."

Nikki dug around in the candy jar until she had a cherry, blue raspberry—*funny, never saw a blue raspberry in my life*—watermelon, green apple, white mystery—*whatever the heck that is*—and a grape. "Here you go. Don't eat them all in one sitting. You'll get sick."

Iris stared at her as if Nikki had sprouted horns. "I'm not dumb. Besides, I've got a bet going with Colby to see who can collect the most Airheads over the summer. I'm winning so far." Iris scooted around the counter, squeezed Nikki's midsection in a hug, and darted to the door.

"Hey, Iris, does your mom know about the kitten?"

Iris grinned. "Not yet." Iris closed the door behind her and skipped down the sidewalk, six pieces of candy clutched in her dirty hand, and turned the corner, vanishing from Nikki's view.

After putting Violet on her mental list of people to pray for, Nikki cleaned up after Iris, and with the café still empty and tables wiped down and cleaned, she was about to refill the empty salt and pepper shakers when the jingle of the bells chimed at another customer.

"Heard you were back in town. Coming to make sure the gossips had it right this time."

Nikki whirled around. "Natasha! How good to see you. You look great."

Natasha Florence, an old friend from high school, beamed a smile and engulfed Nikki in a hug. "It's been forever since I've seen you. How you've been? I thought you shook the farm dust off your shoes the minute you left."

Nikki hugged her back. "That was the plan. Things are kind of up in the air right now." She took in her old school friend's blond bob and blue—*purple?*—eyes. "It's great to see you."

Natasha had always been a solid friend through the quagmire that was high school politics. Everyone had thought them twins, and some teachers had often mistaken them for each other. Not that they took advantage of it.

"Anything new with you, besides colored contacts?"

Natasha giggled. "My mom almost had a heart attack when she saw them. I wanted to try something new. Got tired of the same old. Know what I mean?"

"More than we have time to discuss. And the business?"

Natasha had taken over her father's butcher business after he had suffered a stroke three years ago. Everyone had figured she would sell the meat market. Not only had Natasha defied the blond-haired cheerleader stereotype, but her business savvy and innovative ideas had the business back in the black and expanding. It wasn't uncommon, during the coldest months of the year, for UPS and FedEx trucks to pick up packages of specialty sausages, aged cuts of beef, and gourmet cheeses—crafted by a partnering dairy—destined for far-off places from Florence's Meat Shoppe.

"Going well. I've got this new thing in the works, though, so keep your fingers crossed." She glanced at her phone when it vibrated. "Gotta go." She squeezed Nikki with another hug. "It was so good to see you. We have to catch up sometime. I'll bring the steak." Natasha headed to the door, swung it open, and turned. "Speaking of steak. Almost forgot. I have the Father's Day steaks your mom ordered ready whenever you want to pick them up."

Nikki reciprocated Natasha's farewell wave. It was nice seeing old friends again. Her stomach sank at the thought of Sara all alone in the cabin. She should have forced Sara to see reason and seek the safety of the farm, but as she had predicted, Sara had scoffed at the idea of leaving their roost and her post at the clinic. Besides, Sara had claimed she didn't leave a loaded LadySmith .38 revolver by her bedside for nothing. Not one to argue with a licensed concealed gunwoman, Nikki had hugged Sara goodbye and knocked on the gates of heaven with prayers for her friend.

Time to get back to work before Mabel sent out the search party, and as Mabel was the search party, Nikki wasted no time in swinging back through the saloon doors to become Mabel's sous-chef.

At three, Nikki sank into a chair nearest the kitchen. Her feet felt numb, and her hands were red and cracked from all the dishes she'd washed. Being Mabel's sous-chef was not a glamorous job. No julienning carrots or celery or anything. Just lots of scalding water and soap strong enough to dissolve human skin. Stifling the urge to rip the ponytail out of her hair and dig her fingers into her scalp, she settled for a self-administered temple massage.

"It doesn't get any better."

Nikki glanced at Mabel leaning against the counter. "What?"

"This place will suck the life right out of you."

So much for a pep talk. Nikki cocked her head. "Why do you still do it?"

A harsh laugh erupted from Mabel's well-endowed chest. "It's the only thing I know how to do."

"Oh, Mabel, I'm—"

"Now, before you go getting all philosophical on me, I don't mean to throw a pity party." She chuckled and poured herself a cup of coffee so black it sucked in the surrounding light. After placing the coffee pot reserved for her and one other customer crazy enough to like tar for a beverage back on its warmer, Mabel pulled up a chair next to Nikki and sank into it with a grunt. "Now, where was I?"

"Parties."

Mabel quirked a pencil-drawn eyebrow and took a test sip. "Did you add water to this?"

Nikki shook her head.

Still eying Nikki over an apparently weak cup of coffee, Mabel harrumphed. "I ain't saying I didn't have a good life. The good Lord knows I've done my best." She set her coffee cup down and trailed a gnarled finger around the rim. "If God ever offered me the option to live this life again, I tell you something, missy"—she took the same finger that had circled the cup rim and pointed it at Nikki—"I'd live it the second time around."

Nikki leaned her elbows on the table and cupped her chin in her hands. "What would you do? Where would you go?"

Mabel paused, the coffee cup halfway between the table and her lips. She looked startled at the questions as if no one had ever asked her those before. "Well, I..." The coffee cup met the table with a clunk. "I don't rightly know, now that I'm asked. Isn't that the thing?" Her face screwed up in concentration for several seconds then relaxed, leaving the wrinkles that time and not thought had etched. "Africa. Ever since I learned about that continent when I was a little girl, I've dreamed of going there."

Nikki blinked. "You're kidding."

Mabel's face fell. "Well, you asked, and I—"

"No, I didn't mean it that way." Nikki smiled. "I think it's awesome." For a second, she imagined herself capturing images of Africa's wildlife. Excitement skittered up her spine.

The bells signaled another customer. Mabel creaked to her feet and patted Nikki's hand. "Thank you. It's about time you headed home. I'm good here until Beth takes over." Mabel pursed her lips in indignation at the older gentleman leaning on a cane near the counter. "What brings you here, Oliver?"

Nikki studied the gentleman. This must be Mr. Beaumont. If that was true, Mr. Beaumont must be new to town and, if his blue eyes and full head of silver hair were any attraction to women over sixty, quite the catch.

"It sure isn't your coffee, Mabel." He winked.

And a flirt.

"Now, you either order something that's on the menu or—"

"Now, now, Mabel. I'm not here for any of that, and you know it. Quit being a stubborn old biddy, and come to bingo night with me at the VFW. I hear they're having a live band too."

Nikki observed the stances of the two and took her leave. She grabbed her purse and, before heading out the back, paused at Mabel's side, leaned down, and whispered, "Mabel, this could be your Africa." She squeezed the woman's upper arm in support and walked out the door, a hum in her throat and a smile on her lips.

Author Note: Having grown up in the heart of a small town, I have an appreciation for what they offer. What they don't or can't provide in material worth, small towns make up for in spirit, kindness, and a perfect atmosphere for children to grow up in. I was a bit like Iris—maybe not as precocious, but definitely a free-range chicken like her. There is no greater adventure, at least for a small-town kid, than to leave the house after breakfast and not return home until the six o'clock whistle summoned everyone home. Oh, the trouble found and adventures journeyed. My fictional town of Sandy, South Dakota, is not a real place. It is a combination of three towns near and dear to my heart: Hague, North Dakota, the birthplace of my dad and home to my late beloved Grandma Helen; Artas, South Dakota, a tiny city, which hosted all my childlike adventures as I often rode my bike the two miles from

my house to play with my friends at the park; Eureka, South Dakota, the town where I went to school from kindergarten to 12th grade. My love of small towns runs through my veins.

Chapter 19

Xavier sank into his normal table tucked into a dusty corner in the Other Place, ordered his usual, sans cheeseburger, and nursed his drink. The night was a hopping one full of locals discussing one thing: hikers had stumbled upon the two other missing bodies. Estella brought him a second chokecherry ale and left him to his thoughts and his notepad.

"Need a sounding board?" Thaddeus joined him, waving off Estella's advances, and ordered a Coors Light.

"If you want water, it's free, you know."

Thaddeus grinned and nabbed a fried dill pickle chip from a red-and-white-checkered paper-lined tray. "Have you seen this place? I wouldn't trust the water."

Xavier, having no argument, flipped open his notepad. "The two bodies were pretty messed up. No identification of any kind. We need to wait for the dental records."

"But you're thinking they're the other two missing girls?"

"If I were a betting man—"

"Which you are. And you still owe me twenty from our last poker night."

Xavier waved him off. "I'll buy the next round and an extra order of fried pickles."

"Done." Thaddeus gestured to Xavier's notepad. "If you were a betting man?"

"We found Hallie Crestar and Alexis Stamford."

"Any leads?"

Xavier shook his head and waited until Estella set down Thaddeus's order. "Estella, another round, and another order of pickles."

Estella smiled, her fuchsia lipstick cracking. "Coming right up. Maybe a wait on those pickles though." She eyed the other patrons as if they had invaded her home. "They're flying out of the kitchen like hotcakes. Cook threatened to quit. Just here for gossip over those poor girls. Vultures, the lot of them."

"She's not wrong." Thaddeus sipped his beer as Estella sauntered back to the bar, clearing tables and chatting with customers along the way.

"Problem is, someone in here might have heard or seen something they didn't know was vital to breaking this case wide open."

"Still left with the SUV and nondescript clothing?"

"Well, some tech guy worked his voodoo on the pictures Nikki took—" He swallowed. The idea still chilled his bones. "Got an approximate height and weight. Anywhere from five-nine to five-eleven and weighing in somewhere between a hundred seventy to two hundred pounds. The bulky flannel made it hard to pin down a definite weight. Caucasian."

"That's almost as good as nothing."

"Tell me about it. This guy's power lies in his ordinariness. He fits the profile of at least five men in here." Xavier eyed the bar patrons with undisguised suspicion, and he gripped his glass with a force a hair's breadth away from shattering it.

"The girls aren't her, you know." Thaddeus leaned back in his chair, defying gravity and the age of the chairs.

Xavier scrubbed his hands over his face. The scruff against his palms reminded him he hadn't shaved in two weeks. Hadn't had time. If Nikki were still his, she would have shaved him in his sleep. She always said a beard took away from his gorgeous hair. She also said the combination made him look homeless.

He studied the foamy white bubbles on the top of his dark beer and tried to think of anything but Nikki's fingers in his hair. Grabbing the glass, he chugged the rest, wiped the back of his hand across his lips, and slammed it back down on the table. *All that matters is that she is alive and safe.*

"No, they're not Nikki, but they sure as heck look like her. Doesn't help, you know. Cases like this are hard enough without the added—" Xavier circled his hand in the air as if conjuring the correct word from the air.

"Emotion?"

"Yeah."

Thaddeus and Xavier both nursed their drinks, an unspoken agreement of silence between them.

Xavier broke it first. "Hallie was about to start med school. Alexis had graduated with honors with a degree in chemical engineering. Her fiancé told me she had accepted a position with a company in Boston. They were going to move out there next week."

"Do you think one person orchestrated these four killings?"

Xavier waited until Estella placed their food and drinks on the table and left before answering. "Odds are yes. We're checking into those who knew them, especially men who fit the description, but nothing yet."

Thaddeus raised his glass. "Here's to catching the monster or monsters."

Xavier reciprocated the motion. "And before he kills again."

*A*uthor Note: *My love of fried pickles started years ago when I went to a middle school teacher's conference in Nashville, Tennessee. Sounds riveting, I know! However, I fell in love with Nashville, which says a lot because I'm not a city girl, and I started an unhealthy infatu-*

ation with fried dill pickles. So, thank you, Nashville, for being awesome and dishing up my first round of fried pickle chips.

Chapter 20

Nikki skewered a ribeye steak sizzling on the grill and flipped it over, the juices of the meat causing a flare-up. She attacked the flame with a spray bottle. "Mom, when are you and Dad going to get a new grill? This thing is ancient."

Cynthia sat up in an Adirondack chair and slid her round sunglasses down her nose enough to peer over them. "We got that grill for your dad for Father's Day ten years ago. It's special."

Nikki spritzed another rebel flame. "In the padded room kind of way." Another squirt. "Seriously, Mom, how can I make Dad his special Father's Day steak if this contraption won't quit charring it?"

"Your dad likes a little char. Says it gives the steak flavor."

Nikki poked at the twelve-ounce, twenty-eight-day dry-aged steak. Natasha Florence, if she could see the spasming flames hiccupping all over the steak, would skewer Nikki in retaliation for abusing such an expensive cut of meat. And Nikki wouldn't blame her.

Nikki flipped the other steaks. "Why don't we get the aged ones?" Nikki shot a stream of water at a flame daring to lick at the steak.

Cynthia didn't bother sliding her sunglasses down or raising her head. "You are not a father."

"What's this about Nikki wanting to be a father?" Aaron, TT in tow, ascended the last porch step. They were matching in jeans and T-shirts, one emblazoned with a tractor stating that the wearer Still Plays with Tractors while the other shirt had a toy tractor on it with the words I Play with Tractors. To top it all off, both had on John Deere hats.

"Careful, I'll make yours a flame-broiled aged steak for you." She squinted at his shirt. "Father's Day gift from TT?"

Aaron plucked out a pop swimming in a cooler of ice water, cracked it open, and took a gulp. "Yup, although I'm sure his mother had something to do with it."

Nikki gave TT a high five. "You got your dad a nice present."

TT grabbed the bottom of his shirt and stretched it out, trying to get a look at the tractor. "My tractor's smaller."

Nikki shared a smile with Cynthia and Aaron and ruffled the top of her nephew's hat. "Don't you worry none. You'll grow into a bigger one."

Apparently not satisfied with his aunt's words, TT crawled up into Grandma Cynthia's lap and began chattering to her about his problems.

Aaron let out a visible sigh of relief and leaned against the porch railing nearest the grill. "That boy will be the death of me. I'm too old for kids."

Nikki fought some tiny fires and studied Aaron. He must have shaved, as none of the telltale gray stubble tattled on his age, but his temples were a little grayer than when he first came to help on the farm eight years ago. Still, Aaron in his early forties put men in their early twenties to shame. Nikki bit her lip. Not that she would ever tell him that.

"A little too late for regrets now, wouldn't you say?" Nikki placed the blunt end of the grill skewer on the steaks and pushed. To double-check her estimation, she inserted a meat thermometer into the thickest part of a steak.

"Let me guess, you're right again."

"The day I can't tell the doneness of a steak by feel, sign me up at the nearest nursing home—please make sure it has a birdcage—and leave me there."

Aaron chuckled. "Deal." He gathered up the porch crew and herded them in through the sliding glass doors.

Nikki plopped the steaks in a pan and joined the Lancaster-Tuttle crew at the large dining room table. Surrounding it were the people she loved most in the world. Her mom and dad, while still not the couple they once were before Jake's accident, had climbed out of the mire of their marriage, fingernail by fingernail at some moments, and now sat next to each other, hand in hand.

Corrie, her face pale from a recent bout with morning sickness—or as Corrie called it, day sickness—sat next to TT, her hand on his shoulder more to keep him in place and not bouncing around the room than as a touch of affection. Aaron sat on the other side of TT, his arm around the back of his son's chair, his fingers brushing Corrie's shoulder. Occasionally, his pointer finger performed a curlicue before settling still again on his wife.

Nathan should have been seated on the opposite end as Nikki, but he'd missed so many family holidays that his absence, although noticeable, no longer broke her heart. Nikki remembered far too many Thanksgivings and Christmases and Easters and Fourth of Julys where she had locked herself in her room and cried. She hadn't understood then what she understood now. It was far harsher on Nathan to be away from the farm and family he loved gathered together there than for them to be all gathered together on the beloved farm with no Nathan. She breathed a prayer for the continued safety of her brother.

"I thought Violet, Luke, and Iris would be here too." Nikki nestled the pan among a large glass bowl of tinfoil-wrapped baked potatoes, a tray of steaming corn on the cob, and a basket heaped full of

Cynthia's homemade buns complete with a dish of honey butter and took her seat at the end of the table next to her father.

"Violet's still not feeling well, so Luke and Iris are spending the day with Gerome."

"He'll like that." Nikki couldn't help but smile at how Gerome, Aaron and Luke's dad, had taken to little Iris. He had adopted her in his heart as his granddaughter long before Luke had made it official. Now, when Iris wasn't following Luke around or terrorizing—or helping weed, as Iris reminded them all—the citizens of Sandy, she was Gerome's little shadow. She had, during the chick season, named every single one. Nikki did not want to tell the poor girl what Grandma Mary did to the grown-up versions of those exact chicks in the fall. The family, so far, had gotten away with telling Iris that the chickens went to live on Walter's farm. Who Walter was, they did not know, but it sounded like a good name for a man who took care of imaginary chickens.

"Are we all thinking the same thing about Violet?"

Cynthia shared a secret smile with Corrie and beamed at the rest gathered around the table. "It's official. Violet called this morning and asked me to announce it during dinner. Luke and Violet are expecting a baby!"

No one cared about the steaks getting cold—a taboo in the Lancaster house—as they all took turns claiming they had suspected it or had called it weeks ago. Jake sat silent. The rest of the family noticed the patriarch's silence, and the hum of conversation quieted.

"Dad?" Nikki grasped his hand and squeezed. "What's wrong?"

A tear tracked down his stubbled face. "Happy." After eight years of therapy, Jake had progressed further than his doctors had predicted. His eyes were sharper than they had been since the accident unless he was exhausted. His speech, although slurred, was close to his pre-accident speech patterns. It had been a long time since he had diverted back to one-word answers.

"Dad?" Nikki heard the alarm in her own voice and, after glancing at her family, saw on their faces what she felt. "Do you want to go lie down? We can eat later."

Jake pinned her with eyes as clear and alert as she had ever seen them. "No." His mouth worked to formulate his next words. He closed his eyes in what Nikki guessed was frustration. "I am happy." His eyes snapped open. "And hungry."

The entire room seemed to take a breath, and after a short prayer of gratitude and safety for their loved ones, they ate their Father's Day meal complete with laughter and topped off with upside-down pineapple cake and homemade whipped cream, Jake's favorite dessert.

Author Note: Two of my siblings joined the military after graduation. My sister, Sarah, joined the Navy, and my brother, Joseph, joined the Marines. I couldn't be prouder of them and their sacrifice for the United States. I would be lying, though, if I said I never begrudged the missed holidays and family get-togethers. Their absences always hung like a soft shadow over the festivities and fun. Even though we felt the absence of Sarah and Joseph, I'm sure it was harder on them to not be with the noisy, chaotic horde, to know that everyone was gathered without them. So, to all of you readers who have served this country and sacrificed so many precious moments with family and friends, thank you from the bottom of my heart. To all of you readers who are family to those who serve this great country, thank you for your patience and resilience and dedication to your loved ones.

Chapter 21

"You and Corrie have the same green tint." Nikki gave Violet a gentle hug and settled next to her sister in spirit on a couch straight from the eighties or Mary Tuttle's living room. Either way, until Violet's mother-in-law could no longer come and visit, the large clusters of pink and purple peonies splattered on white upholstery would hold center stage in Violet's otherwise-modern decor.

"Some say pregnant women glow." Violet wiped at her brow, her fingers brushing stray strands of jet-black hair from her ivory skin. "It's a romanticized version of sweat."

"Isn't the AC fixed yet?"

Violet sipped on a glass of ginger ale, a drink Nikki had refused. Only old people and pregnant women drank ginger ale, and Nikki thanked her lucky stars she wasn't either of those. "I'm not scary enough for the repairman to take seriously. Wait until I'm as large as a house and as grumpy as a hippo with bedsores. Then he'll fix it."

Nikki rolled her eyes. Regular Violet was slim and fit. Pregnant Violet, at least with Iris, had been slim and fit and had looked as if she'd swallowed a basketball. Nikki didn't see how this pregnancy would be any different. "By then, you'll need the heater instead of the air conditioner."

Violet rested her head against the back of the couch and groaned. "I have a strange feeling you might be right. I'll see if I can sweet talk Gerome into fixing it."

"That man would crawl backward over hot nails for you."

"He certainly is the father-in-law I never expected or thought I deserved. Funny what driving into the ditch in Podunk, South Dakota, can do for a person."

Nikki clinked her glass of ice water against Violet's outstretched glass. "Here's to happy accidents and planned-for happiness." Nikki gestured to Violet's hand, which lay outstretched on her flat stomach. For years, Luke and Violet had tried to get pregnant, and year after year, they and the rest of the family had given up hope. But now hope blossomed in Violet's womb and the hearts of the family.

"Enough about me." Violet pinned Nikki with a big-sister look. "I hear you almost added killer-hunter to your list of adventurous to-dos."

"You shouldn't believe everything Corrie tells you."

Violet pressed her lips together, which didn't quell her smile. "It wasn't Corrie. It was Luke, who heard it from Aaron, who I'm sure got most of the insider information from Corrie."

"Great, I'm the victim of the telephone game. That never ends well."

"So, it's not true?" Violet quirked an eyebrow and held her gaze steady on Nikki's face.

Nikki gave up trying to maintain a poker face—one of the many reasons she had refused to play Xavier in poker, when they had played games, of course. "Okay, fine. You're not wrong."

Violet snorted. "I guess that's as good of an admission of guilt as I've ever heard from you." Her smile slipped a little. "Promise you won't go off doing something stupid again." She held up a hand to stem Nikki's retort. "I don't mean don't go have adventures or quit following your dreams. There is a difference between going off recklessly half-cocked into danger and seeking adventures of the unknown."

The air in the house thickened. Not because of Violet's words. Violet was right. But the specter of a killer haunting her thoughts and the Lancaster Family House Arrest had stifled Nikki's need for adventure and the ability to seek it for weeks.

"You all right?" Violet laid a delicate hand over Nikki's.

"Yeah. Fine. Late for work is all. You know how Mabel gets."

"The entire town does." Violet walked Nikki to the door and hugged her. "Don't worry. Adventure hasn't left, you know. It's taken a brief vacation. And speaking of adventures, if you see my wayward daughter, send her home."

With or without a kitten?

Keeping that thought to herself, Nikki promised to spread the word if she saw Iris and walked the three blocks to Mabel's Cafe. The breakfast rush over, most of the tables were clear of patrons. Only their dirty cups and plates remained. Nikki paused at the counter, where a note with her name on it leaned against a huge caramel roll. After the Father's Day celebrations the day before, Nikki wasn't sure she would be hungry until next week. With a slight tug of guilt, she slid the plate away and read the note. It was from Mabel, and it informed Nikki to eat before working and that if Oliver Beaumont should come around, to tell him the café was closed.

Nikki chuckled and set the note down next to the caramel roll. Maybe she would have an appetite later. After cleaning and resetting for lunch, Nikki puttered around the kitchen, organizing and hanging pots and pans back on the hanging rack. The door banged, not giving the bells time to do anything more than choke on their cheer.

Nikki poked her head out over the swinging saloon doors. "Mabel? What's wrong?"

Mabel panted and waved her hand in front of her face. "Oh, oh, oh."

"Here, sit." Nikki ran from the kitchen and slid a chair out from a table and held on to Mabel's elbow as the older woman sank into it. "Should I call an ambulance? Are you ill?"

Mabel shook her head violently. "It's not me." She dropped her elbows to her knees, cradled her head in her hands, and sobbed.

Nikki pulled up a chair and scooted close enough that her knees touched Mabel's. She had never, not during high school and not since being back, seen Mabel cry. In fact, the old woman hadn't even cried when her dear friend, Baxter, had died eight years ago of a sudden heart attack. "Mabel, please, you're scaring me. I'm calling 911."

"No. They've already been called."

Nikki's sixth sense quivered. *This is not good; this is not good. Please, dear God...* She didn't finish her prayer. "Why?"

"I just—heard. Oliver—she's dead. Natasha Florence is dead. Murdered."

Dear God, no!

It could have been days or weeks or even years that Nikki sat there in a deserted café, the cracked linoleum of a chair digging into the back of her thighs. All she had registered was Mabel's sobbing and her death grip holding on to Nikki as if Mabel were drowning. And maybe she was. Maybe they both were. It was hard to breathe. Nikki reminded her lungs they needed to inhale and exhale again when the pressure tightened, her lungs squeezing for relief.

The door banged open, and Nikki jumped as if someone had fired a gun next to her ear. Someone called her name and Mabel's, and strong arms encircled her. "Nikki?" The same person shook. "Look at me."

She did. And the tears that she had dammed into submission broke free of their confinement, and she cuddled into the embrace of her brother-in-law. "Oh, Luke," was all that would eke past her tight throat, but by the force of his hug and the kiss he pressed to the top of her head, she knew he understood. He and Aaron had lost their brother in Afghanistan eight years earlier, and sometimes, a look would come into both brothers' eyes that they were thinking of Caleb. She wasn't ready for the quiet wistfulness she saw in Luke and Aaron's green eyes. She was angry. Seething with it.

Nikki hiccupped into Luke's shoulder and whispered, "Don't worry about me. How's Mabel?"

"Don't you worry none about me." Mabel sniffled but didn't relinquish her grip on Nikki's forearm. "I'm too angry to die of shock yet." Mabel seemed to register that she was holding on to something, blinked, and released her hold on Nikki. "I'm so sorry. I didn't—I—"

Nikki patted Mabel's liver-spotted hand. "Why don't you go home? I can finish up here. You could maybe use a nap—"

Mabel flicked the suggestion and a stray tear away as if they were annoying gnats. "Girl, I have not napped since I was three years old, and I don't intend to start now." She crossed her arms over her chest. "Besides, what will I do at home but stew and question the Almighty's sense? I can do that and cook at the same time. Might as well start cooking for what is surely Sandy's darkest day." Mabel pushed herself to her feet and wobbled but shook off Luke's helping hand. "I may not be able to comfort souls like you, Pastor, but I can bring comfort to people's hunger, and I'd like to think it's the same thing."

"Mabel, I want to stay and help." Nikki stood but kept Luke's hand tucked in hers. "Please."

Mabel's eyes shone with tears. In a rare show of affection, Mabel reached up and cupped Nikki's cheek in her hand. "No. The Lord and me? Well, we have some things to talk about, and it wouldn't be fit for you to hear what I have to say to Him." Mabel walked Nikki and Luke to the door, shut and locked it after them, and flipped the Open sign to Closed.

Main Street, the main artery of Sandy, was normally quiet at that time of day, but not this day. People flooded the streets, whether in search of solace or news, Nikki didn't care to find out. All she cared about was that her friend was dead. *Dead. Murdered.* The finality of that word choked her like a piece of unchewed food. Nothing she could do would dislodge it, ease the pain of it.

"Nikki?" Luke untucked her from his side, where she'd been nestled as they walked to his church office. He placed his hands on her shoulders. "Talk to me."

"I don't know if I can," she whispered to the sidewalk. "I can't—I saw her. A couple of days ago. Hugged her. We were planning on—" She snapped her mouth shut, enclosing a cry bubbling up her throat.

Luke drew her to his side and half walked, half supported her the last few blocks to the church. Its white steeple pierced the gray clouds pregnant with rain. As if sensing the mourning community, they pulsated and released their offspring in a deluge of rain.

Soaked through, Nikki and Luke stumbled through the double-wide wooden doors of the church. Instead of shutting out the storm, Luke and Nikki stood in the entrance and witnessed the rain baptize the land. Nikki shuddered.

And wipe away any evidence that will lead to finding Natasha's killer.

Author Note: Small towns, like the fictional Sandy, are often safe places to live, and my dream is to someday move from the cityscape back into the simplicity of rural life. However, I've seen tragedy strike small towns, and I can personally attest to how small-town citizens come together and support each other and the grieving family/families. I know that small-town living may not appeal to all nor be accessible to all, but I believe that we can maintain a small-town mentality living in the middle of a city. As long as we care for our neighbors and rally around those who experience pain and heartache, we've created a little rural neighborliness in the middle of a metropolis.

Chapter 22

Nikki woke at five a.m. with a monster headache. But what else could she expect after a night of weeping? She stretched out her right foot and touched warm skin. She squelched a squeal and yanked her foot away before remembering that she hadn't gone to bed alone. Next to her, Corrie breathed the breath of one deep in sleep. Nikki relaxed and lay on her back, staring at the ceiling. If she were in her old room in her parents' house, she would be able to make out the residual glue that had once held her glow-in-the-dark stars to her ceiling. But with the shades drawn and the sun not yet on the horizon, the ceiling in the guest bedroom was as dark as her thoughts.

The farmyard swirled with red and blue lights; the wail of sirens echoed through Nikki's head as she and Nathan half assisted, half dragged their father back into the house. Gone was the warrior who had brandished a hoe and struck the enemy to the ground. In his place, a shell of a man staggered into the kitchen and fell into the arms of his teenage children.

"Dad!" Nikki pawed at her father's body curled in a fetal position on the floor. Her gaze met Nathan's, and she knew the panic gleaming from them mirrored hers. "Should we get Corrie?"

They both looked out the glass patio doors to the backyard swarming with paramedics and deputies. In the middle of the fray stood Corrie and Sheriff Steve. At their feet, Frank lay motionless.

"She looks busy," Nathan mumbled.

"I don't care." Nikki started to stand, but her father's hand grasping hers brought her back to her knees. "Dad, you need help. Let me go."

He held on. His grip turned her fingers purple and her knuckles white. His glassy eyes never strayed from her face. His lips formed her name, but the only sound to escape was moans that prickled Nikki's skin. With Nathan's help, Nikki situated her father and held his shaking body. She pressed her lips to his graying hair and murmured nonsense, as she would to a toddler.

Needing human touch to comfort her, she slid her foot until her big toe rested against the top of Corrie's foot. Years ago, her big sister had held her as the old Quonset burned. A miracle happened, though, when Aaron and his posse of farmer angels rebuilt the Quonset shinier and newer than the last. Unlike then, there would be no miracle. Nathan wouldn't be running into the room, yelling about an army of angels descending upon the farm to help rebuild. No one could resurrect her friend, erase the violence, the pain, the loss. Today was no different from yesterday. Except that yesterday morning she'd woken up with a light and carefree heart. She thought she had left murder behind her.

She bolted up in bed, tugging the covers with her. Corrie groaned and rolled over, snatching the blanket away and rolling up in it. The fog of a thought that had been hovering in the back of her mind since the horrible news of Natasha's death cleared and burst forth with blinding clarity. *Blond and pretty. Blond and pretty. Blond and pretty.*

Dear God, no! The killer followed me, and now Natasha's dead.

There was no way the killer knew her. *Right?* She had worn that ridiculous hat, had been three football fields away. *But the SUV? Did the driver/killer get my license plate number? Could the information lead to information on me?* The first number on South Dakota license plates designated the registered county of the vehicle. Rather than a twenty-one designating Custer County, a forty-seven was imprinted on Nikki's Bug's plate, telling all who knew or cared that the car was registered in Sandy County. But there were several towns under Sandy's domain. There was no way to pinpoint her exact location. *Right?*

Nikki slipped out of bed and moved the shades enough to peek out into the yard. Black night had given way to a royal blue, signifying the sun was on the rise. Still, shadows lurked, and nothing moved except the farm cats already on the hunt for their breakfast. Nikki unleashed her grip on the curtain, and it fell back into place, blocking her view of the yard she had played in as an innocent child. That innocence was long gone, and she didn't like what replaced it. Fear.

She slipped back into bed and burrowed against Corrie's warm back. Instead of counting sheep to get back to sleep, she told herself that the county courthouse would not, under any circumstances, give out personal information to any Joe Blow off the street. And as she drifted off into slumber, her thoughts asked, *Are you sure?*

Author Note: Let's play a game: Two Truths and a Lie. In this chapter, I have to work some author magic, and let's see if you can figure out where I fibbed.

Option one: The number on South Dakota license plates determines the county in which the car is registered.

Option two: Sandy County is a fictional county that has stolen the number 47 from a real county.

Option three: Sandy County is the county in which I grew up; in fact, my first car was registered under its domain.

What's the lie? If you thought three was a lie, you are correct. In order to make my fictional world make sense, I stole the identity of McPherson County, the county I called home for the formative years of my life.

Chapter 23

There were many days Xavier would never forget. The Battle of Normandy, not because the day held anything special outside the reverence for history but because he had passed his World History semester exam by the hair of his chinny-chin-chin by correctly answering the date of the battle: June 6. Also known in his teenage, hormonal brain as Nikki Lancaster's birthday. Runner-up in infamous days was July 2, two days before he had intended to swear a vow of love and devotion to his bride-to-be. Instead of entering marital bliss, he had spent the 4th of July watching the fireworks he'd intended to surprise Nikki with in his parents' backyard, lighting them off one by one and watching them explode and shatter like his heart.

Xavier parked his Jeep in front of his apartment building and, taking the steps two at a time, reached his door as Mrs. O'Malley and her pink spikes, sharpened to needlepoint sharpness, exited hers. He gritted his teeth and prayed for patience. He couldn't. Not today, the other date he wouldn't soon forget. June 22 was sure to haunt him until he drew his last breath.

Before Mrs. O'Malley could open her mouth, Xavier opened his. "Mornin', Mrs. O'Malley. Sorry, can't chat. Something's come up." He didn't wait for a response and didn't much care that he left her slack-jawed in the hall, her hands on her ample hips and both her eyebrows nearly touching the blond base of her pink spikes.

Something's come up. Xavier tore through his closet and dresser drawers and threw clothes at a duffle bag on his bed. Finished raining clothes on his bed, he shoved them fistful by fistful into the bag.

What did the state of his duffle bag matter when his old high school friend, Natasha Florence, was dead? He slammed his last pair of boxers in his duffle bag and zipped it shut with such force he wondered how the zipper didn't jettison off its tracks. After snatching his vibrating phone from his pocket, he glanced at the text message from his supervisor, Cal Magee.

I've assigned Thaddeus to this case as well. He'll be joining you.

Some weight crushing Xavier's rib cage, making it hard to breathe, evaporated. Taking one large breath to expand his lungs to normal working order, he thumbed out a return text.

He never questioned his orders to get to Sandy as quickly as possible, not when the deceased matched the pretty blond victim profile. He snatched the lone banana—spottier than he preferred—from the counter and a Monster energy drink from his fridge, slung his duffle bag over his shoulder, locked his door, and sprinted down the steps. There was no doubt he was chasing a serial killer. The same serial killer he thought he had kept away from Nikki. Instead, the killer was in her proverbial backyard.

Five and a half hours later, Xavier had never been more thankful for the eighty-mile-per-hour speed limit on I-90. Whether he kept to that speed was between him, God, and the highway patrol officer who had stopped him. Upon seeing his badge and hearing his mission, Officer Gloria Greene had given her blessing and the direct order to "catch the bastard." Balancing safety and speed on the highways leading to Sandy was a different story. He cursed every slow-moving farmer out checking crops and every lumbering tractor, sprayer, or other farm equipment clogging up the roads. It had never bothered him. Until now. He needed to get to Sandy. He needed to make sure Nikki was safe.

At two p.m., he descended the hill leading into Sandy peacefully tucked in the valley. From there, it looked the same. The church steeple pierced an azure-blue sky dotted with fluffy white clouds.

The Sandy River, now more like a stream, meandered down its path and curved around the north and east sides of Sandy as if giving the town a one-armed hug. Trees, planted over one hundred years ago, canopied the town with a protective carpet of green leaves. Below that protection, around the cooling waters, and under the watchful gaze of the steeple, evil had slipped through.

Author Note: There are many perks about visiting South Dakota: the food, the people, the beauty of the Black Hills, the Badlands, and the rolling prairie. Another perk is the speed limits. I know, it doesn't seem much to brag about and gives the sense that we South Dakotans don't get out much, but seriously, once you can legally go eighty on an interstate, you won't want to go back to the measly speed limits on most others. So, if you're ever on I-90 or I-29, and you hit the South Dakota state line, enjoy the ride, and don't let the rolling hills and cropland fool you into thinking we have no sense of adventure or need for speed.

Chapter 24

Nikki sat in Corrie's pickup and gripped the steering wheel until her fingers ached for release. But if she let go, she might slip back into the black abyss of her thoughts, thoughts that had haunted her for the past nine hours. Ever since she had awoken at five, she could not turn off the swirling visions of death, both real and the imaginary concoctions of her own demise. Not able to shake the sensation of eyes watching her, she had even begged Corrie to sit in the bathroom while Nikki showered. An event neither Corrie nor Aaron commented on during a breakfast of bacon and eggs seasoned with furtive looks out the windows at every noise, even familiar ones.

She pried her fingers, one by one, from the steering wheel and, with what felt like leaden steps, trudged to a set of double-wide metal doors. The windows centered in each one welcomed all to Florence's Meat Shoppe. Before she could overthink the situation, she turned the handle and entered a world that used to belong to her friend. A world full of white tiles with dark-gray grouting, rustic hickory butcher block countertops, prime cuts of meat displayed on black trays encased in sparkling glass display cases, and whimsical metal figurines of barnyard animals. An aroma of hickory chips smoking sausage, which from the tantalizing smell of garlic and pepper with a hint of sage, must have been made fresh that morning, wafted from the back smoke room.

"Hello, how may I help you?"

Nikki cut her stare off a galvanized metal cow next to a matching galvanized metal farm truck and returned the friendly smile of the woman behind the counter. A clean white butcher's coat encased the woman's tall frame, and a hairnet covered her ponytail.

"Yeah. I'm... ah..." Nikki squeezed her lips shut. She didn't know the woman. This woman should not be here greeting her. Natasha should be. "Sorry. Um, I'm here to pick up Mabel's order for the café."

"Of course. She called earlier and said you'd be picking up the order. You must be Nikki. I'm Eleanor." Eleanor skirted the meat display case and offered her hand in greeting. "I'm so sorry about your friend. I've only been in Sandy for a couple of weeks, and Natasha was great to me. Offered me a job, even though she didn't need the help, I don't think."

"Sounds like something she'd do." Nikki warmed under the woman's smile. Eleanor's crow's feet around her dark-brown eyes and the horizontal crease indenting her forehead dictated a woman who had experienced both laughter and sadness. *Just like my mom.*

"I'll have the order loaded up. It will be a moment." Eleanor opened the door leading to the real business end of the store and called for someone named Michael.

Nikki sat down in a metal chair softened with a cushion covered in a barnyard-printed fabric and rested her elbow on the matching metal table with a surface the size of a dinner plate and big enough to fit her elbow and a green houseplant. In a few minutes, Eleanor was back and brushed her hands on her white coat. "It's all loaded and ready to go. Tell Mabel I'll put it on her account." The older woman studied her. "Again, I am sorry about your friend. You remind me a lot of her." Her hand came up to Nikki's face as if it wanted to brush stray curls behind her ear. Eleanor blushed, fisted her hand, and nestled it in her lap. "And my daughter."

"We got that a lot growing up." Nikki rose to her feet. "Thank you for keeping her business going. For now."

"I'll do what I can for as long as I can."

Someone called for Eleanor from the back, and she gave an apologetic smile and left Nikki alone in the front display room. Nikki glanced at the wall clock, which surprisingly did not display an image of an animal. Two fifteen. Forty-five more minutes of work, and she could go home, crawl into her blanket fort, and stare out of the breathing hole, on the lookout for killers.

She hopped into her sister's pickup, now loaded with specialty meats and cheeses, and drove the one mile back into town. She almost drove off the road and onto the sidewalk as she passed the sheriff's office on the outskirts of town. A red Jeep was parked in front of the austere brick building. Of all the buildings in town, the sheriff's office was the only one to repel and not welcome. Maybe it was the lack of windows or the architect who had apparently hated frills and swirls and style of any sort. The one thing remotely decorative was the chain-link fencing frosted with razor wire on the back end of the building, which faced the open prairie.

Xavier's in town. The thought both thrilled her and enraged her. There could only be one reason he was there, parked in front of the sheriff's office. She checked her rearview mirror to make sure no one was behind her and slowed down to a measly five miles an hour. A sporty car heading toward her zipped into an empty spot near Xavier's Jeep, and Thaddeus unfolded from the driver's seat. He waved at her before entering the glass doors of the sheriff's department. That meant one thing: the death of Natasha was more than likely connected to the deaths of the four women in Custer State Park.

A spark of fear ignited into an inferno and swirled in her gut the rest of the way to the café. She had two missions in life. No, three. Three missions. Get out of Sandy and on with her life, avoid serial killers—now an arduous task, as apparently, they moved around and had discovered her safe place, and avoid Xavier Palinski. She couldn't bear to leave the safety of the pickup and sat in the air conditioning, the engine still running, for the duration of both "Aquarius" and "Proud Mary" grooving out of the speakers, courtesy of the local oldies station.

Someone tapped on the driver's-side door.

Nikki jumped and knocked her knees on the steering wheel. She swiveled in her seat, pushed the automatic window button down, and glared at Mabel. "You scared me half to death."

"No wonder. You sitting out here, staring at nothing, meat and cheese still in the back."

Nikki slumped and rested her forehead on the steering wheel. "Sorry, Mabel. Just thinking."

"That's your first mistake. I don't pay you to think"—she pointed a gnarled finger down the street in the general direction of the sheriff's office—"especially about a certain blond-haired man."

As Mabel spoke nothing but the truth, even if it did sting a bit, Nikki didn't argue. Instead, she turned off the engine, hopped out, and hauled in box after box, all of which weighed as much as a baby elephant. At least, that was what Nathan would have said if he could see her huffing and puffing after the sixth box.

"Why do I get the impression you're still thinking?" Mabel poked her head out of the saloon doors.

Nikki stacked the last of the Cryovacked strawberry brie, fig blue, and dried apricot gouda cheese blocks in the refrigerated display case along with sealed packages of stuffed pork chops, veal-and-mushroom kabobs, and an assortment of ready-to-cook chicken stir-fry blends, a godsend to most Sandy women if their exclamations of avoiding making another meal were not exaggerated.

"What gives you that idea?"

"You haven't said a word since you quit huffing and puffing like the Big Bad Wolf. Heck, when I was your age, I was out hauling square bales for sixteen hours a day and never once got winded. You young people nowadays." From the sound of thumping, Mabel had returned to beating a dough ball into submission.

Nikki stopped chewing her bottom lip. She thought of her friend and the high likelihood that Natasha's killer was the same man Nikki had photographed, the same man who had run her off the road but failed to kill her. Had he followed her out to Sandy to finish the job but—

A cold sweat beaded on her skin, and her stomach roiled. *No! He had meant to kill me, not Natasha.* She couldn't breathe, didn't know if she wanted to. *I brought the killer to my home.* The chill from the cooler no longer felt cold. It would take an iceberg to cool her fevered thoughts and the anger coursing through her veins. She had to figure out who he was, use herself as bait, and lead him out of town. *And then what?*

"Mabel, I need to go home." Nikki wasn't sure if her voice had been loud enough to cross the café's dining space and into the kitchen, but Mabel popped her head over the saloon doors. After squinting at her, Mabel shooed her away with strict instructions to go home and do something constructive.

Author Note: Mabel is perhaps my favorite character, and I love when she pops up on my screen. Mabel is a conglomeration of all the older, wiser people in my life who have either lost their filter or never had one in the first place. I have had many Mabels in my life, and while their gruffness sometimes stung in my youth, I have no idea where I would be now without their guidance and advice, at times, unsolicited. I'm sure everyone has had or does have a Mabel in his/her life. If you had to pick out your Mabel, who would it be, and what did you learn from this person and how did he/she change your life?

Chapter 25

"Pull." Nikki eyed the clay pigeon as it flew and squeezed the trigger. Orange shrapnel exploded and fell to the ground like orange snow. Twenty for twenty.

Mabel had ordered her to do something constructive, and as soon as Nikki had parked the pickup in the garage, she'd marched to the gun safe in the basement of her parents' house, spun out the combination, and grabbed her pink camouflage shotgun and a box of shells.

She glanced back at Aaron, who had understood her mood the second she'd entered the Tuttles' kitchen, legs shoulder-width apart, shotgun slung over her shoulder like a Continental soldier. He'd helped set up the trap and wrestled out a cardboard box of clay pigeons. After twenty clay pigeons, Aaron stood by the trap, ready to launch another.

Nikki might have snuck the gun from the house, but after one shattered clay pigeon, Jake had shot from the house. Before he could sprint to the shooting site, Cynthia had intervened and now stood by him on the porch, working her magic. Even from where she stood, fifty yards away, Nikki sensed her father's agitation. But the steady presence of her mother and her supportive nod gave Nikki the permission she needed to continue.

She reloaded shells into her shotgun. If only the cement block in her chest would explode as easily as the orange discs. "Pull." Again, a shot and a hit.

"Too bad it's not pheasant season." Xavier slowly clapped as he walked from his Jeep.

Nikki gaped at him, snapped her mouth shut, reloaded, and nestled the shotgun in her shoulder. "Pull."

Nothing.

She glared behind her, where Xavier and Aaron were in quiet conversation. They had seemed to form an organic relationship eight years ago based on nothing but their fear of Corrie. Aaron had feared Corrie breaking his heart; Xavier had been terrified she would break his nose. What had begun as a survival tactic had morphed with time. Until she had broken Xavier's heart. From the smile on Aaron's face, they had bridged the past three years. *Men!*

With a sheepish grin at Nikki, Aaron left his post and sauntered over to the Lancasters' porch. Between him and Cynthia, they must have convinced Jake to go back into the house. Nikki's shoulders loosened.

Xavier loaded a clay pigeon and set the trap arm in place. "Let me know when you're ready."

Nikki narrowed her eyes, trying to decipher his mood. He didn't look angry or upset. He looked calm, which was a dangerous illusion. Everything about him screamed illusion. He looked so professional in his khaki pants and black polo with the DCI insignia emblazoned on the upper-left chest of his black polo. His blond hair pulled into a topknot, however, created the perception that he belonged on the beach somewhere, shirtless and in board shorts.

She blocked that tantalizing image from her mind and readied her gun. "Pull."

An explosion of orange.

"You here because Mabel sent you?" Nikki didn't bother looking at him.

"Went in for cheese buttons, came away with an earful, scolds, which I'm not sure I deserve, and explicit instructions to get my hind end to the Lancaster farm."

"Get your cheese buttons?"

"Sadly, no. She's holding them hostage." He pouted.

Nikki bit back a rogue grin.

Xavier motioned to her gun and the trap. "Care to elaborate on why you're practicing for a hunting season months away?"

"Was Mabel upset I left work early?"

His left eyebrow almost touched his hairline. He tipped his head to the side, and the right side of his mouth ticked up. "Mabel sent no messages of impending doom. Expecting her to fire you?"

"She keeps accusing me of thinking too much. Probably her way of preparing me for the words 'you're fired.' She hasn't gotten around to it is all."

Xavier's half smile grew into a grin. "She likes you too much to fire you. She'll just make your life a living hell until you quit." He loaded another clay pigeon. "I'll play your little game here as long as you tell me what's going on and why Mabel sent me out here instead of feeding me."

Instead of looking into his eyes, she studied the DCI logo embroidered on his polo. Under the intensity of her stare, the letters snaked together, writhing until a white blob remained on a sable sea of cloth.

"Nikki?" Xavier approached her as if she were a wounded animal and set her gun down. One hand cupped her cheek, and his thumb caressed her cheekbone. His other hand clasped hers.

"It's all my fault, isn't it? Natasha's dead because of me." Her voice held no inflection. It sounded as flat as she felt.

His thumb massaging the soft area between her thumb and pointer finger wakened her from her stupor.

Nikki blinked and yanked from his grasp. "Sorry. I, uh, am angry and—sad—and—sorry—"

"Knock it off."

Nikki glared at Xavier. "What?"

"You thinking that you had anything to do with Natasha's death is by far the stupidest thing I've ever heard."

"Wow, your bedside manner could use a little work."

"Listen to me. You had nothing to do with it. We don't even know if the deaths are related. I just got here. It's precaution, a necessary step to either rule it out or—"

"Confirm it." Nikki toed an empty shotgun shell. "It's just that he probably saw my license plate when he ran me off the road and, not getting me the first time, found out who I am."

"And how on earth could he do that?"

"He could call the county courthouse and—"

Xavier held up his hand. "No. No one at the courthouse would give out that information. Ever."

"Then how did—"

"We don't even know if these cases are similar enough beyond the victim profile." He placed his finger under her chin and tilted her face until their gazes locked. "And never apologize for being angry. You have every right to be sad and furious. I am too."

Her heart beat hard against her rib cage at his admission and the iron glint in his eyes.

"She was my friend too." His finger moved from her chin to swoop a stray piece of hair behind her ear. "I promise I will find whoever did this."

Nikki wasn't sure if it was his vow or his touch that caused goose bumps to sprout on her arms. Whatever it was, she didn't care. She felt alive. And like she did at the cabin, she would squelch her fear and channel her anger. No more cowering in the dark or under blanket forts. Lancasters didn't run from problems. They encountered them head-on.

"Pinky swear?"

Author Note: My dad's side of the family LOVES the Fourth of July. The louder and more explosive the better, and this does not just apply to fireworks. You'll know you're in the right farmyard if you see a line of pickup trucks, their tailgates open, with an audience of people watching relatives fire off shotguns in the hopes of making orange shrapnel explode in the sky. While I'm not the best, and I'd rather sit in a lawn chair and drink an alcoholic drink and eat my aunts' glorious food, I've done trap shooting enough to know that it is a great way to forget your worries and live in the present. The only thing that matters in that moment is the shotgun nestled to your body, your finger hovering over the trigger, your eye in the sky, just waiting, anticipating, for the "pull" and the flying orange disc. Not that I've ever hit it! But no worries. I still have my lawn chair, my hard seltzer, and my Aunt Kelly's chocolate mousse to comfort my wounded pride.

Chapter 26

Xavier watched in fascination as her eyes sharpened and zoomed in on him. From experience, her eyes saw what no one else's ever did. Where someone saw an old tractor, she saw a soul, an abandoned and lonely machine left to rot by its owner who should have cared for it and kept it shiny and new. Where someone saw a gutted piano with stiff, unmovable keys, she saw and heard the melodies, happy and sad, echoing from the past.

Wanting to see what she saw, he had bought her a camera for Christmas. Eight years ago, he had thought it the perfect gesture, a moment where she would know how much he cared for her, wanted to dive into her soul and get lost forever. How melodramatic he had been. Instead, he had bought a one-way ticket to the end of their relationship, a trip he wasn't aware he'd been on until the journey had stopped, and she'd booted him out. As soon as she had looked at the world through the lens of a camera, her adventurous ember had sparked into a raging inferno.

Now looking into her eyes, he still felt the pull of them, and like his melodramatic teenage self, he still wanted to slip into her soul, slowly, deliberately, feeling every inch of her presence. His finger twirled a strand of her hair, let it unfurl, and swirled it again.

Her breathing shallowed, and her lips parted. He swallowed and, uncurling her hair, traced his finger along her jawline, down the center of her chin, and settled the tip of his finger in the hollow of her throat, where her pulse beat against his fingertip.

"How about something more binding than a pinky swear?" he whispered, afraid anything louder would scare them both into sense.

He dipped his head, giving her time to run or slap him. She did neither. She met his gaze. His lips touched hers, and like a starving man, he fought the urge to gorge himself on them. It had been too long. Any more than a nibble, and his system would explode. He could feel the tautness in his muscles and the ache of longing in his gut.

Reluctantly he pulled away, her bottom lip the last thing he relinquished hold of. Her eyes, cloudy with dreaminess, gazed at him. Lust told him to take her in his arms and kiss her until they were breathless and panting. Love told him to walk away, get back to work, and give her space.

He squeezed her hand, and without another word, he walked away, hopped in his Jeep, and drove away from the Lancaster farm. He had a promise to keep and a killer to find. Even though he'd told Nikki the odds were slim that the same murderer who had severed the lives of those four women in the Hills area had also ended the life of their friend, his gut told him it was the same man. Instead of sending Nikki away from a lion's den, he'd sent her into a different lair of the same lion. *But how? Who? What is the link?*

Careful not to bring too much speculation into his mind before seeing the evidence, he closed off the endless stream of questions he couldn't answer. Yet.

After the ten-minute drive from the Lancasters to Sandy, he pulled into the same spot he'd left earlier and entered the nondescript building. Its stark brick walls did nothing to brighten anyone's day. And maybe that was the intention. If he compared it to a food, the sheriff's office would come last after bland oatmeal.

He tugged at the glass doors and walked inside, the cool air conditioning a welcome respite to his fevered thoughts and the sweltering day.

The cop at the front desk glanced up and studied his empty hands. "Back so soon? With no cheese buttons? And you promised Agent Cornwall so faithfully." The nasal voice didn't fit the platinum-blond pixie haircut or the jade-green eyes peering under a large sweep of bangs. In high school, Laurel Stewart had been unassuming. It had surprised everyone when she had revealed her post-high school plans of joining the army. Instead of following in her banker father's footsteps, she'd completed her four years, come back, and after completing police academy, worked to keep Sandy County safe. A job now made harder with the first murder in Sandy's collective memory. After the news of Natasha's death, the citizens of Sandy, who used to brag about not locking doors, as there was no need, had all deadlocked their doors that night and the following day.

"Nope. Mabel sent me on a fool's mission. Besides, Thaddeus can get his own cheese buttons."

"There's always supper."

Xavier chuckled. "Don't go destroying my little black rain cloud with your happy silver lining. None of that happiness in here." He glanced at the row of beige seats welded together and the wall clock that resembled every school clock he'd ever stared at, but no matter how fast he tapped his foot, the red second hand ticked time away second by second. A drooping houseplant gave the only color to the entire room. "I don't think it'd survive. Steve and Thaddeus in?"

"They finished up with the ME. Steve said you should go straight back when you arrive." Laurel walked over to the plant and dumped half her water bottle in the pot.

"Good luck with that."

"I might bring in more houseplants. Maybe this one is lonely." Laurel cocked her head, pursed her lips, and touched a wilted leaf.

Or depressed. Xavier scooted around the front desk and rapped once on the door with the small rectangular sign Sheriff's Office.

"Enter."

Xavier did and regretted not taking a deep breath before entering the small windowless office. Elliott Weaver, the county's medical examiner, was a brilliant man renowned for making it his life's work to find justice for the dead. He also had a habit of eating garlic—raw garlic. Elliott claimed it kept him fit as a fiddle, and even though he was easily in his fifties, he didn't look a day over forty with his grayless brown hair, laugh lines, which were the only wrinkles on his face, and the physique of a man in his prime. The only drawback Xavier could see—smell—was the side effects of Elliott's eating habits. Healthy or not, the man stank. And from the look on Steve's and Thaddeus's faces, they also regretted not having this meeting outdoors.

Elliott jumped out of his chair and shook Xavier's hand. "Good to see you again, Palinski. Never thought I'd have the pleasure of working with you again."

The last time had involved the mysterious death of a child. At the lead investigator's insistence, they had called in Elliott Weaver, and with the help of several DCI and local law enforcement officials, the case had soon been closed, the mother in prison for life, and a new face added to the collection of innocence taken too soon that Xavier saw in his nightmares.

Xavier smiled. "Good to see you again, Weaver."

He glanced from the crime scene photos spread on Steve's desk to the man himself, who sat military straight in his rocking office chair. Why Steve had never changed it out for a straight-backed wooden, cushionless chair, was anybody's guess. Corrie, who graduated with Steve, always claimed the military knocked the hair, the fun, and the slouch out of him.

"What've we got?"

After Xavier pulled up an extra chair and sat next to Thaddeus, Steve stretched and placed his folded fingers behind his bald head.

Instead of answering, he nodded at Elliott, his bi-colored eyes signaling the ME to recap the facts.

"What we've got here is blunt force trauma to the head. Perhaps the killer underestimated Miss Florence's strength."

Natasha had been an athlete in high school, but the life of a butcher wasn't an easy one and was more physically demanding than most people thought.

"Why do you say that?"

Elliott opened a manila envelope lying in front of him and handed him some pictures. Xavier's gut flipped. He closed his eyes, refocused, and tried telling himself that the dead body on a cold slab of metal he was looking at was just a stranger's, that he didn't go to high school with her, that he hadn't thought she was Nikki in the hallway and swatted her butt in passing and probably still had the faint bruising of the punch she'd delivered to his bicep.

"If you want to see the body, I can take you to the morgue. It's across—"

Xavier waved away his offer. "Pictures are fine for now." He studied the torn and shattered fingernails. "She fought."

"Miss Florence gave all she had in staving off her attacker. I don't have all the prelims done, but I suspect the initial blow"—Elliott fished out another photograph zoomed in on a wound at the back of Natasha's head—"stunned her and didn't kill her. The fight she put up was a noble but useless one, I'm afraid." Elliott slipped the pictures from Xavier's hand and stuffed them back in the envelope. "That is the only wound I can find. However, there is something odd, and I don't have all the test results back, but I'm pretty sure she was suffocated."

"What?" Xavier was the only one to speak, but from the looks on Thaddeus's and Steve's faces, he wasn't alone in his surprise.

"The telltale signs are there: bloodshot eyes, slight bruising around her mouth, and I'm positive that when I finish my tests, I'll find high levels of carbon dioxide in her blood and glove fibers in her lungs."

Xavier scrubbed his forehead. "So, what, the killer stuns her with a blow and, after realizing he didn't kill her, suffocates her instead of wielding a second blow? That's calculated. That's personal."

"That's evil," Thaddeus growled.

"There's something else." Elliott emptied the pictures from the manila envelope back onto the desk, shuffled through the pile, and chose one that zoomed in on an ear and long blond hair. "See this chunk of hair?" He pointed to a swath of hair, silkier and smoother than the tangled mess surrounding it. "It's almost as if the killer smoothed it on purpose."

"Before or after death?" Thaddeus asked.

"No way to tell." Elliott tucked the pictures back into their folder. "There are no other injuries, except for the broken fingernails, of course."

Thaddeus rubbed the furrow indenting his forehead. "Nothing under the fingernails?"

Elliott frowned. "I haven't gotten to that bit yet. The killer must have been wearing some serious protection. No human skin or hair. Only fibers, which are being tested as we speak."

"But why suffocation?" Thaddeus leaned back in the chair and stopped when it gave its first creak. "You'd think the killer would have delivered another blow."

Steve spoke for the first time since Xavier had entered the room. His voice was raspy. "Do you think Natasha—" Scrubbing his face, he allowed the unspoken question to settle upon them.

Xavier wanted to ask Elliott the same thing: *Had Natasha fought for her last breaths, or had she slipped away into the blackness of unconsciousness after the stunning blow, unaware she'd never breathe again?* But he didn't want the answer, so he didn't finish Steve's question.

Silence permeated the room. None of them spoke. They centered all their attention on the crime scene photos spread across the desk.

Xavier broke the silence. "Do you think there's a connection between Natasha's and the other deaths in the Hills?"

Drumming his fingers on the desk, Elliott shrugged his shoulders. "I'd have to look over the autopsy done on Michelle Osbourne."

The only one of the four women in the Hills to have been unmauled and recognizable. The only one not buried. Something or someone must have interrupted the killer. Was he interrupted or spooked by something the night he killed Natasha? "I'll make sure you have the file by the end of the day." Xavier glanced at Steve. "What about the crime scene?"

"Secured. My deputies are waiting for you and Thaddeus. No one's been in."

Xavier knew how hard it sometimes was for local law enforcement to hand over the reins on a case, especially one as personal as the death of a local hometown woman. "I appreciate it." He rose to his feet, shook Elliott's hand, nodded at Steve, and left the stifling garlic-infused office.

As soon as he and Thaddeus were outside and breathing fresh air, Thaddeus brought his shirt collar to his nose and sniffed. "Let's take your Jeep."

"Why?"

"We're both permeated with garlic, and I don't feel like stinking up my car."

"And you're fine destroying the interior of mine? Besides, there's no way we smell like garlic." Xavier took a whiff of his shirt. "It's probably in our noses."

Thaddeus's eyebrows rose. "One of us must be the sacrifice, and I volunteered your services first."

Xavier swung his keys around his finger. "You owe me."

"Not after that last poker game. I believe you still have a couple of outstanding IOUs."

Xavier sniffed his shirt again and wrinkled his nose, hoping that the smell was stuck in his nose rather than ingrained into the fabric of his polo. "Fine. We're even, then."

"Well, glad that's settled." After setting gold-rimmed sunglasses on his face, Thaddeus sat on the passenger side of the Jeep. He glanced at Xavier, still standing on the sidewalk. "Well? Let's go. We've got a crime scene to investigate."

And like the other ones, Xavier was pretty sure he would find the one similarity linking them all to one killer. A piece of red flannel.

Author Note: One hobby that I wish I had time to hone was photography. I've dabbled in it just enough to know that I am mediocre at best. However, despite my ineptness behind the camera, I love capturing nature's beauty, not that I do it justice. I yearn to show others the beauty of the prairie, the eerie emptiness of ghost towns, the loneliness of old houses, long abandoned by their families. I spent the summer of 2020 at my parents' farm and took hundreds of pictures. I would love to share them with my readers and am currently brainstorming a few ideas on how to do just that. I'm often more of a big-picture kind of gal; the little details often elude me.

Chapter 27

Throughout breakfast, Cynthia, Jake, Violet, Luke, Iris, and Aaron shared furtive glances and never once made direct eye contact with Nikki. TT, not one for social niceties, stared open-mouthed at her. Apparently, the Lancaster–Tuttle crew had decided there was safety in measures. Ever since Violet's ex-fiancé's violent vendetta years ago, Nikki's mother had locked up every night, and now, with Natasha's brutal murder, during the day. Fear had come back and with it the irrational loss of freedom. Nikki predicted the posse before her would soon assign her a chauffeur and bodyguard. She pouted and balanced her fork on her forefinger.

The no-show, Corrie, had a good excuse for being absent from this safety huddle-cum-intervention. Nikki flipped her fork, set it like a small rake, and played with the scrambled eggs on her plate. She wished she had a good excuse like morning sickness to miss this family powwow.

"Nikki?" Cynthia folded her hands on the table next to her plate still full of food.

Nikki snuck a look at everyone else's plates, and all of them, except for TT's, had bacon and eggs and homemade biscuits still steaming. "Yeah?"

Before Cynthia could open her mouth, Iris, near quivering with excitement, blurted out, "You kissed Xavier!"

Nikki's skin felt hot, not from embarrassment but from the memory of his touch, his kiss.

"Iris, that was not kind nor any of your business." Violet smiled apologetically at Nikki. "Sorry." She turned her mother glare back on her daughter. "And where did you learn this, anyway?"

Iris, not defeated or looking a bit sorry, sat up straight in her chair, her arms crossed. "I overheard you and Aunt Corrie talking on the phone last night." Iris beamed a gap-toothed grin at Nikki. "Is he a good kisser?"

All the adults choked on air. Someone kicked Luke under the table if his exclamation of pain and the glare Violet sent him were any proof.

"Iris Rose Tuttle, you apologize this instant." Luke poked his daughter on the shoulder with every word.

Iris rubbed her shoulder and scrunched her nose at her father. "But I didn't mean to be mean. I want to know. Colby claims he's the best kisser in town and wants to show me. I told him he has to trade me at least ten Airheads before I even let him hold my hand."

Nikki covered her smile with a napkin. There was no point in encouraging the girl, but the look of panic and shock on Violet's face and Luke's twitching lip had Nikki swallowing her giggles.

Luke unfolded his napkin, refolded it, set it on the table, and cleared his throat. "Iris, please do not let little Colby Myers near you for anything under one hundred Airheads."

Iris chewed on her lip, scrunched up her nose, and nodded sagely. "You're right, Daddy. One hundred is so much more than ten."

It took several moments before a seriousness veiled the kitchen again, but all too soon, Nikki felt the heaviness of it. If only Iris would say something ridiculous again. But Xavier's kiss hadn't been ridiculous. It had been a golden drop of Pitcairn honey, celebrated for its rarity and purity. Her heart twinged. *In loneliness, in despair, in desperation, in anger, in regret?* So many emotions stewed within her, she knew she couldn't make the right decision if she tried. The last time she'd decided on her relationship with Xavier, it had ripped her heart in two. She rubbed over the aching spot and met her mother's gaze.

"You were about to put me in time-out, I believe."

Cynthia didn't bat an eyelash. "If time-out comprises of you having either Luke or Aaron—"

"Or Xavier." Iris bit into her biscuit and gave Nikki a conspiratorial nod.

Cynthia continued as if her granddaughter had not spoken. "Take you to and from work, then yes, you are in time-out."

Nikki sent a pleading glance to her father. He put his arm around his wife. Nikki looked at TT, who grinned, displaying the uncanny ability to smile with a mouthful of eggs and still be adorable. Violet wouldn't meet her gaze. Luke gave a reassuring smile. Aaron shrugged his shoulders and put his palms out as if to convey he hadn't had a say in this plan either.

The scene before her looked similar to a moment two years ago. The stage had been the same, but the scene was a little different, and the actors, plus Corrie, younger. In fact, Nikki had been one of them, seated in the chair Iris perched on now. The man of the hour, Nathan, had sat in the chair she inhabited currently and announced he was joining the Marines. If she concentrated hard enough, Nikki could still hear the cries of excitement, platitudes of pride and honor, and the overarching respect they had all had for the future soldier.

What hadn't been said rubbed Nikki raw. No one had pointed out the danger, the time away from home, the possibility of never seeing him again. No one had questioned his dreams, his goals, his pursuit of greatness. No one had mentioned the word "safe." What he never heard, she always did.

Her body was primed for a fight. A fight she couldn't win or afford. To ease the pressure building inside her, she stretched out her neck and flexed her shoulders back until her shoulder blades nearly touched.

"Please don't be upset, honey." Cynthia reached across the table for Nikki's hand. "It's that you, well…"

"Match the victim profile. I saw the killer. The killer saw me, yada, yada, yada." Nikki ignored her mother's hand and scooted her chair back, the feet scraping against the flooring. "I'm tired of being afraid, and you should be too." Nikki dropped her napkin on her untouched plate of food, grabbed her phone and purse from the kitchen island, and placed her left hand on her jutted-out hip. "Well, boys, which of you is the lucky winner today?"

Author Note: Airheads come up a lot in my story, and for good reason. When I was a kid, and we visited my Grandma Helen in Hague, North Dakota, my cousins and I would walk to the Hague Café and buy handfuls of Airheads for 25 cents apiece. We left with no money, but we didn't care. We trotted off to the park and traded flavors. Those are the memories that stick with me still today. Years later, my cousins and I are adults now, the original café building is no longer used, and the park where we traded our booty no longer exists, but one thing hasn't changed: the availability of Airheads. They're everywhere! When my own children buy them, I smile softly and decline any offers of a bite because another thing has changed: my tastebuds. I'm not sure what ten-year-old Jessica tasted when she bit into that taffy, but forty-one-year-old Jessica has a much different opinion. I'm sure when little Iris grows up, she will experience the same change. What food did you love as a kid that you can't stand now?

Chapter 28

"You know they care about you and are terrified, right?" Luke parked his pickup in front of Mabel's Café but kept it running. The diesel engine purred.

For a second, Nikki could imagine the late nights in the fields during harvest, her little legs scratched by the wheat stubble, her hands filthy with dirt and the dust of Doritos pilfered from the lunch cooler. Her dad had always kept the pickup running as he blew the combine off after a day of harvesting. It had never taken more than a few minutes for the diesel engine to rumble her straight to dreamland.

Nikki stored that memory away and glanced at Luke. She hadn't looked at him the entire drive into town. There hadn't been the need. He'd been silent. Probably his way of giving her space. "I know." She hopped out and, before closing the door, gave a wobbly smile. "Thank you."

"You're welcome. See you at three?"

"If I'm still alive."

Luke gave her the same look he'd given Iris at her social faux pas that morning over breakfast.

"Sorry." Not feeling one bit sorry for her poorly timed joke, she shut the door then scampered up three stone steps and walked through the café's door.

The bells tinkling announced her presence to a full dining room. A full dining room complete with a corner table of six little old ladies, who from their curious stares through thick-lensed glasses, still questioned her sanity over jilting Sandy's all-American boy. And now that he was in town, the curiosity bordered a little too close to impertinence.

Heat scurried up her neck and nestled behind her ears. Good, it could stay there. As long as her face didn't go scarlet, she would be fine. Anything more than that, and they might suspect what Iris had already known. Nikki shook her head as she entered the relative safety behind the Employees Only sign hanging above the kitchen door so she could gather her thoughts. If Iris knew, it wouldn't take more than a day for the entire town to know. For only being eight, Iris shared the same quirks as the stereotypical elderly curtain twitcher.

"Got several lunch orders already. Today's going to be a busy day." Mabel's double chin trembled with excitement. "Good thing I cooked up a storm the other day."

Nikki opened the large walk-in cooler. "You're not joking." Prepackaged and ready-to-eat or ready-to-cook meals filled several racks along the wall. She glanced over her shoulder at a beaming Mabel. "Have you slept in the past forty-eight hours?"

Mabel shooed that idea away with a flick of her wrist. "I'll sleep when I'm dead. Don't roll your eyes at me, girl." Mabel flicked at a nonexistent speck on her apron. "Besides, if I can provide a meal for the police or Natasha's family and friends, well..." Tears sparkled in her eyes.

"You're a wonderful woman, Mabel." Nikki closed the cooler's door and, on her way out of the kitchen, paused next to Mabel and hugged her. To Nikki's surprise, Mabel wrapped her arms around Nikki's waist and gave one good squeeze before waving her away.

"None of that. I don't pay you to—"

"I know, I know. I'm getting to work." Nikki exited the kitchen and flicked a glance at the corner table laden with lipstick-rimmed white coffee cups and half-eaten muffins.

She set the dirty dishes in a shallow bin, cleared the table of the salt and pepper shakers and bottles of ketchup and mustard, and sprayed the table with cleaner. After wiping the disinfectant spray off the table, she slammed the washcloth back into a bucket of water. She set the shakers back on the table, rearranged the menus, plucked her tip off the black Formica tabletop, and dropped the quarter into the slotted Cool Whip container designated for the Sandy Community Beautification Fund on her way back to the kitchen.

Although she couldn't blame them. Instead of leaving a quarter, they could have at least left a useful tip like "after building a time machine, when you think you want to break up with Xavier, slap yourself silly."

His kiss had awakened her much like the storybook princesses, but instead of Prince Charming waiting by her side, ready to enfold her in a happily ever after, Xavier had walked away. Again, she didn't blame him. She would have walked away from herself.

Nikki opened the kitchen saloon doors with her hip. "Have you ever regretted a decision, Mabel?"

Mabel clutched a hunk of dough from a bowl where it had been rising and slammed it on a floured counter. "Besides hiring you?"

Nikki took small comfort in Mabel's smile and considered it a sign that she wasn't on Mabel's blacklist. For now. "Sure."

Not looking up from her rigorous kneading, Mabel kept thumping and twisting and pulling and pushing. "I also don't pay you to badger me with questions."

Nikki stopped asking questions, but from the slight stoop to Mabel's normally stoic shoulders, Nikki knew that something haunted Mabel. It was the same thing that haunted Sandy. Natasha's death.

Nikki forced the dishwasher door closed and pushed the Start button. "Mabel, do you mind if I—"

The kitchen saloon doors swung open. Nikki jumped.

Mabel clutched a floured hand to her chest, and after seeing who had entered the sanctity of the Employees Only kitchen, she brandished a flour-and-dough-covered rolling pin at Oliver Beaumont. "Can't you read?"

"I was accused of that once and quit." Oliver's smile appeared to work its magic as Mabel allowed him to make a few steps into the kitchen without being bonked over the head with the rolling pin.

Nikki, stuck in a corner between the industrial-sized fridge, gas range, and Mabel's ample hip, stared in wonder at the redness creeping up the old woman's neck. Bingo night had apparently been a successful venture for old Oliver.

"Just because I went to bingo with you doesn't mean you can barge in here all willy-nilly." Mabel had yet to put down the rolling pin.

Oliver's eyes crinkled in a smile. "I called your name several times. Thought I'd take a peek in here before leaving. I wanted to introduce someone to you."

With no visual attempt at hiding her annoyance at a customer entering her sacred domain, Mabel all but slapped the rolling pin down and headed for the saloon doors. She glanced at Nikki. "Might as well come along too. You'll just ask me a bunch of annoying questions about the mystery guest, anyway. This way your curiosity is cured, and you can get back to work."

"Mabel, if the café business doesn't work out for you, you could always pass as a fortune teller."

Mabel hummed a low note in her throat but didn't bother with a rebuttal.

Nikki followed Mabel out of the kitchen and into the seating area. Many of the customers had left, but a few regulars still sat, and would continue to sit for hours, sipping coffee and exchanging news. The late-morning sun streamed through the large windows. Despite the sunshine and comforting sounds of companionship, Nikki shivered. Somewhere out there, a killer might still lurk.

She knew beyond doubt, even though law enforcement officials had not confirmed it, the killer was the same psychopath who had ended the lives of four women in the Black Hills area. And she had seen him. Photographed him. Photography was an intimate act. Whether capturing a ladybug on a stalk of purple alfalfa or a baby's first smile or the personality of an old, abandoned farmhouse standing as a decaying gravestone to the generations who had called its walls home, each photo captured the soul of an individual or object in a single millisecond in time. A time that would never exist again.

Oliver's voice filtered into Nikki's thoughts, and she brought her attention back to reality.

"... my great-nephew, Bryce Beaumont. Bryce, this young lady here is Nikki Lancaster."

Bryce outstretched his hand to Nikki and smiled. "Nice to meet you."

Nikki clasped his hand and returned his firm grip. She met his gaze. The one similarity between great-uncle and nephew was the blue eyes. Bryce's blue eyes seemed bluer somehow. Could have been the thirty-some-year age difference or Bryce's black hair shaved on the sides with the top shock of hair layered and gelled into chunks. The edgy cut gave credence to his beard, well-trimmed with sharp angles. *Dangerous.* Nikki had a distinct impression that a dimple was hiding underneath his dark facial hair. *Could be dangerous.*

She returned a smile. "Likewise."

Oliver slapped his great-nephew on the back. "Ladies, Sandy has gained the newest member of Beaumont's Crop Insurance Agency."

Bryce smiled sheepishly.

Nikki yawned internally. A crop adjuster. *Definitely not dangerous.* "That must be exciting for you. Congrats."

Oliver, rubbing his hands together like a greedy little fly, ushered Mabel to a table in the corner. "You young people converse for a while. Get to know each other. I got some unfinished business with the cook."

Nikki leaned up against the long counter and drummed her fingers against the black Formica countertop, which had survived the last café renovation. "So..."

Bryce hopped onto a barstool. "I apologize for my uncle's heavy-handedness. We can sit here and pretend to talk, or better yet, I'll do all the talking and you nod your head like you agree with everything I say. That way Uncle Oliver will think I'm good at talking to people, and I won't have to suffer any more of his when-I-started-this-business stories."

Nikki chuckled. "Has plenty of those, has he? Want something to drink? It's on me."

"What you got?"

Nikki pointed to the two large coolers behind the counter stocked with Pepsi products, energy drinks, and a variety of iced-coffee bottles. "Or I can get you coffee or fresh-brewed sun tea."

"I'll have what you're having."

Nikki poured two large glasses of sun tea and grabbed sugar packets in case. She liked hers without sugar, but not everyone agreed with her and ended up ruining the beverage by sweetening it. She set the glasses on the counter and wrestled herself onto a barstool next to Bryce's. "Here you go. And some sugar."

He stirred two sugar packets into his tea and took a sip. "That's good. Thank you."

"When did you get to town?"

"A little over two weeks ago."

"So, you were here when... when we got the news."

"Yeah, I'm sorry about that. From what Uncle Oliver says, she was quite the woman."

Nikki sipped her tea to ease her tight throat and played the fingers of her right hand through the condensation dripping down her glass. "She was also a friend."

Bryce rested his hand next to her left one. "I am sorry."

"Thank you." She took a bracing breath and raised her glass to him. "Here's to your new adventure."

He clinked his glass against hers. "May Uncle Oliver never know how inept I actually am at selling and managing insurance accounts."

"You got me to sit down and listen to you. Practice your spiel on me..." She glanced at Mabel and Oliver seated over cups of steaming coffee. "They might be a while."

"You sure you won't regret this?" He dropped his voice to a whisper. "Insurance is boring."

"Won't know until I try. And never admit that what you do is boring... that won't get customers excited to buy anything."

"Solid point. This is paying off already." After taking a sip of iced tea, he cleared his throat, and by the end of his pitch, Nikki wished she needed crop insurance.

But as the only thing she was tending was a soul of discontent, she sent him on his way with free advice and two sugar packets for the road.

*A**uthor Note: Annette Link's Cottage Cheese Button Recipe Dough Ingredients:*
2 c flour
1 egg
Water (enough to make medium-soft dough)
Pinch of salt
Filling Ingredients:
2 c cottage cheese (dry curd ricotta)
1 egg

Salt and pepper to taste

Green onion (to taste and personal preference)

Directions:

Combine dough ingredients and roll out dough to 1/4-inch thickness.

Cut dough into 4" square pieces.

Put about 2 tsps filling into each square.

Fold over and press edges together.

Drop buttons into a kettle of salted boiling water.

When the buttons rise to the top, remove, and either fry in butter on both sides

or make a white sauce as gravy.

Thank you to my good friend, Dalene Tobin, for sharing your grandma Annette's cheese button recipe. I hope it brings everyone who tries it as much joy as it did when your grandma made this German dish for you.

Chapter 29

Nikki sliced into a lemon meringue pie, the knife sliding through the thick cloudlike pillow of meringue and into the velvety lemon-ness. After cutting out five pieces and placing them on plates, she arranged them all on a server's tray and carried the goodies to a group of women.

"You are joining us, right, Nikki?"

At her mother's not-so-subtle command to sit, Nikki cut herself a piece and squeezed in between her mother and Mabel. Joining them was Violet, Iris, who had invited herself after hearing there would be pie, Corrie, and the woman Nikki had met earlier at Natasha's butcher shop.

Cynthia gestured to the woman. "I believe you've met Eleanor already."

Nikki smiled across the table at the woman. "It's nice to see you again." She glanced at the other women crowded around the table meant for four. "What's going on? A secret society meeting?" Nikki gasped and clasped at her chest. "Did I bust a ring of notorious female gamblers bent on spending their husbands' money?"

"Mine would have known to be the better gambler, so I wouldn't have to." Mabel saluted the ladies at the table with her coffee cup.

"Mine is so bent on buying the baby things that he might welcome the extra income." Violet patted her belly.

Cynthia chuckled. "Mine would spend it on board games and peanut butter."

Nikki crossed her arms over her chest when the three matrons pinned her with grins. "Don't even go there with me."

Iris chirped around a mouthful of pie, "I told Colby that he'd marry me someday or else I'd punch him in the nose."

Violet choked on her coffee. "You don't go around punching people. Ever. What has gotten into you?"

Iris, mollified or planning her next attack—it was hard to tell—remained silent and dug into her pie.

"And what about you, Eleanor?" Cynthia asked.

A soft smile touched the corners of Eleanor's lips. She set her coffee cup down and traced the rim with her fingers. "He would have poured me a drink, pulled up a chair right beside me, and tried to win."

"Would have?"

"He passed away two years ago. No, no, it's okay." She pressed her hand over Cynthia's. "My happy memories keep me going, and of course, I have my daughter to think of."

"I'm sorry. I know what it's like to lose a husband. But the important question is who would have won at poker?" Mabel asked.

"Me."

The women burst into laughter, and for a moment, it was as if a cloud of uncertainty lifted only to settle back down when the last chuckle and sigh died. For the first time, Nikki heard the silence, and she looked around at the otherwise-empty café.

"First, what are you ladies doing here? And second, where is everybody?"

Mabel pointed at the sign on the door, the word Open facing the inside. "I made an executive decision and want to plan something nice for Natasha's family. Figured I'd recruit some help along the way."

The café's doorknob turned, and the door thunked against the deadbolt.

"Can't people read?" Mabel muttered, swiveling in her chair and glaring at the illiterate interloper. "Well, well, look what the cat dragged in."

Nikki turned her head and froze. Xavier pressed his face against the door's window, and his hand shaded his forehead to cut the glare. Thaddeus peered in the side window.

Xavier caught sight of Mabel and mouthed the words, "Let me in."

Mabel shook her head and turned her back to him. Nikki followed suit.

Tap, tap, tap.

"Men." Mabel glared at Xavier, but before she could mouth a retort, he pressed his badge against the windowpane.

Muttering under her breath, Mabel trudged to the door, flicked the lock, and yanked the door open. "There's no need to flash that fancy badge of yours around. You could have knocked."

Xavier smiled. "It's good to see you too." He glanced around the dining area, and his gaze landed on Nikki's. His body tensed, and his hands fisted at his sides. "Nikki."

Nikki's heart skipped at his husky greeting. "Hello, Xavier."

It was the snort from Iris that broke the spell, and Nikki swore she could hear the little whippersnapper whisper-singing, "Xavier and Nikki sitting in a tree, k-i-s-s-i-n-g."

Feeling heat crawl up her neck, she shook Thaddeus's outstretched hand and returned his smile. "It's good to see you again." She motioned to the group around the table. "Ladies, this is Agent Thaddeus Cornwall. Agent Cornwall, Sandy's female mob."

"Always wondered what that looked like." Thaddeus grinned at them and saved his brightest smile for Mabel. "And I assume, ma'am, you are the mob boss."

Mabel tutted. "Don't ma'am me, Agent."

Unfazed, Thaddeus asked, "And the mob boss part?"

"Pfft. Have a seat, and I'll get you a piece of pie." Without offering Xavier pie, Mabel waddled off to the counter replete with glass-dome-covered pies.

A twinge of guilt over the pieless Xavier pinched Nikki's heart. "Can I get you anything?" *Please say yes. Please say me.* She almost slapped a hand over her mouth, afraid she'd said those words out loud. Sitting around, doing nothing but leeching off her family and waitressing had rotted her brain. *I need to get out of here. Do something.*

"No, thank you. Just here to talk. Had a couple of questions." Xavier pulled up a chair to the already-crowded table, and between the manipulations of both Mabel—who had sat down after gifting the new guy with a large pie slice—and Cynthia, he ended up hip-to-hip, thigh-to-thigh with Nikki. Thaddeus perched on a barstool outside the circle, pie plate balanced on his knee, fork primed for the first bite.

Trapped between her merciless mother and a man who rattled her senses, Nikki slouched in her chair and fiddled with a balled-up napkin.

"Xavier, Agent Cornwall—"

Thaddeus wiggled his fork and swallowed. "Please. Call me Thaddeus."

"Of course." Cynthia gestured to the woman across the table from them. "This is Eleanor St. John. She recently moved to Sandy."

Xavier smiled at Eleanor. "It's nice to meet you. I understand you worked for Natasha."

"That's right."

"For how long?"

"A couple of weeks, if that. I am so shocked that someone would want to harm her. She was the nicest person you could ever meet."

Xavier dug out a small notebook and made notations in it. "Where are you from?"

"Sorry?" Eleanor played with a ring encircling her pinky.

"Where did you move from?"

"Ah, Keystone."

"That's right next to Mount Rushmore." Iris, who had been too busy pilfering her mother's pie to notice the boring adult conversation, perked up.

A small smile touched Eleanor's lips. "That's right. I got to see the fireworks every year for free from my cabin."

Before Iris could invite herself to a cabin the woman no longer inhabited, Xavier cleared his throat and gave Iris a look that had the girl settling back into her chair and diving into her pie.

"When did you move to Sandy?" Xavier's thigh muscle tightened against Nikki's.

Nikki's ears heated. She nudged Xavier's knee with her own. He glanced at her, and his left eyebrow arched.

In forced playfulness, Nikki put her hand on his shoulder. "Sorry, Eleanor. Xavier is always in cop mode. Natasha was a good friend of ours during high school. He's been asking everybody that question, even ones who grew up here." Even though her smile felt as fake and melty as margarine, Eleanor didn't seem to notice.

"Oh, yes, sorry. I understand. Brain fog's been pretty serious ever since poor Natasha's death." Eleanor's face screwed up in thought. "Let me see. Today is the twenty-fifth, right? And I moved to town on the eighth. So, two-ish weeks ago."

Xavier, his knee pressing back into Nikki's, scribbled something on his notepad and turned his attention to Violet. "Violet, did you notice anything? Hear anything?"

"I've been racking my brain, trying so hard to think of something. But nothing comes to mind. Isn't that crazy? The last time I saw her was two days before she—"

Iris, abandoning her dessert, grabbed her mother's hand and brought it to her cheek. No words passed between mother and daughter.

The tightness around Violet's mouth relaxed, and she inhaled. "Sorry. It's hard, you know."

Xavier clicked his pen closed and rested it on his notepad. "I don't want to put any burden on you, but anything you can think of. Something that stuck out, something out of the ordinary."

"Iris?" Cynthia rarely, if ever, used the *mother tone* on her grandchild.

Iris straightened from a near under-the-table slouch and plucked her finger from her mouth, a habit she indulged in when scared or nervous. It didn't take long for all eyes to focus on her.

"Did you see something? Hear something?" Xavier asked, his voice gentle.

Iris hovered her finger near her mouth, glared at it, and sat on her hand. "I... I don't know if I should say. He could get in trouble."

Thaddeus pushed off the barstool he'd been sitting on and knelt beside Iris, taking her hand in his. "I can't make any promises. But what if this person saw something important or heard something? Like you did. I'm sure he'll want to help find who killed Natasha."

"But what if he killed her?" Iris's voice was little more than a scratched whisper.

Nikki's throat burned. Her arms ached to hold her niece, to protect her from the evils of the world. No eight-year-old should ever have to speak those words.

"It's okay, sweetie." Violet snuggled her daughter into her side and pressed a kiss to the top of her head. "If you don't want to, we understand—"

"Oliver's nephew. The new guy," she whispered.

"Bryce?" Goose bumps exploded on Nikki's arms.

Xavier shot her a look before concentrating on Iris. "What did you see? Hear?"

After burrowing deeper into her mom's side, Iris closed her eyes and inhaled a shaky breath. "I didn't mean to. Really, I didn't. I was supposed to be sleeping." She peeked up at her mom under wet eyelashes. "I'm sorry, but Colby told me he'd seen a glow-in-the-dark butterfly, and I wanted to prove he was lying—there's no such thing as a glow-in-the-dark butterfly, you know." Iris cocked her head to the side and played with her bottom lip. "When I got to the park—"

"Which one?" Xavier asked.

"The school park. Where Colby said he'd seen it."

"That's in the Beaumonts' backyard." Nikki chewed on her bottom lip. Oliver had been an easygoing fellow and had never once complained when stray balls or stray students ended up in his backyard.

"What happened?" Xavier asked.

"She kissed him. On the cheek."

Xavier scribbled on his notepad. "When? Father's Day night?"

"No, not that night. It was earlier." Iris's bottom lip curled out. "I'm sorry. I don't remember." Tears rolled down her cheeks, and she swiped at them as if they stung her.

"You did a great job, Iris. Thank you." Thaddeus shook Iris's hand as if she were a little lady, and she rewarded him with a toothy grin.

Xavier snapped his notepad shut, stuck the pen through the spirals, and stood. "Well, ladies, you've all been a great help. I'll have to talk to each of you again. Separately." After patting Iris's head—and receiving an eight-year-old-girl glare—he crooked his finger at Nikki.

She followed him and Thaddeus out the cafe's door, crossed her arms over her chest, and glared at Xavier. "So, what? We're suspects now?"

Thaddeus's gaze flicked between Nikki and Xavier and, as if sensing the incoming storm, he walked to Xavier's Jeep.

"Nope. Just doing my job." After pulling out his notepad, he thumbed through the pages and stabbed at the middle of the page with his finger. "Ah, yes. What can you tell me about this Bryce Beaumont?"

"Nothing much. Met him last week when Oliver introduced him to me and Mabel. Seems like a nice enough guy."

"Bryce Beaumont just moved here."

"So?" She squeezed her arms tighter around herself.

After gripping her hands in his, he met her gaze. "Bryce Beaumont moved here from Custer."

Author Note: There is nothing more American than pie, but pie is as old as Egyptians and didn't make its way to American shores until the colonists showed up. In fact, the crust, which most people eat nowadays, used to be a "coffin," and was so hard you couldn't eat it even if you wanted to. The crust was, up until the Revolutionary War, meant as a container for the filling and not part of the edibleness. After gaining freedom from England, colonists started referring to the "coffin" surrounding the filling as "crust." Over the generations, the pie evolved into what we know and love today. Most people have their favorite, and you guessed mine if you said lemon meringue!

Chapter 30

Xavier released his hold on Nikki's hands when she backed up.

"So? People move all the time." She bit at a cuticle on her thumb. "Eleanor moved here from Keystone. And we all know that she of all people didn't do it. Should we amend the Welcome to Sandy sign and put Except West River Men?"

"I can't say anything right now." After clicking his pen closed and slipping it and his notepad into his pants pocket, he was about to serve his normal scold to be safe. The sheer panic glistening from her eyes froze those words on his tongue. "Oh, Nikki." He pulled her to him, and for a moment, he wished he could keep her safe like this, burrowed into his chest.

His hands slackened their pressure on the small of her back. Nikki wasn't burrowing. Her spine, ramrod straight, hadn't slackened, slouched, or shivered. After holding her at arm's length, he studied her face. It was like flint. He was sure that at that moment, if something struck her, it would shatter by touching her skin.

"Nikki, I promise I'll—"

"What? Catch him before he catches up to me?" She slanted her right shoulder away before he could rest his palm there. "Somehow, someway, he followed me here, and I hate to burst your fancy cop bubble, but you can't keep me safe."

His jaw tensed. Ever since meeting and falling in love with Nikki Lancaster, that had been his goal: keep her safe. And she had rewarded him with a broken heart and a shattered future. But he wasn't about to change now, not when her safety truly was threatened and not just a figment of his stupid hero-complex imagination. "Leaving at three?"

Nikki's right eyebrow almost touched her hairline. "Stalking me now?"

"That's illegal... as you are well aware after your brief foray into that crime in Custer." He wanted to kiss the scowl off her face but knew she would slap him. Instead, he stuck his hands in his back pockets and jerked his head toward the cafe's door. "I'll see you at three."

After she slammed the door with extra gusto, the tinkling bells singing out her anger, he made a mental note to have Steve post a deputy out the back for when she gave them the slip.

"Shut up," Xavier growled as he approached his Jeep and the chuckling form of his best friend.

"I didn't say anything."

"You don't need to." Xavier jammed the key into the ignition. "I've got it under control."

Thaddeus glanced at the spot where Nikki and Xavier had been arguing. "Sure you do."

A few minutes later, after dropping Thaddeus off to question the Sandy residents holed up in the town bar, Xavier collapsed into the chair opposite Steve's desk. Someone had sprayed a generous dose of air deodorizer, and now the funky aroma of garlicky lilacs filled the small office. He wrinkled his nose.

"Deputy Stewart tried." Steve blew his nose into a tissue.

"And failed." Laurel's voice seeped through the crack in the door.

Xavier had heard of olfactory fatigue and hoped that his nose tired quickly of smelling. "Got the crime scene photos?"

Steve swiveled in his chair, pulled open a drawer in a file cabinet as tall as the room, and plucked out a file. "Here you go."

"Got a whiteboard or something and markers?"

A snicker slipped through the crack.

"For your diligent observation skills, Deputy Stewart," Steve called, "why don't you accompany Xavier to the basement and help bring up our... whiteboard?"

Suspecting he wasn't retrieving his exact wishes, he traipsed down the steps to the bowels of the county sheriff's office. He wasn't sure what was housed in the depths under the building, but from the murky, dusty darkness, he wouldn't be surprised if a few troll families called this place home. Laurel flicked on a few light switches, and fluorescent tubes buzzed to stuttering life.

"It looked a heck of a lot less creepy with less light." To investigate his claim, he flipped the lights off. "But"—he flicked them back on—"I suppose we need illumination to do our job."

"You're telling me. As the lowest on the totem pole around here, I'm the sacrifice sent down here."

"Well, where's this 'whiteboard'?" His fingers hooked air quotes, and he scanned the metal shelves decorated with file boxes, old office equipment, and an odd assortment of shade-less desk lamps.

Laurel followed his gaze. "Don't ask. No one knows where they came from or what they're doing down here. They've been here since the beginning of time."

From the pillowy layer of dust on the lamps' bases, Xavier couldn't argue.

"This way." Laurel crooked a finger and led the way between the narrow path splitting the metal shelves. "There's a room back here—"

"Where the trolls live?"

"How did you know?" She smiled over her shoulder as she stopped in front of a time-eaten wooden door.

Xavier ignored the scratches on the door. There was no such thing as trolls. Especially in Sandy, South Dakota. "Educated guess."

She snorted, turned the bronze doorknob, and used her right hip to convince it to open. It creaked on its hinges and exposed a cluttered room full of office and cop stuff that had been obsolete since the fifties. Utility belts were slung over abandoned overhead projectors and an old film projector slumped in the corner. Cardboard boxes, overflowing with dusty film reels, squatted on top of and next to it.

"I have a strange feeling my whiteboard isn't here."

"Nope. But never fear. We've got something better."

Better turned out to be a jerry-rigged green chalkboard attached to a squeaky wooden frame with wheels.

Laurel took the lead and wheeled it out the door and down the aisle to the base of the steps. "The school donated this a few years back when they cleared out their own creepy basement."

Xavier bit back a grin. He knew all too well the ins and outs of the Sandy High School basement. He had abandoned his naughty activities, however, the moment Corrie Lancaster had gotten her clutches—or her fingernails—into his earlobe one fateful night. Somewhere under the furnace or hot-water heater lay a few poker chips and his grandfather's pocketknife he'd lost in a scuffle when his opponent had called him a cheater.

After grasping the wooden frame and lifting his portion of the chalkboard, he followed Laurel up the stairs and back into the land of the living. "I don't suppose there's an extra room where I can set up."

"Today's your lucky day." Laurel continued past her desk, and before it looked as if she were going to go straight through the cinder block wall, she hooked a sharp left and dragged both the chalkboard and Xavier into a small office—a small, sunlit office.

"You might be my favorite person in the universe right now."

She settled the chalkboard against the wall farthest from an olive-green metal desk that looked familiar. "Another kind donation from the school."

He rocked the swivel office chair with matching green leather armrests, back, and indented cushion. In his first free moment, he was ordering an office chair online. "Got any chalk?"

"Thought you'd never ask. Be back in a jiffy."

A few minutes later, Laurel entered the room with several boxes of chalk in hand. "Here you go. Got some pinks and greens, even. If you're feeling colorful, that is." She dusted her hands together, and a tiny cloud of chalk dust puffed into the air. "If you need anything else, holler. I'm right around the corner."

After Laurel left, Xavier stood in the middle of the tiny space. He was sure it was two feet wider than his wingspan. Testing that hypothesis, he spread his arms out. Sometimes, he didn't like being right. But he had a window. He pressed his forehead to the windowpane. Cars and trucks loitered down Main Street. He slid his forehead as far right as he could and slanted his gaze down the street. He could make out Mabel's Cafe.

After running out to his Jeep and gathering his laptop and files, he spent the next hour setting up his office space and running a routine search on Eleanor St. John. One speeding ticket. Law-abiding citizen and owner of a 2012 Toyota Corolla.

A knock sounded on the doorjamb. Thaddeus entered, clutching a brown paper sack. With him came the tantalizing aroma of cheese buttons, Mabel's cheese buttons.

Xavier's stomach growled, a reminder that he was on the cusp of starvation, and his mouth salivated.

Thaddeus held the bag out of arm's reach. "Nope. I was lucky enough to get on that dear woman's good side and was told in very clear words not to share with you. You did not do the job she gave you earlier."

"But... but—" Xavier snapped his mouth shut. "I did that woman's bidding. The job she tasked me with isn't some errand. It's Herculean."

"You must be speaking of Nikki. In that case"—Thaddeus opened the bag, pulled out a Styrofoam container, and opened the lid, releasing curling wisps of steam—"it'll be a while before you taste these again." He forked a generous amount into his mouth and chewed. "Man, these are good. I hope your taste memory is good. It must suck to be you right now."

"When are you out of my hair?"

"When we solve this case." Thaddeus tucked into the last cheese button.

"Good." Grinning, Xavier pointed at the green chalkboard attached to a D-minus-shop-project wheeled frame. "Got us a 'whiteboard' and"—he tossed Thaddeus a piece of pink chalk—"some whiteboard markers. Careful, they'll leave a mark." He wiped at his forehead, conscious of the fact that he had wiped his brow with green-chalked hands.

Over the next several minutes, Xavier and Thaddeus revisited the Custer State Park murders. "So, we have four victims"—Xavier tapped the women's names written in pink chalk—"Lucy Porter, Michelle Osbourne, Hallie Crestar, and Alexis Stamford. All blond, all pretty. All killed by blunt force trauma. Also, toxicology reports came in from both Custer CSI for Michelle and Weaver's too. Traces of chloroform in both Natasha's and Michelle Osbourne's systems. Between coyotes and decomposition, the use of the stuff is inconclusive with the other three victims found in the park." He made another bullet point under Michelle's and Natasha's names and added *chloroform* behind them.

"Killer uses the chloroform to incapacitate his victims first. Why?"

"Make it easier? Less risk of getting caught if the victim can't make noise or escape."

"But apparently, that didn't work in Natasha's case." He pointed his fork at the words *flannel fibers under her fingernails* under her name. "Unless he used chloroform after the fact." Thaddeus chewed another forkful of cheese button. "Maybe that's how he suffocated her. I'll check the surrounding suppliers. See if any buyers match the description."

Xavier scanned the board. "What's the link between them?"

"Professional?"

"Nope. Lucy worked as a hostess for the Silverado Franklin Hotel and Casino in Deadwood." Xavier abbreviated the name of the establishment under Lucy's name. "Michelle was a baker from Tulsa, Oklahoma"—the chalk squeaked as he bulleted that under her name—"Hallie was starting med school, and Alexis had earned her degree in chemical engineering and was about to move out to Boston with her fiancé." Nothing but the scratching of chalk filled the office for several seconds while Xavier scrawled out his notes until he highlighted it all with a pointed stab of chalk to finish off the *i* in fiancé. The chalk stick snapped in half.

Thaddeus picked up the severed half from the floor and bounced it around in his hand. "No shared alumni? No mutual friends? Nothing that connects them?"

"Nothing." To the board, Xavier added the fact that Michelle had been seen at a Sturgis gas station buying whiskey—which she hadn't drunk—a bag of Takis, and Diet Coke, both of which were found in her stomach during the autopsy. "Oh, almost forgot." Under all this, he scrawled *Missing ring?* and made a mental note to call Michelle's parents to double-check the ring's backstory.

"I find it odd that if she were under duress or any stress at all that she'd have eaten anything, especially those."

"I agree, which is why I don't think she knew she was in any danger. The gas station attendant recalled her as being hoity-toity, not nervous or fidgety. She probably had no clue she had purchased and eaten her last meal." Xavier ended his notes with the words *dark-green SUV.*

"So, she trusted whoever she was with." Thaddeus played with the sides of his mouth, leaving a trail of pink-and-green chalk dust in a perfect Fu Manchu mustache.

Xavier bit back a grin at his friend's acquired facial markings. "That's the theory I'm going with. For now."

"Any ID on the SUV?"

"None. The attendant assumed a man drove it because it was a manlier-looking vehicle, but he never got a plate number."

Thaddeus made an asterisk by the picture taped to the chalkboard that Nikki had taken of the suspect. "Sure looks like a man. Caucasian would be my guess."

"That's the theory." Xavier bit at his thumbnail and scowled. "Did kids really eat this stuff? Tastes like..."

"Chalk?" Thaddeus set his chalk on the beveled tray. "So, where are we now? How does Natasha fit into all this? And how much police protection does Nikki need?"

"The only things that connect the victims, at least in West River, are their looks and the location of their bodies: all in Custer State Park. That has to mean something. Could very well be the clue that breaks this wide open."

"You got something, don't you?"

"Just a supposition is all. Nothing definite." Under the victims' names, he scrawled the name *Bryce Beaumont*.

"You're kidding me. He's a game warden, part of the law enforce—"

"And you've never met or at least heard of a dirty cop before?" Xavier circled the name. "All I know is that he, as a game warden, would know the ins and outs of the park, the secluded spots where he wouldn't be interrupted, and his job would make him seem trustworthy." After he put Custer State Park in all caps, he underlined it twice. "Custer State Park brings in thousands upon thousands of people every year, especially during the summer months. I am certain the park connects the women. They were there for a good time, to see the sights, maybe a buffalo or two. Case of wrong place, wrong time."

"And Nikki?"

Xavier paused in his note-taking. The chalk, suspended between his fingers, shook. "I have no clue. There is no way the man she photographed could follow her. The car he followed her in and tried to—" His breathing hitched, and he rubbed at the spot over his sternum. "Her car was totaled after that. And I've spoken with both Custer and Sandy County Courthouse treasurers, and no calls ever came in concerning the plate registered to Nikki's car. But because of his job, he could look up who a license plate number was registered to, making it simple for him to follow Nikki across the state."

"So, Natasha's murder wasn't a random act?"

Circling Bryce's name, Xavier ground out between his teeth, "And we're back to Mr. Beaumont, aren't we? We could chalk"—he stared at the piece of chalk in his hand and grinned—"it up to coincidence that a few weeks after he moves to Sandy, there's a murder whose victim matches the victim profile, or we—"

"I don't like coincidences."

Xavier slammed the chalk into its tray so hard it shattered. "Neither do I."

*A**uthor Note: As a teacher with the latest technology at my fingertips, I often look out on my students, with also the latest and great technology, and wonder if they're missing out on the "good old days." I distinctly remember the smell of chalk in the classroom and how my classmates and I would vie for the coveted job of taking the huge erasers down to the custodians' "lair," where we would use the industrial vacuum to rid the erasers of chalk dust. Perhaps it was the tunnel we had to travel down that made the job so interesting. I may have lost the reason for craving this job, but I have not forgotten the roaring of the vacuum,*

the smell of chalk dust, or the gritty fineness of the powder. What memory of school do you have that you think younger generations are missing out on?

Chapter 31

It was in a twisted dog yoga pose that Nikki realized she shouldn't have unearthed her old yoga DVDs from the bowels of her parents' media collection. She also shouldn't have snuck out of work early to escape the calvary of Xavier and Thaddeus's minions. What started as a meditation and relaxation exercise had twisted her body as much as her mind.

Bryce Beaumont, aka game warden, aka benevolent nephew come to rescue his uncle suffering from the early stages of Alzheimer's, was at the top of Xavier's suspect list.

Easing from a plow pose, Nikki felt her abs tighten and shake until her heels touched the carpet. Tired in both body and soul, she lay in the corpse pose and stared up at the living room ceiling. A fitting position for someone who saw a murderer. *Probably gave him an iced tea too. I should have known when he dumped two packets of sugar in his drink that I couldn't trust him.*

She needed more than yoga. She needed to escape behind the lens of her camera. After taking the steps two at a time, she rounded the corner of the Tuttles' guest bedroom and dug through her unpacked suitcases. There was no need to unpack when she didn't plan to stay long.

She descended the porch stairs. Corrie's pickup was alone in the yard. An odd loneliness crept around her middle and squeezed. She sprinted to her sister's pickup, slammed herself inside, and locked the door. For what could have been seconds or minutes, she sat straight, her hands wrapped around the steering wheel like a boa constrictor suffocating the life from its victim.

Her phone pinged in her pocket, and she screamed. Cursing under her breath, she wiggled her phone free and glared at the screen. *Xavier!*

His text offered no signs they'd shared a kiss the other day, or ever for that matter. *Where in the hell are you?*

She glanced at the clock display on the dashboard. 3:02.

Her phone beeped and vibrated in her palm, and after a brief pause, a text notification pinged. *Nikki! Answer your phone.*

Every moment of people ordering her about, questioning her decisions, her goals, replayed in her mind. Knowing full well she should answer, she plopped her phone on the passenger side and rammed the pickup into gear. She would reply when she was good and ready to. And quite frankly, she wasn't good and ready to do anything but escape to the world she zeroed in on with her camera lens.

A decrepit Allis-Chalmers tractor slumped in dejection. Partially protected by a rotting roof, the tractor's frame had survived the years of neglect. The less hardy bits—the tires, seat, and wires—sagged in age or had been gnawed away by time and mice. Where splotches of rust hadn't spread, orange paint managed a feeble gleam from the sun rays streaming through holes and cracks in the roof.

Standing in front of the tractor, pointing her camera at the broken grill grinning at her, Nikki focused in on the glory that once was. She wanted to concentrate on the beauty under it, that part where a story could still be seen. And from the dents marring the tractor's surface, Nikki was sure this Allis-Chalmers had quite the story.

After picking her way around the debris field of old tractor parts, rusted cans, and an assortment of abandoned tools littering the inside of the dilapidated shed, she exited the empty doorframe and back into daylight. Next to the old shed, an old house rose above a sea of weeds, which Nikki assumed used to be a manicured lawn and some sort of driveway leading to the front door. There wasn't much of a front door now. What was left hung off its rusted hinges, and a scrap of tattered, yellowed lace clinging to an old curtain rod fluttered in the breeze, a reminder of some woman's attempt to make her house a home. A planted wheat field surrounded the old farmstead and encircled the property. The house, the tractor shed, and the accompanying barn with a collapsed roof was an island of the past amidst the modern world.

Nikki cued up to take a picture of a ladybug crawling on a stalk of purple alfalfa and paused. A rumbling sound broke the stillness. Weeds as tall as her chest impeded her movement as she waded toward the edge of the homestead island to see who had disturbed her solitude. She wasn't sure who owned this land, but as she was trespassing, she worked up a grand apology to whoever was driving a beat-up, old blue pickup down the section line and toward the old house. After all, it was easier to ask for forgiveness than permission, or at least that was what she hoped as she struggled free from a tricky patch of Canada thistle.

The pickup came to a rocking halt. The driver's-side door opened, and out stepped Bryce Beaumont.

Her heart hammered in her chest, and for a split second, she visualized Xavier standing over her dead body unearthed from some hole or even the basement of the decaying house behind her, asking the same question she asked herself now. *Why didn't I answer Xavier's phone call?*

A *uthor Note: Bad decisions. We've all made them or been victims of someone else's bad decisions. As a farm kid, I was often subject*

to my father's hare-brained schemes like putting a nine-year-old in a manual, one-ton pickup and telling her to drive her little sister back to the camper. True story and one of many where I performed adult tasks before even reaching puberty. When I was a child, my parents were custom combiners. In May, we'd ready the camper, load combines and headers on trailers, and start the journey to Walters, Oklahoma, and work our way up with the ripening wheat harvest. My first time driving happened in Attica, Kansas, and my sister and I had been out with my dad. He finished the field and needed an extra driver, so he put me in the driver's seat, slid it all the way forward, put the pickup in low gear, and told me to drive. And that's what I did. I'm not sure how we made it safely, but my mom was very surprised to see me rolling into the camper lot with my little sister in the passenger seat, her head hanging out the window, screaming.

Chapter 32

By the time Nikki figured she had 2.2 seconds to run, Bryce stepped over the threshold between planted wheat and wild weeds. A green ball cap embroidered with the gold words Beaumont Crop Insurance Agency shaded his face and softened the sharp, clean lines of his Wolverine-esque beard.

"Hey, Nikki, what brings you out here?" His gaze flitted from her face, which from the warming sensation was flushed, to her arms clasped behind her back.

"Nothing. Just..." She clutched her camera tighter. Maybe if he didn't see it, he wouldn't get the photographer connection, wouldn't realize she was the one who snapped his picture at a crime scene. *But maybe he's not the one? But what if he is?* While her internal thoughts played angel and devil, Nikki breathed a prayer of gratitude that in her fear of being alone at the farm, she'd forgotten her orange fishing hat. Hopefully, she had a chance to ask forgiveness from her father. If that ugly thing had been splayed on her head, Bryce would have to have been an idiot—*if he is the killer*—to not recognize the orange monstrosity. *Act normal!* Entrusting her immediate survival to a shaky sense of anonymity, Nikki plastered a smile on her face and brought her camera into view.

"Taking some pictures. A hobby, really." She waved the camera about as if it wouldn't shatter her bank account if she dropped the darn thing. After stashing it back in its case before he could scrutinize the obvious quality of her "hobby's" equipment, she placed the strap across her chest. "I could ask the same thing of you. What are you doing here out in the middle of nowhere?" *Besides, of course, possibly burying a body.*

He studied her for a second longer before smiling and tapping the clipboard pinned between his side and left arm. "Work."

Her lungs deflated. "You mean you're not here to—" *Lord, shut my stupid mouth. Please!*

"To what?"

"Ah... reminisce about the good old days." She gestured to the elderly buildings in the background.

Snorting a laugh, he stepped closer. "I'm not as old as that, but I love old houses. Think we can go in?"

"Don't you have a job to do?" She pointed to the wheat field. Far from the mature, golden-bearded stalks ready for harvest in late July, the wheat resembled overgrown green grass.

"Last field of the day. Besides, I've been behind the wheel for a grand total of 217 miles today. Legs and hindquarters wouldn't mind a traipse through an old house. A bonus if it's haunted."

"But... but that's trespassing." Never mind the fact that she'd wallowed in that crime for a good thirty minutes before his arrival.

He cocked his head and studied the obvious trail of her struggles into and out of the weeds. "Looks like you're an expert at it. Shall we?" Holding out his arm, he gestured for her to show the way.

Two choices lay before her. One, run and make a fool of herself if he was an innocent man. Two, stay and become his next victim if he was as nefarious as Xavier had alluded to a few hours ago. *Or three, you ninny, stay and enjoy traipsing through an old house with a man who has only shown you kindness.*

Her phone pinging in her pocket disturbed her warring thoughts. Huffing, she snatched it from her pocket and glared at the all-caps text message from Xavier.

Where in the—she ignored the creative adverb or adjective... or possibly a noun or verb—*are you? Please, Nikki!*

She'd taken it too far. Again. She'd wanted to escape from... everything. *Sorry. Just got this.* Little white lies didn't count. *Taking pics at that old house two miles south of the old Lutheran church.* Swallowing her pride, she tapped out *Bryce is here.*

"If you can't go through the house with me now, I understand. Maybe you can show me all the haunted spots later." Bryce glanced at the phone clutched in her hand then at the weathered house. "I should get back to work, anyway." He turned to leave.

"Wait." Nikki tucked her cell phone in her back pocket, readjusted her camera case strap, and jerked her head toward the past. "No time like the present, right?"

Her doubt slipped away at his boyish and alluring smile.

"Really? Because only if you want to. No pressure." His left eyebrow quirked when her phone pinged and vibrated in her back pocket. "Someone must want to talk to you."

"No one important." Those words burned the back of her throat. "Let's see if we can find some ghosts."

"During the day?"

"Maybe some of them are more ambitious than others. Why leave scaring humans to the nighttime?"

Bryce laughed as he followed her through the pre-trampled weeds and long grasses. "Never thought of that before, but that is a great question. Let's hope I have the wits—before they're scared out of me—to ask when a daytime ghost appears."

They stopped short of the two front steps, if they could be called that. At one time, they may have been a safe way into the house, but the steps had rotted away, leaving the center and edge stringers.

Bryce placed his foot on the inch-wide stringer. It groaned. "Think it's safe?" He stepped away and looped his thumbs through the belt loop on his jeans.

"Nope." Nikki relished the adrenaline pulsing through her system. It had been too long since she'd felt the rush, the spin in her stomach, the giddiness from an unknown adventure. For the first time in a long time, she felt alive. "Let's go." Straddling the two outer stringers, she inched her way up to the hanging door and gripped the white-splotched metal doorknob to regain her balance. "I think I may or may not have touched dried bird poop."

"Best not to think of such things. Pretend it's dried icing or something." Bryce came up to her side and teetered on the opposite stringer. "Home sweet home."

As she was behind the door, he led the way into a long hallway that must have served as a sort of front entrance and a place to hang coats. Before taking a step, he tested the raccoon-poop-infested wooden floorboards with a hearty push of his booted toes. She followed his lead, her heart skipping every time the floor creaked under her feet.

"You okay?" He glanced over his shoulder after a few steps.

"Never better." She resisted the urge to hurry him into the house. They had plenty of time for discovery and possible close calls with ethereal beings or spongy floors.

He grinned and continued forging a path until the hallway ended and opened into a kitchen—not that it inspired Nikki to cook. Whatever had been of value or small enough to loot had been removed or stolen long ago. All that remained were cabinets, half with their doors missing or doors clinging to their moorings by rusty hinges. A chair, gutted of stuffing and stripped of upholstery, lay upside down, its springs exposed to the discolored and moldy ceiling. Small pyramids of animal feces covered the floor.

Nikki tiptoed over debris and gunk to the sink. Instead of clean white porcelain, the two sides of the sink housed mouse droppings and leaves, feathers, and other bric-a-brac the wind had blown in through the broken window above the sink. A tattered piece of curtain still clung to its rod. Time and weather had melted a once-bright-blue gingham together, morphing the various blue checks into a dingy gray.

"Nikki, you've got to check this out." Bryce's voice echoed through the empty house.

Nikki spun around to find herself alone in the kitchen. "Where are you?"

"I think I'm in the living room or maybe the parlor. I don't know. Come here."

More than adrenaline pricked up her spine as she moved toward the doorway separating the kitchen from the rest of the house. *He just wants to show me something, not kill*—she heard his warning and the snap of boards too late. She screamed.

Author Note: I love exploring—to the detriment of my poor ankles—old houses. Something about their eyeless windows, shuddering bones, and dust-covered memories stab me right in the heart. I want to know who lived there; I want to know who hung the curtains, now tattered and colorless; I want to know why they left their belongings behind; I want to hear the last song played on a piano now muted by time and decay. As part of my summer of photography, I explored many houses and came away with different emotions for each. Some houses felt lonely, some sad, some nostalgic, some bitter and angry over being left to rot in the prairie wind and snow. Perhaps I'm crazy or maybe all houses have souls just waiting to be discovered. What do you think? Have you ever been in a house or building where you felt this presence?

Chapter 33

Xavier pulled up at the edge of the abandoned farmyard, behind a beat-up old pickup and the car Corrie had loaned Nikki. He called in to have the pickup's plates run and stepped out from the air-conditioned cab into the late-afternoon sunshine. A voice crackled over the radio he'd borrowed from the Sandy County Sheriff's Department. He pulled a pen from the spirals on his notebook to jot the registered owner's information down.

A scream ripped from the house.

Nikki!

He dropped the pen and notebook, sprinted through the weeds, and jumped up the decayed steps. Setting his back against the peeling plaster of the wall, he slid down the hallway, and gun drawn, surveyed the kitchen. Five steps in, he paused and listened. A man's voice murmured something, and footsteps scuffled on the wooden floorboards. Nikki's text informing him of Bryce Beaumont's presence flashed through his mind. It hadn't been a good idea to leave Thaddeus in town to continue questioning the residents. The floor bowed under his foot. On second thought, maybe it was a good idea Thaddeus wasn't there. There was no way his partner would have gotten two steps in without falling through the floor.

Nikki cried out.

Xavier picked his way across the rest of the kitchen, and after positioning himself with the cleared kitchen to his back, he rounded the corner and fixed his gun sight on the man pinning Nikki to the floor. His stomach plummeted to his feet.

He slipped his gun back into its holster and launched himself at the man. "Get off of her."

Nikki's pale face and dilated pupils were the last things he saw before he and the man tumbled to the ground and fell through the floor.

For several moments, Xavier lay on his back, his breaths coming in gasps, and stared at the water-damaged first-floor ceiling instead of the basement ceiling. The cannonball that had been him and Bryce next to him hadn't done a thorough job, though, of bringing the whole thing down. All he could see of Nikki were her legs and feet dangling in midair. She was still stuck in a Nikki-sized hole. She kicked her feet and, from her tone of voice, was cursing his name and maybe the man's beside him too. If this was the thanks he got for rescuing her—not that he'd done that—he was done getting her out of scrapes.

"What is wrong with you?" the man lying prone next to him wheezed.

Xavier twisted his head to the right and glared at the dark-haired man with ridiculous facial hair. *Who does he think he is? Hugh Jackman?* No doubt about it, though, the man matched Bryce Beaumont's law enforcement photos. Somewhere along the fall, Bryce had lost his ball cap. Xavier opened his mouth to arrest the man, if just for touching Nikki, but the sound of a broken squeaker toy escaped his throat.

Bryce chuckled, coughed, and panted for breath.

It took all of Xavier's self-control—a commodity he was running out of—to not punch the man in his smug face.

Nikki shouted again, but the echoing old house and half the floor keeping her from falling muffled the words. Xavier was sure he wasn't missing anything too earth-shattering, but taking an extended nap among the decaying old things in the basement wasn't an option.

After clearing his throat, Xavier pointed his finger at Bryce and rasped, "You are under arrest."

Bryce stared at him, struggled to a sitting position, then climbed to his feet. He wobbled and steadied himself against a rotting cabinet. Cocking his head, he held his hand out to Xavier. "For what?"

After glaring at Bryce's hand until it should have shriveled to a stump, Xavier grasped it and hauled himself to his feet, then doubled over in pain. His vision grayed, and fuzzy stars danced along his peripheral vision. He gripped an open cabinet door with one hand and clutched at his right side with the other. Thank goodness for forgotten furniture.

He looked down at Bryce leaning against the cabinet's side. "I'm arresting you for—" His mind whirled with stats and numbers and facts and pictures. There was no way Bryce clocked in at anything over six feet tall. And from the tackle move Xavier had done on him, he fit the weight profile, too, of a suspected serial killer.

Knowing he shouldn't show all his cards at once, he croaked, "I'm arresting you for assault."

"You've got to be kidding me. Who did I assault?"

Nikki hollered and kicked so hard that a sprinkle of dirt and one feather rained down on Xavier and Bryce. This time, her voice cut through the flooring. "Xavier, you idiot, get me out of here. Now!"

Xavier eyed Bryce. "This conversation is not over." At another stream of Nikki's commands, Xavier let go of his side long enough to point to her kicking feet. "Help me get her out?"

"That's what I was trying to do before you came charging in."

"Likely story." Xavier scoffed and limped to a set of rickety stairs. "You stay down here and push at her feet while I pull."

"Ask her yourself. She'll tell you I was trying to help her out of the hole."

"Still, not done with you—"

"Xavier!" Nikki yelled. "Are you ignoring me?"

Fat chance of that. "Coming. Hold your horses." Xavier picked his way up the steps, one hand clutching his side, the other searching out handholds to secure his shaky progress. By the time he got to the top of the stairs, his breaths came in deep gulps, and with each one, searing pain shot through his side.

"Xavier." Nikki's voice cut through the fog of pain. "Are you okay?"

He met her gaze across the gaping hole in the floor. Dark circles rimmed her blue eyes. Dirt smudged her face, and her disheveled blond hair reminded him too keenly of the hit-and-run that could have killed her. Whatever annoyance he'd felt in the last few minutes dissolved, leaving fear twisting in his gut.

"Don't move. I'm coming."

She rolled her eyes. "Like I'm going anywhere."

"I meant don't move around. I don't want you impaling yourself on something." Goodness knew what rusty, nasty things were kissing her skin already. He inched his way around the perimeter of the living room, testing each step before dedicating his weight to a spot.

"Christmas is coming too."

He was about to snap out a retort but caught the mischief in her eyes. "Probably won't have time to shop for your present either. You'll have to forgive me." His chest expanded at the thought of having a reason to get her a present. Pain exploded at his side.

"You even remember what I like?" Her eyes were no longer teasing.

Did I ever really know what she liked? What she wanted? Probably not. He'd never taken her cues for something bigger, grander, wilder. "How about we consider me getting us out of this house without it falling on us a present for now?"

Another eye roll and an added grunt. "Thought so."

Bryce's voice floated up from the hole. "You about ready?"

"You sure are in a hurry to get arrested, aren't you?" Xavier caught Bryce's gaze and tapped at the DCI insignia on his chest.

"Why are you arresting Bryce?" Nikki's face drained of color. She whispered, "He didn't ki—"

"For assaulting you. You're welcome."

He made it to the outer edge of the room next to Nikki and lay on his belly to a combined chorus of "I didn't assault her" and "He didn't assault me."

Xavier ignored them and edged closer to the hole until his right hand grasped hers. His side pinched. He sucked in a breath only to regret the extra dose of pain that came with it.

"You okay?" She eased a strand of hair behind his ear that had escaped his low ponytail.

"Just dandy." He didn't have the leverage lying down to lift her from the hole, so he situated into a squat behind her and placed his arms under her armpits. "Ready, Bryce?"

"Yup."

"On the count of three. One, two, three."

Xavier pulled, and Bryce pushed from the bottom. The floor cracked, and Nikki whimpered.

"It's okay," he whispered as her feet cleared the hole. Not waiting around for the floor to decide whether to stay intact, he shuffled backward out of the living room. Nikki's dragging heels left two tracks in the dust.

Upon reaching the relative safety of the kitchen, Nikki twisted in Xavier's arms and crushed him in a hug. She might as well have been wearing a suit of knives, but he swallowed the screaming pain in his chest and wrapped his arms around her.

The sound of Bryce's footsteps in the basement reminded him of his duty. "Nikki," he whispered in her hair. "Did he hurt you?"

"No," she mumbled into his chest. "He was just trying to help me out of the hole."

"But I heard you scream."

Her body shook with a laugh. "I fell through a hole. Next time I'll do something else. Maybe try out a yippee or woo-hoo."

Relief flooded through him, enough to numb the pain in his chest. Barely. "Listen, I don't trust him, but I don't have enough evidence to arrest him for anything. Yet. Until I can question him, find out more, I want you to stay away from him."

Instead of putting up an argument, she nodded. Her nose rubbed up and down on his sternum. Another emotion that wasn't fear or pain coursed through his body.

"You going to arrest me now?" Bryce held out his hands, his wrists placed for a pair of handcuffs. "That is if you have anything to arrest me for."

Ignoring Bryce's grin, Xavier eased himself from Nikki's bear hug. "I misunderstood the situation. Nikki explained what happened. But I would like to talk to you down at the station."

"For?"

"Just routine questioning over the death of Natasha Florence."

Bryce's Adam's apple bobbed. "Sure. Anything I can do to help."

Xavier glanced at his wristwatch. Almost six. "Tomorrow morning. Eight." He turned and smacked into the doorframe separating the living room and kitchen. He sucked in a wheezy gasp.

"You're not okay." Nikki latched on to his hand. "Let me drive you to the hospital. Please." She squeezed his hand when he shook his head.

"I'm fine." He grunted and doubled over.

"Liar." Not so gently, she lifted his black polo, exposing his side and an explosion of purples and blues spreading over his ribcage. "If you don't come with me willingly, I'll arrest you myself and drag your sorry butt to the ER."

Bryce chuckled and offered a helping hand to Xavier.

Brushing the gesture away, Xavier straightened until his teeth nearly bit through his lower lip. "I've got this. Tomorrow morning. Nine sharp."

"Wouldn't miss it."

Motioning for Bryce and Nikki to exit the house, Xavier followed them, clutching his side and imagining the satisfying click of handcuffs around the ex-game warden's wrists.

Author Note: A strange sensation happens when you fall through the floor of an old house. One part terror, one part surprise, one part bracing for impact, which leaves your body feeling elongated. Want to feel taller? Do you yearn for the feeling of your legs leaving your body or your torso lifting off your hips? Ever wonder what it feels like when your heart slides down your body and lives in your big toe for a split second? I wouldn't advise following in my footsteps or the misguided footsteps of Nikki, Xavier, and Bryce, but if you're looking for a cheap adrenaline rush and have an old house nearby—no, what am I saying? Don't do this. Don't try this at home or any home for that matter. What is the cheapest or freest thrill you've ever experienced that made your life flash before your eyes? Give me all the "deets" at https://www.jessicabergbooks.com/contact.

Chapter 34

Xavier wasn't sure what could be worse than a woman nursing him back to health—unless it was four women. That was definitely worse.

He had a slight reprieve from the ministrations of Nikki, Corrie, Cynthia, and Violet and used the quiet of the Lancaster living room to breathe as deeply as his two cracked ribs would allow and to readjust the bag of frozen peas resting against his bound side.

"If you want to get the true rest the doc ordered, you better come over to my house." Aaron grinned from a mahogany-colored recliner across the coffee table from Xavier. "Got some cold beer in the fridge, and I'm sure there's a baseball game on."

Resettling himself in a recliner that matched Aaron's, he winced. "I'm afraid they'd find me... us. Besides, I'm sure Corrie knows where the hide-a-key is. We couldn't even lock her out."

Luke chuckled from the matching love seat. "Don't look at me. Violet wouldn't let a locked door stand in her way either." He saluted Xavier with a glass of iced tea. "Looks like you're trapped."

"As long as you two are trapped with me, I'll be okay."

"My, my, look at the time." Aaron checked his nonexistent watch and kicked the recliner's leg rest in.

Luke set his glass on a coaster. "Yeah, I should start working on my Christmas Eve sermon."

Thunder from an approaching evening June storm rumbled in the distance.

Xavier snorted. "Wouldn't surprise me if that's done and in the bag already."

Instead of answering, Luke sprawled back on the love seat, turned on the television, and channel surfed. After going through the entire channel rotation twice, he stabbed the power button on the remote. "Nothing on."

A silence settled over the men, and the soft sound of women's voices filtered in from the kitchen.

"By my calculations, we have about two minutes to escape." Aaron flipped the leg rest back up. "But as we have someone on the injured list, our chances of getting out alive are slim to none. Might as well surrender now."

There was nowhere to hide, and Xavier's bag of peas had warmed enough to feel more like a bag of goo than an ice pack. Hitching himself up enough to kick the leg rest down, he grimaced.

"And where do you think you're going?" Nikki rested her hand on his shoulder and pushed him back into the chair. "The doctor gave strict orders to limit your movement and get plenty of rest."

After a clean bill of health and a shower, Nikki looked refreshed and, from the sparkle in her eyes, alive. He shook his head against that ridiculous thought—*of course, she's alive, you moron*—but there was no other word to describe the vivacity radiating from her, a vivacity he'd never fed. No wonder she had left him. If she had married him, he would have unwittingly snuffed the life from her.

Shaking off his invitation-only pity party, he forced a smile. "Don't worry. I've had much worse things happen to me than two cracked ribs." The moment those words left his mouth, he wished he could reel them back in.

Her smile slipped into a frown.

"But, hey, I'm here, and I saved your life."

"After you almost killed Bryce and me with that little stunt of yours." At least she wasn't frowning at him anymore. The arms crossed over her chest and her gaze staring down at him was much more her style.

He plucked the bag of now mushy peas and held them out to her. "I thought he was hurting you. What did you want me to do, stand around and wait until he'd finished the job to make sure?" When she ignored him and the bag, he jiggled it. "More frozen peas, please."

She snatched the bag and stomped from the living room, calling for backup. "Mom, your patient is being unruly. Your turn to deal with him."

Before Xavier could tell Aaron and Luke he didn't need their help—if what they were about to offer was help—the front door slammed open. He couldn't see the door from his spot, but he heard TT and Iris's high-pitched chatter, Thaddeus's booming voice declaring it wasn't his fault, and a strange woman's laughter in the foyer.

Both Aaron and Luke went to investigate and wrangle their children, who had been sent outside after supper to wear off some energy. Poor Thaddeus had unwittingly volunteered for babysitting duty, and Xavier felt slightly guilty about shackling his would-have-been niece and nephew to his best friend. To be fair, Thaddeus had thrown Xavier's Jeep under the garlic bus more than once. He glanced at the wall clock. Eight p.m. The last couple of hours felt like an entire day. Scrubbing his hands over his face, he relived Nikki's text, her scream, seeing Bryce—his gut roiled.

After the incident, on the way to the ER, he had called Steve and Thaddeus and filled them in on the situation. A deputy was monitoring Oliver Beaumont's house. If his great-nephew left, Xavier would know about it.

That didn't mean he could sit around like an invalid. He had a job to do. He would take a bag of peas to go and—

"I can hear your thoughts from here." Corrie leaned against the open doorway separating the living room from the entrance hall. A slight swell of her belly tattled on the baby growing inside her.

"Never could fool you, could I?" Even after eight years, Xavier's respect—and if he was being honest, fear—had never waned. "Who's here?"

"Oh, Eleanor. Gossip travels fast around here. She thought she'd come out and see if there was anything she could do for Nikki." She walked into the living room and settled on the old-barn-wood coffee table in front of Xavier. "Wanted to check in on you too."

He grimaced.

She grinned and patted his knee. "I told her you were napping. You owe me."

"I love helpful neighbors." He scratched his head and lowered his voice. "Do I have to pretend I'm sleeping for the rest of the night?"

"Like that would be a hardship. But no, Eleanor took pity on Thaddeus and offered to help him entertain the kids in the backyard. Apparently, they still have energy. I sometimes pray for winter just for the early darkness, and so I can put TT to bed at seven without him being the wiser."

"You're an evil woman."

"That's what Aaron says." She cocked her head. "What's eating you?" She held up a finger, stemming the obvious answer. "Besides the murders. And your cracked ribs."

He scrunched his face. "Nothing."

"I remember a time when I hauled you to your feet by your earlobe. I often wonder if I still have it in me to do again."

Odds were she did, and Xavier was a betting man. He inhaled, exhaled, buried his face in his hands, and spoke through the cracks of his fingers. "I never was the man for Nikki, was I?" As the silence stretched longer than he had expected, he set his hands on his thighs, met Corrie's brown eyes, and braced himself for the hard truth.

"No, I don't think you were the right boy for Nikki."

Hearing it was much worse than knowing it. Hearing it meant that someone besides him knew the truth. He wanted to say something, defend himself, but no words could squeeze through the tightness in his throat. Instead, he gripped his kneecaps and watched in fascination as the color leached from his knuckles.

"But…"

He raised his head and met Corrie's intense gaze.

"I think, now, you are the man for her."

Despite his heart thumping in agreement, he scoffed. "I didn't think you were the one to speak in riddles."

She made a pinching motion with her thumb and index finger. "Careful." Grinning, she scooted closer to the edge of the coffee table. "As a boy, you didn't know what Nikki needed. To be honest, none of us did. Now, as a man, you do. And it's your responsibility, if you want to earn her back, to ensure she gets what she needs."

"But what if her needs, her desires—"

"Are risky? Adventurous? Doomed to fail?"

He nodded.

"That's life. None of us are guaranteed success or happiness or fulfillment of dreams. Most of us go through life a passive participant in it, hoping and praying and wishing that hardships take a detour around us." She paused and glanced at the baby pictures hanging above each of the Lancaster children's high school senior pictures. Her gaze centered on three-month-old Nikki's gummy little grin beaming from chubby cheeks. A wistful fondness clouded Corrie's eyes before they cleared and met his. "Nikki was never like that. She embraced life, wanted to be an active participant in it. She was never content with life happening to her. She happened to life. That's where we all screwed up."

Shame heated his cheeks. For years he'd swaddled her with his affection and called it love. She didn't need his protection or his ego. She needed his respect for the person she was. Still, the idea of her in danger had his hands fisting.

Corrie laid her hands over his fisted ones. "And when she gets hurt or frustrated or one of her grand schemes explodes in her face, which will happen, I'm sure she won't need your I-told-you-sos or other safety sermons—"

He grunted.

"She'll need you to be there. That's it."

His mind whirled, and his insides quivered at the thought of proving his worth to Nikki. Fear, hope, and a healthy dose of pessimism swirled in his gut. "You're a wise woman."

"I thought I was evil." She grinned and hoisted herself to her feet. "You're both."

Voices, one of them Eleanor's, wafted from the kitchen and increased in volume as they neared the living room. Quicker than his ribs appreciated, Xavier reclined in the chair, and Corrie, playing the caring nurse, tucked a blanket around him and nestled it under his chin.

"Shh," she whispered to the invading guests, which from the variety of voices, Xavier assumed was every living Lancaster in a five-mile radius. "He's sleeping and needs his beauty rest."

"Then we better not disturb him for at least another two years." Thaddeus chuckled.

The chorus of laughter faded, and Xavier peeked an eye open. Seeing no one around, he disentangled himself from the blanket and recliner and tiptoed to the front door. After gathering his things, slipping on his shoes with several whispered exclamations of pain, and texting Thaddeus, *Make up an excuse to leave and meet me at the sheriff's office*, he walked to his pickup as fast as his ribs would allow. The time for napping was over. It was time to catch a killer.

*A*uthor *Note: I wonder how many bags of peas are purchased for vegetable ice packs. Odd question, I know, but my brain is full of*

odd questions on the best of days. What makes bagged peas better than a standard ice pack? Is it that after you are done icing your injury, you can microwave them, and have a snack? These are questions that I would like answers to, so if you have the answers to my ridiculous questions, please let me know. I'm dying to find out! So, tell me all about the iced peas at https://www.jessicabergbooks.com/contact.

Chapter 35

Nikki swerved around the corner of the living room doorway, clutching a bag of cold peas, and skidded to a stop. Her patient had escaped. She squeezed the frozen bag so tight it popped open. Pea buckshot exploded in the air and landed on her mother's white carpet. *Who puts white carpet in their house, anyway?*

Fearing her mother's wrath over the carpet more than the loss of a dollar's worth of peas, Nikki fell to her knees and gathered up the tiny green pellets. She would never eat peas again. Not that she ever did, but after plunking them in Xavier's abandoned cup, there was enough hair and dust to create a real-life dust bunny with peas for a skeleton.

"Need help?" Eleanor knelt next to her, pinched a wayward pea, and plopped it in the glass.

"No. Yes." Nikki sagged from a kneeling position to her butt and brought her knees to her chest. She clutched the glass of peas between her hands and stared at the hairy mixture. "This glass is my life."

Eleanor laughed and bit her lip. "Sorry. Didn't mean to laugh." She poked at the glass. "I think that can be said for a lot of us." After plopping another green orb into the glass, Eleanor mimicked Nikki's position. "Care to talk? I believe the two Energizer Bunnies have been drained of all their power and are watching SpongeBob in the family room." She shook her head. "It's been a long time since I've entertained small children, and then, I only had one. I can't imagine how your mother raised three." The wrinkles around Eleanor's eyes told of more hardship than raising just one child.

"Where are the rest of the horde?"

"They're in the kitchen, planning who has you tomorrow."

Nikki groaned. Her life was like the contents of the glass—a trapped mixture of mush and hair, especially when she forgot to shave her legs for weeks on end. "Tell me they're planning on leaving me alone."

"They're just worried about you." Eleanor took the glass of peas from Nikki and set it on the coffee table. Large tears pooled in her eyes and squirmed on her lower lids before cascading down her cheeks. "Trust me, if I could have protected my daughter from the dangers of the world, I would have. I learned that lesson too late."

"What happened?" Nikki scooted closer to Eleanor. "That is if you want to talk about it."

"It's okay. I regret not acting before my daughter got hurt. It seems like I've been playing catch-up ever since, especially after—" A hiccup wracked Eleanor's body, and she placed her hand over her mouth and closed her eyes. "Sorry, it happened so long ago but feels like yesterday."

"You don't need to tell me. I shouldn't have pried. I'm sorry."

Eleanor waved off her apology, opened her eyes, and swiped at her tears. "I was the one who brought it up. I can't, you know. It's still too deep." After taking a couple of bracing breaths and blowing her nose in a tissue Nikki offered her, Eleanor focused on Nikki. "They tell me you saw the killer in Custer. That must have been terrifying."

"Not Custer. Custer State Park. And, no, not really. I thought he was an idiotic tourist until he started running after me."

"And being run off the road, I imagine, was terrifying." Eleanor shivered.

"Let me guess. They filled you in on all the gory details so you'd be on their side about the Lancaster Family Protection Order."

Eleanor gave a shaky smile. "Maybe." She leaned over and nudged Nikki's shoulder with hers. "So, tell me. Did you get a glimpse of this man, this killer?"

"Well, from the pictures I took—"

"You got pictures?" Eleanor's eyes widened. "That's so... useful, right? I'm sure the police can use them to identify the guy?"

"Nope. One would think that with the camera I used and the crime scene technology, we could get a good visual. Right now, all they have is a Caucasian male of medium height and build. Oh, and wearing flannel and a red ball cap. That's it."

"That could be anybody." Eleanor frowned and picked at a carpet pile tuft.

Groaning, Nikki lay back and spread her arms. "I'm going to be stuck here forever, aren't I?"

Eleanor laughed. "Well, if my bones and aching joints have anything to say about it, I'm stuck on your parents' floor forever too." As if on cue, Eleanor's right knee popped as she struggled to her feet. "See, told you." She held her hand out to Nikki. "Come on. I'll buy you a drink from your parents' fridge."

"In that case, I'll take two glasses of wine, stat."

Two glasses of wine and an hour later, Nikki sat around the kitchen table with her parents, Eleanor, Corrie, and Aaron and was losing big-time at Shanghai Rummy. She should have taken TT up on his offer of cuddling on the couch. If she had, she would be asleep and drooling on herself like her nephew. She'd gone set three times in a row, and if her score would have been lottery winnings, she would be smiling instead of glaring at her ridiculous excuse for a hand.

Aaron, sitting beside her, leaned over and peeked at her cards. "Need this five of hearts?" He tapped a card in his hand.

"Wouldn't hurt," she muttered. *Wouldn't help either.* But that didn't keep her from snatching it from the discard pile before anyone challenged her ownership of it. Sliding the card between her two of hearts and six of hearts, she caught Bryce's name being whispered across the table between her mother and Eleanor.

"What about Bryce?" Nikki asked.

"Nothing, dear. I was filling Eleanor in on the details she missed about your near-death experience today."

Nikki rolled her eyes before yelling, "Buy it!" when a four of hearts landed on the discard pile. "First, I did not almost die." She rearranged her cards and placed the new one with its other heart family. "Second—"

"Xavier nearly did, then." Cynthia laid down two runs and one set. "Besides, with the suspicions about Bryce—"

Nikki gaped at her mother. "Do you have little messenger pigeons that bring you the latest and greatest tidbits of gossip? Besides, where did you find out about these suspicions?"

Waving her hand in the air as if conjuring a good excuse, Cynthia huffed. "Everyone in town is talking about it. Saying how he came from Custer, where all those other murders happened, then Natasha being murdered after he showed up. Tell me that's not at least fishy. And"—she pointed at Nikki—"Iris said she saw them together."

"She was also on the hunt for a glow-in-the-dark butterfly. Since when have you stopped sprinkling a major dose of salt on what Iris says?" Nikki growled at the card she picked up off the pile and flicked it onto the discard pile without remorse. "Besides, we of all people should know not to make assumptions about someone. Remember how we thought George was the one setting fires and destroying our property."

Corrie, who had been silent throughout most of the game, grasped Aaron's free hand. "George turned out to be a jerk, not a homicidal maniac like Violet's ex-fiancé."

"See, Mom, we were wrong before. Nothing says we're not wrong now." Nikki squealed with joy when she pulled the card that completed her run, and with a hoot, she laid down her run of hearts, run of spades, and three aces. "And to be fair to George, he has been working hard on not being a jerk."

"Sometimes," Corrie muttered.

Nikki had never been prouder of her sister than after hearing she'd punched George, the Lancaster's ex-hired man, after he'd scared the wits out of Violet. That was years ago now, though, and occasionally, George would pop in for a visit. Corrie sometimes referred to him as her pet project. But some old dogs couldn't be taught new tricks, and from the updates via text between Nikki and Corrie over the course of the last eight years, George took to manners like Kentucky took to strangers. Not a good success rate, as Kentucky resorted to pecking first and asking questions later. George wasn't much different.

Aaron played his last card and splayed his empty hands in victory. "I suggested a shock collar once. Corrie didn't say no."

Everyone around the table chuckled except for Eleanor. Nikki was about to explain why George should wear one when tears sprouted in the woman's eyes.

Cynthia must have noticed as well because she grasped Eleanor's hand. "What's wrong?"

Eleanor sniffled and waved away the concern. "Nothing. I'm being foolish, that's all."

"You're among friends." Cynthia motioned around the table. "Please, let us help. Even if it's by offering a shoulder to cry on."

"It's that... I'm afraid."

"Of what? Or should I say who?" Cynthia asked.

"I'm being silly. I shouldn't talk out of turn. But"—she fiddled with the cards in front of her—"Bryce came into the meat market right before closing today, and I couldn't shake the feeling that his was the last face poor Natasha saw before..." A large tear rolled down her cheek. "I'm afraid that one of these days, I'll be alone with him."

"Have you told Steve about this, or Xavier?" Cynthia asked.

"I told Steve. And now I feel like a foolish old woman."

Amid incoming soothing remarks from her family, Nikki replayed the events of the afternoon through her head. If Eleanor was a foolish old woman for mistrusting Bryce, Nikki was a foolish young woman. And Nikki feared that in the end, Bryce would make them all look like fools.

Author Note: My family loves to play Shanghai Rummy. It is the perfect card game for large family gatherings (just put a leaf in the table and add a few decks of cards) or small groups. There are plenty of websites out there with directions on how to play this card game. We also love to play other card games and board games. Here are a few of the Krumm family favorites: whist (card game), The Farming Game, Clue, Tri-Ominos, Dominos, Apples to Apples, and Pictionary. What are your favorite card or board games? If you had one game you wanted my family to try, which one would it be? Fill me in on the best game ever at https://www.jessicabergbooks.com/contact.

Chapter 36

Xavier woke the next morning with grumpy ribs that made it known in no uncertain terms that his actions the day before were foolish at best and dangerous at worst. Bleary-eyed and hunched like an old man, he hobbled from one of the hotel's queen beds to the paisley curtains swishing in the air conditioner's fan. He poked at the royal-blue amoeba shapes swimming in an ocean of burgundy. Most of his professional life centered around hotels, but he was pretty sure that the curtains hanging before him were the ugliest he had seen. Ever.

The bathroom door clicked open, and Thaddeus stepped out, polo shirt crisp, khaki pants without a wrinkle, and a scowl that stopped the "good morning" forming on Xavier's lips. Giving his friend a wide berth, Xavier stepped into the bathroom, locked the door, and sagged against the pink-and-cream-marbled counter. *Coffee.* That was what his brain demanded, but from the state of the in-room coffeemaker, the last person who had used it had attempted to make ramen.

As quickly as his ribs would allow, he prepared himself for the day and hoped that this would be the day a clue would break free from the jumble and point to a murderer. His money was still on Bryce, but he had nothing substantial, nothing to hold him for. And he was pretty sure Bryce would not crack as easily during the interview as some of Xavier's suspects did.

He opened the bathroom door to a still-scowling Thaddeus. Normally, his hotel mornings were unimpeded by others. However, when a June weekend wedding—or any other month, for that matter—hit Sandy, the one hotel in town burst at the seams. He and Thaddeus had been lucky to secure a room at all. So Xavier not only got a roommate, but one who did not wake up cheery and bright-eyed. He caught his reflection in the full-length mirror outside the bathroom and winced. Thaddeus was not the only one not bright-eyed and bushy-tailed.

"'Bout time." Thaddeus sat on the edge of his queen bed and tugged on black tennis shoes.

"Who peed in your Cheerios?" Xavier grinned at Thaddeus's derisive snort. "Let me guess. It's not work related."

Thaddeus grunted and tightened his laces with such force Xavier was surprised they didn't snap in half.

"I bet you one of Mabel's caramel rolls that I can, with one guess, name the perpetrator of your *pleasant* mood."

Thaddeus stashed his wallet in his back pocket, slipped his gun in the holster at his side, pulled his ID out of a dirty pair of pants, and stowed it in his other back pocket.

Accepting the silence as indirect permission to proceed, Xavier gathered his own things, secured his gun in its holster, and followed Thaddeus out the hotel room door. The hallway smelled of stale cigarettes and the vestiges of cheap liquor. His booted foot clinked against a glass bottle. Boone's Farm Strawberry Hill. The wedding party might not be so bright-eyed and bushy-tailed either.

After scooting past another bottle of cheap wine, Xavier hurried to catch up with Thaddeus. Before they neared the opened doorway leading to the white-tiled lobby, Xavier offered his guess. "Sara."

Thaddeus, for his linebacker size, had the agility and reflexes of a cat, and it shouldn't have surprised Xavier when his partner stopped, spun around, and gaped at him in one fluid motion. After staring at Xavier's raised defensive hands, Thaddeus pointed a finger at him.

"How... why... who...? Never mind. I don't want to know. And shut up."

"I wasn't going to say anything." Xavier followed his partner out the lobby doors and into the bright Friday-morning sunshine. He slipped on his sunglasses and gestured between his Jeep and Thaddeus's car. When Thaddeus sat in the Jeep's passenger seat, Xavier shrugged, jumped in, and started the engine. "Want to know how I figured it out?"

Thaddeus grunted. "You want to play Sherlock Holmes? Don't let me stop you."

"Well, after I sent you on watch duty at the cabin, you've been silent about Sara. And the other day, when your phone rang, Sara's name came up on the caller ID." Xavier drummed his fingers against the steering wheel as he waited for a tractor lumbering down Main Street to pass before he could cut across the road and into a parking spot in front of the café. "Am I right?"

"You're not wrong."

That was as good of a concession as Xavier would get, and after putting the Jeep into park, hopped out of the driver's seat. "Great. You owe me a caramel roll. And coffee. Must. Have. Coffee."

They entered to the tune of bells and Mabel's gruff welcome. Xavier took it as a sign of her affection and snagged a table in the corner by the large window facing Main Street. After settling himself with his back to the corner, he searched for the one face he wanted to see: Nikki's. He heard her before he saw her. And when his gaze narrowed in on her flushed face, blond wisps that had escaped from her chignon, her blue eyes round with surprise at whatever the four old men she was serving had told her, his heart gave one jump before settling into a rhythm to break the hundred-meter speed record.

"Good morning, boys." Mabel set two cups of steaming coffee on the table and whipped out a green order pad from the front pocket of her apron. "What'll it be, handsome?"

Tearing his gaze from Nikki, Xavier pretended to look at the menu. "I'll take two eggs—"

Mabel poked Xavier's shoulder with her pen. "Wasn't talking to you."

Thaddeus grinned at Xavier and spread his hands out in a don't-know-why-this-happens-to-me-all-the-time manner. "Well, in that case, surprise me. I'm sure anything from your kitchen is as good as gold."

A pink blush bloomed on Mabel's cheeks. "Go on with you now." After swatting Thaddeus with the order pad, Mabel pinned Xavier with a look caught somewhere between exasperation and perturbation. "Two eggs..."

"Sunny-side up, hash browns, and sausage." He gathered the two menus and clicked them against the table to even out the tops. "And *handsome* over here"—he flicked the menus in Thaddeus's direction—"is buying a caramel roll as well."

After Mabel waddled off, Xavier leaned back in his chair and crossed his arms. "What's with you and women? You don't even try, and they melt to goo before you." When Thaddeus didn't give up his secret, Xavier plunked down the feet of his chair and leaned across the table. "So, what's with you and Sara, and why are you so...?" He waved his hand in the air as if to conjure the right adjective. Not finding one, he grabbed his coffee cup and brought the rim to his lips.

"She's coming here."

If ever there had been a bad time to take a sip of scalding coffee, it was then. He had two options. Either swallow and possibly choke on lava or spit it out and make an ass of himself. He chose the first option, and after liquid heat slithered down his esophagus, he nursed his wounds by chugging a glass of ice water. Fishing three remaining ice cubes from the bottom of his glass, he slipped them into his coffee. He wasn't one to make the same mistake twice. Unless, of course, it involved Nikki.

His gaze sought her out again. This time, it met hers. The room shrank. The sharp clinks of silverware on plates, coffee cups on tables dulled as if someone had shoved cotton balls in his ears. She smiled—at him. Everything sharpened back to pinpoint focus. The world still spun, and there was a slight possibility that maybe, just maybe, she still had feelings for him. A customer in need of a coffee refill interrupted the moment. Swallowing whatever emotion was trying to claw its way up his throat, Xavier turned his attention back to Thaddeus.

"Sara, Nikki's Sara, is coming here. To Sandy."

Thaddeus closed his eyes as if in pain and rubbed circles on his temples with his index fingers.

"Why?"

One derisive snort and swig of coffee later, Thaddeus plunked his half-drank cup on the table. "That's what I would like to know. She won't listen to reason. Doesn't care there's a madman on the loose, claims the United States Constitution gives her the right to bring and use her gun, and the United Nations' Universal Declaration of Human Rights gives her the right to travel unimpeded. Says Nikki needs her, and that is that." With a sigh heavy enough to draw attention from the neighboring tables, Thaddeus tapped a few icons on his phone and slid it across the table. "See for yourself."

Xavier peered at the screen, blinked, and squinted at the dialogue exchange. Curiosity got the better of him, and he swiped farther down the message feed before Thaddeus snatched it from his grasp.

"First of all, Sara has proved she's an absolute delight. Secondly, tell me, *Teddy Bear*, when should we expect Sara's arrival?"

If looks could kill, Xavier wouldn't have had the chance to eat the breakfast coming his way on a tray held aloft by Mabel. But as he was still alive, he dug into his eggs and ignored his friend sawing his steak slathered with the runny yolks of two eggs.

After several moments of silence and eating, Xavier put his fork down. "Look, man, I'm—"

"Forget about it." Thaddeus waved the attempted apology away with a swish of his fork. "I should have told you sooner. But with everything going on and crap hitting the fan, there never seemed a good moment. Besides"—he scratched the back of his neck and winced—"I'm not sure how to put how I feel about Sara into words, you know? I've never met anyone like her, and the last thing I want is for her to come here, but I don't want her anywhere else except here. Doesn't make sense, I know."

Xavier knew all too well the mental torment when the perfect and perfectly irritating woman invaded one's life. "Trust me. I know." He snuck a look around the room. No Nikki. "So, when does she get here, and does Nikki know?"

"Tomorrow afternoon sometime. And no, she wanted to surprise Nikki."

Mabel brought the bill and a to-go container for the uneaten caramel roll. "Be sure to stop in for lunch today, boys. Made extra strudels."

Xavier's stomach, full from breakfast, managed a growl of anticipation. "Wouldn't miss it."

With a grand tsk, she set two bills on the table and walked away.

"How did you get on her bad side?" Thaddeus picked up both to the tune of Xavier's protestations.

Giving up trying to get his bill back, Xavier frowned. "I believe the only way I will ever get back into that woman's good graces is by marrying Nikki."

"Good luck with that." Thaddeus slipped his debit card from his wallet, tapped the corner of the table, and scrunched his face in thought. "Why don't you take her out tonight?"

"I think we're a little busy, don't you?"

"A few hours won't hurt, and besides, you have me to pick up your slack. Pretty used to it by now."

"I'm so glad I have an understanding and helpful friend." Xavier stood, pushed in his chair, and looked again in vain for Nikki. "Well, I want to ask Iris a few follow-up questions before interviewing Bryce. Meet you at the station in about thirty minutes?"

Echoing Xavier's remark to Mabel, Thaddeus slapped him on his shoulder. "Wouldn't miss it."

When Mabel's back was turned, Xavier slipped through the saloon doors leading to Mabel's inner sanctum. Before Xavier searched all of Iris's haunts for the girl in question, he first had to find Nikki. He had a proposition to make.

Author Note: One of my favorite desserts, if you haven't been able to tell, is caramel rolls. The following recipe is in honor of Alice, a dear woman who was the picture of small-town hospitality and a wonderful cook and baker. Thank you, JoAnn, for sharing your mother's recipe.

Caramel Recipe:
**Mix together equal amounts of heavy whipping cream and brown sugar (start with at least ¾ cup each)*

Dough Recipe:
**2 packages dry yeast, dissolved in ½ cup warm water*
**4 cups lukewarm water*
**1 cup lard, melted*
**1 cup sugar*
**1 Tbsp salt*
**About 15 cups flour*
Directions:

*Mix the dough ingredients together and let sit for two hours.
*Work down and let sit another hour.
*Work down, let sit for 1 hour more.
*Shape into rolls.
*Pour caramel into a greased baking pan
*Place rolls on top of caramel.
*Let dough rise
*Bake at 350 degrees for 20-25 minutes
Serving:
*When the rolls have cooled slightly, flip the baking dish over onto a tray.

For lazy bakers like me: buy frozen dough, follow the thawing instructions, shape it into rolls, follow the above recipe's directions, and enjoy!

Chapter 37

From her hiding spot between a refrigerator and shelf housing huge tin cans, Nikki glanced at the rooster clock hanging over the industrial stove range. Eight thirty. Surely the man had eaten his breakfast and was now busy saving the world or, at least, this little chunk of it.

She couldn't face him, not yet. Not while she was still under the influence of their locked gazes. The look on his face when she'd smiled at him—*goodness knows why*—made her light-headed. Closing her eyes, she placed her hand over her racing heart. The look was a heady cocktail of love, desire, need, desperation, and topped off with a garnish of wild abandon.

Her skin tingled as if he had touched her. She slid sideways out from her spot, nearly knocking canned carrots off the shelf. If she could believe the label, six pounds of chopped carrots swam around in there.

"Never understood why anything in industrial-sized cans looks so unappealing."

Nikki jumped, whirled around, and glared at Xavier. "You scared the living daylights out of me."

"The question is why were you wedged back there, anyway?" Leaning against the kitchen's island, he looked relaxed, but from the firmness of his jaw and the clenching and unclenching of his right hand, Nikki knew all was not right in his world.

Risking a closeness she'd avoided for years, she stepped to him until two squares of cracked linoleum separated her tennis-shoed feet from his booted ones. "The question is how is that any of your business?"

He plucked a dust bunny displaced from the back corner of the fridge from her hair and flicked it off his fingers. "Who knows? You might have found a wayward clue or something."

"No, just a family of dust bunnies." After swiping the parts of herself she could reach, she took another step toward him. "If Mabel finds you in here, she'll never feed you again."

His fingers captured a strand of her hair, and he twirled the curl around his index finger. "It's a risk I'm willing to take."

Nearly purring from the combined powers of his husky voice and his finger twirling her hair, she concentrated on his mouth, the shape of his lips, the stubbly proof that he hadn't shaved for a day or two. He would look homeless before too long, but that didn't stop her from wanting to feel his five-o'clock shadow with her palms. "She might think I allowed you in here and fire me. The guilt would eat you alive."

He grinned, and her stomach yo-yoed between her toes and her clavicle. "In that case, I'd better go." He made no move to leave.

Mabel's voice broke the electric silence between them.

He grabbed her hand. "I'll be at your parents' house tonight around seven. Say yes. Please."

"To what?"

Mabel's voice neared the saloon doors.

"Please." His gaze flicked from her eyes to her lips.

"Yes." Breathless, she watched him dart out the back door leading to the alleyway.

"You'll never guess what that old codger—" Mabel stopped inside the saloon doors and planted her hands on her ample hips. She squinted at Nikki. "What's gotten into you?"

Patting the hair Xavier had caressed back into place, Nikki took a fortifying breath. "Nothing. Just busy this morning, isn't it?"

Mabel backed up a few steps, peered over the saloon doors at the half-full dining room, and back at Nikki. "Hmm. I don't pay you to moon around with men in my kitchen."

"Moon? Men?" Slapping a hand over her heart, Nikki pretended shock. "Me?"

"Never mind." Mabel threw a clean dishtowel at Nikki. "There's work to be done."

As Mabel turned away, Nikki glimpsed a smile on the old woman's lips. Nikki followed Mabel out to the dining room, a matching smile on her lips.

Author Note: It is clear that the ice is thawing between Nikki and Xavier. Whether you are Team Nikki or Team Xavier, they both have some work to do to figure out this thing called love. If you could give them one piece of advice on overcoming obstacles and obtaining lifetime love, what would it be? Let me know at https://www.jessicaberg-books.com/contact.

Chapter 38

As Xavier had expected, Bryce showed up at nine a.m. Dressed in jeans and a T-shirt, Bryce looked ready for a day in the field doing whatever crop insurance adjustors did. Xavier had no clue and didn't care to know. All he cared about was breaking loose a clue that would move this case forward.

"Tell me again where you were the night Natasha Florence was murdered."

Bryce flicked a look at his wristwatch. "Look, I've answered your question already."

"Answer it again." Xavier never thought his tiny makeshift office could feel any smaller. Crammed with three grown men, the office seemed more fitting as part of a doll's house than a sheriff's department. Even if he wanted more air to breathe, his lungs, still sore from his escapade at the old house, wouldn't take too kindly to it.

Linking his fingers behind his head, Bryce sighed. "I was with my uncle. We were watching *I Love Lucy* reruns. Way too loud, of course."

Xavier did not return his conspiratorial grin. "Could your uncle vouch for you?"

"Why don't you ask him yourself?"

"We did." Thaddeus leaned forward in his chair, bracing his elbows on his thighs. "He said he doesn't remember you being home. Said he first saw you when he woke around midnight."

Bryce's face flushed, and he pushed his fingers through his hair and pulled. "Of course he doesn't remember. He has early-onset

Alzheimer's. Why do you think I left my post as game warden to be a"—he flung his arms out, which in the small office, nearly ended with his finger poking Thaddeus in the eye—"crop insurance adjustor? Do you think I enjoy the long hours, the endless miles, the farmers? My great-uncle has worked hard his entire life and needed—no, deserved—some help. I couldn't let his life's work mean nothing in the end."

"Did he see you at midnight?" Xavier asked.

"Of course. That's when I woke him up. He must have nodded off somewhere between Lucy doing something stupid and Lucy doing something else stupid."

"Who's to say you didn't leave your great-uncle happily snoozing in his recliner while you—"

Bryce's hand cut through the air and Xavier's statement. "Nope. If this questioning is going where I think it is, I want a lawyer. I tried cooperating with you, but this is where that stops."

Pretending not to hear Bryce, Xavier leafed through several pages of his notepad and tapped his pen on a line of chicken-scratched handwriting. "I have a witness that claims she saw you kissing Natasha." Not quite true, but Xavier wasn't above breaking one moral code to get the truth.

Bryce's mouth gaped open, and he seemed to forget his request for a lawyer. "Me kiss Natasha? I barely knew her."

Xavier shrugged. Thaddeus crossed his arms across his chest.

"This *witness*, as you call her, must be blind or some—" His face bleached of all color.

"Yes? Would you like to change your story?" Xavier readied his pen to jot down notes.

"Yes. No. Look—" Bryce splayed his hands on his thighs. His fingers trembled. "She kissed me." He waved away Xavier's arched eyebrows. "No, really. The Friday night before Father's Day, she asked my uncle if he could come to the butcher shop and look at an air compressor that was acting up. He wasn't feeling the best, so I went instead. She drove us out there, I jerry-rigged it for her until a professional could look at it, and she drove us back to my uncle's. She walked to the house with me, and before I knew what was happening, she kissed my cheek. Said it was a thank you for my time, as I wouldn't take the cash she offered me. Simple."

Xavier wasn't so sure simple was the correct word but jotted down Bryce's statement. "Out of professional courtesy, I'm telling you not to leave town."

"That's part of my job description."

"I want your daily itinerary every morning."

Bryce's grin resembled more of a wolf showing off its canines than a fellow officer of the law smiling. "You'll need to talk to my lawyer about that."

"And who would that be?"

"You'll find out when he—or she—contacts you. Until then, I have nothing else to say to you." Bryce, not giving Xavier a chance to sneak in another question, marched from the office.

Too angry to sit, Xavier walked the few steps to the chalkboard and stared at it. The chalked words meant nothing as they faded in and out of clarity. He focused on the crime scene photos taken of Michelle's body in Custer State Park and Natasha's body found behind her butcher shop. Something was similar about how the bodies were shaped after death. If he could ignore the blood and trauma done to the bodies, it looked as if someone had tucked them into bed and had forgotten to cover them with a blanket.

Author Note: My favorite I Love Lucy *episode is tied between two. In the first one, Lucy and Ethel get jobs at the chocolate factory and have to package the chocolates. If you haven't seen that episode, all you need to know is chocolate-1, Lucy and Ethel-0. In the second one,*

Lucy and Ethel's capers get them locked inside a freezer with an ill-got-ten meat stash. Despite the years between the original airing and my lifetime, the fact that this show still makes viewers laugh gives credence to its title as a classic. If you've watched I Love Lucy, *which episode is your favorite? Or if you're a fan of another classic television show, which one is it and why? Reach out with your answer at https://www.jessicabergbooks.com/contact.*

Chapter 39

Nikki perched in a wicker rocking chair on her parents' front porch, her eyes and ears alert for the first sight and sound of Xavier's Jeep.

Her phone pinged. Too intent on watching, she ignored it and scowled when it pinged again five minutes later.

Two messages from Sara:

Hey, my mom's here and says she has a feeling. Are you all right?

My mother says that if you do not answer my text right now, she will get in her car and start driving. Her "feeling" is strong.

Nikki wasn't sure if she could ever tell her own mother to get a grip, much less Mama Kelly. After checking the driveway for signs of life and finding none, she tapped out a text. *Everything is fine. Xavier's taking me somewhere. Maybe that's why your mom is getting her feeling.*

Ping. *SQUEEEEE!!!! So, you've finally come to your senses. Good. Because if Thaddeus hadn't bumbled into my life, I'd have ripped that blond-haired sexy man from your idiotic clutches, shrunk him down, and stuck him in my pocket for whenever I wanted to play.*

Wow. Remind me to tell you what a great friend you are when I see you next, which could be never if my family has their way. A distant rumble and a cloud of dust alerted Nikki to an approaching vehicle. Xavier's Jeep. With more force than necessary, she texted: *S.O.S. He's here.*

Ping. *Kiss him and get it over with. You know you want to.*

Such texts were not helpful, so Nikki stowed her phone in the back pocket of her dark skinny jeans. As his Jeep turned into the quarter-mile-long driveway, Nikki noticed a trailer towed behind it with two ATVs. Smoothing her white off-the-shoulder empire-style shirt embroidered with wildflowers, she sensed she had overdressed for the surprise occasion.

The closer the Jeep got to the porch, the drier her mouth became. If things kept progressing, she would have a hard time moving her tongue to say even the most rudimentary of greetings.

Gravel crunched under the Jeep's tires as it came to a stop. The four-wheelers tied down on the trailer rocked back and forth a few times with residual momentum. Out hopped Xavier. Instead of his normal crisp polo and khakis, he wore ripped jeans splotched with old grease stains and an old Sandy High School Mustang shirt, which strained against muscles that hadn't been present when he'd worn it as a senior. Nikki couldn't see the emblem on his backward snapback hat. Dark sunglasses hid his eyes, eyes that had looked as if they'd wanted to devour her hours ago.

Well—was about all Nikki could think and decided that thinking normally got her into trouble, anyway, *So why continue that habit?*

He took the porch steps two at a time, slipped his sunglasses on top of his hat, and grabbed her hands in his. "You look beautiful," he whispered.

The intensity of his gaze made her feel translucent, as if he could see every inch of her, inside and out.

He blinked, shook his head, and gestured to the four-wheelers. "We can do something else. I can take you—"

"No." It had been forever since she'd ridden an ATV. After she had broken her arm in a freak accident, her father had banned her from the four-wheeler and, if Corrie hadn't needed it around the farm, would have sold it. No matter how she'd begged and pleaded, post-poetry Xavier had refused to go behind her parents' back.

After the hell her family had been through, they had come out stronger and alive, but they had also seen the face of death and destruction, had experienced the life-changing consequences a moment, a breath in time, could cause. Xavier had seen it, too, had been there when a violent arsonist had prowled outside the Lancasters' door. She closed her eyes and remembered how he had held her hand and requested to stay the moment Violet had revealed the monster bent on destroying Violet and her newfound family.

No wonder they had all overcorrected the wheel. Instead of keeping Nikki under wraps to protect Jake and the family from his breakdowns, they had bought into the irrational fear stalking them all and wrapped a trouble-seeking Nikki in metaphorical bubble wrap. But now, standing on her parents' porch as a twenty-five-year-old woman, she could see what an eighteen-year-old Nikki couldn't. They hadn't meant to stifle her or suffocate her with rules and regulations and safety. In not being able to conquer Jake's invisible and imaginary enemy, they hadn't been able to deal with their own.

A familiar hand clasped hers and drew it to a T-shirt-clad chest as it had all those years ago. With her eyes still closed, Nikki concentrated on Xavier's heart pumping beneath her palm. This heart had never stopped loving her, even when it had every right not to. She opened her eyes and met Xavier's gaze.

"Tell me, Mr. Palinski, are you defying a direct order from my parents, from *Corrie*, to never take me four-wheeling? That's very..." She pursed her lips and relished how his body shivered under her palm and how his blue eyes darkened with dilating pupils. "Irresponsible of you."

"I would... ah..." Xavier cleared his throat from the obvious frog lodged inside it and tried speaking again. "I would like to think Nikki Lancaster capable of making her own decisions." He plucked her hand from his chest and pulled her to him until her ear, instead of her hand, rested over his heart. "All I ask is that I'm there for them, no matter where they take us."

Us. He had used that word, probably knowing full well she had the power to fling it back in his face. Burrowing her ear deeper into his chest, she put to memory the sound of his heart pounding, his blood swooshing like ocean waves. She couldn't speak, not yet. Too many words had left her lips in the past that had done irretrievable damage. To her, to Xavier. Time would tell. But for now, her body melted to his.

After giving herself a few more seconds curled into him, she pulled back and smiled up at him. "Well, let's take *us* for a four-wheeler ride."

She darted into the house, sprinted up the stairs, and plowed through her old dresser, which still contained farm clothes. Within minutes, clad in ripped jeans and tennis shoes so worn her socked big toe stuck out, she rejoined Xavier on the porch, a duffle bag of extra clothes slung over her shoulder.

"Nice shirt."

She gazed down at the yellow shirt, a replica of Xavier's. "Old school is cool school, you know."

"Come on." He grabbed her hand and ran with her to the Jeep.

She hopped in and peeked in the back seat. "You thought of everything, didn't you?" A picnic basket, an Igloo cooler, and two helmets.

After clicking his seat belt, he scowled. "It is possible to have fun and be—"

She laid a finger over his lips and giggled when he looked cross-eyed at her fingertip. "*Safe.* I know." She replaced her finger with her lips, and heat coursed through her at his surprised moan. Pulling away, she ran her thumb along his bottom lip. "Thank you."

His gaze never left her mouth. "For what?"

"For trusting me to have both." Settled back in her seat, she gripped his free hand. "Let's get into trouble."

*Author Note: *Sighs and places hand over heart**

Have Nikki and Xavier just compromised? Looks like they have. Hopefully, this will engender something more, but for that, you will need to wait until the next few chapters. For now, let's discuss Nikki's clothing ensemble of old farm clothes. I do not exaggerate in this scene. I believe I've worn the exact same thing when I know I'm in for a particularly dirty job on the farm. I'm pretty positive that my students, who see me in professional dress 180 days of the year, would have a hard time recognizing me, Mrs. Berg, in my farm clothes. But, hey, whenever I can let loose and wear ratty jeans, T-shirts with holes, and tennis shoes with little to no material left, I am in my element. Basically, the dirtier the job, the holier the clothes! Let me know if your coworkers would have a hard time recognizing you outside of work because of your "get dirty" clothes at https://www.jessicabergbooks.com/contact.

Chapter 40

Whether or not Xavier and Nikki found trouble might be debatable, but they found mud—lots of it. It was a good thing Old Man Maverick, known more for his pet fainting goats than caring for his pastures, didn't care that local teenagers or adults with the mentality of teenagers sometimes used his most useless pasture as a mudding extravaganza. As long as trespassers left gifts of food for himself or his goats outside the gate to his property, Maverick left the troublemakers to their own devices.

After an hour of slipping and sliding through mud, Xavier and Nikki parked their four-wheelers next to a copse of cottonwood trees where an old homestead must have stood if the rock foundation meant anything.

If he and Nikki looked anything like their ATVs, they would need to use the water from the collapsible five-gallon container he'd brought along before climbing back into his vehicle. Love had its limits.

After dismounting from her four-wheeler, Nikki strutted toward him, every inch of her body covered in mud. *Maybe love doesn't have limits.* She flashed a grin, and her teeth looked whiter against the mud splattered like freckles around her mouth.

Fighting the urge to kiss her, he set the container on a foundation rock and handed her a roll of shop towels he'd stolen from his dad's house at that same time he'd absconded with the four-wheelers and trailer. "While you get cleaned up, I'll set up the picnic."

"Such gallantry. How will I endure it?"

He playfully lunged for her, but she eluded his grasp.

"Don't get used to it."

Sticking out her tongue at him, she sauntered to the Jeep, grabbed her duffle bag, and pointed her finger to the other side of the car. "Scram."

"As you wish." He winked and settled on the other side of the Jeep, careful to keep his eyes where they belonged. The food. The only sign he had that she was changing came in verbal spurts of "How did I get mud there?" and "Good grief, that's a first."

With more energy than necessary, Xavier snatched the food Mabel had prepared for him. As soon as she'd heard his plans to take Nikki on a picnic, she'd pulled out all the stops—fancy Black Forest ham sandwiches complete with colorful-frill-topped toothpicks, deviled eggs, macaroni salad, and two large slices of apple pie. The drinks he'd provided himself, and he popped the cork on a bottle of white wine secured from the on-sale, off-sale bar on Main Street.

"Your turn." Nikki, clean and wearing a fresh pair of fray-kneed jeans and a tank top speckled with daisies, threw a towel at him. She'd even washed her hair. Xavier hoped she'd left enough water for him.

"Don't worry. I've left enough water for you. Barely." Grinning, she snagged a deviled egg and popped it in her mouth. "Better hurry. Can't guarantee you'll have anything to eat if you dawdle."

Taking her warning to heart, he washed in the water she'd left him—which wasn't much—changed, and interrupted her swig from a plastic wine glass. "Hopefully you left more wine than water."

Rolling her eyes, she scooted over on the red-checkered blanket he'd brought. "Too bad you can't wash up in wine."

His skin grew hot and felt too tight for comfort. He shouldn't be imagining her body dripping in wine, so he nabbed a sandwich and stuffed half of it in his mouth.

"Hungry?"

You have no idea. Swallowing, he wiped his mouth with a napkin Mabel had thrown in along with tiny paper salt and pepper packages and a handful of wet wipes. *She thought of everything.* Except to tell him what to do when he got Nikki all to himself. She probably would have had a few ideas. None of them good or proper, but he could have at least scraped the acceptable bits off and put them together to form a somewhat-good plan.

Nikki touched his arm, and his thoughts screeched to a halt. "Thank you." When he couldn't move words past his tightened throat to ask for what, she scooted closer until their thighs and shoulders touched. "Today was... different... good." She spidered her fingers down his arm and played them over his as if she were playing piano. "It gave me hope that maybe..."

Xavier wasn't sure if his heart had ever beat harder or faster. Surely, this was a sign of heart arrhythmia or something equally deadly. She met his gaze and smiled. Nope. It was a severe case of loving Nikki.

Rubbing at the thumping in his chest, he leaned down and rested his forehead against hers. "Maybe what?" he whispered, terrified anything louder would break the spell she had cast.

Instead of answering his question, she hopped to her feet and faced the setting sun painting the cotton candy clouds in rainbow-sherbet colors. With closed eyes, she spread her arms and tilted her face to the sky. The breeze fluttered at her blond tendrils and seemed to erase the wrinkles worry had etched across her brow. He stood next to her but didn't touch her.

"Am I broken?"

Her whispered question speared him, and he studied her serene face. She had never looked so unbroken. Unsure of the answer, or even if there was one, he slipped his hand in hers. Her long dark eyelashes fluttered against her cheeks.

"Why do you think you are?"

Chattering leaves, whispering grass, and chirping birds filled the silent void between them.

"Because I feel more alive out here than I do anywhere else. I feel connected to God in nature but not in a building. I hear him in the simplicity of a bee sucking nectar from a flower or when adrenaline pumps a hundred miles per hour through my body." Her hand trembled. "That's not normal."

He played his thumb over her skin. "If that's the case, then I wish I weren't normal."

Her eyes snapped open, and she locked gazes with him. "What do you mean?"

"Out of everyone I know, you are the only one who has ever *experienced* God. I only wish I were brave enough to live life like you do, unimpeded by worry or what-ifs. And that you live your faith outside the four walls of a church speaks more than the most pious person who isn't brave enough to live the one life he's been given, sitting in any pew anywhere in the world. People like me. If anyone's broken, it's me. You"—he cupped her cheek—"are not broken. You need to give yourself permission to be the Nikki God made you to be."

Her body shuddered with an exhale, and she rested her forehead over his heart. It took him a moment to register her sobs. Enfolding her in his arms, he held her and envisioned every tear was a mangled lie she'd told herself or, worse yet, the lies her family and he had allowed her to believe.

"I am so sorry I ever allowed you to believe otherwise. I'm sorry for all those moments where I expected you to be my version of Nikki." His throat burned. "And most of all, I'm sorry I betrayed you, that I went behind your back and canceled all your plans for our honeymoon. I have no excuse, and as I made my decision in fear"—he traced his finger along her tattoo—"I can't hide behind my reasoning either. I was a complete idiot, and I'm sorry. Can you ever forgive me?"

She straightened and locked gazes with him. A whip-poor-will sang his call. Another answered. Acid burned his stomach and sizzled up his throat. He dropped his hands to his thighs and rubbed his clammy palms on his jeans.

Her glistening eyes darkened, and her lips parted in a tremulous smile. "Yes."

With a whoop, he caught her around the waist and spun her in a circle. Whatever had cemented itself around his lungs and weighed him down for three years shattered, leaving him weightless. Dizzy, he settled them both to the ground and nestled her head under his chin.

"Thank you. I've thought myself broken for so long. How could God love someone who constantly hurt her father? I lost more than my father in that accident. I lost my partner in crime, my adventurous sidekick. We even had a secret code when we didn't want Mom to know what we were up to. But even after I knew how he would react, I still desired to do things that would make him go crazy. What does that say about me?"

"It doesn't say anything about you. It says everything about the traumatic brain injury your father will suffer for his entire life. Your father can't live without fear, but you can. You must live your life, not your father's." He twirled one of her curls around his finger. "Besides, he's made massive strides, and your mother seems to have some tricks up her sleeve to calm him."

She traced a heart over his pectoral muscle. "Do you think we could... you know... pick up where we left off?"

"I have a better idea." He pulled her into his lap and enjoyed her squeal of delight. "Instead of starting from our past, why don't we start from our beginning? Now. You and me on the same page. Finally."

Doubt flooded her eyes. "What if I want to go skydiving?"

He held her at arm's length and cocked his head. "Do you?"

"Yes."

"Well"—he swallowed his fear of flying and, in this case, falling—"if you don't get a two-for-one deal, I'll be waiting for you on the ground, with at least two ambulances."

"Nothing will happen."

"I'm not talking about you. I'm referring to the medical attention I'll need from a probable anxiety attack."

Her fingers crept around his neck and undid the low knot he'd put his hair in. He swallowed a groan. No need to let her in on the power she held over him. By the gleam in her eye, she knew well what she was doing.

Threading her fingers through his loose hair, she whispered. "Bungee jumping?"

"What's next, BASE jumping?"

"Nah, that's for people with a definite death wish." She nipped his bottom lip. "I don't have one of those. I just like to feel my blood pumping, you know?"

He couldn't stop the grin spreading across his face. He knew several ways to get her blood pumping, but he promised himself to control whatever wanted to unleash itself from his core. "Can't we meet in the middle?"

"Swimming with sharks?"

"Dolphins?"

Her face screwed up in thought, and he kissed her furrowed brow.

"Deal," she said.

"Don't you think we should seal that deal?"

She held out her pinky. "Like this?"

"No. Like this."

He lowered his lips to hers and took a few tentative dips before diving in. Blood roared in his ears, deafening him to the chattering leaves on the cottonwood trees. Pleasure bordered on pain, and when Nikki bit his lower lip, he couldn't stop a primal, guttural sound from escaping his chest. When a breathless Nikki pulled away, he nearly wept.

"Good idea," he said. "Someone has to be the smart one."

"No." She wriggled off his lap and pointed to his hip. "You're vibrating."

Crap. Raising his hip, he wrangled his phone from his back pocket. The screen lit up with a text message. He cursed.

Nikki dropped to her knees next to him and grasped his free hand. "Another one?"

"No, thank God." He cradled her to him and wrapped his hand around her wrist, resting his index and middle finger on her radius pulse. "Test results are back. No DNA evidence. Nothing. It's as if the killer's a ghost."

"But that's not possible."

"No." He scrubbed at his forehead. "But we're missing something."

"I wish I could help."

"You have. Your testimony. The pic—"

"And yet the killer is out there." She shivered.

He knew she'd thought of Natasha and pressed a kiss to her temple.

"He's here. I went back to the pictures the other day, fiddled with the digital files. Something doesn't add up."

"Should I be concerned that you're sticking your—"

"Nose in police business? Of course I am. But only in your presence. Not behind your back." She flicked at an imaginary speck on her clean tank top.

That was good enough for him. For now. "What do you think we're missing?"

"I don't know. Something doesn't feel right." Her shoulders squirmed. "I keep seeing him walk toward me, that ridiculous flannel. Who wears flannel in June?"

"Someone who kills five women."

"Someone crazy?"

"Quite the opposite. I think we're dealing with a cold, calculating killer who won't easily slip up the next—"

"No, say it. You think he'll kill again." Nikki placed her hand on her neck.

"Odds are yes."

"And you've always been a betting man."

There was nothing left to say besides the normal scolds to be safe, so he used his mouth in a more productive way and kissed her until he wasn't sure he remembered how to spell *safe*.

Author Note: I'm afraid I'm more like Xavier than Nikki when it comes to having adventures. I really don't want them. Give me a book, a comfy chair, and a delicious beverage, and then you can feel free to go on all the adventures you want. I will listen attentively to all of them when you get back. I promise. However, you might be like Nikki and crave adventure. If you are a Nikki, what's your ultimate adventure so far, and what is your dream adventure? Let me know at https://www.jessicabergbooks.com/contact.

Chapter 41

Xavier sipped at his to-go container of coffee and stared at his chalkboard. He and Thaddeus had added more information, and still, all they had was five dead women, unconnected except for a scrap of red-and-green flannel left as some macabre token of death and their blond hair. No matter how he spun it or rearranged it, nothing made sense.

Grinding his teeth, he walked the half a step it took to get from the chalkboard to the window. He flicked open the makeshift curtains created with an assortment of beach towels stolen from his dad's house to keep all the lookie-loos away from his business. No wonder Steve didn't use this office. Careful not to dislodge the pushpins securing them to the drywall above the window frame, he peeked through the crack between woven seashells and what could have been half-naked mermaids.

Outside, life went on. A bride and groom were marrying today. He checked his watch. At two, if he could believe town gossip. Signs of the impending nuptials were everywhere. A few bridesmaids, their hair already done in impossible updos, stood outside the beauty salon, laughing. The bride must be getting her finishing touches. A limo drove past and turned toward the church.

He leaned against the window casement and blew on his coffee. In a few days, when the ME cleared Natasha Florence's body for burial, another type of vehicle would take the same turn toward the same church for a different purpose. Turning back to his board, he frowned, sipped his coffee, and pulled at the sides of his mouth. This case was going nowhere, and from the email he'd received from his supervisor, Cal Magee, the powers that be weren't too thrilled. But with Bryce Beaumont, the one guy he suspected most of all, and his pain-in-the-butt lawyer, the case had slowed from turtle speed to snail.

His phone rang. It was Deputy Morrison.

"What'd you find out?" Xavier stood, primed with chalk, ready to jot down Morrison's intel.

"I don't think you're going to like this."

"Have I ever liked anything you've said?"

"I got off the phone with Bryce's boss. The bodies of all the women found in Custer State Park were on his particular route. He would have known that terrain like the back of his hand."

The piece of chalk snapped in Xavier's fingers. "And would have known where the quiet spots were, the spots that tourists didn't even know existed." Xavier picked up a new piece of chalk and jotted the information under Bryce's name. "He must have crapped his pants when he saw Nikki. He hadn't expected to be interrupted." Her proximity to death that day had his blood pooling in his feet, and saying her name in relation to the killer had his teeth grinding.

"Oh, and the fibers of the flannel found near Natasha's body match the flannel fibers found near the other women."

It was official. No more speculating. They had a serial killer on their hands.

"No other DNA, though? The crime scene techs couldn't find anything?" Assuming a negative answer, Xavier set down the chalk.

"Nothing."

"Were you able to talk to Bryce's colleagues?"

"Some were pretty tight-lipped. You know how that goes. No one wants to rat out a fellow law enforcement officer, but those who talked spoke highly of him. Said he was a stand-up guy. Would be the first to take up an extra shift for someone if needed."

"Very altruistic of him. Probably gave him more ground to play with." Xavier dug his fist into his cheek to keep his teeth from grinding to a pulp. "How was he with women?"

"According to his friends and coworkers, Bryce was charming and seemed to enjoy the role of knight in shining armor. He'd often change a flat tire for stranded tourists before AAA could get to the scene."

"Girlfriend?"

"Not a current one that anyone knew of. Though when he first accepted the job and moved to Custer, he brought his girlfriend with him, a Beatrice Hansen, who not only left him, but left the area. According to the gossip mill, one day she up and left. No word."

The hairs on the back of Xavier's neck stood at attention. "Don't tell me. No one has heard from her since."

"No wonder you get paid the big bucks." Morrison paused and, from the slurping sound over the phone, was sipping something through a straw. "Care to guess Beatrice's hair color?"

"Blond?"

"Wrong."

Xavier's gut slid to the floor, and he scoured his forehead. "What?"

"Miss Beatrice Hansen was a brunette."

After a few more shared tidbits, Xavier sat in his office chair and swiveled back and forth. "Thanks, Morrison. I'll be in touch." After hanging up, Xavier plunked his forehead on the edge of the desk and watched his feet propel his chair back and forth. Maybe if he were in a trance, he could figure this out. Nothing lined up. Nothing added up. Just blondes and flannel. That was it.

It was a waste of time to call Bryce in. According to Sheila Price, Bryce's lawyer, he had cooperated fully with the investigating officers and would continue to do so only with Ms. Price present. She sure was taking her dandy old time getting to Sandy. And according to town gossip, Bryce was doing his crop-adjusting thing in a small town fifty miles away by the ghost town Greenway.

He opened his laptop to begin a search on Beatrice Hansen. If she was alive, she could be the key to breaking this case wide open. If she was dead—Xavier inhaled through his nose and blocked that thought from his head. He tipped his to-go container for more caffeine. A lukewarm drop touched his tongue.

"Laurel?"

Silence.

"Deputy Stewart?" Still not receiving an answer, he walked out of his office, empty cup in hand. He peeked over the edge of the counter, now resplendent with fake potted succulents. Apparently, she had given up on trying to keep real green things growing and had transitioned to fake ones.

Not finding her at her desk or under it—not that he had looked there—he poked his head into Steve's office. She wasn't there, and neither was Steve. She'd announced hours ago that she had a call to go to and had wanted to make sure he wouldn't be scared by himself.

He checked his watch. *Call must be serious.*

Somewhere in one of the back rooms used as a makeshift break room, an old refrigerator hummed to keep a couple of cans of Mountain Dew and Diet Coke cold. After nabbing a Mountain Dew and a cheese stick nearing its expiration date, Xavier entered his office and stuttered to a stop.

"Eleanor, what are you doing here?"

She didn't answer or turn from the board. One hand dug into her hip, the other cupped her chin. He couldn't quite see what she was zeroed in on, but by her stance, he assumed she was staring at the grisly face of death, either Michelle Osbourne or Natasha Florence.

He set his pop and questionable snack on his desk. "You shouldn't be in here."

As if hearing him for the first time, Eleanor jumped and spun around. "Sorry. I... uh, was driving through town and wanted to talk to the sheriff, and well, your door was open, and when I saw all this, I couldn't help myself." Despite being told five seconds before to leave, she stepped closer to the pictures, the chalked bullet points, the chalk lines intersecting and triangulating facts and evidence.

"Eleanor, please. You need to leave. You can't—"

"They remind me so much of my daughter, especially Natasha. Such a pity. All so young."

When Eleanor's fingers raised toward the pictures of death, Xavier grabbed her forearm and pulled her from the small office. After closing the door, he marched her to the uncomfortable plastic chairs inside the main doors. He plonked down next to her, rested his elbows on his knees, and scrubbed at the back of his neck.

"I'm sorry." Eleanor sniffled and wiped her runny nose on her short-sleeve T-shirt.

Not good with blubbering women, Xavier distracted himself by finding a box of tissues and, upon a successful hunt, proffered her the entire box. "Seeing death, even through pictures like that, can get to the hardest cops."

"This could have all been avoided. If only..."

"If only what?"

She waved away Xavier's question with an unused tissue. "Never mind. Just a middle-aged weepy woman who sees her daughter every time she thinks of those poor girls."

"Tell me about your daughter."

"She's beautiful. So full of life, you know? It's been a while since I've seen her; she... uh... moved and hasn't been home since." She pressed the tissue to her nose. "I guess that's why I'm so upset. Natasha reminded me so much of her that I got them confused sometimes." A hiccuped laugh escaped her throat. "Sometimes I'd call Natasha by my daughter's name. Natasha never minded, though. What a sweet girl."

"Do you have any other children?"

"No. Just my sweet baby girl."

"And your husband?"

"He died several years ago. It's a burden I must bear alone, I'm afraid."

"But I don't understand how this could have all been avoided. Do you know something?"

Pressing her hand on top of his to stop him from writing in his notepad, she shook her head. "I meant bigger picture. That somewhere down the road, someone could have seen the devil inside the man, you know?"

He slid his hand out from under hers. "Ah, yes. If we could only identify the scum of society before they struck. That puts a kibosh on the whole innocent before proven guilty thing, doesn't it?"

"Some people are guilty!" Spittle flew from her mouth.

Xavier leaned away from her vehemence. "Look, you've had quite the shock. If you want to talk about it, Pastor Luke Tuttle has one of the best ears in the business."

"No." She stood and wiped her palms on her jeans. "I'm sorry about that outburst. I'll be fine. Just emotional is all."

"Well, if you're sure." He walked her to the main door and opened it. "Please take my advice to talk to Pastor Tuttle. He's always been there for me when I need guidance."

"I'll keep that in mind." Her lips hinted at a smile. "And sorry again for the blubbering and... uh... looking at what I shouldn't have been looking at."

"I trust you will keep what you saw confidential." He crossed his arms over his chest and maintained eye contact for longer than normal.

She blushed and looked away. "Of course. Trust me. Some would say I'm the vault of secrets."

"Good." After she left, he went back to his office and studied his crime chalkboard.

No wonder Eleanor had a breakdown. Seeing pictures of the dead was never easy. He stepped closer until his nose nearly touched the first picture—the man Nikki had captured on film—tacked to the wooden frame next to the photos of the victims. The bulky flannel and nondescript red hat hid the man's identity so perfectly that Xavier wouldn't be surprised if there wasn't a man in there at all. Maybe ghosts existed. That crazy idea would at least explain the lack of forensic evidence. Going with crazy, he sent Morrison a quick text to do a more thorough background check on Eleanor. Definite crazy vibes coming off her, but then again, she was a grieving widow with an absentee daughter. Maybe slightly crazy was the woman's norm.

Time to find Beatrice Hansen, and as Xavier sat down and began slogging through files, he prayed he would find her alive and sipping a Mai Tai on a beach somewhere in Bora Bora and not buried in a shallow ditch in Custer State Park. After longer than normal, he found her.

Bora Bora had not been Beatrice's destination, final or otherwise. Housekeeping staff had found her body six months ago in a cheap motel room in Billings, Montana. All they had to work off was a fake South Dakota ID with the name Beatrice Hansen. There was no other information about her. It was as if the ME had ruled it an overdose.

Suicide? Murder?

"Mr. Palinski?"

Xavier jumped, knocking his knees on the bottom of the desk, and bit back a curse upon seeing his visitor. "Iris?" He grinned despite the throbbing pain in his knee. "What brings you here?"

"I'm afraid."

"Come on." He led her from the room, hoping she hadn't taken in the photos stuck to the chalkboard. "Here, have a seat. What's on your mind?"

"Keeping secrets is bad, right?"

He followed her furtive look outside the windows. There was nothing. "It depends if keeping the secret will hurt someone."

She giggled at his quirked eyebrow. "My Aunt Corrie does that. Daddy says it terrifies him when she does." Her face contorted to mimic his facial expression. Everything but her eyebrows twitched. "Did I get it?"

"Not quite, but practice makes perfect, huh? So"—he slapped his hands on his knees and bent forward—"do you have the right kind of secret where it will help someone and is okay to tell an adult?"

Iris studied her hands clasped in her lap. Her teeth worried her bottom lip. "I think so," she whispered.

He leaned back. "I'm all ears."

"Aunt Nikki—" Tears swam in her eyes. She swiped at them with the back of her hand and, holding her hands over her mouth, mumbled, "knows who the killer is."

His mouth went dry. Instead of firing a barrage of questions that would send the girl flying out the doors, he forced himself to relax. "Really? You might earn a deputy badge yet."

Her cheeks pinked.

"How did you sleuth out this little tidbit?"

"I... uh... I was—" The blush in her cheeks worked its way up to her ears until the tips turned purple.

"Collecting evidence? Like any good detective should do, by the way."

"Yes... I was doing what you said, and I overheard her talking to Eleanor."

"You were right to use all your senses. What did she say?"

Again, her teeth took her bottom lip prisoner. "She said... Aunt Nikki said that she took the guy's picture."

Xavier's lungs imploded in his last inhale and cemented against his ribs. He still remembered the hardest hit he had received in football. The impact of the opponent and the brutal landing on the ground had driven out all his air, his ability to breathe, and what had felt like part of his lungs.

Iris laid her hand over his. "You okay?"

Breathe! He concentrated on Iris's little hand, the dirt wedged in the tiny ridges of her skin, the cuticles stained green with what must have been a recent bout of weeding. If he concentrated on that, his mind couldn't concentrate on Iris's little factoid. Then he could breathe. Stretching his chest until his muscles spasmed in pain, he forced the air out of his lungs and, ignoring the burning sensation in his chest, pasted a smile on his face. "I'm fine," he croaked.

She tried to raise one eyebrow and looked up at her eyebrows as she gave it another go. "Close?"

"Better."

"Will Aunt Nikki be mad that I told her secret?"

"No, she won't." He rifled through his pockets and came up with two quarters. "Here." When she reached for it, he held it out of reach. "You told me a secret it was okay to tell because keeping it would have hurt Aunt Nikki, right? Well, I have a type of secret that it is not okay to tell because telling it will hurt Aunt Nikki. Can you promise me you won't tell anybody else what your aunt said?"

"No one? Not even—"

"Not a single person. Please, Iris, it's important."

"I promise."

After handing her the coins, he walked her to the main door. "Thank you. You were very brave in coming here and telling me, and I think that's pretty darn cool."

She beamed a smile, and as if remembering the crux of the meeting, she clenched her lips shut, zipped her fingers across them, and threw away an imaginary key. Half tripping, half running down the sidewalk, Iris sped away and made a beeline for the café.

Xavier wished he could have the childlike innocence that Iris embodied. Instead, he slunk back to his desk and leaned over it, bracing his hands on the surface. Drawing a deep breath and forcing it out again did nothing to ease the tightness building in his chest.

For the price of two Airheads, he had tried to buy a nine-year-old's silence, but even if he could trust her to keep the secret safe, someone else already knew it. If one person knew Nikki had taken a photograph of the killer, it wouldn't take long for everyone in Sandy to know it. Including the killer.

It was time for something drastic. Time to move in with the Lancasters.

*A*uthor Note: *Unlike Iris, my children are horrible secret keepers. Not a single one of them can keep presents or surprises quiet. Not even the four-year-old. She's cute, but Do. Not. Trust. Her. No matter how she tries to wiggle her way into your affections, she will turn on you when you least expect it. I'm sure this is a kid thing, and that I, too, at one point sucked at keeping secrets. What is a secret that your children, nieces, or nephews let out of the bag? Do spill the beans at https://www.jessicabergbooks.com/contact.*

Chapter 42

Saturday mornings normally meant lying in bed until the last possible moment before she wet her pajama bottoms or the Midwestern guilt stemming from not using every moment of sunlight to work drove her from her blanket cocoon. This morning, it had been her mother who disturbed her dreams, and as Xavier was in them, repeating the kisses they'd shared the night before, Nikki swung her hoe with a little more force than necessary at a patch of weeds.

Her mother's garden—no, more like a two-acre vegetable field—took hours to weed. The sun at eight in the morning had felt warming in the cool of dawn. The sun at two p.m. beat down on her with searing intensity, reminding her to reapply SPF-fifty sunscreen. Nikki stretched and kneaded her fists into the small of her back. Maybe if she hadn't taken so many breaks, leaning on her hoe, and replaying Xavier's healing words, sincere apology, and kisses the night before, she could have finished before lunch. But, alas, she had misused her time and now beads of sweat dripped down her back. Her fault. And Xavier's. Her core tingled at the flame he'd ignited. Problem was, she didn't know what to do with it. Should she stomp it out for the safety of all concerned, or should she blow on it, giving it the life it needed? She chopped the last remaining weed in half. Time for a nap and a snack.

TT, with his habitual string attached to nothing, zoomed by her, Bacon and Kentucky in tow.

"TT, hold up. What you got there?" Nikki leaned down to rub Bacon's graying muzzle. The old dog kept hanging in there, seeking shade whenever TT didn't require a partner in crime in the summer and demanding to be let in the heated garage in the winter.

With the pride only a four-year-old could possess over a dirty plastic cup, TT tipped it so she could peek inside. "Cheerios," he lisped.

"Does Mommy know you have these?"

He laid a dusty finger to the middle of his lips and whispered around it. "Nana gave them to me."

Nikki had long since worn off her eleven o'clock lunch. Her stomach rumbled. "Your Nana is a wise woman." She pecked his cheek, which he rubbed off before skipping off to his swing set.

Five minutes later, Nikki sat at her mother's kitchen table, a bowl of Cheerios before her. She ate a spoonful and scowled into the dish.

She poked at the yellow cardboard box—which probably had more flavor than the oat circles floating around in her milk—until the front of the box faced her. "Since when did you stop buying the Honey Nut ones?"

"Since no one living here eats them." Cynthia poured herself a glass of iced tea, sat across the table, fished out one Cheerio, and popped it in her mouth.

"I eat them."

"You don't live here."

Nikki spread her arms out and gestured to the four corners of the kitchen and to herself. "Am I invisible?"

"Even if you were invisible, we'd still be able to hear you." Corrie, who had entered the kitchen, nabbed a seat next to Nikki and ruffled her hair.

Scowling, Nikki leaned away from her sister's attempted noogie. "Did you know that TT is on the prowl?"

"Yup, saw the posse comprising a boy and his dog and chicken out the kitchen window about the same time I saw you mooning about something in the garden." Corrie grabbed the cereal box and, pretending it was a hoe, rested her hand on top of the box and her chin on top of her hand. "What does a girl think about while hoeing?"

Nikki felt heat creep up her neck. If her ears looked as red as they felt, there was no way she was getting out of this interrogation with her secret tryst just that. She clutched the spoon harder in her hand. "Shush. You're getting batty in your old age, you know."

Corrie swatted that comment away with a flick of her wrist. "Older and wiser. And if I'm not mistaken, a certain individual who I ran into this morning at the store was looking a little red too." She cocked her head and grinned. "Xavier must have spent too much time in the sun. Just. Like. You." Three pokes to the back of Nikki's hand accompanied those words.

Nikki wasn't sure she'd ever heard her mother squeal. Ever. But before Nikki could put her spoon down, her mother crushed her in a bear hug. "Is this true? Are you and Xavier back together?"

With her spoonless hand, Nikki tapped her mother on the back. "Mom, I can't breathe."

Cynthia relinquished her WWE-worthy hold on Nikki but still held her hand prisoner. "Tell me. I always knew you and Xavier would work things out." She wiggled Nikki's hand. "Is it true, or is Corrie suffering from pregnancy delusions?"

"Does Corrie have to be pregnant to suffer from delusions?"

"Hardy har har." Corrie stuck her tongue out, stood up, and rummaged through the cupboards and drawer for a bowl and spoon. "All I know is that I've never seen two people more in love yet more determined to fight it."

Nikki wasn't sure if she feared or respected Corrie's ability to be right. All. The. Time. Either way, big sister was right again. Abandoning her now-soggy Cheerios, Nikki studied one as it drowned in a sea of milk. "I guess I'm afraid."

"You? Afraid?" Corrie's grin faded as soon as she turned toward Nikki. She set her bowl and spoon on the counter and took her seat next to Nikki again. After turning over Nikki's arm, Corrie circled her finger around the tattoo on Nikki's skin. "Last time I checked, this Bible verse didn't go: There is no fear in love *except when it comes to Xavier*."

Cynthia pulled up a chair and flanked Nikki on the other side. "What are you so afraid of?"

Blowing out a breath, Nikki bit her bottom lip. "Failure. Breaking his heart... again. Not being enough for him. Him realizing he made a mistake and breaking my heart this time. You name it, I fear it." She fiddled with her spoon. "The Xavier situation is the one thing in my life I can't control."

"But you can't control other situations you put yourself in." Corrie stilled Nikki's fidgeting with a gentle touch. "You can't control the plane you go skydiving in or the bungee rope strapped around you when you jump off a bridge. Why is the Xavier situation different?"

Nikki felt hot tears pool behind her eyes. Biting her lip wasn't doing the trick, so she clamped on to the inside of her cheek. "Because..." *Breathe, Nikki. Breathe!* "When I do those things, get my adrenaline rush, and something goes wrong, the only person affected is me—" She held up her hand, stemming the retorts she saw forming on her sister's and mother's lips. "Yes, I know. That's not what I mean. Please, hear me out. If Xavier and I were to get back together for real, and something goes kablooey and I make a mistake or pull a normal, everyday Nikki move and Xavier gets hurt too?" One tear escaped. She bit her inner cheek harder. "I couldn't bear it."

"So, you think the easiest thing to do is not reignite an adventure with him. Don't you think he's man enough to decide what adventures he chooses? What gives you the right to make that choice for him?"

"Mom, I didn't—"

Cynthia grasped both of Nikki's hands and played her thumbs over the tops of her daughter's hands. "You might not realize you're doing that. Like I didn't realize I was doing that to you."

The kitchen, even the fridge, went silent. Somewhere outside the cheery kitchen, TT ordered Kentucky to sit and roll over. Corrie's mother instinct must have kicked in because she went to the patio door leading out to the garden and peered out at her son. That or she was giving Nikki and their mother space.

"Mom, you don't have to explain or apologize. I know why you—"

"You always were the stubborn one, weren't you?" Cynthia speared Corrie with a look when the eldest Lancaster child snickered. "On second thought, Corrie wins first prize in that one." Returning her gaze to Nikki, she squeezed her hands. "I'm sorry I didn't bother understanding the real you to appreciate what made you tick, what made you want to conquer the world. I ignored your individualism to ease your father's fear—no, I must be honest—my fear as well. If I didn't allow you to do those things that terrified me, my fear had nothing to taunt me with. Or so I thought. I didn't give you a choice. I fenced you in with my fear and called it love. And that is what you are doing to Xavier. You're fencing him out, not allowing him the chance at one of the greatest adventures of all time. Trust me, there is no greater adventure than marriage and children."

She let go of Nikki's hands and pressed a hand over her heart. "When your father had his accident, it changed everything. Nothing has been or will be the same. I live with that every day. I have to wake up every day and make the conscious choice to stay on this adventure with him, to not abandon my partner in life." Smile lines creased around her teary eyes. "Nikki, I'm not like you. I never asked for an adventure. I wanted security. Normal. I have a strange feeling that if roles were reversed, and you were in my situation, you'd make Xavier's life exhilarating despite a life-altering handicap. You'd figure out how to backpack him up Mount Everest, for all the strength that's in you. You would ensure that he *lived* not just survived." Cynthia cupped Nikki's cheek. "That's what makes you special, and I am so sorry that I didn't celebrate that integral part of you when I should have."

For a second, Nikki forgot to breathe, and when her lungs had enough, she expelled a huge breath and launched herself into her mother's arms.

She wasn't sure how long she clung to her mom, but Corrie's voice soon broke into their mother-daughter moment. "Now, don't go thinking this gives you permission to go do something stupid for the sake of being stupid."

Nikki wriggled free of her mother's embrace and scrunched her nose at Corrie. "And when have I ever done that?" As soon as those words were out of her mouth and Corrie's face lit up, Nikki knew she was in for a lengthy list of Stupid Nikki Moments. It was a hobby of Corrie's, and once a year, she would give Nikki and anyone else unfortunate to be around a recap.

Corrie held up one finger. "Nikki, age six, creating a homemade tightrope from the barn loft." A second finger ticked off another moment. "Nikki, age eight, tying kites together to test the theory of flight... again from the barn loft." Finger number three joined the other two digits. "Nikki, age ten—"

"Enough." Cynthia chuckled. "The only adventure I need details on is the one where Nikki takes the plunge and marries Xavier."

"Did I hear someone say, 'marry Xavier'? Good, because it's about darn time."

Nikki jumped to her feet and spun around. "Sara!" For the second time in less than five minutes, she jettisoned herself into another set of arms, ones that smelled of vanilla bean.

Author Note: One of the most divisive concepts among society is how people eat their cereal. No, seriously, it's true. Most have very strong opinions on cereal and how one should ingest it. I, for one, will not eat cereal if milk has touched it. Yes, I eat my cereal dry. And the only cereal I eat is Cinnamon Toast Crunch or Frosted Mini Wheat. I believe the vast majority of people pour a little milk into their bowl and then consume the cereal before it congeals into a stew of grains and milk. Ewww! Then, you have people, like my dad, who crush their cereal, drown the crushed grains with milk, walk away for about five minutes, and come back and chow it down. So, which person are you? Are you a dry cerealist, a moist cerealist, or a gooey cerealist? Share your cereal preference at https://www.jessicabergbooks.com/contact.

Chapter 43

It wasn't until Xavier turned into the Lancaster's driveway that he knew he'd already screwed up. Here he had barreled out of town and nearly torn up the gravel driveway, all to command Nikki's next moves. Apparently, he was a slow learner, and if Nikki knew his initial intentions, her analysis would be more severe. Which he deserved.

He coasted his Jeep to a stop in front of the Lancasters' farmhouse and next to a battered, old pickup—*Sara must be here already*—and sat in the air conditioning, praying the cold air would cool his emotions. Knowing he couldn't sit there forever, he turned off the ignition and moved to open his door.

A tiny face popped up in his driver's-side window.

"Holy—"

TT grinned and, from the movement of his lips, was talking to him.

Xavier pointed his finger to his ear and mouthed, "What?"

Like a little suckerfish, TT planted his mouth on the window and yelled something through the glass. From the condition of the boy's tongue licking the glass, he had eaten a recent snack. TT brought a dirty cup into view, shook it, and tipped it enough to show off his wares.

Xavier chuckled and eased open the door.

TT jumped off the running board and chirped, "Want some?"

Knowing he had no choice but to accept the proffered snack, he held out his hand. As soon as grubby little fingers placed one Cheerio in the center of his palm, he prayed a small prayer and popped it into his mouth.

"Mm," he hummed and chewed a moist Cheerio. Forcing himself to swallow the questionable item, he patted TT's head. "That was just what I was hungry for."

"Good. Bacon wasn't hungry for them." TT sprinted off, calling for Bacon, who hobbled out from under the shade of an evergreen tree, and Kentucky, who darted out from under the porch. Both animals followed the boy to the swing set.

Not wanting to give any more thought to where the snack Xavier had eaten had been, he ascended the porch steps and knocked on the door. He couldn't count the times he'd done the same thing as a teenager to bask in Nikki's glow or seek sanctuary from his home life. He would never forget the first time he stepped into the Lancasters' house. A sense of warmth permeated the place. It had been years since he had experienced that sensation at home.

A day after Xavier's tenth birthday, his mother had left with no excuse except for a scrawled note stating, "I can't." That night, over leftover birthday cake, unbeknownst to Xavier, he and his father had their last genuine conversation. After that, Xavier's dad had crawled into a self-made prison and rotted away from the inside out until drink took his last breath.

No matter the good memories of the Lancaster family, he couldn't escape the one moment when he had closed the Lancasters' door, descended the steps, gotten in his vehicle, and driven off, thinking he would never see the inside of their house again. Never see Nikki again. Never feel that sense of home.

But here he was. This time, it was him bringing sanctuary to the Lancasters, him working to reestablish the sense of a safe place amidst a storm of uncertainty and fear.

The door opened, and out whooshed feminine laughter and the unmistakable scent of vanilla bean.

Corrie grabbed Xavier's hand, pulled him inside, and grinned wickedly. "If I have to suffer, you have to suffer too."

"What did I do to deserve said suffering?"

"You ordered Sara to come here, didn't you?" Corrie crossed her arms and gave him the same look Iris had tried to imitate earlier.

"Me? I don't think anyone could order Sara around." He held his hands up in innocence. "I swear I had nothing to do with this."

Nikki's laugh floated from the kitchen, followed by a donkey's braying. "Is that—"

"Sara's laugh?" Corrie grabbed his arm and dragged him toward the kitchen. "Yup." As soon as they crossed the threshold, Corrie presented him as if he were a prize. "Look who showed up on our doorstep."

Cynthia's eyes widened, and she clasped her hands together and nuzzled them under her chin. *Odd.*

Sara stopped mid-bray and flashed a smile so big it showed off her gums. *Doubly odd.*

Nikki, standing in the center of the kitchen, holding a bowl of cereal, gaped at him. Color crept up her neck and spread like pink blossoms across her cheeks. Her gaze held on his, and for a moment, the other women disappeared, the kitchen disappeared, the bowl in her shaking hands vanished, and all that existed was her.

A throat cleared. Someone snickered. A sigh.

The front door slammed open, and bare feet slapped against the tiled floor. "Nana! Kentucky rolled over. I need a treat."

Trance broken by TT's demands, the world zoomed back into focus. Cynthia was still there. Her gaze, doe-like and dreamy, flicked from him to Nikki. Sara, smile still as big, began humming a tune under her breath. Xavier cocked his head to the side. He'd heard that song somewhere. The pink splotches on Nikki's face turned crimson.

TT, undeterred by no response the first time, tugged on Cynthia's shirt until she looked down at him. "Nana. I need a treat. Kentucky did a trick."

"I suppose this means a treat for you too." Cynthia sprinkled some mini marshmallows in TT's snack cup. "And these are for Kentucky." She shook a small bag of Corn Nuts and placed it in his hand.

"Thanks, Nana."

After the front door slammed closed, Cynthia offered Xavier a seat. "Care for lemonade? Iced tea?"

"No thanks." Waving away her offer, he locked gazes with Nikki. "I'm here to talk to Nikki." When no one moved, he sighed. "Alone."

Nikki rolled her eyes and snorted. "Being as these people won't leave, let's go for a walk."

"Great idea."

"I have those sometimes." She grabbed two root beers from the fridge and slid open the patio door leading from the kitchen to the backyard. "I've got the perfect spot."

She smelled of dirt, sweat, and sunshine. Her fluffy ponytail hung crookedly, and her makeup-free face smiled up at him. Strings hung off her tattered shorts, and an oversized orange tank top that probably belonged to her brother, Nathan, flashed occasional peaks of her black sports bra.

"What? What's wrong?" She stopped. Her smile dimmed, and she fussed with her hair. "Sorry, I was working in the garden, and I haven't had a—"

"Stop." After capturing her wrist, he brought it to his lips and kissed her pulse point. For five pulses, he held her there, his eyes on her. Raising his lips a hair away from her skin, he whispered, "You are beautiful."

Her other hand pawed at her hair and readjusted the slipping tank top strap. "You are delusional."

Grinning, he pulled her to him until there was nothing between them except their shirts. "Maybe. Probably. Usually. But never with beauty. I'd like to think I'm an expert."

She licked her lips. "What else are you an expert at?"

"A few things."

"I'm more of a visual learner."

"Well, in that case." He dipped his head and captured her bottom lip lightly between his teeth and nibbled. At her gasp of surprise, he captured her top lip and sucked.

Someone from inside the kitchen whooped.

"They're goofy." Nikki grasped his hand and jogged until they came to the base of the windmill. "There. Finally, away from prying eyes." Instead of falling back into his arms as he'd hoped during their mini-run, she stepped back, crossed her arms, and tapped her foot. "Now, before you woo me with your voodoo, which by the way, is very voodoo-y and lovely and worth exploring again, I assume you came here for business."

"Guilty as charged." He leaned against the windmill's rusting metal skeleton. "A little bird told me today that you may or may not have let slip that you took the killer's picture."

She looked everywhere but at him. "Can I have one guess who that little bird is?"

"No." He ignored her pout.

"But I didn't mean it. It... popped out, like the little moles in Whac-A-Mole, you know. Bang, and there it was, and before I could—"

"Nikki, I'm not blaming you. It's okay. Now that that *little* factoid is out there, I'm afraid it won't be long until the entire town knows it as well."

"I only told Eleanor."

"Who will most likely suffer from the same Whac-A-Mole syndrome, and before night falls, *everyone* in Sandy will suffer from the same contagion."

It took several seconds for his words to sink in. And when they did, steely resignation replaced the earlier playful blue. "So, it won't be long now until he knows who I am." She rubbed her hands up and down her arms. "I made a mess of things." Her gaze locked with his. "What now? What should I do?"

He squinted at her. He could count on one hand the number of times she had ever asked for his advice or opinion. Taking her hand in his, he drew her into his arms and rested his chin on top of her head. "I was wondering if you would mind if I camped out here, at your parents' house. You don't have to say yes, but I want to be closer in case..." He closed his eyes and swallowed the lump forming in his throat.

Nikki wriggled from his embrace but kept her hands tucked in his and studied him. "Thank you."

"For what?"

She cupped his cheek and played her thumb over his several days' growth of facial hair. "Giving me a choice."

"And what is it?"

"That when it comes to who I want and need by my side, it's you."

His heart thumped once against his chest before settling into a racing stride. He leaned into her hand and nuzzled it until her palm rested over his lips. He kissed that spot once before grasping her hand in his. Words would not squeak past the lump in his throat. He had waited so long for those words that, once he heard them, he didn't know what to do with them. "Nikki, I... ah..."

She giggled and kissed him. Like she used to. She started with his top lip, moved to his bottom lip, and dove in with abandon. Blood pooled from his head to his core, and he couldn't breathe. Not that he wanted to. Breathing meant breaking the kiss. His body reminded him that if he suffocated to death, he wouldn't be able to kiss Nikki anymore, so he captured her bottom lip one more time before releasing her.

Nikki licked her lips. "Well, that was..."

"Delightful?"

"Scrumptious."

"How 'bout we compromise and call it 'delightfully scrumptious'?"

She held out her pinky finger. "Deal. See, we make a great team."

He hooked his pinky around hers. Reality shattered the iridescent fog of Nikki's kiss.

Her smile slipped. "Yes. Back to the task at hand. How do we deal with this?"

"I think, right now, you live normally. Come and go as you normally would. Let's not awaken suspicion by giving you a bodyguard or anything like that."

"Tell that to my family."

He kept his grin to himself. "Not an official bodyguard. I'm not brave enough to tell your sister or your mother to stand down."

She palpated his biceps and smiled. "Strong man like you terrified of two women?"

"Have you met said two women?" His skin tingled where she'd touched him.

"Right. Family-appointed bodyguards remain." She chewed her bottom lip. "What else?"

He marked each suggestion with a raised finger. "One, keep your phone with you at all times... and answer it once in a while"—he ignored her furrowed brow—"two, try not to go anywhere by yourself—"

"Sara's here now. I don't think I could be alone even if I wanted to."

"Three, let me know any suspicions you have, no matter how small. Four"—tucking a stray blond hair behind her ear, he gazed into her eyes—"let me know the moment you feel hemmed in. I don't want history to repeat itself."

After studying him for a few moments, she smiled. "Deal." And instead of sealing the agreement with a pinky swear, she kissed him.

He lost track of time, but eventually, hand in hand, they ambled back to the Lancasters' home. While she admired the blooming flowers, commenting on how well she had weeded the garden, he scoped out the yard and house, making mental notes of where a killer could lurk and gain access to Nikki's sanctuary.

Author Note: I cannot give many pointers on baking as God did not equip me with the baking gene. I can tell you what NOT to do and, I promise, this will be the best baking advice you ever get. Who needs the Great British Baking Show when you have my mistakes to learn from? Never, ever, melt the square caramel candies and pour that ooey, gooey caramel goodness throughout the chocolate cake batter and then bake it. Why should you not do this lovely-sounding addition? Well, the caramel hardens into something like cement, the knife will break when you go to cut the cake, and you will have to soak the cake pieces in milk just to make it edible. This is how I ruined one of my brother Joshua's birthday cakes. Sorry, buddy! What's your worst baking mistake? Please share at https://www.jessicabergbooks.com/contact.

Chapter 44

All too soon, after an ops meeting with Cynthia, Corrie, Sara, and Nikki, Xavier left with direct instructions to act normal.

Nikki eyed her family and best friend, who all began chatting about what Xavier had interrupted earlier: her wedding to Xavier. *He could have given us an easier task.*

Not able to take any more planning, without her input, of course, Nikki dragged Sara from the house and introduced her to the resident pets. Bacon licked Sara's hand, and Kentucky, showing her true sassy colors, pecked at Sara's big toe sticking out of her Chaco sandals. Before Sara could make true on her threat to incorporate Kentucky into a stew, Nikki bundled Sara into the pickup and headed into Sandy.

As soon as they pulled onto the highway, Sara twisted in her seat. "So, my mother's feeling has not been unfounded."

Nikki snorted, but her hands clutched the steering wheel tighter. "Why do you say that?"

"Girl, I don't need my mom's spooky sixth sense to feel the angst coming off you." She waved her hand between her and Nikki as if swooshing away visible fumes.

"I'm fine."

"In that case, I'm the queen of England, and as my first royal edict, you must tell the whole truth and nothing but the truth."

"Do they say that in the English court?"

Sara rewarded her with an imperiously arched eyebrow.

"Okay, fine, I'm not fine."

"Want to talk about it?"

"How much time do you have?"

"Well, from the sign updating us on our proximity to Sandy that we just passed"—she leaned over and squinted at the speedometer—"and the land speed record you are attempting to break, I'd say about seven minutes."

For the next seven minutes, Nikki brought Sara up to speed on everything from details surrounding Natasha's death to her house adventure with Bryce. As she slowed from an over-the-sixty-five-mile-per-hour speed limit to a snaillike twenty-five, her blood sprinted through her body at the retelling of her make-up session with Xavier both the night before and moments ago under the shadow of the windmill.

"And this is where you ask me to be your maid of honor." Sara eyed the small shops lining Sandy's Main Street.

Without the need to attract tourists, most East River small towns lacked the "cute, rustic factor" that West River tourist towns needed to entice customers through their doors. Instead, brick-and-mortar shops in Sandy were rather utilitarian, there to serve a purpose the citizens depended on to survive when the closest Walmart or Target was an hour-and-a-half drive away.

"Xavier's got to ask me to be his bride first—ah, for the second time." Nikki pulled into a parking spot in front of the Sandy Sundry and Supply Store. "And with my track record, I'm sure he's not champing at the bit to ask me again."

"Whatever, still calling dibs on being the maid of honor."

Knowing there was no point in arguing, Nikki hopped out of the pickup, tripped up the curb, and stumbled into an elderly man stooped over a cane and a cat on a leash.

She reached out a steadying hand. "Sorry, Mr. Graham. You okay?" At his nod, her gaze followed the pink leash gripped in arthritic fingers to the cat attached at the end. "Are you and Tobias out for an afternoon stroll?"

Mr. Graham smiled, showing off discolored dentures. "The missus thinks the old cat is fat so insists I take the poor thing for walks. I think she thinks I'm the fat one and uses Tobias as an excuse to get me out of the house."

Nikki chuckled and leaned over to scratch Tobias between his droopy ears. The cat butted her hand, sat on its haunches, and used a back claw to scratch at the rhinestone-encrusted collar. Nikki often witnessed Mrs. Graham herself half dragging, half cajoling the poor creature on these "walks."

"Mr. Graham, please meet my dear friend, Sara. Sara, Mr. Graham."

"It's nice to meet you, Mr. Graham." Sara shook his offered hand and eyed the pink sparkly collar around the cat's neck. "Isn't Tobias a boy?"

A pair of bushy eyebrows furrowed. "Yes?"

Sara smiled. "Never mind."

Mr. Graham hiked his pants up, checked his watch, and grunted. "Well, Tobias, exercise is over. Time for a nap." After nodding at Nikki and Sara, he waddled down the sidewalk, towing Tobias behind him.

"That old man had a cat on a leash."

"Your eyesight hasn't failed you yet, I see." Nikki grinned and opened the door, gesturing for Sara to enter first.

"But I don't think the cat enjoys it."

Nikki snagged a shopping cart and before starting down one of four aisles in the store, she peered through the store's front window. Mr. Graham hadn't made it far, as every few feet, he had to pause, shake his finger at the cat, and begin again. Every time, Tobias sat on his haunches and stretched all four paws out and skidded along on his backside.

"Poor cat," Sara whispered behind Nikki.

"Yeah. They used to have another one, but I'm pretty sure it ran away."

"I like a cat with some sense of self-preservation."

"You like any old cat." Nikki kicked at the squeaky shopping cart's wheel, hoping to dislodge the annoyance before her ears bled. The Sandy Sundry and Supply Store boasted everything from ten-pound bags of sunflower seeds to the occasional frozen lobster but didn't specialize in carts that worked. Either they squeaked, squawked, or rattled down the narrow linoleum-tiled aisles in a cacophony of noise.

"What can I say? I have a soft spot for strays."

Grinning, Nikki glanced at the shopping list her mother had entrusted her with. "Is that why you took me under your wing? Ten cans of tuna, please."

"Nah, you were willing to pay the rent I was asking." Sara counted out ten cans of tuna and dumped them in the cart. "Should have known you were crazy then, but it's too late now, and I refuse to miss out on being in your wedding."

"Careful, or I'll pick out the ugliest bridesmaid dress ever. Something in puce."

"It'll be your fault when I look like a walking prune."

Nikki snorted and continued shopping, calling out items for Sara to pluck off the shelves and set—or throw—in the cart.

"Hey, Nikki."

Nikki halted at Bryce's voice behind her. Tuna cans sustained trauma from the sudden impact with the front of the cart. Snippets of conversation she'd had with Xavier the night before and his suspicions about Bryce replayed through her mind. Doubt clouded her thoughts, and for a moment, she considered abandoning her cart, grabbing Sara's hand, and running.

Sara mouthed, "This guy?" and Nikki nodded.

Taking a deep breath, Nikki forced a smile and faced him. "Hey."

His smile slipped. "You think I killed Natasha, too, don't you?"

"What? Um... ah... sorry. Look, I—"

"No need to apologize. Just thought you were different, is all. My bad." He turned his cart around in the narrow aisle and bumped into a display of Little Debbies.

"Bryce, I... um..." Nikki exhaled and stuck her hands in the back pockets of her jeans.

After completing a three-point turn to escape the cardboard boxes, Bryce nabbed several and threw them in his cart. "With all that trouble, might as well make it worth my while."

"Wait... uh..." Sara snatched a box of Swiss Rolls off the shelf and handed it to him. "You can't walk out of here without these."

He eyed the peace offering as if it would bite him and eyed Sara as if she would take a chunk out of him too. Nikki didn't blame him. He didn't know what was in Sara's purse nestled next to her vanilla bean lotion, but Nikki did: a concealed handgun. Sara only smelled the part of a delicious baked good. Inside, she was as solid as a rock with nerves of steel.

Sara's hand, still clutching the proffered box, shook. *Maybe nerves of steel wire.*

Taking the box, Bryce nodded. "I appreciate it. Most people around here would rather hand me a rope and point to the nearest tree. A kind of DIY hanging, I suppose."

Nikki scrubbed at her neck. "Look, I am sorry. People around here are finding it difficult with who they can trust and who they can't."

"Well, you might want to tell them that so far, they're trusting the wrong person."

Without realizing it, Nikki grasped his upper arm. "Who? Do you know who—"

She followed his pointed gaze at her hand white-knuckling his bicep. Relinquishing her hold, she stepped back.

"I don't know any more than the next person. All I know is that a young woman is dead, and I had nothing to do with it." Clear of the Little Debbie roadblock, he walked away, his tennis shoes squeaking, his cart creaking.

From the lack of breathing sounds, Nikki assumed Sara was also holding her breath.

Inhaling sharply, Nikki placed her hand over her heart. "Well, that went well."

"Has the face of a killer," Sara whispered.

"Sara!"

"Does not have the aura of one though."

"And how do you know? Met many killers recently?"

Sara patted her purse. "You never know, but I'm always prepared. Don't roll your eyes at me. You're the one who went through a haunted house with him."

Nikki was about to correct her friend about the presence of ghosts, but the reality of her vulnerability with a could-be killer had her swallowing bile instead.

Author Note: I have two personal connections to this chapter. First is the cat-walking. I tried it when I was little with my cat, Fraidy. She clearly loved it—not. She, in fact, mutinied and refused to walk. So, how did I fix this recalcitrant feline? I simply dragged her around the farmyard until my mother put a stop to the nonsense. Second is the Little Debbies. I had to include this as a shout-out to my youngest daughter, Emma, whose love for these little snack cakes I used to bribe her to take naps. Hey, a mom's gotta do what a mom's gotta do. To all you moms out there, what was your go-to bribe with your children? Share your powers at https://www.jessicabergbooks.com/contact.

Chapter 45

Grocery shopping for the Lancaster household complete, Nikki and Sara piled into the pickup and drove a couple of blocks down Main then parked next to Xavier's Jeep in front of the sheriff's office.

"Oh, I didn't know we were stopping here." Sara wiggled her eyebrows and made a kissy face.

"You said you wanted to see all of Sandy's wildlife. This is part of the tour. Besides, I need to tell Xavier about our run-in with Bryce."

"Ooh, I enjoy seeing wild things in their habitat." Sara flipped down the visor and checked her reflection in the mirror. She scowled, rummaged around in her purse, plucked out a tube of fire-engine-red lipstick, and applied it to her lips with precision. "Just in case my Teddy Bear is here too."

"Good grief." Nikki hopped out. "Does Thaddeus know that's your code name for him?"

"Of course. Want to know what he calls me?"

"Nope. Not one little bit." Before opening the door to the sheriff's department, Nikki checked her reflection in the glass doorway and patted down her fly-away hair. In the hubbub of wedding planning and store-list making, Nikki had not completed the one task she wanted to do: shower. Not that Xavier had minded earlier. Warmth oozed through her veins and set a fire in her belly.

"Earth to Nikki." Sara waved her hand in front of Nikki's face. "You going to open the door, or stand there and hold it closed?"

Nikki blinked at her hand grasping the door handle. "Oh, yeah. Sorry."

She yanked it open and wrinkled her nose against the layer of odors as soon as she entered the building. It was a lasagna of smells: old plastic chairs, a dusty, decaying houseplant, day-old lavender, and a recent attempt to cover it all with a coating of dollar-store cinnamon apple spray. And a dollop of vanilla.

"It smells like sadness in here." Sara turned full circle in the empty waiting room in front of an abandoned front desk. "And loneliness."

"Hello?" Nikki called out, almost afraid of the silence.

Xavier poked his head around the corner of the hallway leading away from the front desk, his scrunched-up face relaxing into a lazy smile. "Miss me that much?"

Nikki wasn't sure about the physics at work inside her body, but she was pretty sure they weren't healthy and that some of her organs swapped places for a couple of seconds. "Not one little bit."

Sara snorted and inserted herself between Nikki and Xavier. "She's lying." She peered around him. "Thaddeus here?"

"Nope. Sorry to disappoint."

"Who says I'm disappointed?" Sara's lips puckered as if she'd sucked on a lemon, and she gestured to the plastic chairs in the waiting area. "Those seats comfortable?"

"Not even the slightest."

She huffed, sat herself in a chair, and started texting, her thumbs flying over the screen.

Xavier chuckled. "Poor Thaddeus."

"Where is he, by the way?" Nikki asked.

"Out double-checking leads and re-questioning people on our list." Leaning against the wall, he crossed his arms over his chest. His gaze fluttered between her eyes and lips.

"Would Bryce be one of those people?"

His relaxed stance hardened. "Why?"

"Ran into him at the grocery store." She burrowed into his waiting arms. "Something doesn't feel right. I keep running the morning I took the picture of the killer through my head. I know I'm missing something."

"Just a second. Wait here." He walked away and came back seconds later with a print of a photo she'd taken. He handed it to her. "Take another look."

Nondescript red ball cap, flannel, grass too long to see the cut of jeans or shoes, a shadow of facial hair under the cap's bill. Nothing.

"It could be anyone." She closed her eyes and relived the moment. Dawn had broken over the horizon. A mother bison and her calf were basking in the quiet of an undisturbed moment. Wildflowers woven through the green tapestry of prairie grasses enticed bees to their scent. Inhaling through her nose, Nikki could almost smell the waist-high yellow clover waving in the gentle breeze. *Movement!*

She opened her eyes and grasped his hands. "It's not a thing I'm missing. It's a moment." At his quirked eyebrow, she tugged at his hands. "Don't you see? Pictures aren't just pictures. They represent a moment in time. A moment complete with movement. Every item has a presence, an aura—"

"Thought you didn't believe in that," Sara called from her seat.

Nikki ignored Sara's comment and Xavier's eye roll at the interruption. "You see, whenever I snap a picture, there is movement before and after and during. I need to piece my pictures back-to-back by time stamp. Give them motion, per se, maybe that will help me recall what is on the tip of my brain."

"Nikki, I think you—"

"But I can't leave this alone. I know. Police business is police business, and I should keep my—"

His lips on hers shut her up. And if this was how he would do that from now on, she didn't care if he shut her up more often. He retreated enough to rest his forehead against hers. "Do me a favor, next time. Don't assume you know what I'm going to say." He grinned. "Or else, you wouldn't have heard me tell you that you're brilliant."

She circled the embroidered logo on his black polo. "And don't you forget it." Tipping up on her tiptoes, she whispered in his ear, "Besides, I have a witness."

His breath tickled her ear when he whispered back, "I don't believe a fiery-tempered redhead more invested in hunting down an MIA DCI agent than in the whispered sweet nothings between lovers would be seen as reliable in a court of law."

"What about a court of love?"

He held her at arm's length and, by the twinkle in his eye, enjoyed watching the heat she could feel crawl up her neck. "Nikki, my love, that was the cheesiest thing I've ever heard you say."

"Remember, you called me brilliant a few seconds ago."

"Did I? Must have been the wind through the rafters or something." His cheeky grin melted into a sensual smile, and his head dipped down to meet her rising lips.

His phone rang.

He answered it without looking at the caller ID. "Hello?"

Nikki couldn't hear the speaker, but from the color leaching from Xavier's face to the way his hand scrunched around his phone until his knuckles whitened, she assumed the news was not good. She gripped his free hand and didn't flinch when he squeezed back. Even Sara left her spot and joined them to slip her arm around Nikki's waist.

"Be right there." Xavier stuffed his phone back in his pocket. His eyes had gone dark and emotionless.

His outward calm did not fool Nikki. His body shivered under her touch.

He kissed her forehead. "Go home. Straight home. Lock the doors. And for the love of all things good, do not, under any circumstance, allow Bryce Beaumont into your house or even on your front porch." He grasped her upper arms and waited until she met his gaze. "Please."

"What happened?" Nikki croaked around the lump in her throat.

"It's Laurel. She's dead." Without another word, he zipped into his office, came back out several seconds later, and after a quick buss on Nikki's cheek, ran out the main doors to his Jeep.

It wasn't until the roar of the Jeep's engine faded that Nikki and Sara locked gazes. They swiveled to face the abandoned front desk. A gold-plated nameplate stamped Laurel Stewart's possession of the welcome center for the sheriff's office.

Laurel Stewart. The same Laurel who had helped Nikki pass Algebra II, some of it ethically, most of it not. Laurel Stewart. The same Laurel who instead of being a shoo-in for her father's bank dedicated her life to the military, protecting America's people, and came home to protect Sandy's people.

The engraved name on the nameplate swirled in Nikki's vision. Too soon, her name would be engraved in granite.

Stupid thoughts darted through Nikki's brain: *What happens to the pictures she has in cute frames? Who gets her coffee cup stamped with "Badges? We don't need no stinkin' badges?" Is it all crammed in some brown office box and handed to her parents with pomp and circumstance?*

Nikki picked up one of the tiny potted fake succulents and turned it over. Laurel hadn't even had time to remove the price sticker from the bottom.

Sara eased the potted plant out of Nikki's hand and set it back to complete the neat row Laurel had created. "Come on. Let's get you home." She stuck her hand out. "Keys?"

Squaring her shoulders, Nikki swiped at her tears with the back of her hand. Tears were useless and would blur the images she needed to piece together a shadowed clue. "I'm driving."

Author Note: Blazing Saddles *is an irreverent parody of Westerns, and one that I watched growing up. While there are many parodies out there, including* Spaceballs *and* Robin Hood: Men in Tights, Blazing Saddles *will always have a spot in my heart, not because of the plot or the characters or the satirical lengths they went to when producing this movie. I remember this movie as the source for my mother's all-time favorite movie quote: "Somebody's gotta go back and get a sh*tload of dimes." Yes, this is my mom's favorite movie quote, and she doesn't even like this movie! What is your all-time favorite movie quote? Let me know at https://www.jessicabergbooks.com/contact.*

Chapter 46

Forty-five minutes later, Xavier joined the calvary outside the decaying wooden elevator, a lone sentinel among gnarled trees that used to shade houses. Houses now long gone.

Even in the late-afternoon sun, Xavier fought a shiver before entering the rotting edifice. If he were in a movie, some manic violin would accompany his footfalls as he stepped over holes in the floorboards. But this was not a movie. This was real, and the closer he got to the hulking frame of Thaddeus, the closer he moved to the body of Laurel.

The sunlight did not penetrate past the entrance and exit points and into the middle innards of the elevator. Xavier accepted a flashlight from a uniformed officer, flicked on the light, and directed his beam to the floor. Even though the elevator hadn't seen business for years, remnants of past crops stored here littered the floor. Kernels of corn and wheat, leaves, and debris blown in had settled into cracks in the floor. A film of dust covered every surface. Disturbed by human feet, the dust danced through the air and shivered in the flashlight beams.

Xavier coughed. Someone handed him a dust mask, which cut the dust and not the smell of rotting grain left to mold away, mouse droppings, and rusty oil cans. Crinkling his nose against the smell, he walked toward the body lying in the middle of the elevator on top of the metal grate that once received thousands of bushels of grain per year.

He stooped next to the body and, with a gloved hand, inspected the surrounding area. All evidence would have fallen through the cracks and into the pit below. He swallowed the bile rising in his throat at the thought of climbing down there into years' worth of muck. "Who found her?"

Thaddeus crouched on the other side of Laurel's uniformed body. "A couple of teens. I'm sure they were up to no good, but before they had a chance to get into trouble, they found Laurel's body." He pointed at the exit. "They're out there if you want to question them too."

"Later." Xavier glanced at his watch. "Weaver here yet?"

"He'll be here in five."

"Good. Let's search the area." Eyeing the grate, he sighed. "One of us will have to go down there."

A swear word filtered up from the abyss.

Thaddeus plucked a strand of hair from the floor with tweezers and placed it in a small plastic evidence bag. "Steve is down there."

Grunting his acknowledgment, Xavier pulled on a second glove and examined Laurel's body. Resting in a fetal position, it matched the position of the other three women. It was as if the killer had tucked them into death. Whoever had brutalized these women had rearranged their corpses as if he'd cared for them after death.

Xavier squinted at Laurel's hand tucked under her chin. "What's this?" Not waiting for an answer from Thaddeus, he pulled at a bit of fabric sticking out of her fist. A piece of flannel. After tucking it into an evidence bag, he scanned the rest of the area. "Whoever killed her took her gun"—he double-checked her utility belt—"and everything else."

Anger surged through his veins, gathered in his gut, and swirled.

He fought the urge to straighten her crumpled and bloodied uniform. "What was she doing all the way out here, anyway?"

"Not sure. An officer is looking into calls that came through. It is odd, though. We're on the literal edge of the county. Sandy to Greenway is not a small jaunt. Killer must have made the call, lured her out here, pretended to need her help, then..."

"What did you say?" Xavier's mouth went dry.

"I said a lot of things." Thaddeus tweezed a fiber into a baggie.

"Where are we?"

"Greenway. According to Steve, this used to be a hopping railroad town." He shrugged. "Now nothing's left but a few rotted-out basements and this elevator." The sound of a far-off tractor buzzed through the air. "And fields." Thaddeus looked up and blinked. "Why? You look as if you've seen a ghost."

"Not a ghost. A killer." Xavier scrambled to his feet and paced. Clues clicked together in his head. "Steve," he called through the grate, "get a judge on the phone. I have a search warrant request to make."

"Who?" Steve and Thaddeus asked.

"Bryce Beaumont."

Author Note: Greenway is an actual place. Well, it was an actual place. Nothing remains anymore of this railroad town on the South Dakota prairie. When I was a little girl, all that remained were a few old, rotting houses scattered among overgrown trees and a proud elevator that reached into the sky. A local farmer actually still used the ancient elevator to store his grain. A few years ago, however, this once state-of-the-art elevator from the early 1900s toppled to the ground (with the help of explosives). Now, trees and the cemetery are all that populate a town once bustling with life and activity. Ghost towns intrigue me, and while I would never stay overnight in one, I love to venture forth during the day. Somehow it makes me feel connected to the past, a past that made me who I am today. Do you love ghost towns?

Would you stay overnight in one? Let me know at https://www.jessi-cabergbooks.com/contact.

Chapter 47

"How long do you plan on keeping me in here?" Bryce tapped his feet against the metal legs of his chair, breaking the heavy silence choking the room after Steve had read him his Miranda rights.

The small cinderblock room at the back of the sheriff's department with one window large enough for a toaster to squeeze through shrank with every breath the men took.

"That depends." Steve's phone vibrated. He looked at the incoming text and grinned. "Search warrant came through for your great-uncle's house and your pickup. Care to tell us what we might find? Save us some time? You were in Greenway this morning. Got opportunity already. Means and motive won't be too far behind, I'm thinking."

Bryce eyed the empty folding chair next to him. "I'm waiting for my lawyer."

"Suits us fine. At the rate she's getting here, you might earn yourself a sleepover. We've got room for you." Steve summoned a deputy standing guard at the door. "Take him to the cells, and let me know the moment his lawyer steps through the front doors."

Xavier followed Steve from the room, and within five minutes, Steve entered Oliver Beaumont's house, and Xavier stood outside Bryce's pickup. Bryce being in Greenway the morning of Laurel's murder was circumstantial evidence. Bryce having the murder weapon or something linking him to the crime scenes would be gold. Pure gold. Anticipation skittered along his spine, and sweat beaded on his forehead as he snapped on gloves and opened the driver's-side door. A few sunflower shells fell out and sprinkled the ground, a half-empty bottle of Coke leaned out of the cup holder, and a brown, leather-textured Little Trees dangling from the rearview mirror coated everything with a smell of leather.

Compartment after compartment revealed nothing except evidence that the man had been logging serious miles on the road. Napkins from different restaurants, candy and food wrappers, a phone charger, caffeine supplements, Tylenol. Nothing to mark a murderer.

Abandoning his search of the front seat, Xavier moved to the back seat. An extra pair of clothes, a pair of overshoes encrusted with mud, and a toolbox. He grabbed the box, brought it to the paved driveway, and opened it. He sat back on his haunches and stared at the red-and-green flannel smashed into the top tray. Emotions warred inside him. Fear, anger, relief. He stood and stretched his shoulders to ease the knots settling in. He had expected to feel different, to feel elation. The hunt for a killer was over. But he didn't.

After snapping pictures of the incriminating flannel, he lifted it and held it out. Pieces had been torn from the shirt, and though it was still wearable, its frayed and worn fabric hinted that it was once well used. Lab results would tell the shirt's history. Xavier tucked the shirt inside an evidence bag and searched for Laurel's gun. Nothing but a few more candy wrappers. He secured the evidence and searched for Steve. Time to show Bryce the ace up their sleeve.

The blast of air conditioning as he walked behind Steve into the sheriff's department was not enough to cool his body or his mind. A different deputy, by the name of Henderson, manned Laurel's old post, and after giving a negative answer about Bryce's lawyer, he went to fetch Bryce from his cell.

Xavier and Steve sat silently in the same room they'd been in before. This time, the room felt smaller, and Xavier struggled to keep his breathing even. He'd dealt with society's scum often enough that he had become calloused to it. Now, in a few moments, he would come face to face with a man who had evidence linking him to the deaths of six women, two of them Xavier's old friends. That Bryce had almost killed Nikki and had been alone with her in the old, abandoned house had his vision going blurry. He blinked until his vision cleared. Now was not the time for emotion.

Footsteps echoed down the hallway. Xavier took one large breath for good measure before Bryce walked in, handcuffed, escorted by Deputy Henderson, whose face betrayed his hatred for the suspect.

"My lawyer's not here yet." Bryce stood beside the chair he had sat in earlier.

"Doesn't mean we can't chitchat a bit." Steve scrunched down in his chair and, with one foot, kicked the folding chair from under the table. "Sit. Agent Palinski has a story to tell."

After glancing between Xavier and Steve, Bryce sat, scooted up his chair, and placed his handcuffed wrists on the table.

"Consider this story time, a perk of being here." Xavier set his notepad on the table and opened it. "Once upon a time—"

"I don't have to sit here and listen to this."

"Then don't listen." Xavier rechecked his notes. "Now, where was I?"

Steve leaned over and peeked at Xavier's chicken-scratched notes, indecipherable to anyone but Xavier. "Looks like you were about to introduce the characters."

"Ah yes. There were a few—six, to be exact—innocent girls, living life, minding their own business until someone—let's say Villain Number One—came along and killed them. Along his path of destruction, he laid a trail of not bread crumbs but flannel pieces. Odd choice. Bread crumbs would have fit better in my story." He laid his palms on the table and pushed himself to his feet and leaned across within an arm's length of Bryce. "But here's the problem. This is not a story. This is real life, and someone brutally murdered six women. And from the evidence found in your pickup, I believe Villain Number One has a name." He leaned down, grabbed the evidence bag containing the flannel, and slapped it on the table. "Yours."

Bryce's flushed face bleached. His eyes widened, and his pupils dilated. "Where did you—"

Xavier sat in his chair and folded his hands together in his lap to keep them from slamming into Bryce's face. Besides, he was sure Steve didn't take too kindly to outsiders assaulting prisoners. But after finding the incriminating evidence in the back seat of Bryce's pickup, he wasn't too sure he cared about justice or the law. He wanted to hear the crunch of his fist impacting Bryce's nose. He fisted his hands harder in his lap.

"Mr. Beaumont, it is in your best interest to cooperate with Agent Palinski and me."

Xavier leaned back in his chair, glad Steve's bicolored eyes weren't peering into his soul right now.

But, really, does Bryce even have one?

Bryce squirmed under Steve's stare.

Maybe he does.

Composure regained, Bryce snapped his mouth shut and stared at the shirt encased in plastic. "Lawyer," he ground out between clenched teeth then looked at the wall behind Xavier and Steve.

"Suit yourself. Deputy Henderson, please escort Mr. Beaumont back to his cell. Story time is over."

After Henderson took Bryce from the room, Xavier rubbed his temples. "Ever get a feeling that something's not over?"

"Part of the job sometimes." Steve grunted as he rose to his feet. "Been a long day. Headed to the bar. You coming?"

What little light had squeezed through the tiny window during the late afternoon had long vanished. Exhaustion seeped into him. The cure wasn't a drink. It was a woman. "Nah. Thanks, though.

See you tomorrow morning. Oh, and if Fancy-Pants Lawyer contacts you, let me know."

"Scout's honor."

After grabbing his stuff from his office, he hopped into his Jeep and headed out of town. Time to tell Nikki he'd caught the killer. His questioning gut roiled. *Maybe.*

Author Note: *If you're looking for a reason to celebrate on June 13th, you could bake a cake, light a few candles, and sing "Happy Birthday" to Miranda Rights. Yup, on June 13, 1966, the Supreme Court made its final decision in Miranda vs. Arizona. Even though American citizens have the Miranda Rights nearly memorized thanks to the myriad of cop shows, the story behind these words is not nearly as well known. If you're curious as to the backstory of the justice system's Miranda Rights, head on over to History Channel's "This Day in History" page to read all about it.*

Chapter 48

Nikki glared at the photographs she'd printed from her parents' printer.

"Anything yet?" Sara stepped into the Lancasters' office, sipping from a hot-pink straw. She plopped a hip on the edge of the mahogany desk and stirred her lemonade. Ice cubes clinked against the glass.

Nikki's idea of making a moving picture book had died as soon as her parents' ink had. On top of having a four-picture movie, she now owed her parents printer ink. "I need to be there. See it for real. I don't know. Maybe even smell it. Doesn't smell trigger memory?"

Sara's straw hit bottom with a gurgle. After one last suck for good measure, Sara grinned. "Once had an ex of mine tell me that the memory of my lotion would haunt him in his dreams." Shrugging, she bit the tip of the straw. "Not unhappy about that."

Nikki squinted at the grainy quality of the prints. "I need to go back."

"Back where?"

"Back home. The cabin."

"You sure? I'm not sure your family —"

"Look, I need to do this. Something about all this doesn't make sense." She slid a hand through her freshly washed hair and tugged. "I think going back to where it all started could trigger something."

A knock sounded behind them. "Do these plans include me?"

Nikki spun at the sound of Xavier's voice. She wasn't sure about weapons any longer, and as for the heat... well, that settled in her stomach and hummed.

The old Nikki would have rolled her eyes and told Xavier her plans and added the caveat "whether you like it or not." The new Nikki still wanted to, but holding up her side of the bargain, sealed by a couple of kisses—kisses that made her insides go squishy—she ignored Sara's snickers and led Xavier from the office.

With family lurking everywhere inside, she pulled him from the house and claimed the rocking chair next to the one he sat in. She leaned her elbows on her knees and cupped her chin in her hands. An industrious ant had found an abandoned Cheerio, courtesy of TT, and was busy carting it toward his home. Nikki guessed by the number of Cheerios littering the yard like confetti that the ant had found an abundant supply for his winter food stash. She watched it, and the Cheerio disappear through a crack in the porch decking.

"What's wrong?" Xavier's fingers caressed the back of her hand, beckoning her own to turn and intertwine her fingers with his.

"Nothing... it's just that I think I need to go back to... that place." Still staring at the crack where the ant had disappeared, she braced herself for the knee-jerk safety precautions, the imminent no. Through her peripheral vision, she saw his Adam's apple bob. *Probably in panic.*

"Okay." He rolled his eyes when she pressed the back of her hand to his forehead. "I trust you."

"How long did you practice that in the mirror?"

Ignoring her comment, he continued. "If you think being there will bring back a memory or shed some light on this case, you should go. I would..."

"Yes?"

"I would like to go with you."

"Mind being trapped in a car with me… and Sara? Definitely listening to my Boy Bands of the 90s Pandora station."

He grimaced. "Is there such a thing?"

"Oh yeah. Backstreet Boys, NSYNC, 98 Degrees—"

"Okay, okay. I get it. And trust me, I've been stuck with worse. As long as I get shotgun, I don't care."

"That's between you and Sara. My money's on Sara." Returning his grin, she cupped his scruffy jawline, played her thumb over the bristly whiskers, and whispered, "You need to shave." At his frown, she kissed the dimple in his chin. "It's my turn to ask you what's wrong."

"We arrested Bryce."

Her thumb stopped its roaming, and she studied his face from his wrinkled brow to the worry clouding his blue eyes. "You have your doubts though, don't you?"

His laugh lacked any mirth. "I thought I'd feel ecstatic. Maybe even do a jig right there in Oliver's driveway when I found the—ah, evidence—but it's not sitting right. Something feels off."

"What does he say?"

"Won't talk until his lawyer gets here." He checked his watch. "His lawyer is vying for the slowest land speed record of any attorney."

"Can't you shake him down? Play some good cop, bad cop with him?"

"I imagined smashing his face in. Does that count?"

"It's close enough. For now."

A silence settled between them, and as twilight faded into night, Nikki found herself curled in Xavier's lap. She pressed her ear over his heart. In that moment, hearing the heart that beat only for her race under her touch, she chose her biggest and scariest adventure. Him.

Trailing her finger up and down his arm, she whispered, "I'm sorry."

Even though she couldn't see his face, his chin moving along the top of her head signaled his contortion to see hers. She buried her face in his chest.

"Nikki?" He lifted her chin with his index finger and met her gaze. "What could you possibly be sorry for?"

"Breaking your heart."

He rested his forehead against hers. "I broke yours first. But I'm thinking I broke your spirit long before that."

Pressing her finger against his lips, she shushed him. "We'll be sitting out here all night arguing about who's the worst one." She grinned. "I'd rather spend our time more wisely."

He trailed kisses along her ear. "As long as you admit we are both F-average students at relationships and promise to strive for at least a C-average relationship with me."

Goose bumps exploded on her skin as his kisses detoured from her ear to her neck. "That's the most romantic thing anyone has ever said to me."

"There's more where that came from. Just you wait." He nipped her collarbone.

"What are the chances of us getting an A?" Now her goose bumps had goose bumps.

"Fair to middling, but if I were a betting man—which I am—I'd say that practice makes perfect."

To stop her skin from igniting from his kisses, she smooshed his face between her hands until his lips resembled a kissing fish. "First lesson for both of us. You living under my parents' roof and not having Corrie drag you to good behavior by your earlobe."

"Have any easier lesson to get our feet wet?"

"No." She released his face, snuggled back into his chest, circled her finger over his heart, and sighed. "I want to know that even if my latest and greatest shenanigan blows up in my face, you will still hold me like this and keep the see-I-told-you-so to a quirk of your left eyebrow."

His chuckle rumbled through his chest and echoed in her ear. "What about my right? That's got a better quirk to it."

"Deal."

"I have to check with McGee and okay it with him, but you're right. Something about this doesn't feel right." He rubbed over where she'd completed several circles. "I have a few loose ends to tie up, but barring any calamity, it shouldn't take long, and we can head out tomorrow sometime." He kissed the top of her head. "Maybe we should leave Sara here. Someone to keep Thaddeus in check. He gets into trouble when left unsupervised."

"You are a very wise man."

"I should have recorded that."

"Your loss."

Author Note: Ah, the Boy Bands of the 90s. Is there anything better? Probably, but you'll have to do a lot of convincing first, so let's skip that mission and talk about the best of them all: The Backstreet Boys! Now, I know there is a strong Team NSYNC out there, and while I give them some credit, my boys will always be Backstreet. I was supposed to go to one of their concerts in 2020 but the event that shall not be named interrupted that, and I now wait for summer of 2022 to see the Backstreet Boys in concert. Tell me, are you Team Backstreet Boys, Team NSYNC, or Team Other Boy Band? Let me know at https://www.jessicabergbooks.com/contact.

Chapter 49

Xavier sank into his office chair and thunked his forehead on the desk. Five a.m. wake-up calls were never his favorite. Five a.m. calls that disentangled him from his dreams of Nikki based on the real snuggles shared the night before were definitely not his favorite. Honey-tongued lawyers with the personality of an angry hornet also made the blacklist. Especially at six in the morning. After an hour of his questions being batted away like the wet-behind-the-ears detective she clearly thought he was, he needed caffeine. He rotated his head until his temple rested in the spot his forehead had been, and he stared at his coffee cup. *Scratch that... more caffeine.*

Despite the nonanswers and evasion tactics, the identity of the flannel was clear. It was Bryce's. But one he hadn't seen for years. The last time he had seen it was in high school.

Xavier raised his head and squinted at the chalkboard.

"Knock, knock." Thaddeus entered, clutching a coffee cup in both hands. Apparently sensing Xavier's eagle eye on one of them, he brought them closer to his chest. "Nope. Both of these are for me. After that interview, I might need a whole pot. Steve headed to Oliver's house. Wants to see if he can get anything out of him."

Xavier grunted and came around his desk, leaned against it, and scowled at the chalkboard. "How does a guy lose his shirt only to have bits of it pop back up at the crime scenes of six women? And deny any part in the murders?"

Thaddeus opened his mouth and snapped it shut again. Grunting, he shrugged and took a sip of one of his coffees. "Do you believe him?"

"Yes," he ground out between gritted teeth. Everything in him, except his gut, told him Bryce was guilty. Like Nikki, he felt off about this case. Too many variables. Too many oddities. As a law enforcement officer, if morals hadn't played a role in not murdering six women, Bryce should have known better about the evidence. It was as if he wanted to get caught. All paths led to Bryce. So, that meant one of three things. Bryce was either an idiot—*not discounting that one so quickly*—or so ashamed of his actions that he wanted to get caught or so arrogant he didn't think he would get caught. Or as Bryce emphatically stated, he was innocent.

Xavier glanced at the clock hanging above the door. 7:10. Knowing Nikki, she would have packed for the trip complete with road trip snacks and was probably standing by the front door, her foot tapping with impatience. He didn't blame her. His own limbs twitched with anticipation at the trip. They would both have to wait, though, several long hours for her to figure out the answer to her gut instinct. If she found an answer at all. More than that, he wanted this all to be over with. He wanted to put murder behind him and blow some much-needed oxygen on his rekindled love with Nikki. But until he solved this case, life was on hold and murder took precedence. Scratching at his facial stubble, he bent over his coffee cup and frowned at the tiny dot of dark-brown liquid sitting at the bottom.

"Here." Thaddeus held out the second cup he had been holding.

Xavier nodded his thanks, took a bracing sip, and sighed. "Up for round two?"

Ten minutes later, Xavier and Thaddeus sat across from Bryce. His bright-eyed lawyer, Sheila Price, sipped on something that smelled like green tea. Xavier hated green tea.

Sheila folded her hands and rested them on the table. Her bright-red nails popped in color compared to her gray-and-light-blue-pinstripe suit, white collared shirt, and chestnut-brown hair pulled back into a ballerina bun. A single diamond pendant lay an inch below her clavicle, and a matching set of diamond studs winked from her ears.

"Agent Palinski, Agent Cornwall, I must object to this. My client was just questioned." She studied Xavier's face. The sharpness of her green eyes showed a hunt for any tells. Bad for her and good for him, he was an excellent poker player. "Unless you have something to offer or another line of questioning that does not deal with your recent accusations, I will have to ask that this interview be over."

He leaned back in his chair and linked his fingers behind his head. Ignoring Sheila, he directed his attention to Bryce. "Quid pro quo?"

"Agent—"

Paying no attention to Sheila's outburst, he spread his arms out. "Mr. Beaumont, this is my last offer. The evidence against you is, for the lack of a better word, damning. The head prosecuting attorney is itching to take this to court. And trust me, she's a bulldog in the courtroom. Isn't that right, Agent Cornwall?"

"Hasn't lost a case yet."

Sweat beaded on Bryce's forehead, and his tongue flicked out and licked his lips, but he remained silent.

After grabbing the manila envelope Thaddeus handed him, Xavier opened it and laid out six pictures of the victims, lining them up so they faced Bryce. At the end of the row, he set the evidence bag enclosing the flannel. Bryce eyed it as if it were a cobra wriggling to free itself and bite him.

"The theatrics are a little unnecessary, don't you think, Agent?" Sheila's gaze flicked over the pictures and held steady on the flannel.

"Mr. Beaumont, in true quid pro quo style, I will go first. From what I understand, you were an upstanding officer of the law, and that you gave it all up to help your ailing great-uncle is admirable. I respect that."

Bryce blinked but remained silent.

"I also think the evidence against you is a little too damning. A little too convenient."

Bryce sat up straight, his shoulders so rigid, it looked as if they would shatter. But still, he did not speak.

Xavier pointed to each of the pictures. "Each one of these women had their lives ripped away from them. You once took an oath to protect people, women like these six. When I first came to town, you told me you would do whatever you could to assist. Now is your time to keep your side of the bargain."

"I—" Bryce's voice cracked. "I didn't kill them. I wouldn't—couldn't—do that to anyone."

"But this is your shirt?" Xavier tapped the plastic evidence bag.

"Bryce, I recommend you do not answer any more of his questions."

Brushing away Sheila's advice, Bryce nodded. "Yes. That is my shirt. But I do not know how it got into my toolbox or how pieces of it are at the crime scenes. I haven't seen that shirt since high school."

"Where did you donate it?" Thaddeus asked.

"I didn't."

Sheila cleared her throat and opened her mouth to speak.

Bryce held up his hand to stem whatever she was about to say. "It went missing. That's all. One day, it was in my closet, and the next time I wanted to wear it, it was gone."

"Who had access to your room?" Xavier set his pen to his notepad, primed to jot notes.

"You're serious? You think someone stole my shirt and years later—"

"I don't think anything right now. I need the facts. Tell me all you remember. Do not leave any detail out. Understand me?"

"It was after a huge fight with my girlfriend. Now that I think about it, more than my shirt went missing. She'd taken back anything she'd bought me. An act of revenge?" He shrugged. "Anyway, we got back together a couple of weeks later, kissed and made up, and life seemed pretty good."

"Girlfriend's name?"

"Beatrice. Beatrice Hansen."

Xavier's lone poker tell he had weaned from his system—a twitchy top lip—flickered to life. "What happened after that?" But he already knew what happened to Beatrice Hansen, or the woman calling herself that. Xavier glanced at Bryce's stoic face. He either didn't know she was dead or didn't care... or had done the deed himself and staged it as self-inflicted.

"We were together off and on for a couple of years. Toxic, really. Looking back, I should have never made up with her after she stole all my stuff. It ended two years ago when I moved to Custer."

"Why?"

Sighing, Bryce rubbed the back of his neck. "Not proud of it, but life with her stopped being an adventure and more of a job, you know? She only took jobs that paid in cash, so she was constantly mooching off me. And I was so tired of her manipulative behavior that I looked for comfort elsewhere, if you know what I mean. Well, before I could tell her, apologize, and discuss ending our relationship, she found out. Without a word to me or anyone else, she left Custer. I haven't heard from her since. I stopped calling and texting after one hundred messages went unanswered."

"What about her family?"

"What family? Her father had died before I met her, and Beatrice hated her mother, wanted nothing to do with her. I never met the woman."

"That didn't seem strange to you?"

"At the time, I was so intoxicated with her beauty that I could hardly see straight. Not meeting her mother didn't even register on my radar. Then, after we had seen each other for a while, whenever I brought up the subject of meeting her mom, she would fly into a rage, accuse me of wanting to see her confront the woman who had ruined her life, even claimed the thought aroused me." He shivered.

"Did she ever elaborate?"

"No. All she ever said was that her mother was a manipulative woman who would do anything, no matter the cost, to get her way. It took me too long to realize the apple hadn't fallen far from the tree."

No one said anything for several moments. Xavier's pen scratched along the notepad.

"The woman you cheated with?"

Bryce's eyes squinted. "I can't. I won't."

"May I remind you what's at stake here? That there's apparently a person out there that hates you so much he or she wants to frame you for multiple murders." Xavier worked his jaw back and forth to relieve the building tightness. "What did she look like? Hair color, body style?"

Bryce closed his eyes as if exasperated and snapped them open. His blue eyes sparked with anger. "Her name is Cecilia Montgomery. I haven't heard from her since I broke off the affair—no—I can't believe—no, it's not possible."

"What's not possible?"

"Cecilia is beautiful, slender build, and..."

"And?" Xavier pressed the tip of his pen so hard into his notepad it speared several sheets of paper.

"Blond." He pressed his palms together as if in prayer. "Please, I need to know if she's okay."

Thaddeus took down all the information Bryce had on Cecilia and left the room.

Doodling in the margins of his notepad, Xavier curled a circle around the word "mother." "You sure there's nothing you can tell me about Beatrice's mom? Maybe she slipped up with the name? Think. Anything."

Bryce's face screwed up in thought, and his fingers drummed on the tabletop. Seconds ticked by and expanded into minutes. Xavier was about to call for a break, when Bryce's fingers stilled, twitched, and pressed hard on the table's surface.

"There was one night. We were still in high school—well, I went to high school, she was 'homeschooled,' and this was after the big fight. I had stolen some whiskey from my dad, and we were half the bottle in when we played truth or dare. On one of the times she selected truth, I asked her the craziest thing her mother had ever done." He rubbed his hand over his mouth as if wiping away the taste of whiskey. "She... uh... was pretty drunk, and I'm sure if she'd been sober, she never would have told me."

"What did she say?" Sheila surprised Xavier—and Bryce—if raised eyebrows meant surprise for him. By now, Bryce had silenced Sheila so many times that she had busied herself with jotting down notes. What she wrote, Xavier had no clue, but he had never seen a black pen cursive itself across and down pages and pages of a yellow legal pad at such speeds before.

Bryce inhaled, held his breath, and exhaled slowly through his nose. "When she was a freshman, this was before she moved to town, her boyfriend had tried to take advantage of her at a party. When she told her mom about it, her mom ordered her to keep it a secret and not talk about the assault. Within one week, the boy's neighbor's dog was found mutilated, and all evidence pointed to the boyfriend. He was charged and spent a year in juvie."

"Don't tell me, the boyfriend didn't do it." Like Legos snapping into place, evidence and clues clicked together in Xavier's brain. Anticipation swirled in his gut, and his body was hyperaware of every sensation, every touch. The ridges of the individual weaves of his polo shirt pushed against his skin. The backside of the embroidered DCI logo scratched against his pectoral muscle. He wriggled his toes against a sock that had shifted a millimeter off-kilter.

"Her mom did it all. Killed and mutilated the dog and planted the evidence. Beatrice hated her mother after that. Refused to talk about her or introduce anyone new to her mother. She also refused to go to school. Said she did better teaching herself. Fear, I guess." Bryce massaged his temples. "That was the last time... only time she ever talked about her mother."

Thaddeus entered the room, and from the look on his face, Xavier sensed the news was not good. Bryce must have noticed it too. His face bleached, and he nibbled at a cuticle.

"Cecilia Montgomery died five months ago in Topeka, Kansas. The case file says her friends claimed she'd gone back home after things didn't work out in Custer. Blunt force trauma to the head. Traces of chloroform in her system." Thaddeus slapped a piece of paper on the table and slid it over to Bryce. "And the only thing missing, according to the parents, was a cross necklace she'd gotten the day of her confirmation."

Bryce stared at the jotted-down information so long Xavier feared shock had paralyzed him.

"Bryce?"

He blinked and wiped the back of his hand across his mouth. "I... ah..."

"What kind of vehicle did Beatrice drive?"

His eyes squinted. "Um, an SUV. It was a dark color. Don't remember the exact color. She didn't have it long after we met because her mother took it away from her for some reason. After that, I had to drive Beatrice everywhere."

Xavier nodded to a waiting deputy, who escorted Bryce from the room.

Xavier didn't need to ask for the mother's name again. He knew how to find it. And as a betting man, he knew what name he would see. He would see the name of Beatrice's mom and the name of a killer.

A*uthor Note: Coffee, otherwise known as the elixir of the gods. Oddly enough, I hated coffee up until a few years ago, and now it is my only breakfast. Probably not healthy, but I'm sure there are other things I could be ingesting that are much worse. I like flavored coffee, and I take it black. If you're a coffee drinker, how do you take yours? And, if you're not a coffee drinker, what's your hot beverage of choice? Let me know at https://www.jessicabergbooks.com/contact.*

Chapter 50

Nikki was down to one unmaimed cuticle. The morning sun had already risen past sunrise and was powering up to bake everything in sight. Or maybe the sweat beading on her skin was nerves. That would match her queasy tummy.

"Nikki!"

Pinky to her lips, Nikki spun around too quickly and grasped the porch railing for balance.

"Mom, you scared the living daylights out of me."

Handing her a heavy cardboard box, Cynthia grinned. "That's too bad. Thought it might scare some sense into you."

"Ha ha." Nikki jiggled the box. Jars rattled. "What's this? I won't be gone that long. Xavier and I should be back tomorrow if everything goes as planned."

"Not for you. Eleanor mentioned the last time she was here that she liked the canned venison I had made for supper. I also threw in some of last year's canned applesauce. Without Nathan here to eat it, the jars stare at me whenever I go into the pantry. Thought it'd be nice to share with her." Cynthia rested her hand on Nikki's shoulder. "I think Eleanor's been through some pretty tough times. Would you and Sara mind running it into town before you go? Might cheer her up a bit."

"But—"

"You two will have plenty of time to get there and back before Xavier shows up. Trust me. When men say two hours, they mean four. Besides, if I have to watch you chew your fingers anymore, I'll go berserk. And don't forget to take Sara."

"But—Sara's playing so nicely with TT. I'll just leave her here. Like you said, it'll be a quick trip."

Cynthia readjusted the slipping box in Nikki's arms and placed the pickup keys on top. "Are you sure about this? We promised Xavier so faithfully." Her teeth worried her bottom lip.

"Mom, I'll be fine. It's only Eleanor. Maybe I'll stop and say hi to Violet and Iris too. That's it."

"I—ah—are you sure?"

"Mom, remember what you said about fences?"

Cynthia bowed her head. "You're right. Just be quick, and don't stop anywhere besides Eleanor's and Violet's, okay?"

All the way to Sandy, Nikki's stomach squirmed like a ball of worms. Crossing into city limits, she eyed Mabel's café. Maybe she was hungry. She hadn't eaten yet, and Mabel's caramel rolls always delivered the desired effect of a full belly and sugar high. If her mother was right about Man Time, she had a few extra moments to spare.

After zipping into a parking spot, she entered the café, reciprocated the waves sent her way, and hopped onto a bar stool.

"Ah, finally come into work, have you?" Mabel's voice scolded before the woman made an appearance through the saloon doors.

"I know. I'm so sorry. I promise to make it up to you."

Mabel's harrumph and heaving bosom told Nikki everything she needed to know. *Buttering the old woman up might not be a bad idea.* After praising her caramel rolls and general cooking wizardry, Nikki ordered one.

Xavier's comment about the entire world knowing about her run-in with the killer all because she told Eleanor niggled at the back of her mind.

She swallowed her last bite of caramel roll. "Mabel, you outdid yourself again. That was delicious."

Mabel shooed the compliment away and reached for her dirty plate and fork.

"Say"—Nikki leaned over the counter, resting her forearms on the Formica top. "Heard any juicy gossip lately?"

Mabel's wizened eyes pinned her with a quizzical look. "Since when are you into gossip?"

Since a killer may or may not know that I took his picture.

"Just wanted to keep my nose to the ground. See if I could sniff any clues out. You know, help out Xavier."

"You help out Xavier?" Mabel squinted at Nikki. "Since when—" Her gnarled hands grasped Nikki's. "You mean, you two are..."

"Now don't get too excited. Don't go planning the wedding supper."

But it was too late. From the gleam in the old woman's eyes, Nikki suspected she'd already created the menu down to the different pies she would serve alongside the wedding cake. Looked like everyone had their wedding planned except for the unasked bride and clueless groom.

Before Mabel could plan anything else, Nikki tapped the back of her hand. "So, any gossip around the place?"

"Don't suspect you care about the Ladies' Aide Society and how all the women are blaming voter fraud for Maude getting Ladies' Aide Society president."

"Not sure I care in the slightest."

"Hmph... in that case, I got nothing for you."

Other than the bar, Mabel's Café was the meeting place for Sandy's most notorious gossipers. If Mabel hadn't heard that the killer had been captured on film, her secret was still safe. Eleanor hadn't blabbed.

A weight lifted off her shoulders, and the pressure that had built up in her chest released. "Good. Just wanted to be sure we weren't missing something. You'll let me know, though, if something comes up?"

"If you ever get your butt back to work." Mabel didn't wait for Nikki's response and waddled off to serve customers who walked in.

Nikki plunked down some cash and left the café. Time to drop off the jars, head back home, and wait.

A few minutes later she parked her pickup in front of the two-story house two miles out of town that Eleanor rented. During hunting season, it was a prime hunter's lodge, but during the summer, it was left to molder in the sunshine and heat. Built for utility instead of beauty, the square building squatted on its plot of land with no adornment except for one lone pink flamingo.

What used to be white paint had grayed with age, and dark splotches betrayed spots where the paint had chipped off, exposing the wooden siding to the elements. The owner of the rental house had tried to spruce things up by painting the window trim evergreen, but he had either hired toddlers to complete the job or done it himself after a night out at the Pheasants' Roost, the bar in town.

After navigating the cracked sidewalk, Nikki rested the heavy box on her bent knee, rested both against the doorjamb, and knocked. Seconds ticked by. Then minutes. Her leg quaking from the weight of the box, she knocked again. Harder.

The doorknob twisted, and Eleanor, clad in black yoga pants and a pink T-shirt, opened the door. "Nikki, what a surprise. Come on in."

"My mom sent this box for you. Venison and applesauce." She stepped over the threshold to the kitchen and set the box on the red-and-black-speckled lacquered tabletop. The metal legs squeaked under the weight of the box.

Eleanor had attempted to make something of the retro kitchen, but when orange covered every surface from the sink to the cupboards to the countertops and even to the orange specks in the green linoleum, there was only so much a girl could do.

"Hope you like the color orange." Nikki opened the box and took out a jar of applesauce. "Where would you like me to put these?"

"You can keep them in there. I'll find a place later."

Shrugging, Nikki went to put the jar back when it slipped from her fingers and shattered on the floor, splattering applesauce and glass feet away from the impact zone. "Crap! I'm so sorry." She grabbed the garbage can, fell to her knees, and began picking up the bigger pieces of glass.

"Don't worry about it. Here, let me. I would hate for you to cut yourself."

Cold heat sliced through her palm. She hissed in pain and clenched her hand into a fist. "Too late."

Eleanor reached for her wrist and pried open her hand. Blood oozed from the deep cut etched into her palm. "Let's get you bandaged up. Leave it. I'll get it later," she scolded after Nikki grabbed another piece of glass and chucked it in the garbage.

Following Eleanor through the tiny living room, empty except for an old box-style television and tattered couch, Nikki closed her fist and cupped her good hand under to catch any drops of blood.

They both squeezed into the bathroom, and Eleanor pointed to the pink toilet. "Sit."

Nikki shut the lid and sat down, cradling her stinging fist in her lap. "Sorry to be such a bother."

Waving away her apology, Eleanor opened the mirrored bathroom vanity, shuffled around bottles and tubes, and unearthed bandages and a brown bottle of peroxide. "I'm not sure how old these things are. Must have been left by hunters. But they'll do for now." Bathroom almost too small for one person to move around comfortably, Eleanor half leaned, half sat on the pink counter and rested

Nikki's hand on her thigh. She tutted. "This is pretty deep. You might want to go in for stitches." Eleanor sprinkled the antiseptic on the cut.

Hissing through her teeth as the peroxide bubbled and sizzled over her wound, Nikki shook her head. "Can't. Don't have time."

Eleanor wiped the foamy blood from the cut with a cotton ball and poured some more peroxide on the wound. "This looks serious, though. You should make time. What's so important you can't get this looked at?"

"Leaving for—" *Idiot! This is exactly why people don't think I can take care of myself.* "Just a road trip."

"Anywhere special?" Eleanor dabbed the cut again, waved her hand over it to dry any moisture away, and unpeeled the packaging away from the Band-Aid and stuck it over the cut. "This isn't going to work. These will fall off the first time you do any movement with your hand." Her face scrunched. "Oh, I know. I'll be back."

Alone in the bathroom, Nikki eyed the matching pink sink and pink-tiled shower. She was trapped in a bottle of Pepto Bismol. Before she succumbed to the sensation and tasted the chalky liquid, she left the pink nightmare. "Eleanor?"

Silence.

To her left was a set of stairs leading up to the second floor. Might as well save Eleanor a trip. The wooden steps creaked as she ascended. Reaching the top step, she turned the corner and peeked into the first bedroom. Empty. The second room proved the same. The last door off the hallway was half-closed.

"Knock, knock." Nikki pushed the door open. "Sorry, I was totally creeped out by all the pink..."

Eleanor spun around, slammed a dresser drawer shut, and clutched a sock to her chest. Her face paled.

"Sorry. Thought you heard me."

The room was shabby chic, but more shabby and less chic. Chipped baby-blue paint created odd shapes on the walls, and the navy-blue shag carpeting that hadn't been the rage since the sixties looked as tired and worn as the drooping curtain rod doing its best to keep a translucent-blue swag curtain from tumbling to the floor.

Nikki eyed the bed covered with folded clothes. Two empty suitcases lined the wall. Just like the rest of the house. Empty. Nothing personal. Nothing to make the place a home. How awful to have nothing to make a space hers. Eleanor deserved better than that.

"Moving out?"

Still clutching the sock to her chest, Eleanor skirted the edge of the bed until her hip knocked up against the bedside table. A picture frame sitting on the table shook with the force. "Yeah, Natasha's family is selling the butcher shop."

"That doesn't mean you have to leave. Why don't you stay awhile, see what else Sandy has to offer?" She pointed to the framed picture of a young, pretty brunette. "Is that your daughter?"

Without following Nikki's gaze, Eleanor approached Nikki with the sock. "Yeah. Here, hold out your hand."

Nikki did as ordered. As Eleanor wrapped the sock around her hand, Nikki studied the woman's bent head. Graying roots tattled on the woman's dye job. Uncomfortable silence filled the air. *Say something!* "I bet you're going to see your daughter. Don't blame you, especially with everything that's been going on."

Eleanor sighed. "Wish I could. She died two years ago."

"I'm so sorry! Me and my big mouth. I assumed... with how you've spoken of her... that... never mind. I'm shutting up now."

"Don't apologize. I'm afraid I deal with my daughter's death in a rather unorthodox way." Eleanor finished wrapping Nikki's hand and tucked the end of the sock under the wrapped sections. "There, you are all fixed up. Probably not enough for your mysterious road trip, though."

Nikki couldn't imagine being all alone in the world, with nothing and nobody. She would have gone postal. "Look, I meant to thank you as well for keeping my blabbing about the photograph to yourself. I'm sure if I had said that to anyone else, everyone in the county would have known."

"I understand the importance of secrets."

Nikki's phone buzzed in her back pocket. Probably Xavier. "Oh, I'm being summoned. Spent too much time gabbing... and bleeding all over your kitchen floor. I should go. Xavier's waiting for me."

"Are you and Agent Palinski going somewhere?"

She'd done it again. Tempted to slap herself silly so her family wouldn't have to, she grinned sheepishly. "Look at me. I can't keep a secret to save my life."

"That's too bad. Secrets are sacred, don't you think?" Eleanor stepped over to the dresser and opened another drawer.

Something in Eleanor's tone made the hair on Nikki's neck rise. "Yeah, sure. I might not get into as much trouble if I knew how to zip my lip." Forcing a smile, she glanced again at the picture of Eleanor's daughter and froze. Sticking out of a pile of clothes Eleanor's body had blocked was a pattern that had haunted Nikki's thoughts. A red-and-green checked flannel.

No matter how her brain tried to reconcile seeing it on Eleanor's bed, her muscles tightened, and her heart throbbed, pumping tsunami waves of blood through her body. "Look." Nikki wiped her dried lips and forced her gaze away from the shirt. Maybe if she pretended she hadn't seen it, hadn't recognized it, Eleanor would be none the wiser. "I, ah, got to get going. I'll let my mom know about the applesauce jar. I'm sure she'll give you a different one. She's constantly cleaning up after my messes." If her voice sounded as high-pitched and panicky to Eleanor as it did to her, she was in trouble.

Her gaze locked with Eleanor's.

She was in trouble. Big trouble.

"I wish you hadn't seen that." Eleanor took one step toward her.

"See what? Oh, the flannel. I was thinking that I have the same in my closet at home. Did you get yours at Walmart?"

"I wish you would have stayed in the bathroom."

Me too. "What can I say? I don't like pink." Nikki grabbed the closest thing to her, the picture frame, chucked it at Eleanor's face, and ran from the room.

Glass shattered, and a shrill scream echoed as Nikki's feet thundered down the steps and through the kitchen. Her hand clenched the doorknob, twisted.

White-hot heat punched her in the soft flesh of her shoulder. An explosion burst in the air. She staggered to the ground, and her good hand smashed into shards of applesauce-covered glass.

Her ears rang. Her shoulder burned. Her hands tingled.

A clammy hand stuck to her forehead.

A blur of flannel cloth.

A too-sweet fruity odor.

Each of Eleanor's victims flashed through Nikki's mind. Just as quickly as they appeared, they evaporated, leaving shadows of faces then darkness.

Author Note: Small-town gossip earned its popular stereotype for a reason. Often enough, my parents knew what I did before I even knew it. Here are a few other "you know you're from a small town when" moments:

When asked where you live, you give the nearest town with a Walmart.

Driving twenty minutes to get groceries or go out to eat is considered nothing.

Traffic jams usually occur due to a slow-moving farm implement.

Directions are given in landmarks and not street names.

High school sporting events are a big deal and source of entertainment for the whole community.

You can list the first and last names of your graduating class.

The university you went to after high school had double or triple the number of people as your hometown.

The closest shopping mall is over an hour away.

You are an expert at driving on gravel roads.

All you past or present small-towners, what else can we add to this list? Let me know at https://www.jessicabergbooks.com/contact.

Chapter 51

Xavier jammed the Return key on his laptop. The death certificate belonging to Jane Doe, aka Beatrice Hansen, proved useless, so Xavier dove into old *Rapid City Journal* articles, scouring news of Keystone, South Dakota, that included St. John. Within minutes, a picture of Eleanor and a teenage girl standing in front of a flower garden smiled from the screen. The caption read "Eleanor and Kendra St. John, mother and daughter, win local gardening contest."

His fingers flew across the keyboard in search of Kendra. A search that dried up. Nothing existed after her sixteenth birthday.

He checked his phone for the fiftieth time that morning. Nothing from Nikki. Growling, he plunked it down on his desk and stared at his computer's screen. A thought niggled at the back of his mind. Kendra's face looked oddly familiar.

He scanned the file the lead officer on Beatrice's death had sent him and clicked on the photos attached. Even in death, the two women looked startlingly familiar.

If he'd been standing, he might have stumbled backward, but as he was sitting, he leaned forward and stared at the faces of death. If his eyes weren't playing tricks on him, Kendra St. John and Beatrice Hansen were the same woman.

Eleanor St. John. He wasn't sure how she did it or why she did it, but his cop gut told him Eleanor St. John had more to hide than crazy.

He jumped to his feet, snatched his phone, and made two phone calls—one to a judge issuing a search warrant and the other to Nikki.

After her voicemail message told him to have an adventurous and fun-filled day, he pleaded, "Please, Nikki, when you get this, call me. I think the killer is Eleanor. Please..." He paced the room and swallowed the fear clogging his throat. "Please. Call me."

Within minutes, the search warrant came through, and in under ten, he and Thaddeus, followed by two deputies, parked in the driveway of Eleanor's house. After peeking inside the windows of Eleanor's car, he stalked up the front steps, fisted his hand, and pounded on the door.

Silence.

He knocked again.

Thaddeus circled around the back and, before long, came back. "Back door is locked. No signs of life."

Biting back a swear word, Xavier made a few calls, and after speaking to the owner of the house, found the hide-a-key in a hole bored into the underside of a pink plastic flamingo.

His heart thundered in his chest as he slipped the key into the lock and twisted the door handle. No ominous creaks accompanied the spidery nerves crawling up and down his skin.

"Hello? Eleanor? This is the police. We have a warrant for your arrest and a search warrant to search the house, property, and your vehicle."

After drawing his gun, he opened the door inch by inch. And froze. A stew of brown goo, shattered glass, and splotches of red littered the kitchen floor. His heart dropped to his feet. His gut churned. Sweat beaded on his skin.

Low and slow, Xavier crept into the kitchen, stepping over the debris. "Clear."

He and the rest of the officers cleared every room of the house.

No sign of Eleanor.

After leaving another voice message on Nikki's voicemail, Xavier cracked his knuckles and gathered his evidence kit. With clear instructions and the house and property broken up into quadrants, the four men set to work gathering evidence. The two deputies headed outside to search the two small outbuildings. Thaddeus began his search of the basement.

Ignoring the cardboard box on the table for now, Xavier crouched and scooped up a glob of the brown goo and smelled it. *Applesauce.* After collecting a sample of the applesauce, he used his tweezers to pinch a few glass shards into an evidence bag. He squinted at the red blotches and followed the trail into a bathroom so small he could have used the toilet and washed his hands simultaneously.

An open bottle of peroxide sat on the counter, and the flimsy white backing of bandages and pinkish-colored cotton balls littered the floor. He collected a sample of the peroxide, slipped the pieces of trash in a bag, and headed for the stairs.

Xavier took the steps two at a time and bypassed the first two empty rooms. The farthest room from the steps must have been Eleanor's, as it was the only one to have a bed or any furniture at all. Clothing was strewn over the cream-colored chenille bedspread. He pinched the collar of a wrinkled hot-pink T-shirt between his fingers and inspected it. From the condition of the kitchen and the bandages in the bathroom, Eleanor had probably cut herself on the broken jar and changed.

A shattered picture frame lay in the middle of the floor. Xavier flipped it over. His blood ran cold.

Beatrice Hansen.

Marks indented into the ugly carpet matched the dimensions of suitcases.

Eleanor St. John obviously didn't plan on returning. And she hadn't bothered cleaning up after herself.

His spine tingled, but he pushed the sensation aside and opened a narrow door on the far side of the room. It led into a closet bigger than the door foretold, and Xavier stepped in and searched for a light switch. His hand fluttered above his head and swatted against a metal chain. He pulled it, and light flooded the small closet large enough for three of him. Sticky residue littered the walls. After snapping pictures of the walls, he scraped at different patches of goo and collected them for evidence. Probably nothing more than standard clear tape, but cases were sometimes broken or made on innocuous-looking evidence. He measured the spots and guessed the tape once adhered at least twelve standard five-by-eight pictures to the wall.

The shag carpet of the bedroom leached in the closet. Several indentations in the woven blue pile marked where objects had squished the carpet. Before obscuring them in his search, Xavier took a few pictures of the indents. On hands and knees, Xavier slipped off one glove and trailed his hand over the fluffy carpet. His fingers brushed up against a small, hard object. Glove back on, he pinched it between his thumb and forefinger and stared at the aquamarine gem stud earring. After placing the earring in an evidence bag and labeling it, he plowed the carpet for more clues but came up empty-handed.

Search complete, Xavier checked his phone. Nikki should have called him by now. Knowing service was sketchy on the Lancaster farm and that a text rather than a phone call might squeak through, he shot off a text. *Nikki, I need to know you got my message. Please!*

Thaddeus and the two deputies, Henderson, who had proved an excellent officer, and a newbie on the Sandy County Sheriff's Department, Kelley, were gathered around a red-and-black-speckled lacquered tabletop.

The metal legs squeaked when Xavier set his kit next to the closed cardboard box.

Each shared their finds. Henderson found a charred piece of denim in a burned-out five-gallon metal drum. Whoever had set fire to the objects had not stayed around to ensure a complete job. Kelley had searched the outbuildings and found nothing out of the norm for a gardening shed. As a newbie, he'd gotten the short end of the stick and had searched the garbage bin.

Xavier read down the list Kelley handed him. He squinted at a few of the items. Several Takis bags, empty twenty-ounce bottles of Diet Coke, and two bottles of Jack joined a menagerie of other household trash. To Xavier, this was conclusive; to a good defense attorney, this would be circumstantial. Just because Michelle Osbourne bought the same combination at a Casey's gas station in Sturgis wouldn't win the case alone. But Xavier wasn't Eleanor's future defense attorney, and his gut told him that the same person who had ingested the questionable concoction in Sturgis and probably killed Michelle Osbourne was the same person who had called this rental house home for several weeks. The same person who had weaseled her way into the Sandy community and Lancaster family and had discovered the one person on this planet who had photographed her.

Almost afraid of what he would find in the box, he peeled back the four flaps. His stomach careened to the kitchen floor. There was one woman he knew of that put her initials and the date on each lid of the jars she canned. Cynthia Lancaster.

Ignoring the questioning glances of Thaddeus and the deputies, he whipped out his phone and did what he swore at himself for not doing earlier. He called the Lancasters' landline and waited. Each ring meant seconds he didn't have. Each ring lasted for minutes.

"Hello?"

"Cynthia, is Nikki there?"

"No." Something in his voice must have alerted her. "Why? What's happened?"

"Do you know where she went?"

Please don't say Eleanor's. Please don't say—

"Eleanor's." Silence. "Xavier, what's going on, please—"

"Stay by the phone. And as soon as Nikki gets home, call me." Not waiting for an answer, he ended the call and ran outside.

Nikki's pickup was not parked alongside Eleanor's car.

Bile rose in his throat.

He had failed at the one thing he'd thought he could never fail at: keeping his Nikki safe.

Author Note: Keystone, South Dakota, is a gorgeous town in the shadow of Mount Rushmore. If you're looking for adventure, nature, exploring caves, or tourist-y destinations, Keystone has you covered. Hopefully, by now, you've included the Black Hills on your travel bucket list, but if you haven't, maybe looking into Keystone will clinch the deal. Trust me. This is the hub of most Black Hills adventures and smack dab in the center of the Black Hills. While this is one of my favorite vacation spots, I understand that everyone has different preferences. If you could go anywhere in the world, money and time are no issue, where would you go and why? Let me know at https://www.jessicabergbooks.com/contact.

Chapter 52

Blackness faded to gray. A dull sense of pain throbbing throughout her body evolved into pulsing, screaming points in her shoulder and her hands, and her brain felt two sizes too big for her head.

Nikki forced her eyes open and snapped them shut. *No!* She couldn't be back here.

Knowing the truth, no matter how awful, was much better than believing in a lie, no matter how enticing, she opened her eyes again. Two holes, a gaping one that Xavier and Bryce had created and the mid-sized one she'd been stuck in days ago. Sunlight bathing the upper floors in light and warmth did not penetrate the dank darkness. Groaning, she rocked her head side to side, more to check if her head was still attached to her body.

"Careful," Eleanor crooned from the darkness. "We want you in good condition when you meet my daughter."

Nikki's mouth went dry. Even if she had a retort, her tongue could not cooperate.

"It'll be a bit longer. Then all will be ready."

With her head tilted to the side, Nikki could barely make out an Eleanor-sized shadow among the larger shadows of the farthest corner. Her world turned blurry. Blinking against the unconsciousness coming upon her, she breathed deeply, concentrating on every breath.

A band of pressure squeezed around Nikki's upper left arm. She reached across her body and played with the frayed threads of a rag.

"What kind of mother would I be if I let you bleed out before it's time?" Eleanor stepped from the shadows.

Unconsciousness almost won out over will. Nikki bit back a scream. No longer clad in black yoga pants and a pink T-shirt, Eleanor was decked out in jeans and a red-and-green flannel, and her long brown hair was tucked up under a red baseball cap shading her face now covered with tufts of hair.

"Shh, it's okay," Eleanor whispered and kneeled next to Nikki's head. Her shaking fingers stroked a strand of Nikki's hair. "It'll be okay in the end. I promise. It won't hurt."

Nikki shook her head to ward off Eleanor's stroking. Pain exploded behind her eyes, and stars flickered in her peripheral vision.

"See, now you've gone and hurt yourself again." Eleanor bent down, her lips touching Nikki's earlobe, and whispered, "It's almost time. But I don't want you hurting yourself. You've forced me to put you in time-out."

The ludicrous words snaked into her ear and vibrated down her spine.

Eleanor left her side. The darkness hid her movements, but tin pinged against tin. Fibers swept the floor. A wooden object fell and splintered on the hard dirt floor.

It was clear the woman was insane. What was not as clear was how Nikki would escape. Nobody came back to the old house. Except for Bryce, of course, but he was locked in a jail cell. And Xavier, but he was interrogating Bryce.

More noise rustled from the dark. Nikki slithered her hand down her side, hissed when the sock bandage caught and tore at her cut, and fished in her pocket for her phone. A sense of dread dropped like a cement block on her chest. She couldn't breathe. Empty-handed, she cradled her palm between her breasts and pushed down to remind her lungs to inhale and let up to guide her lungs in the opposite direction. She would not die down here in a decrepit basement in the bowels of a decaying house. And if she had to remind her lungs about the plan, she would.

Eleanor gave a small victory cry. She must have found what she wanted.

Nikki channeled her anger, her fear, her will to live. Her heart felt two sizes too big for her ribs, and she glanced down at her chest to double-check that her heart wasn't escaping out of her breast.

"There, knew I had it somewhere. Mind must be going. Age does that, you know." She retook her spot next to Nikki's head and threaded a piece of Nikki's hair between her fingers. "Here, now be a good girl and give me your hands."

After clasping her hands together, Nikki rested her elbows on the ground and raised her arms right above her chest.

Please, God, please. She'd never been one to give credence to God's audible voice, but somewhere, somehow, she felt the word *yoga*. Of all the answers she expected, that was not it, but it hit her. If she had abs to control her legs going down, she had the strength to go in the opposite direction. She nestled her elbows in tighter to her sides.

"That's a good girl. Like all my daughters. Such a good girl." The loose tassels of a rope slid over Nikki's forearm. "There, now hold still for Mommy, and we'll be done, okay? All the bad things will go away. I promise."

Tightening her abs and anchoring her elbows on the basement floor, Nikki hefted her legs up and, spiraling a little to the right, kicked at Eleanor's face.

A crunch, a scream, a crack. And silence broken by Nikki's desperate gasps for air. After rolling to her good side, she struggled to her knees and swayed. Pain exploded in her right arm. Seconds later, warm liquid oozed down her arm and dripped off her fingertips. They pinged against a piece of tin on the floor. *Ping, ping, ping...*

She snatched at the loose rag and, using her teeth, tied the material as tight as she could.

In the murky light leaking through the holes and broken teeth of the above floor, Nikki kneed herself over to a support pillar and, digging her fingernails into the rotting wood, clawed herself to a stand.

Her head felt weightless. She rested a hand on top of it to keep it from floating off her body.

Eleanor groaned.

Nikki's heart stopped, skipped double time, and thundered in her chest. She grabbed the rope Eleanor had unearthed, and before she let pain or dizziness stop her, she rolled Eleanor onto her stomach, wrestled her arms behind her back, and tightened the rope around Eleanor's wrists.

Nikki staggered backward, caught herself on the support pillar, and pushed herself into a stand once again.

Eleanor's groans turned to whimpers. "Don't leave me," she whispered. "I need to see my daughter. Don't take her away from me." She breathed an animal-like, guttural moan into the floor. "Please. Don't abandon me. We were going to meet her together, you and me. She would have loved her new sister." She turned her head, sliding her nose along the floor until her dilated gaze bored into Nikki. "Wouldn't you have liked that? Having a sister?"

Nausea swirled in Nikki's gut. Using various odds and ends rotting away in the basement, Nikki walked herself over to where Eleanor had rooted around earlier. Her fingers brushed against fiber. She grasped the rope with her good hand, limped over to Eleanor, sat backward on the woman's thighs, and wrapped it around her ankles several times before tying off the coil.

"Don't you want a sister?" Eleanor whined and bucked underneath Nikki.

Woozy and lightheaded, Nikki scraped herself off Eleanor. "I already have a sister."

She stumbled to the steps, caught herself with her bad arm, and screamed. Blinking against the starbursts threatening to blind her, she crawled, hand over hand, knee over knee, up the rotting steps. Eleanor's strangled cries followed her.

After climbing what felt like Mt. Everest, she collapsed on the remaining edge of the first floor.

"Kend—Beatrice," Eleanor panted from the depths. "Please, come back, Beatrice." A wail pierced the air. "I'm sorry."

Using her good arm to military crawl along the edge, Nikki made it to the kitchen's entrance and solid flooring. Not wanting to take the chances of falling back down into the abyss with a delusional serial killer, she crawled through the muck and dirt and animal droppings all the way to the house's crumbling front door. With no energy left, she rolled down the step and landed on her back.

At least she wouldn't die in rotting darkness. She would meet death here, with the sun shining warm on her face, a robin serenading her with a death song, crickets scraping a funeral dirge with their back legs, and yellow clover and purple alfalfa offering a sweet incense to heaven along with her soul.

Xavier!

Her breath hitched with unshed tears, but she didn't have the energy to remind her lungs that every exhale needed an inhale.

Something buzzed in the distance before her ears tuned out even that sound. *Probably a bee...*

Author Note: Oftentimes, love and hate share a razor's edge. As odd as it seems that love can drive someone to do awful and violent acts upon someone they supposedly love, it happens more often than it should. If you're a true crime addict, like myself, then you know full well how love can easily turn into a nightmare. What is the craziest true crime story you've ever heard and what about it sticks out in your mem-

ory? Let me in on the story at https://www.jessicabergbooks.com/contact.

Chapter 53

Xavier slammed his palm against his Jeep's steering wheel. An hour after Steve called out an APB on Eleanor and Nikki's pickup, people had called in claiming suspicious activity. None had panned out. Following a lead called into dispatch, Xavier turned into a section line leading to a secluded spot famous for high school parties. As he approached the copse of trees, his phone rang.

Xavier swiped the green phone icon. "Thaddeus, tell me something good."

"We found her. A farmer spraying the field next to an abandoned house found her, called it in."

Relief kicked him in the chest. He brought the Jeep to a rocking halt and sat, frozen. Paralyzed by the answer he didn't want, it took several seconds for his tongue to work enough for him to ask, "Is she...?"

"She's alive."

His body trembled, and he scrubbed his face with shaking hands. A sob ripped from his chest.

"Xavier, she's... uh... not doing so well. The ambulance is taking her to Sweetwater as we speak."

Xavier's body stiffened, and his vision grayed.

"Go." Thaddeus's voice broke through his fog. "I'll take care of Eleanor until you can get away."

"You found her?"

Thaddeus chuckled. "Didn't have to. Nikki had her all tied up for us."

Pride surged and, for a second, overcame his fear. "That's my girl." He hung up the phone, slammed his Jeep into Drive, and broke a few speed limits on his way to see for himself that the love of his life would come out of this alive.

Xavier sprinted into the hospital, and after demanding to see Nikki, a harried nurse directed him to the waiting room. Clenching his fists to keep his temper and agitation in check, he walked through the doors and into Corrie's embrace.

He wanted to think he was comforting Corrie, but as he broke in her arms, he was sure he was sucking every ounce of comfort from her. She detached herself from his hold, led him to a couch, and handed him a box of tissues.

"Sorry." His voice, raw from his gut-wrenching sobs, cracked. Heat burned his cheeks. He hadn't cried like that since... well, the day his mother had abandoned him. His throat closed. *Dear God, don't let Nikki abandon me too!*

She swiped a tissue under her nose and gave a wobbly smile. "I'd think you were a robot if you had any other reaction. And I don't approve of my sister marrying a robot."

"Well, it's good to know you have standards." He rubbed the back of his neck, blew out a steadying breath, and glanced around the empty waiting room.

"Mom took Dad outside for a while. He was holding together pretty well, especially with the magical incantations Mom murmurs to him, but a tone went off in a nearby patient room. Things went downhill from there."

"How is Nikki?"

"The doctor thinks she'll pull through. She lost—" Corrie's breath hitched, and she pressed a balled-up tissue to her mouth. "A lot of blood and might have severe head trauma." She pressed her hands together in prayer and rested her forehead on them. "I don't—I can't—what if she...?"

Xavier tucked Corrie's quaking frame to his side. "Nikki is the most stubborn person we know. If anyone can go tell death to fly a kite, it's our Nikki. She doesn't do what she doesn't want to do. Remember that."

A doctor wearing teal scrubs entered the waiting room. "Mrs. Tuttle?"

Corrie stood on wobbly legs and splayed out a hand, catching herself on Xavier's shoulder. "Is she okay? Please..."

"You may come back and see her." His gaze took in Xavier. "Family only, I'm afraid."

Corrie placed her hands on her hips and straightened to her full height. "He is family. My parents are outside. Please tell them they can see Nikki now." Without waiting for the doctor's rebuttal, she grabbed Xavier's hand, pulled him to his feet, and jogged down the corridor.

As soon as he entered the room, his lungs constricted, and his blood pooled in his feet.

Nikki, small and weak, lay in the hospital bed. Tubes and IVs streamed from her body.

Corrie rested her hand on his shoulder, and they walked to the edge of the bed. He reached for Nikki's hand but paused before taking her fingers in his. Guilt stabbed him in the gut, nearly bringing him to his knees.

If only he'd been fast enough to get to her, smart enough to figure out the true killer, she wouldn't be here, wouldn't be hooked to a machine charting out the rhythm of her heart. His job was to protect, to keep the innocent safe from the world's evil, and he had failed the one person who mattered most in his world.

"Stop it," Corrie whispered.

He slid his gaze from Nikki's ashen face to Corrie's tear-streaked one. "Stop what?"

"Blaming yourself." She entwined his hand with Nikki's and moved to the other side of the bed where she gripped Nikki's bandaged other hand.

He rubbed his thumb over the soft spot between her thumb and index finger. Her nails, though cleaned by nurses, still bore the battle scars of her fight to live. Torn and jagged, they proved she had fought—and won—without him.

The boulder of worry and fear and doubt that had grown in his chest ever since someone—*probably Eleanor*—had tried to run Nikki off the road shattered in his chest. He inhaled sharply.

"What's wrong?" Corrie stared at the heart monitor.

"Nothing. Nothing's wrong."

For the first time in a long time, nothing was wrong. Nikki didn't need him to be her bodyguard, safety manager, or savior. He was free to be what she needed him to be—her partner in crime, her best friend, her adventure-seeking sidekick, and if she was willing, her partner in life.

Author Note: Can we give three cheers for Xavier for learning that he wasn't and never was Nikki's knight on a white horse? I waited a long time. Fifty-three chapters, as a matter of fact, for him to come to his senses, and I'm sure you were too. Men! We'll just have to wait and see if Nikki decides to let him tag along and partake in her adventures.

Chapter 54

Nikki sensed before opening her eyes that she was not alone in her old bedroom. From the potent smell of dirt and grass and sweaty boy, Nikki also guessed she wasn't sleeping alone. She cracked open one eye and smiled. TT lay on his side, facing her, his eyes closed, and his face relaxed in the innocence of sleep only a four-year-old could enjoy. A cup gripped in his little hand tilted, nearly tipping out its contents of mini-marshmallows, Cheerios, and a few corn nuts.

As gently as possible, Nikki slid her arm out from under the covers and slipped the cup from TT's fist. He groaned, pursed his lips, and nestled deeper into the pillow. Her heart pinched, and she tucked the covers around his shoulder. She rested her fingers on his shoulder and matched her breaths with his. His lips twitched in his sleep. Not wanting to disturb him from a rare nap, she scooted to the side of the bed, allowed herself several seconds to acclimate to a sitting position, and pushed herself to her feet.

It had been one week since coming home, and she still wobbled around like a newborn colt.

Enough is enough. Time to quit healing and do some living.

After quietly gathering clothes, she eased herself to the bathroom, sliding her good shoulder along the wall for support. Not positive she wouldn't fall to her death in the shower, she washed as best she could from the sink, doused her hair with dry shampoo, brushed her teeth, and slipped into her first pair of jeans in two-and-a-half weeks. Her shirt was another issue. Biting back a yelp the second time she raised her right arm, she threw her T-shirt on the bathroom floor and, in jeans and a sports bra put on last night with the help of her mother, scooted along the wall to Nathan's old room. She nabbed a blue-and-red-striped dress shirt off a hanger. She knew she looked an absolute nincompoop, but she had dressed herself without the aid of her mother or Corrie—she shivered—or both.

Mexican aromas from the kitchen wafted up the stairs and teased her nose. Her stomach grumbled. Tacos. One of her favorites. Still unsure of her footing or the stairs, she sat on her backside and slid down the steps as she had seen TT do before conquering steps. No sense in pride breaking her neck. That would be an ignominious ending. She could imagine the local paper's front-page headline: "Local Girl Survives Serial Killer Only to Die After Falling Down Stairs."

"What in the Sam Hill do you think you're doing?" Cynthia, one hand on a hip, the other brandishing a spatula, leaned against the kitchen doorway.

"I'm hungry." Nikki, using her left arm, pulled herself up. "Feed me?"

Her mother ignored her exaggerated pout and circled the spatula at Nikki's shirt. "And what are you wearing?"

"Stole it from Nathan."

"Glad to see you're back to normal." Cynthia pressed a kiss to Nikki's temple and ushered her into the living room. "There's someone here who really wants to see you."

Xavier jumped to his feet the moment Nikki turned the corner. Before she could say anything or smile, his fingers were in her hair, and he pulled her to him and nestled her ear over his heart. It didn't matter that she couldn't understand the words rumbling in his chest. The intensity of his hold, the beating of his heart, told her everything. He still loved her, although only God knew why. She would have given up on herself years ago. Hopefully, he would give her a lifetime to make up for the most idiotic decision she'd ever made.

She squirmed from his hold, clasped his hand, and anchoring to his strength, walked him to the porch.

"Are you sure you're up for this?" He guided her to a wicker rocking chair and helped her sit.

"If I have to stay cooped up in the house or my bed any longer, I will go postal. Besides, I have a Goldilocks in my bed." She smoothed out his quirked eyebrow. "If Goldilocks were a smelly four-year-old boy."

"Nikki—" He clasped her hands in his and played his thumb over her skin. "With everything that's been going on, I haven't had a chance to... um... tell you I—"

"Wait."

He blinked, and his thumb froze.

"There's something I need to do... say... both." She was sure he could see her heart jumping out of her chest. Blood coursed through her veins. This is what she imagined it felt like before jumping out of an airplane. And she was taking a plunge, and the ending would either kill her spirit or leave her feeling invincible.

Before she chickened out, she slipped from the chair, waved off Xavier's concern crinkling his forehead, and propped herself up on one knee. Her lips quivered as his eyebrows arched. "Xavier, the pain I caused you, the years I stole away from us is unforgivable, and I am sorry. The one thing I can't apologize for is my love for you. I don't think I ever stopped loving you. Even when I thought that's what I wanted, I couldn't. I'm not sure how to make up for the heartbreak I caused, but I want to spend the rest of my life trying." She swallowed the emotion clogging her throat. "Will you, do you want to... I mean, I totally get it if you don't... but will you marry me... again?"

Xavier's eyes darkened, and he slid to the porch flooring to cradle her right cheek in his hand. "Under those conditions, no—"

The breath she sucked in burned her throat. His rejection shot through her heart and landed with a sickening thud in her stomach.

His thumb traced her bottom lip. "You didn't let me finish. I don't want you with all the trappings and baggage of what used to be. I don't want you chained to any guilt you feel. I want you. The you I discovered because you had the brains enough to leave me in the first place. Imagine if you had married the old Xavier, the one who thought I was the knight meant only to keep you safe? I would have done more than break your heart. I would have broken your spirit."

Nikki refused to undam the flood of hot tears burning her eyes. "Is that a yes?"

His kiss set her core on fire, but it was his whispered yes against her lips that made her skin tingle and her body weightless.

Despite the hardness of the porch decking, she made no move to leave the spot. Snuggling deeper into Xavier's embrace, she rested her ear against his chest and counted out the beats of his racing heart. "Don't go dying on me now. I would be seriously displeased."

"It'd be your fault." His laugh rumbled through his chest.

"Want me to leave?" She swirled a curlicue over his pectoral muscle.

"Don't you dare. I've wanted you here for three years. I don't think your parents would mind if we became permanent fixtures on their porch."

"My backside would, though. Starting to get numb."

"Here." He untangled from her arms and led her to the porch swing. After he sat, she lay down and rested her head on his lap. His fingers playing through her hair set her core humming.

A shadow soon darkened her spirits. A shadow that took the form of Eleanor St. John. "Xavier, can I... speak with Eleanor?"

The porch swing stopped mid-swing, and his thigh tensed under her cheek. His fingers swirled faster through her hair.

In the two weeks of lying around and doing nothing, Nikki had heard all the gossip. Her mother, especially, didn't seem to give two figs about what the Bible said about gossip. Not when Eleanor nearly killed her daughter. When her mother had pulled up a chair and started venting, Nikki had zipped her lips and allowed her mom to release all the pent-up rage and venom. Better out than in as Nathan was fond of saying. That's where she had learned Eleanor's death count had increased by one, making a grand total of seven. And it was over Oreos and a glass of milk she learned that on Eleanor's daughter's sixteenth birthday, she had informally changed her name from Kendra St. John to her paternal great-grandmother's name, Beatrice Hansen. That was also the year she moved, met Bryce Beaumont, and started life living off the grid and on a fake ID.

Silence permeated the air. Not even the squeak of the porch swing chains broke the unwelcome stillness. She braced herself for the immediate no, convinced herself she would be okay with the answer.

After a drawn-out exhale, Xavier tipped his feet up, and the swing began its gentle rocking. "Yes, but on one condition."

Nikki sat up and studied his face. "Name your price."

"I go in with you. I won't say a word. I'll just sit quietly by your side."

"Oh, so instead of playing bad cop to my good cop, you'll be the silent, brooding one?"

He chuckled and cupped her right cheek. "I'd like to consider it teamwork."

She snuggled back into his chest. "I like the sound of that better."

Under the promise of Xavier by her side, the Eleanor-shaped shadow lifted. From the strength of his arms, she knew he promised more than teamwork in finding closure with the past month's tragedy and destruction of lives. He also promised a lifetime of working through an adventurous life they would travel together.

Author Note: Everyone's learning lessons it seems! Nikki has finally learned that being independent doesn't mean having to go through life alone and unsupported. I'm not sure how she'll hold up when she comes face-to-face with the serial killer who not only killed her friends but also tried to kill her as well. We'll just have to wait and see how the "Interview with Evil" will go.

Chapter 55

The stifling room shrank as the audible ticking of the clock's red second hand marked each second. Sweat dripped down Nikki's back, and she played her thick tongue over the insides of her dry mouth.

A door clanged. Nikki jumped.

Xavier rested his hand on her shoulder. "It'll be okay. The moment you want the conversation to end, you end it. If you change your mind the moment she walks through the door, you let me know."

Words would not eke past the lump in her throat. She nodded and clasped his hand.

The door opened, revealing a deputy and Eleanor St. John clad in an orange jumpsuit, her wrists handcuffed behind her back and her ankles shackled by leg cuffs. Another deputy followed.

Nikki dropped Xavier's hand and clutched her fists in her lap. No need for Eleanor to see them shaking.

The two deputies flanked Eleanor before sitting her in a chair opposite Nikki and Xavier. One released her hands and, after she sat, clipped the handcuffs to a ring under the table.

The last time she had looked into Eleanor's eyes was in the decrepit basement of a rotting house. Then the woman's eyes had gleamed with insanity. Her screams for her daughter echoed through Nikki's mind. Nikki clenched her fists. The fingernails biting into her flesh reminded her that if she could feel pain, she was alive. Eleanor had failed.

All the questions she had wanted to ask dissolved. The one remaining—*Why?*—seemed stupid, insipid. The banality of that one word fits situations ranging from why TT put crayons down the sink disposer to why the sky was blue. Asking that of the woman across from her who had singlehandedly murdered seven women and had attempted to strip Nikki of life reeked of naivety.

But in the end, that was all that squeaked out of Nikki's throat. "Why?"

Eleanor cocked her head like a bird, and her glassy gaze flitted from Nikki's nose to her forehead to her chin and settled on her eyes. Nikki's eye muscles twitched to blink, but she refused them their wish. She would not blink in the face of fear, and she certainly would not show weakness to the predator feet away from her.

Eleanor's lips pulled back in a smile, revealing white teeth. The smile stopped short of welcoming. Under the cracking veneer of teeth and red lips, hatred lurked. Eleanor shrugged. Metal clanked against metal. "If you would have hung around longer, you'd know. But you abandoned me in that basement." She moved to cross her arms. Chains stopped the trajectory. She cursed and settled her hands in her lap. Her gaze bore into Nikki's, and the gleam in them gave an illusion of tears swimming in her eyes. "How could you abandon your mother?"

Xavier pressed his thigh against Nikki's. The pressure of his thigh on hers had her straightening her spine and settling her shoulders back. "How could you abandon your daughter?"

Eleanor's head jerked back as if Nikki had struck her. And maybe she had. Xavier had filled her in on Beatrice's teenhood with a narcissistic mother. The episode of dog torture and the framing of a teenage boy, who perhaps deserved punishment, served the wrong one, the endless manipulation causing an irrevocable rift between mother and daughter, leading the daughter to take the final and deadly plunge: suicide.

"How dare you?" Eleanor ground out between clenched teeth. "She abandoned me." Her tongue darted out and licked her bottom lip. "And then *he* came. Bryce broke her heart. He killed her. Don't you see? I had to destroy him." She strained against the chains, groaned, and plopped her hands back in her lap. "He should be the one chained like an animal."

Nikki concentrated on the warmth of Xavier's thigh seeping into hers. "Is that why you did it? Why you killed them? Framed Bryce? Why you tried to kill me?"

Eleanor's hand shot out across the table. Metal grated. Her hand poised midair between them, her fingers straining, wiggling as if wanting to stroke Nikki's face. "Not you. You were never part of the plan. But then you gave me no choice. But... I would have been gentle. As a good mother should. You would have felt no pain. You would have loved meeting her." Her hand dropped to the table, palm up, welcoming Nikki to lay her hand in hers. "Kendra," she whispered and gazed into Nikki's eyes.

Knowing that Eleanor no longer saw her but the form of her daughter, Nikki nudged Xavier's knee with hers. Xavier nodded to the two deputies, who flanked Eleanor, secured her arms behind her back, and lifted her from her chair.

Cut from her trance, she bucked between them. "No!" Spittle sprayed from her mouth. "Don't take me away from my daughter. No. Please," she whimpered and collapsed back into the chair. "Kendra? Beatrice?" She cocked her head again and studied the girl across the table. Her eyes shimmered, and her skin paled. "Kendra, don't leave me again."

The deputies strained against her deadweight but got her to her feet again and dragged her from the room. Her voice pleading for her daughter echoed down the hallway until a heavy metal door clanged shut and killed the sound.

Nikki wasn't sure how long she sat in the cold metal chair in that tiny cinderblock-walled room. Time, which had previously announced its presence, quieted until that, too, stopped existing. The one oblong-shaped pitting in the wall, which had saved her from sinking into the abyss of Eleanor's gaze, faded from sight, even though her eyes still rested on the spot. She lost the feeling of Xavier's thigh, which had been her foundation during the interview. It became part of her much like her own skin.

"Nikki?"

The second hand ticked again. The cinderblock wall came back into focus, and the warmth of his thigh heated hers until she thought it would combust. She rested her folded hands on the table and scowled at the healing scar on her palm. A scar that would always remind her of her run-in with death. "She's going to plead insanity, isn't she?"

Xavier exhaled a deep breath. "If I were her attorney, that's what I would push for."

She swiveled, swung her arms out, and gaped at him. "What? Are you saying that she's not guilty, that she doesn't deserve to be punished, to be locked in a cage for the rest of her life?"

He gathered her spread-out hands in his and brought them to his chest. "That's not what I'm saying. All I know is that our part in bringing her to justice is only halfway complete. No matter what her attorneys throw at us on the witness stand, when we're called to testify, all we can do is tell the truth. If we do that, no matter if Eleanor spends the rest of her life in a penitentiary or spends it in a psych ward, justice will be served."

"Are you sure we can't go back to the Old West days when horrible people were executed in the town square?" Hot tears burned the back of her eyes. She clamped down on her inner cheek. She would not cry for the likes of Eleanor St. John. Eleanor deserved none of her tears.

"Could you pull the lever?" Although he asked it gently, the question cut to her core.

She wanted to spit out yes, but her tongue could not form the words. Faces that had haunted Nikki's dreams shimmered before her. *Lucy, Michelle, Hallie, Alexis, Natasha, Laurel, and Cecelia.* Even so, she could not say the word. While their journeys had ended tragically, Eleanor's journey had just begun. Even though Nikki could never pull whatever lever or push whatever button to end Eleanor's life, she would do what she could to ensure that Eleanor got the justice she deserved, in whatever form that looked like.

Resting her head against Xavier's shoulder, she whispered, "Take me home."

Author Note: This chapter was perhaps the most difficult of them all. Getting into the head of a serial killer is one thing, getting into the head of a female serial killer, and one who acted so maternal, took the energy right out of me. As soon as I typed this chapter's final word, I sat at my desk and stared at my computer screen. Even though I, through Xavier, asked if Nikki could pull the lever, I did not and still do not have the answer. That's the tricky thing about justice, isn't it? All too often justice looks a lot more like revenge. I believe if I had to answer that question, I would be with Nikki on this deep and murky question.

Chapter 56

Xavier peeled off the last of the photos from the chalkboard and tucked them into labeled manila folders. He would have to re-arrange and sift through the evidence to prepare for the imminent trial, but for now, a folder labeled Eleanor St. John would have to do. He tucked the folder next to the large items of bagged evidence consisting of the jeans, flannel shirt, red ball cap, and fake beard, which when tested would surely prove Eleanor the sole owner and wearer of it, and Laurel's police-issue gun that Eleanor had stolen off the deputy's body.

Eraser poised in his hand, he studied the board's chalked evidence. It had all been there, staring at him, taunting him. The tender positions of death, the smooth tendrils of hair stroked by mutilated love, and the use of chloroform for an easier kill, a seemingly painless death for her victims all pointed to a motherly figure. He glared at the word *jewelry*. Deputies had found all the missing jewelry after searching Eleanor's luggage and person. The ring stolen from Michelle Osbourne's body had been on display the whole time on Eleanor's pinky. It had been there when he'd first questioned her at Mabel's café. *Idiot!*

"How long are you going to blame yourself for this one?" Thaddeus leaned against the desk and crossed his arms over his chest.

Xavier pinched the bridge of his nose. "Won't be one I forget."

"That's not what I asked."

"I thought you said you were out of my hair after this was all over."

"Tough luck. Especially since Sara and Nikki appear to be inseparable."

Xavier slid Thaddeus a glance and grinned. "She caught you in her snare, didn't she?"

"Who said I mind being caught?" He gestured to the board. "None of this is your fault. You know that, right?"

"You sound like someone else I know."

"That person must be wise."

Wiping the eraser over the board, Xavier chuckled. "You have no idea."

He dusted his hands free of chalk and stared at the now-empty board. If only erasing death from his thoughts—and dreams—was that easy. But this time it was different. Yes, he would stash this away, keep the victims in a safe and sacred spot within him, but he no longer felt the weight of them. If Nikki had taught him anything, it was that life, not death, mattered. More than anything he wanted to live life—no—experience life with Nikki. For too long, he had allowed a job that dealt with death and destruction to shackle him to fear.

"You okay?" Thaddeus clapped him on the shoulder.

"Yeah. More than okay. Let's go."

Between the two of them, they carried boxes overflowing with documents and stuffed briefcases out of the tiny office and into Xavier's Jeep and Thaddeus's car. The case wasn't over, and sleepless nights lay ahead for both, but for now, justice had been served to the residents of Sandy and Custer. Now the biggest task lay ahead: surviving a six-hour road trip with Nikki's promised Boy Bands of the 90s playlist.

*S*nap!

Nikki jumped and placed a hand over her heart.

Snap!

She abandoned her suitcase and the pile of clothes slotted for eventual rolling and stuffing and walked to the spare bedroom's window. Below, Sara, tucked up against Thaddeus, Xavier, TT, and his pets sat on the cement driveway littered with what looked like spitballs with tails. TT chucked something to the ground. *Snap!* Bacon never moved. Kentucky ruffled her feathers, pecked at the white fluff, and settled back against TT's thigh.

If she didn't get a move on, she would never be ready to leave in time for the Fourth of July celebration at Mount Rushmore. Leaving the assembled company to their Snaps, she settled back into packing and opened the drawer to the side table. She crinkled her nose at the empty drawer. Unless her Bible had grown legs and walked off as her mother always accused inanimate objects of doing, it should be where she had left it the night before. Reading her favorite passages had rekindled an ember inside her; no longer would dust blanket her Bible or her soul. She looked under the bed and investigated all the drawers to the big dresser but came up empty-handed.

A knock on the doorframe interrupted her search in the closet. She stuck her head out from the small space. "Dad?"

He shuffled his feet and scrubbed the back of his neck.

"Come on in. I'm just looking for my—"

He held out his hand.

"Bible."

His face reddened, and his gaze refused to settle on her.

"Here." She led him to the bed and sat next to him.

With a shaking hand, he gave her the Bible. "Open."

The air in her lungs thickened. She opened the cover and read the new inscription scrawled with an unsteady hand: *For my Nikki. May God keep you safe on your new adventures! Love, Dad*

Her father's handwriting blurred.

"Mom helped me."

Forgetting the book in her lap, she curved into her father's chest. His arms came around her, and for a moment, it was as it had always been. His strength, his support, his fearlessness all for her.

"I'm sorry," he murmured into her hair. "I... ah... I don't know how to... I can't..."

Repeating what she witnessed between her parents, Nikki placed her hand on her father's cheek and his hand on hers. "It's okay, Dad. It'll be okay. I'm okay." And it was. It was her turn to give strength, support, and fearlessness not for herself but for her father. "Are you any good at packing?" Nikki smiled and gestured to the clothes still awaiting suitcase space.

"Never was." His eyes twinkled.

"Good. I like knowing what to expect."

For the next ten minutes, they worked on getting her all packed up, and before she knew it, she was on the front steps of her parents' house, wrapped in Xavier's arms. Her house. She'd come to the farm in a flaming ball of tattered shame and was about to leave it probably still a flaming ball but one of adventure and hope for a future she thought she had destroyed.

Sara patted Sampson on its rusty hood. The diagnosis had been fatal; Sampson would rest in peace in the Lancaster tree belt. "Well, at least I'm riding back in style." Her tears betrayed her smile as she slid into the passenger seat of Thaddeus's sports car.

Thaddeus closed the door, walked around to the driver's side, and waved at the assembled group of Lancasters and company. "Thanks again. For everything." He glanced at Xavier and Nikki. "Ready to roll?"

After hugging and kissing her family goodbye and loading the back seat of Xavier's Jeep with goodies from Mabel, who had sent them with the kind words that Nikki hadn't been the worst employee, Nikki hopped into the passenger seat. In front of her stood everyone she loved and held dear, everyone who represented stability and unchanging love. Whatever she threw at life, no matter how she screwed up or missed the mark, Nikki knew one thing: her dad, mom, Corrie, Aaron, TT, Violet, Luke, and Iris would be here. With such a firm foundation and with Xavier at her side and God in her wheelhouse, she couldn't wait to explore uncharted lands.

As Xavier put the vehicle in reverse and backed away from her childhood home, she blew kisses at her family. TT, mimicking those around him, caught one, peered at his empty palm, and placed it on his cheek.

"Ready?" Xavier asked before shifting into drive.

Nikki took one more look at all she loved and reached over to grasp his hand. "More than I ever have been."

The Jeep's wheels took her closer to the mailbox at the end of the gravel driveway and farther away from her family. Their forms in the side mirror shrank until the Jeep crested a dip in the road and they disappeared from her sight. But not from her heart. Behind her lay her past. In front waited her future. Beside her, the man she chose as her most exhilarating adventure yet.

Author Note: Fireworks are the coolest thing since, well, anything before the invention of fireworks. The more the merrier, the louder the better, the more colorful the bigger the oohs and aahs. Here are some of the coolest fireworks facts I found from Americanpyro.com:

The first fireworks were bamboo sticks thrown into fire.

Man-made fireworks were created somewhere between 600-900 AD.

Colonists celebrated the first Independence Day with fireworks.

John Adams wanted future generations to celebrate the Fourth of July "with pomp, parade...bonfires and illuminations from one end of this continent to the other."

Thunder Over Louisville is one of the largest American fireworks displays, bringing in more than 56 million dollars!

I don't know about you, but I just might make my way down to Louisville one of these Fourth of Julys!

Chapter 57

"You look a little green." Nikki smoothed the lapel on Xavier's dark-gray suit coat surrounding a sunflower-and-purple-bachelor-button boutonniere. Despite the green hue lurking under his skin, his blue eyes mirrored the cloudless early-afternoon sky over Glacier National Park. The breeze tousled his blond hair, and he swiped at it with his left hand. His platinum wedding band glinted.

"Not thinking about cutting it, are you?" She twirled a wayward strand behind his ear. Her updo was sprayed with enough hair spray that it didn't even shiver in the brisk autumn wind. She wrapped her fur stole tighter around her strapless cream-colored wedding dress.

"Nope. Thinking about my imminent death." He narrowed his eyes at the hot-air balloon ready for the final part of the wedding ceremony: sealing the deal at three thousand feet in the air over the Rocky Mountains.

She twirled his ring around his finger. "If this is something you really don't want to do, we don't have to." She stepped closer, placed her hand over his racing heart, and whispered in his ear, "Besides, we do have a jacuzzi in our honeymoon suite. And I forgot my swimsuit."

A hiss escaped his lips as she licked his earlobe. "Well, if that idea didn't kill me, a hot-air balloon probably won't."

Heat coursed through her body and settled in her core. "Are you saying that I'm more dangerous than flight?"

"Absolutely."

"Good." She poked him in the chest. "And don't ever forget it."

He brought her left hand to his lips and rubbed his finger over her diamond-encrusted wedding ring. "Something tells me you won't let me." After kissing her until her limbs went squishy, he pulled away and jerked his head toward the balloon. "Shall we?"

"Till death do us part, right?"

The underlying green hue seemed to leech from his pores, and his pupils dilated.

"Too soon?"

"Is it too late for the hot tub?" He swished his finger between his shirt collar and neck.

"How about the hot balloon first? Then the tub. Plus, champagne and chocolate-covered strawberries."

He squinted at the balloon and back at Nikki and held out his pinky finger. "Deal."

"I got something better in mind." She dodged his descending lips. "But you gotta wait a bit." Picking up the hem of her dress, she trotted as fast as her heels would allow to the basket of the hot-air balloon. Xavier settled a fur mantle over her shoulders.

The ground crew undid the lines, and with a lurch and sway, the basket began its ascent. The wedding group consisting of close family and friends waved from the ground, their smiles and cheers diminishing with every foot the balloon rose. Soon, they were little more than ant-sized humans.

Trees that had towered over them during the outdoor ceremony looked like mere toys, fit for a model train setup. From thousands of feet in the air, the oranges, flame reds, and yellows of leaves melded together into a thick carpet broken sporadically by dark green swatches of ponderosa pines. Looming to the east, the peaks of the Rocky Mountains, already covered in a snowy blanket, touched the azure-blue sky.

As the pilot worked his magic, Nikki and Xavier, who had one hand strangling the basket's edge, the other gripping a plastic champagne flute stem, clinked their mimosas together.

"To our first adventure as man and wife."

Xavier glanced over the edge, and his Adam's apple dipped. "Maybe our next adventure could be on the ground."

"It sounds to me like you need to take your mind off where we are."

His knuckles whitened as the balloon dipped. "And how do you suggest I do that?"

"Like this."

Being careful not to rock the basket, she stepped into his one-armed embrace, cupped the back of his neck, and captured his lips. He tasted of oranges, and she moaned as his tongue explored her lips and mouth. His hand that had strangled the basket now rested on the small of her back, and he pressed her into him.

At three thousand feet in the air, they sealed the ultimate deal. A life of adventure. Together.

Author Note: Anyone else terrified of heights and just the thought of going in a hot air balloon gives you the hives? Well, you are not alone. I'm right there with you. I know that I should think hot air balloon rides are romantic and sexy, but I'm like Xavier, and I'd have one thought in my head if my husband coerced me into a hot air balloon basket: get me down. Now! But, as you can clearly see, Xavier changes his mind rather quickly.

Thank you so much for coming along on Nikki and Xavier's journey. I've enjoyed this ride, and I hope that you did as well! If you enjoyed their story, please check out Corrie and Aaron's story in Amber Waves of Grace. *Get a sneak peek at the synopsis and reviews on my website: https://www.jessicabergbooks.com/books.*

Acknowledgments

To my siblings: you taught me the importance of family, and even though miles separate us, our bond is closer now than ever.

To my parents: you taught me to follow my dreams and to work hard for my goals. This book and my author career are proof that your guidance (and sometimes cajoling) worked.

To my husband: without your support, this book—and the others before it—would not be possible.

To my children: you are the reason I push myself, so I can prove to you that if you have a heart for something, you can and will accomplish it.

To my publisher: thank you for your support and remarkable ability to gather up all the "ducks" I've managed to misplace and order them all nicely in a row and create a beautiful book all around a little idea I had.

About the Author

Jessica Berg, a child of the Dakotas and the prairie, grew up amongst hard-working men and women and learned at an early age to "put some effort into it." Following that wise adage, she has put effort into teaching high school English for over a decade, being a mother to four children (she finds herself surprised at this number, too), basking in the love of her husband of more than fifteen years and losing herself in the imaginary worlds she creates.

Read more at https://www.jessicabergbooks.com.

About the Publisher

Dear Reader,

We hope you enjoyed this book. Please consider leaving a review on your favorite book site.

Visit https://RedAdeptPublishing.com to see our entire catalogue.

Check out our app for short stories, articles, and interviews. You'll also be notified of future releases and special sales.

www.ingramcontent.com/pod-product-compliance
Lightning Source LLC
Chambersburg PA
CBHW031308210726
48287CB00005B/1469